THE SHREW

Book Three of The Dark Series

Charnae

Sonder Skookum Publishers, LLC

ISBN: 978-1-962695-08-4 (Digital)
ISBN: 978-1-962695-09-1 (Paperback)
ISBN: 978-1-962695-10-7 (Hardback)

Library of Congress Control Number: 2023923150

Cover Photo Credit: Irina Bg/Shutterstock.com
Cover Creation: Canva.com

This is a work of fiction. Names, characters, places, brands, media, and incidents are the product of the author's imagination or are used fictitiously. Any resemblance to actual persons, living or dead, business establishments, events, or locales is entirely coincidental.

FIRST EDITION: May 2024

Published by Sonder Skookum Publishers, LLC
Sandy, Utah, U.S.A.
www.charnaesbooks.com

To Dad.
After long days at work, you read me stories on
that old red chair. Those were good days.

CHAPTER ONE

I pass Nacole another square cloth since her current one's soaked with tears and snot. She attempts to give me the used one, but I withdraw my hand quickly.

Gross.

She doesn't notice my disgust. The soggy handkerchief hangs suspended in the air as, for what must be the tenth time, she chokes out, "Annibeth, I just don't understand."

I'm her best friend, so I attempt an expression of pity, but it's hard to maintain. She's cried for an hour, at least. And that's just today. Don't get me started on yesterday. And it all stems from the recent discovery that the love of her life loves someone else. I mean, it sucks for her, but what am I supposed to do about it?

"I don't understand, either," I say as my attempt at sympathy. The statement is factual, not emotional—not exactly what Nacole's looking for—but it will have to do. I brush a hand across my freckled cheek to feign a tear, but I'm positive my blue eyes—dry behind long lashes—betray the truth. I'm not so much sympathetic as ready for a new topic.

Last summer, Nacole announced to me that Siman Harcort owned her heart. At the time, I approved. We're of an age where it's natural to pair off. He's well-respected, and socially, they're a perfect match. Whether she actually declared her love to Siman is unknown to me. I didn't ask because, frankly, I didn't care. If she wanted to tie up her emotions with that boy, it was her business, and I didn't need to talk about it. I'm no gossip.

But based on the evidence—by which I mean basic observation—they locked lips enough times that they could have had a love conversation somewhere in their trysts. After all, I'd had that conversation with Cully on multiple occasions. Regardless, yesterday, Siman told Nacole the terrible news—that his affections reside elsewhere. Since then, she's subjected me to her endless moaning.

Elsewhere! That's the part where I find fault.

Elsewhere is Tesha Dale.

I shudder because… Tesha Dale, *of all people!*

I'm apprenticing to become a reckoner—an enforcer of the law in our community—and it's become natural for me to analyze things. Using those skills, a logical comparison of the two women proves my point in Nacole's favor.

Nacole is beautiful, and Tesha is frizzy.

Nacole has a sweet voice, even if she whines too much. Tesha is whistly.

Nacole *can* be funny, whereas Tesha is too serious, without a bit of humor.

Nacole is next in line as Sector Leader of Manufacturing and Distribution—following her mother, Alace Rupret—while the only title Tesha can claim is the community witch.

And finally, Nacole is my friend, and Tesha doesn't have friends. Well, that's not entirely true. Siman and Vale Rennick have associated with her over the years, entering her crazy world. It makes some sense because Vale's world is crazy too. But, Siman? Well, Siman could be something. With minor effort, he could make a perfect life for himself, so I don't understand his choice to align with them. Or make one his girlfriend.

Another bad move on Siman's part is he's recently chosen to support those from the Dark. The strangers from a place called Tenebris insist they're our allies, but those of us in the Government and Law Sector aren't so sure. Siman's gone so far as supporting their causes over the desires of his own people, and it's not helping his community prospects.

As for Tesha, the three brothers from the Dark seem to have a soft spot for her. Well, the gloomy one—who's quite a looker—seems tolerant of her. It's probably his effort to stay in Vale's good graces since there's some interest between those two. As for the big guy, I couldn't gauge his level of devotion to the witch. He's usually quiet and disturbingly light-footed for his size unless he's casually (and inaccurately) demeaning my character—calling me *mindless* and such—so I'm unsure of his stance on Tesha. The young one, though, who teases and jokes more than saying anything important, dotes on her. Maybe men are attracted to uselessness.

Even if the brothers from the Dark found some value in associating with Tesha, there's still no competition. As far as I can see, between Siman's two leading choices in girlfriend, there's only one winner. I'd tell Nacole the same, but she'd only cry harder.

It's easy to understand why Nacole's so upset. I mean, if a guy you like chooses someone far inferior, it can only make you feel bad about yourself. It's never happened to me, although there was a time I thought it might. Cully Clarc—who I claimed as mine when our mothers bathed us together as toddlers—had started spending time with Vale Rennick. I wasn't sure at first, but he convinced me it was an act so she'd give up information about what he suspected was happening in the Dark. It turned out his suspicions were correct—something was going on—and it involved Vale far more than Cully realized. She even left the community and traveled with the strangers into the wasteland. It was a bold move—admirable in a way—but mostly, I was relieved Cully's attention was in pursuit of information, not Vale herself. Still, I monitor her. She might have the hot guy from the Dark all twisted up for her, but that doesn't mean she won't try to steal Cully from me. Basically, I don't trust her.

Nacole's still going on about her loss. I partially listen to her rambling, giving random input while brushing my hair.

The long blond strands were in knots after my morning trip to the bathhouse. We're low on everything since the usurper, Captain Malum, initiated fear-based disruptions in community operations. Consequently, there's no almond oil to condition my hair, and it's in a proper state. I've pulled half of it from my head, trying to get a brush in there.

I long for a return of order—to have the provisions I need and luxuries I enjoy. I miss our controlled environment where my status guarantees I can keep everything precisely as I like. My life was perfect before all this disorder, and I'll do whatever is necessary to get it back to the way it was. If it means discrediting the people from the Dark, I'll do it. Or if it's better to work with them, I'll take that route. I'm not picky as long as the outcome is to my satisfaction. And if Nacole would shut up, I could begin the undertaking now since I intend to search out one of the Dark brothers to start my negotiations.

As luck would have it, after an hour of suffering through the noise, Nacole's stuttering rant seems to be ending. "I just—" Nacole hiccups. "Don't." She sniffs. "Understand."

I mean, it must be ending, right? How many more times can she repeat the same statement?

I let out an unsympathetic breath—my usual type of breath. "There's not much I can say," I tell Nacole, laying out the facts as I see them. "Tesha's a weirdo. I don't understand the workings of Siman's mind. But I can tell you one thing." Nacole goes silent—even the sniffling stops—as she waits for me to impart my wisdom. "Crying won't help. And it's giving me a headache. Let's go see what's happening in the Common."

Nacole blinks. "Oh-h, okay," she stutters, sounding stunned —possibly from hearing a voice other than her own. She slides down from her perch in my window and wipes her runny nose with the saturated cloth, asking, "Want me to do your hair first?"

I want you to wash your hands first, I almost say, but pinch my lips closed. Instead, I nod and point Nacole toward a water pitcher on the table in my room. She washes her hands and dries them on a towel before picking up the square of cloth again and wiping her nose.

"Nacole!" I complain and push her in front of the pitcher again. "I don't want your boogers in my hair."

"Oh. Right," she says, putting the material with the rest of my laundry before rewashing her hands. "Sorry," she mumbles when she's done, but I'm already sitting on the chair, so she stands behind me and starts.

Nacole is an expert with hair. Curls. Braids. You name it, and she does it with precision. It looks like I'm getting a braid today, which I appreciate because of my unoiled hair. While most girls might do braided tails or a tight plait to the head, Nacole will create an intricate pattern of large and small braids. She's always been good with her hands.

We're both seventeen, but I'll turn eighteen in under a month. Her day will come a few months later. Like everything in life, Nacole's always a little behind me.

"Annibeth," my mother says, popping her head into my room and interrupting my thoughts.

"Yeah?" I ask, turning just enough to see her while letting Nacole keep control of my hair.

My mother smiles but falters when she sees Nacole's flaming red nose and dark, water-rimmed eyes. "Sorry to interrupt, girls. Annibeth, I need your help with a few things. If you have time."

"I have time. What with?"

"The increase of meetings in the Well is starting to show. I need to get the cleaning crew together, but I'm not up to coordinating it."

I turn a little more, and Nacole accommodates the angle. My mother, indeed, looks tired. She's been doing too much.

Again. Why won't she slow down? I tell her repeatedly to let me step in, but she seldom does. She must be feeling much worse today if she's requesting my help.

"We're almost done," I tell her, facing forward so Nacole can keep going.

"Yeah, and I need to go home and do my chores," my friend adds. She's excellent at accommodating my needs, which is precisely why I keep her around, but I'm not done with her today.

"Nacole's staying over tonight," I tell my mother. I don't ask her because that's not how my household operates. We don't request. We state our intention, and if there's an objection, we note it.

"Okay," my mother responds.

I also don't ask Nacole if she wants to sleep over. Again, I just announce it, and it's up to her to say if it doesn't work. But she'll never decline because she doesn't want to upset me. Also, she enjoys staying here because the size of my family's quarters is rare in the community. Our apartment has two separate bedrooms—one for me and one for my parents. Cully's family quarters are like that too, but we're the only ones in the entire community. Nacole enjoys having space to ourselves, and she knows I've never invited anyone else to spend the night. Besides, she'd never decline because then I might not ask her again—it's an unspoken contract between us, showing how well Nacole gets me that our deal can go unsaid.

Within a few minutes, Nacole finishes the braid. My mother inspects it, remarking, "It's lovely."

"Thanks." Nacole dips her head, her cheeks flushing with the compliment. (You'd be right to think her cheeks now match her nose and eyes.) "I'll see you tonight," she says, then scurries to vacate the room.

"Mother, you look exhausted. Let me finish up today's

chores."

Again, going against her nature, she nods. "I need cleaners for the Well, as I mentioned, and we need some water in the kitchen. The rest can wait."

"I'll see to it." Beyond her spoken list, I intend to complete any other tasks needed for the meeting. It's essential to reduce her stress and keep her from overdoing it.

When we leave my room, my mother goes straight to hers, which I'm happy to see, and I grab the empty jug in the kitchen and head out for water. Most citizens go to the platforms near the Upper River Bridge to get their water, but we have a private one near the Lower River Bridge, so I don't go far to scoop fresh, chilly water, but it's tiring hefting it up the slight incline. Then I have another climb up the outdoor stairs to reach our second-floor housing. I'm almost at the top, slightly out of breath, when my name is spewed disparagingly.

"Annibeth Petters. What an *unpleasant* surprise," says the youngest of the Dark brothers, leaning against the railing. He delivers the comment with his natural swagger, smirking and brushing back his dark brown hair that's short and curls around his ears.

His name is Evans, and he seems a very transparent person —always searching for adoration and approval while joking away anything serious. He tries to maintain the middle ground while his family expects he'll do more with his life. It's a weak move. I'd never present myself as being so inadequate.

I intended to search out and converse with a Dark brother, but Evans was never my top choice. Besides, now's clearly not the time to discuss inducements for making them leave because Siman is with him—not an unusual sight of late. The citizens are on the verge of considering Siman more aligned with the Dark strangers than a member of our community, especially since he's now dressing like them, wearing a gray longcoat. Evans wears one too—his is dark brown.

"What are you doing here?" I ask, though it's a stupid question. When they're not in the Dark, they're here at the Well, though it's usually downstairs in the meeting area, not on the second-floor landing leading to my living quarters. I can't help adding, "Did you see Nacole? She just left."

I glare at Siman, but he doesn't react, remaining stoic behind his black eyes and hair. He stands there with his thumbs hooked inside his pockets, saying, "No. We missed her. But we're here to talk to you."

Evans grumbles. "We drew the short stick, is all," he mumbles, shaking his head.

Siman grins—white teeth against his pale skin—and, knowing my direct proclivities, gets right to the point. "There's a meeting tomorrow at the Well between our people. The Coastals think involving more of your citizens would be beneficial, but Lucan's against it." Lucan can be narrow-minded, though he's right to be cautious regarding the people from the Dark. Siman continues, "He doesn't want the sector leaders involved yet, but I suggested they include the reckoners. It only makes sense if we're discussing long-standing policy regarding the Dark."

"So then, what's the problem?" I ask. Siman might be a natural leader, but he's also long-winded, as they all tend to be.

"They're not convinced. But because of how you're positioned, we hope you can persuade them."

"How am I positioned?" I ask.

Siman shakes his head. He knows I don't need him to spell it out, but I'm making him. "Because you're an apprentice reckoner. Because Lucan respects you." Siman bites his lip and then spills the actual reason. "And because of your father."

My father. Yes. One of the long-winded leaders.

"I'd like to be there, but if he's against it, it won't happen." My father's one of the few people I listen to. If he hasn't said anything, he doesn't want me there.

"Oh, come on, Anni," Siman says, using the nickname my mother despises. Coming from him, a former friend, I sort of don't like it either—Siman's lost the right to call me that. I scowl, but he continues, "No one in the community can keep you from doing anything you set your mind on."

My mind. Not my heart. There's a difference, and Siman knows which one I use to get my way. But because my mind is acutely adept, I know this is manipulation. This is what he wants, not what I want, and his attempt to trick me into thinking otherwise is annoying. Presumptive. Conniving. And I hate all three devices unless I'm the one wielding them.

"That's true. And your scheming tactic has me leaning toward *not attending*."

But the minute I say it, I feel a twinge of guilt—not because I've been dishonest with Siman but because I've been dishonest with myself. In my experience, I'm the only person to whom I owe complete honesty, and I just tried to convince myself of a falsehood—one of my own making. Truthfully, Siman's calculated maneuver hasn't turned me off as it should. No, I want to be there. I want to be involved and help with these decisions. Though I'm only an apprentice, I'm their best reckoner, and they need me.

And when Siman doesn't reply, only smiles, I'm sure he understands my conundrum.

"Gah!" I blurt out after a long silence. I hate assenting, but maybe a small concession will benefit me later. Still, I can't give in completely, so I leave them with a vague, "I'll consider it."

CHAPTER TWO

I could have been a nice person. At least, I've considered the possibility when I see the evidence stacked against me.

"Annibeth, you're so cruel," Nacole says, drawing out each word, then giggling.

Cruel. I think on the descriptor.

I guess I am. On the outside, I'm not bothered by the label, so I smile in agreement. Inside, the word scratches lightly, just a brief scrape on my conscience, reminding me I could act differently—could *be* different. Instead, I return Nacole's giggle with a laugh and continue tormenting my target.

Who is the target?

It doesn't matter. It's the principle you should note—no one is safe from me.

Nacole smiles, and the expression is false—she doesn't enjoy being mean. In fact, she doesn't even like me. Not really, but she knows it's too easy for me to take one of her flaws and turn it on her. She's seen me do it to others, so she's afraid. And she smiles through her fear.

Only once did Nacole find the courage to go against me. She sided with Siman during a night of rooftop games on Building Fifteen. And I was proud of her. Hurt, but still proud. It was nice to see and confirmed why I chose her as my primary friend. Afterward, when she came groveling, I didn't let her back in. Not at first. She felt my ire for a few days until I gave my forgiveness. And then she fell under my control again.

So easily.

That's how it works. I'm the expert here. I turn everything my way.

It's sad how efficiently I can ruin someone. It's disappointing how fake I am. I could have been nice... but that was before tyranny became a part of me. It didn't happen because I enjoyed it... not at first. Or because I was afraid... *never*.

No, I evolved into who I am because they taught me to be this way.

"Shouldn't we get back before it's too dark?" Nacole asks, which is her way of saying the target has had enough.

I shrug and brush my hair behind my shoulder. Nacole watches the jangle of my bracelet. I see the envy in her brown eyes over the precious item but pretend I don't. Then I walk away, and Nacole takes quick steps to follow me. It's ridiculous I still act this way. I'll be eighteen soon, and it seems the right time to stop playing control games with others. Honestly, the time was a couple of years ago, but I'm not sure I can stop. At least, not until I have somewhere else to wield control. I have to have power somewhere, and until they make me a full-fledged reckoner, I'm not sure I'll have enough of an outlet.

We arrive at my quarters well before the light is gone. We enter the gathering room, and the door to my parent's room is closed. I take light steps and open it to peek inside. My mother is asleep under her blankets, so I pull it closed with a soft click. Hopefully, tomorrow will be a better day for her.

Entering my room, Nacole asks in a low whisper, "Is your mother okay?"

I feel the first signs of moisture in my eyes. The thing is, I don't know if she's okay. Her life was perfect. She was unstoppable—until she wasn't. And the clinicians can't find anything wrong, but she gets exhausted frequently. Her energy and drive used to be without match, and I could barely keep up. Now she's drained most of the time. I want to help, but I don't know how. I do what I can, but it's never enough.

"She's tired," I say, but Nacole's expression says she thinks there's more, but she's smart and knows I won't tell her anything, so she doesn't press.

"Maybe it's not a good night for me to stay over," she says, looking at our thin walls.

"Nah. We'll just be quiet."

We're already whispering, but Nacole's voice drops when she asks, "Do you want to go rung climbing tomorrow morning?"

It's something we started a year ago. We both enjoy exercise, but a confined community doesn't provide many opportunities for strenuous activity. The Hem is about the only place to run or jog—a traditionally nefarious prospect with the Dark so near. So, instead of tempting the unknown, Nacole and I used the ladders and irrigation flumes built for our rooftop aqueduct. We climb up, run across the buildings, climb down, and find the next ladder to go up again. We do it early so we're not seen, not wanting to start a trend and defeat the entire purpose. Though trending isn't the real concern. It's more likely that if Lucan or Devid Herrington—our friend Melton's father, who's the Sector Leader of Construction and Lumber—knew what we were doing, they'd stop us. Worry over damaging the flumes is real, but we're always careful.

"I can't. I have somewhere to be," I say, but I don't elaborate.

After talking to Siman and Evans, I didn't go to my father like they wanted, instead using the relationship with Cully's father, Lucan, to get the reckoners invited to tomorrow's meeting. It wasn't difficult. The biggest hurdle was managing Lucan's anger over my knowledge of the meeting. Of course, he didn't aim his frustration at me. It was entirely on Evans after he learned about the two boys providing the information. "I should have known. That one can't keep his mouth shut for a worthy cause," Lucan had said, removing any blame from Siman—a mistake in my mind.

Nacole looks disappointed I'm unavailable in the morning,

so I attempt to soften the blow. "I'm gonna head downstairs and get some bread and cheese."

"Ooh," Nacole says, her consternation disappearing at the impressive suggestion. The others don't have these items available like we do. Lucan keeps the quality stuff on hand for meetings or important meals. It's easy to run to the kitchen next to the large Well meeting room and get something.

The best part is, if Lucan were to see me, he wouldn't even mind. He'd call me his darling girl, advise me not to let his son do anything dumb, and send me on my way.

"Anything else you want?" I ask, opening the door.

"Some water?" Nacole asks coyly, not wanting water in the least.

"Apple juice," I say, and she grins, silently clapping her hands.

"Thanks, Anni," she whispers as I slip out of my room.

I don't make it far. Rounding the corner to exit our quarters, my mother's standing on the landing above the stairs. It takes only a second to realize she heard my exchange with Nacole. Not the one about my mother's health. Not about ladders and flumes or getting food from the kitchen. No. It was the last part she heard as Nacole gave me her thanks. The second I see her face, I brace for her anger, mentally working on my rebuttal.

"Why didn't you correct her?" she asks. It's an old argument. One that frustrates me, mostly because I shouldn't have to care. It's a stupid fight. Every time we have it.

"Nacole meant nothing by it," I say, not bothering to tell her that all my friends call me Anni when we're together. They know to call me Annibeth in front of my parents, but it was a harmless slip when Nacole did it just now. She thought my mother was asleep, and she's been upset about Siman. It was an accident.

"Your name is *Annibeth*. It's not proper for people to call you otherwise, and you must be sure to correct them."

I purse my lips. I actually like Anni better, but after years of the same instructions, I've given up arguing the point. Instead, I say, "I know. I'll remind her." And I expect my mother to drop it, but this time, she doesn't.

"We have a reputation to uphold. We can't show weakness or be casual with any of the citizens. Remember our place in the community system."

I release a frustrated sigh. (Frustrated sighs are my go-to of late.) I want her to back off, so I can get snacks and begin a relaxing, enjoyable night with my friend. But until I discuss this with my mother, she won't let it go.

"I know my role and what I'm supposed to do. I'll be sure Nacole maintains the proper boundaries."

My mother nods and blinks slowly. I almost wonder if she'll open her eyes again or fall asleep standing here on the landing.

"I need you to follow the rules without having to remind you. I promise there's a good reason for them. We've taught you these things from your earliest years, and we did it to keep you safe. It was the only way."

I used to ask what it all meant—her vague comments about keeping distant to keep safe—but my father would always give her a look, and she'd maintain her silence. Then she'd promise to tell me when I'm older.

And now I'm older. Isn't this the time?

What slight amount of energy she had when we started this discussion has waned. I can't press her for answers tonight. I must lighten her worries, and nothing she asks of me is worth disrupting her precarious health.

"You taught me what I need to do. I promise I'll do a better job of it, with no need for reminders."

"Daughter," she breathes out with a quivering lip. I reach around her in an encompassing hug, holding her to me. She relaxes, and I take some of her weight. "Thank you. These men from the Dark... I'm just so afraid. And I'm just so... tired."

"I'll help. You can depend on me. I'll do everything you taught me and more."

Years of instruction run through my mind. I'll be the perfect daughter. I'll maintain control in every situation and never get taken advantage of. Never look like a fool. Act better than them. Be better. I'm above the community and answer to no one but my parents. I direct what happens around me. Never get too close. Uphold the mask of flawlessness. Make Lucan cherish me. Make Cully choose me.

"You need to get back to bed," I tell her, fatigued by the long list of all I need to do and be.

She pulls back. "I'm tired but don't know if I can sleep."

I brush her face and wisp away a hair stuck to her cheek. "You should probably try."

"I need your help again tomorrow morning," she says.

Requests for my time during that period are coming like lightning. "I can't. I have a meeting, but I'll help later."

"To what meeting are you referring?" she asks. She was once a reckoner like I plan to be, and her words occasionally come out like she's requesting evidence or giving a verdict. Now she plans events, which is likely where she needs my help.

"Lucan asked for me," I answer, saying the magic word. Any connection to Lucan makes my mother happy. "I'm not sure of the details, but it concerns the people from the Dark. All the reckoners and apprentices will be there."

"Good for you," she says, smiling and patting my cheek before kissing the same spot. "I'm sorry I've kept you. Get your treats so you can go to bed. It appears you have a busy morning."

She walks into our quarters, a slow shuffle to her step. As curious as I am about tomorrow's meeting, I hope it's short (though, we all know there's no such thing) because I want to get home and help her with everything she needs.

I hurry down the outside steps, re-enter the Well, and go to the kitchen. I find the items quickly and am heading back with my arms full, when I encounter three late-night visitors. It's Siman and Evans, and this time they brought the big guy, wearing his black longcoat that makes him look like a thunderous cloud blown in on a storm. While the first two have a smile and mischievous glint, respectively, Ronen doesn't look happy to be here.

"You're here again?" I ask but don't get a reply, so I look at Ronen and add, "You draw the short stick this time?"

"Aye. Somethin' like tha'," he says with a wince. He's a head taller than the others and double their width. The thick beard covering his face—rich brown with a subtle red tint—only makes him look bigger. It's trimmed short—maybe an inch long—but it's not only the hair on his face that's maintained. The hair on his head is cut that length too. Also, the fuzz on his arms and the tufts at the neckline of his shirt. He's covered in hair—there are even little groupings between his knuckles —but he keeps it all controlled, so instead of looking like an overgrown goat, he's sleek and powerfully appealing.

Though I get the feeling he doesn't approve of me. Not that the others do, but I believe I irritate him to a more considerable degree. I decide his annoyance with me is equal to his size and feel rather proud of the accomplishment.

"He's here to be the voice of reason, is all," Evans says with a chuckle. "Considering he doesn't talk much, I don't know how that will go."

Ignoring Evans, Siman asks, "Did you do it?"

"To what are you referring?" I use the same phrasing as my mother. She taught me well.

The big guy groans. "Mindless lass."

"Gah! Stop calling me that, Big Scruff," I bark back, and when the little boys laugh, I bite my smile. Then I consider calling them *little boys* out loud—because there's nothing like an insult to get someone's attention—but I settle on, "Just because I prefer a transparent question to get a precise answer doesn't make me mindless. And, yes, I did *do it*. What's the meeting about anyway? Lucan was tight-lipped."

Evans grins. "You're gonna love it." But he looks more like he'll love it. Like they've planned the event and secured my attendance, especially to witness my torture.

I look at Siman, who's possibly more reasonable than the other two. "Tell me."

"I can't."

"Right," I drone. "If I stutter or cry like your beloved Tesha, you'd tell me, wouldn't you?"

"No," Siman answers, nonplussed.

"Don't care that much anyway," I say, hoping my disinterest will inspire some words, but they don't bite, staying silent about anything important.

When it's clear they're just playing with me, I twist to go up the stairs, and the group watches me take the risers two at a time. I reach the top, and turning back, they're gone. Standing outside my home, I'm no wiser, with only an armful of food and a headache.

CHAPTER THREE

I t's a frigid December morning. The sun entered our cloudless sky hours ago, but the towering pines near the bathhouses cast a long, low shadow. The early frost is still on the back steps as I move down them, leaving outlines of my shoes. My father left identical shapes when he left our quarters fifteen minutes ago. Well, not identical since the mark of his left foot is elongated compared to the right. But the point is, he's the only other person to leave our home this morning—Mother and Nacole are still in the bedrooms, sleeping.

I wasn't responsible like Mother asked, and instead of getting sufficient sleep, I stayed up late talking with my friend, but the lack of rest gives me an edginess I enjoy. We'll see if I feel the same by the end of the day.

I wish we had indoor stairs down to the Well like the Clarcs do. They have a set outside and inside, but we're not so lucky. I shiver and rush to the front of the building. Here, at least, the sun has found a path through the trees to warm the ground. Entering through the large doors, I'm engulfed with heat, feeling instantly thawed. I'm even ready to take off my wool sweater.

The comforts we've enjoyed since the people from the Dark showed up are remarkable. We keep an almost-constant fire in the rock hearth of the Well, warming the rooms above and making this space more of a gathering spot than ever. The presence of the Coastals is still disturbing, but I won't complain about the benefits.

Crossing the room, I gather by my people, noting that Vale is here. She's my nemesis, though we're no longer in competition for Cully. So maybe that demotes her from nemesis to merely an opponent, which is how I view most people. I'm either devoted to them, or they have something I want—even if it's their docility. Or allowing me to have my way without contest.

It's meaningful that Vale isn't standing with the people I consider my own, and it feels like her alliance is fully with the Coastals now, though I don't know her well enough to be sure. I've barely seen her lately, as she's been in the Dark, and it's been nice to have free access to the community without her frequent intrusions into my business. But now, here we are again. I can't help but wonder if it will be more of the same— each of us arguing our point, unwilling to budge. I don't like her but admire that she doesn't back down. Still, it doesn't mean I won't decimate her if I have an opening.

She's watching me—her green eyes locked on my face, studying me—though I can't guess the purpose behind her intense gaze. Her hand rests at her throat, rubbing a wooden pendant hanging on a ratty cloth chain. She's worn it since we were children, but not because it's pretty—not in the least. She drops it to her chest, then brushes her black hair over her shoulder before looking away from me.

"Thank you for coming," Lucan says, tilting his chin in greeting. His dirty blond hair brushes his shoulders with the gesture. "If you'll all take a seat, we'll begin." His tone is formal while ushering us to fill the seats around the sturdy table.

When choosing our seats, we take sides, so to speak. The five Coastal representatives are on one side—the three Dark Brothers, Vale, and her father, Laso—and four community representatives are on the other. We fill every chair at the table with no one left standing, which makes no sense because not all the reckoners are here. It's just me, an apprentice, and the senior reckoner, Balee, who is my mentor.

"Where are the other reckoners? And Cully?" I ask. Surely, Lucan wouldn't have this meeting without his son. I note that Captain Rhed isn't here either, which seems odd.

"You're very astute, dear," is Lucan's response, not bothered by my interruption. "At first glance, it would appear we're missing key people, but we're assembled as planned. Captain Rhed and I agreed we're crunched for time, so we divided into two groups. I'm leading this exploratory information session while he's with Cully, the sector leaders, and the other reckoners, seeing the lamlight and a Coastal guard demonstration. We'll convene this evening to make decisions based on our discoveries."

It's disappointing to learn the others are experiencing the lamlight since I've yet to see the miracle light source myself, but Balee nods beside me, content with the situation. She's a pleasant woman with a sharp mind and a natural smile, highlighted by a small mole on her upper lip. Like me, she was attentive during Lucan's explanation, but the rest seem already informed about our division.

"Let's begin," says the man our community calls Lucan's assistant. The man I call Father.

His proper name is Marven Petters, though you'll rarely hear it. The man who does so much for the community barely has an identity of his own. In the citizen's eyes, his primary worth is his connection to our leader, and they address him accordingly—a fact I abhor.

He's a dutiful man and deserves more credit. It bothers me endlessly, but I really get riled up when I notice it bothering him. So, he's learned not to let me see it because I can't keep my mouth shut where family pride is concerned—a trait I don't find shameful in the least. Why should I concede to another's opinion of me or mine when I don't agree?

And while Lucan—a man I think well of—overshadows my father's identity, there's no doubt my father's the more capable of the two. He's excellent at what he does. The two men are not close in age—Lucan's a decade his junior—but my father looks and acts younger, even with his perpetual limp and balding head.

I observe the row of faces on the other side of the table, and I'm happy the one causing Nacole's tears to saturate all my good handkerchiefs isn't here. (You'd feel the same if you'd suffered through his apologetic smiles as much as I have of late.) Evans sits across from me with his unnerving black lenses. His equally intimidating brothers flank him—Ronen opposite Lucan and Geric opposite Balee. Vale sidles up to Geric —her hot boy toy with the rigid posture—and my father faces off with Laso on the other end, sitting next to Lucan and Ronen, respectively.

Their positioning makes sense because my father is always squaring off with Laso. They don't get along—always scowling at one another—and it's been worse lately, possibly because of Laso's involvement with the Coastals. It's the only solution I've come up with since my father won't speak about it.

I asked him once if he had an issue with Laso Rennick, and he nearly bit my head off, demanding I never let my mother hear me say that, though what she has to do with it is a mystery. I'm not one to let things go, so I've continued watching their interactions closely but covertly. I've even eavesdropped a few times but have had no luck discovering the source of their discord.

It's strange to be in this room with the people from the Dark. I've seen them plenty of times in the community. A group of us even learned ways to defend ourselves from Evans and then later from members of the guard. But, until now, I've never interacted with them in my capacity as an apprentice reckoner. I'd never reveal my feelings, but it's thrilling to get the chance.

"We bring this exploratory session to order," my father says to start things officially. "The topics discussed in this meeting should not be repeated outside of this room without express permission from Lucan." He slices his hand through the air, as is his way—he always uses his hands when he talks. "Is that understood?"

"We're accustomed to your secret pacts. No need to worry we'll spill the soup," Evans says.

I look at the faces around the room as I try to decipher the strange comment, which is a mixture of frustration and amusement. But Lucan is the one who looks *really* frustrated, so much so it outweighs Evans's amusement.

"We agreed you wouldn't be a mouthpiece at this meeting," Lucan says with a growl.

"Oh, you're right. I'm not. That's his job." Evans pokes Ronen. "Doesn't mean I'll not talk." Evans scoffs, then grins.

Lucan doesn't like the brothers, but he tolerates Ronen the most. Our leader runs a hand down his face and sighs. He's not looking at anyone, just mumbling behind his hand before telling my father to continue.

"It's agreed that Lucan Clarc, myself—Marven Petters—Balee Nordup, and Annibeth Petters are representing the interests of Harwell." He rolls his hands, listing the names.

Interestingly, my father uses the name the Coastals call our community—Harwell. Lately, he's adopted the term more frequently. And where Lucan used to be opposed, he seems to have no objection now. If that's the case, I may start using it because it's much simpler.

"Representing the Coastals are Ronen Wynne, Geric Dover, and Evans Dirby."

I swear I was told they were brothers, but maybe Coastals have different customs for surnames. I'm curious, but it's not the time to ask. The boys are without their longcoats, making their bodies look smaller, though no less intimidating. The attitude they put off behind their black lenses spurs my need to dominate, and my lips fidget, wanting to use words to conquer them. But the need subsides as my father claims my interest with what he says next.

"Laso Rennick and Vale Rennick have asked for neutral representation at these proceedings."

Neutral? Does that mean they have no say? Or does it mean they speak for both sides? More importantly, where do their loyalties lie? And maybe that's exactly the point. They don't have a firm commitment to either side. It seems rather cowardly when I consider it that way. Do one or the other, but not both. *Take a stand.* Their middling attitude is bothersome, and I can't stay quiet.

"What exactly does being neutral entail?" I bite out, and Ronen's mouth disappears in his beard as he presses his lips together disapprovingly. He can silently decry my question all he wants. I equally decry the stand Laso and Vale are making, but I do so vocally.

Laso's the one who addresses my concern. "It means we possess knowledge of both sides—our history living in Harwell and our experiences traveling in the Dark."

His answer is overtly political, which may be a ridiculous observation since this meeting is entirely political. Still, I'm not in the mood, so I press my point. "Why not be honest about which side you're on?"

"I believe that's the entire point of neutrality," Vale says, drawing my attention to her. Her green eyes flash with confidence. "We don't wish to be on a side at all. We wish to advocate the interests of both sides."

I open my mouth to give a reply but am cut off.

"Daughter, that's enough for now. Let's continue."

I purse my lips and turn away, scowling. *That's enough*? How am I supposed to be a reckoner if I don't speak? And if there was an issue with my inquiry, why didn't my mentor, who's sitting right next to me, make the objection? I did nothing wrong. I wasn't badgering, belligerent, or unreasonable. In fact, I was ready to concede to Vale's argument. It was sound. Instead, my father stepped in, berating me like a silly child. I love him, but I can't believe he'd purposely make me look foolish.

The meeting starts, and I don't feel like I can do my job. I'm supposed to inquire about details and search out meaningful questions. Instead, I can't look anyone in the eye while I try to prevent the blush of embarrassment from covering my cheeks.

But I don't let the reaction linger. I always rally. That's my way.

My father turns the meeting over to Ronen to navigate our topics. The big guy rarely leads the discussion but directs his brother what to present next.

Evans opens with information regarding the surrounding civilizations. Our region has four territories led by people of the Dark—the Northern, Southern, Desert, and Coastal. Within each are various Dark cities, falling under the laws and protection of their respective territory. There are also light bubbles of many sizes and population densities within the boundaries. Some are ruled independently, of which Adlumen, Torquent, Hamo, Circes, and Patera are the largest. It goes without saying that Harwell lies within Captain Rhed's Coastal Territory.

The details are overwhelming when presented to a group accustomed to a single civilization comprising three thousand people. I've always enjoyed the closeness of the community. It's been my stage. The people watch me perform, and I direct what they do. I own every facet of the production. But in the world outside Harwell, what part do I play?

It's suddenly clear my pleasant existence isn't returning. It's ended, though it's the last thing I want. The realization momentarily makes me unsteady, and I feel unsure of my place but compelled to find it. All I know is I'll be influential in what's happening. I'll create a role if I must, but I won't get left behind, no matter how concerned I am.

But the men from the Dark are very convincing and excel at delivering their points. Begrudgingly, I respect their presentation while continuing to struggle with how the revelations impact my life.

Based on Lucan's questions, he has similar worries, but he's too transparent, not waiting for proper openings to make his move and secure his role. A brief glance from my father shows he's noticed Lucan's errors too. Our thoughts aligning makes sense because Father taught me how to think—calculating and decisive.

Geric talks about threats and alliances, and from my limited viewpoint, it seems there are more of the former than the latter. Their only ally seems to be the Southern Territory, and, after a lengthy back and forth about Captain Rhed's handling of some minor squabbles, Lucan comes to the same conclusion, saying, "It seems you have one avenue of support against multiple threats."

"Aye. Tha' would be the look o' it," Ronen agrees blandly, his statement not one to stoke confidence. The man would be terrible in a debate. Indeed, I'm not convinced he's a viable candidate to lead this meeting, but he improves my opinion slightly when, after an uncomfortable pause, he adds, "But the threats er little 'n the support, big."

"Ronen's right," Evans adds. "And Raider believes some issues we're facing might be Adlumen creating diversions."

Adlumen—the light bubble that hired Captain Malum to find Harwell. Raider—a leader in the Southern Territory. I'm more easily linking names and places, expanding my ability to process information and shape conclusions, and it has me realizing alliances and threats aren't our problems.

"The political posturing and sheer volume of people outside of Harwell are intimidating," I say with a nod to Lucan. "But the real issue is lamlight, isn't it?" I ask, looking at the Dark brothers. "Without it, the balance of power would remain unchanged, and our community would mostly remain out of harm. But the lamlight not only changes Harwell but changes every other settlement—whether a Dark territory or a light bubble. So, there's no point dwelling on alliances and threats. Those were yesterday's problems. Starting today, they're nothing but an interesting side note. Because they're temporary. Everything's about to be redrawn."

"It pains me to admit, but that's the brightest thing you've ever said," Evans says with a dry smile.

I keep my expression neutral (a practiced and perfected skill) while bristling inside over the blatant insult. But Evans agreed with me, so starting an argument serves no purpose. Still, Lucan must think it's an option because he groans before saying, "I hoped to avoid a quarrel today. Before that hope is destroyed, we should break for mid-day meal. Maybe some food will help me tolerate you for another hour."

"Aw, thanks," Evan says, hopping to his feet. "Someone point me to the grub."

CHAPTER FOUR

Needing a relief break more than food, I leave the Well, and when I return, I'm the only one not seated and focused on eating. The group remains divided, which is more evident during mealtime, with the Coastals at the kitchen table and the community members returning to the main meeting table. Laso and Vale remind me of goat's head stickers, adhering to their new friends like the painful clinging weed.

I've barely entered the room when my father pushes off his chair and hobbles to my side. His limp is pronounced today—a sign he's been sitting for too long. It's an old injury from before I was born. Living in second-floor quarters is difficult for him, but the prestige of his position is worth any pain. He doesn't like to talk about how it limits him, discomforts him, or how it happened, so I barely consider it most days. But today, the brothers from the Dark are noting his struggle, making my anger simmer. They better not think of him as weak. He's the most determined man I know.

"You're doing well today," he says, keeping his voice low. "I'm proud of you. I'm sorry if my earlier reprimand made you uncomfortable."

"It should have come from my mentor, not you. But I understand your desire to end the topic."

"And I understood your need to press them on it. It wasn't without merit. I just didn't know how Lucan would react."

"He seemed fine," I say, recalling the moment.

"He did. And I'll do better to let your mentor guide you."

"You're fine, Father. Don't let it concern you." I lean over and kiss his cheek. Glancing up, the Dark brothers are still watching. Laso and Vale too. I wish they'd mind their own business.

I enter the kitchen and take the last bowl of food, already dished out for our mid-day meal. It's a soup with fish, potatoes, apple slices, and peas. We've had more soup lately with the increased availability of open fires. (Two words and a contraction: It's been divine.) We've also had a few citizens nearly burn down their buildings, so there's that downside. I'm still getting used to the smell of trees when they burn. The leaf logs smell dusty, putting off a lot of smoke, whereas the tree logs smell clean.

"Annibeth!" With food in hand, I turn to find Vale motioning me to their table. I hope she doesn't think I'll sit there. I glance into the other room, locating the empty seat beside Balee. It's like Vale knows my thoughts. "I just have a quick question," she says, but questions are never innocent between us. There's always a deeper meaning.

Nearing their table, I consider it's one against five. I never purposely enter a situation with bad odds. This move seems a critical error, but I still grant Vale's summons. Though wary, I walk until my thighs hit the tabletop.

"When's your birthday?" she asks, and my immediate response is a scowl. Why would Vale Rennick care when I was born? And how will my answer trap me in whatever plan she's concocted to make me look stupid?

Not compliant by nature, I can't quite bring myself to tell her the date. I'm never submissive unless there's a return benefit. "Planning to sabotage the day?" I ask, remaining collected and watching their faces. Those lenses! They give nothing away.

"What? Of course not." Vale's answer seems forced, though not necessarily false. She seems resolved and unsurprised by my reaction. "We've lived together all these years, and I don't know much about you."

"A fact you've never found issue with until now," I state. "What's changed?"

"I just wondered," Vale responds with a shrug and a frown.

Does she want my pity? Trying to make me look pitiful is more like. I roll my eyes, keeping the answer to myself.

"You're a proper piece of work, aren't you?" Evans asks, and my eyes flash to him.

"If you mean I'm not one to get duped by a stupid ploy, then yes, I am."

"That's not what I meant at all," Evans sneers.

Big Scruff grunts next to him. "Leave it alone, Kid. Let the lasses find their path."

I'm surprised when Evans takes direction and stays quiet, but Vale goes mute too—I've shut her down. I stand stupidly for a few moments. The only ones looking at me are Ronen and Laso. The others are too busy eating their food, which is precisely what I should be doing, but I can't let this go. I'm always strategizing, and the question of my birthdate has me doing just that. I can't have them think I'm afraid, and the date of my birth isn't any secret, so I blurt out, "February first," before spinning on my heel to leave.

"Lass!" The word vibrates from Ronen's throat, stopping me. He's on his feet, rounding the table and facing me. I've rarely stood this close to him, but I get the same sensation each time—he's gigantic. My eyes fall level with the wide expanse of his chest, and I straighten my spine to feel more like an adult than a child.

He holds up his thick hand in a meaty fist. "Fer yer soup," he says, waiting on me to offer my bowl for some purpose. I hesitate, but strangely enough, the thing that decides me is when I take in the expression on Vale's face. She's giving Ronen a tender smile. She doesn't even see I've noticed her.

I lift my bowl, and he opens his hand. A dusting of items

resembling dry, crumbled leaves and sand drop into my soup. I wrinkle my nose and stare up at him.

"Trust me. Ye'll like it." Without further explanation, he spins away. (I feel an actual breeze when he moves.) Returning to his table, he relaxes onto the unprepared chair with a creak.

Joining my people, I look over the stuff floating in my bowl. I slowly drop onto my seat, spying on the other meals and noting no one else got the addition from the Coastals. I stir my soup, mixing it in, barely listening to the table conversation. It's a minute longer before I dare try it. I lift a spoonful of broth and sip it. It's not bad. The next time I dip my spoon, I put the entire thing in my mouth, this time with a potato. "Mmm," I say, chewing the flavorful vegetable. I've never liked potatoes, but these are wonderful.

"What was that, my dear?" Lucan asks, tilting his head and watching while I reload my utensil.

"Just thinking how good the soup is today."

He winces, and I notice a slight shake of his head. "I thought it was rather bland."

"Oh. I'm sorry."

"No. I'm glad your portion is good," Lucan says, and I glance into the kitchen at the one who altered my soup. Ronen catches me looking at him and puts his thumb in the air. I don't know what the gesture means or how to respond to it, so I turn away and keep eating my meal.

Soon we're finishing up, and the main door opens. Cully enters the room, his dirty blond hair hanging in his eyes, so it's difficult to see where they're focused. He may have noticed me in the room, but he doesn't make any sign of happiness about seeing me. We have an understanding while performing our community jobs—we keep things professional. It's just easier. Though, sometimes, I wish he'd forget himself and give me a grin or wink. But today's not that day.

I twist my gold bracelet under the table while he approaches Lucan. "Hello, Father. We've concluded our business in the Dark. Should I ask the others to enter the Well to join your meeting?"

"Uh," Lucan looks at my father, who gives our leader an imperceptible headshake. "No. That won't be necessary. We'll finish up with the group we have."

"Father?" Cully asks, flipping his hair to the side and scowling between the two men.

"We don't need any more logs on the fire," Lucan says by way of explanation, and I agree with him. Having the sector leaders and other reckoners could create even more conflict within the room. Some of them might attempt to posture to look valuable in their leader's eyes. I can see the wisdom in Lucan's decision, but I'm still surprised by what I hear next.

"Did you want just me to return?" Cully asks.

"No. We'll finish up soon, and I'll connect with you." Only we won't finish up anytime soon. From what I know of the agenda, we'll likely go late. "We'll get both groups together later as planned."

"I'll tell them," Cully says, but his voice is stern. His eyes fly to mine, staring. *I'll see you later*, his expression says. He figures I'm his personal information source, but if I want to be a proper reckoner, I'll tell him nothing. To get him moving, I give him an imperceptible nod—the Petters have that motion down pat—but I hate the idea of anyone believing I'm easily swayed into revealing confidences.

As Cully slips out the door, I see Siman outside with Tesha. They're holding hands, and I roll my eyes, dropping my spoon into the bowl with a clatter before throwing back my chair and taking my dirty dish into the kitchen.

The break is over, and the meeting reconvenes, going on for hours. Lucan called for mid-day meal to improve our moods with full bellies, but it doesn't prove to be enough.

The slight tension from earlier becomes more pronounced. Motives are questioned regarding things of little consequence, and conditions go from bad to worse. Tempers flare on all sides. I only keep an objective mind from force of habit. Show of emotion is a weakness. Understanding an opponent's mind is vital in any argument, almost to the point of believing it oneself. Only then can you come out on top. But no one is winning today.

"We're going in circles," I say after I can't keep quiet any longer. I've listened in silence long enough. "We need to do something different because we're not making progress."

"By the Dark, she's right again," Evans grumbles.

Ronen ignores his brother, saying, "We're all tired," and no one can argue that point—the yawning has been constant for the last half hour.

"We'll stop for the evening and start fresh in the morning," Lucan announces. "The same group. No additions," he says, looking around the room for acknowledgement. Once he has it, Lucan waits for the Coastals and Goat Heads to leave before turning to us. "Tomorrow, I hope the strangers will be more willing to bend to our thinking."

Unlikely, but I guess there's no policy against having hope.

"Annibeth," Lucan says to get my attention. "I upset Cully when I didn't invite him to stay. He'll be in your room waiting for details." Lucan doesn't miss a look or gesture. "If I add more people, they'll feel like they can too. And I want to keep Captain Rhed out of our meetings. The boys are more loose-lipped when he's not around."

"They've seemed fairly transparent today," I say, reflecting on everything they said in our sessions. "More so than in the past."

"Maybe so, but there's something they're not saying. I can feel it." Lucan reaches out and gives me a fatherly pat on the cheek. "Help Cully understand. You always know the right way to get through to him."

Yeah, I think with a smile, *I boss him around and don't give him any choice.*

The sun isn't down, so there's plenty of light when I enter my room. The west window has a view of the sunset above the Dark, where the void is nebulous. It's a pretty sky, and I'd rather stare at it than talk to the boy sitting in my room.

"You gonna tell me about your meeting?" he asks, picking at the edge of my blanket.

"It was long," I say with wide eyes, and Cully snorts, knowing that's all he's getting. "Learn anything inside the Dark?" I ask, pulling my hair off my neck and into a tail high on my head. Cully watches as I brush the strands with my fingers, smoothing them along my scalp.

"Counted close to one hundred of them, though I bet there are more. There were even some new arrivals during our meeting. At this rate, they'll soon outnumber us."

I look curiously toward the Dark, amazed so much is happening out there of which we're mostly unaware. "What else?"

"Learned that Rhed's guard isn't as scary as Malum and his Six. Not nearly. The fancy clothes really set them apart."

But appearance isn't everything, and it's good to remind Cully of that. "Yeah, but who's the one that's dead?"

Ignoring my question, he says, "I asked to spend more time with them tomorrow in the Dark. Figured I wasn't wanted elsewhere, so I might as well dip my jug and see if I get water."

"Your father will like that."

Cully groans, but his disgruntled attitude doesn't last long. His eyes brighten, and he swoops my feet off the floor, holding me around the waist. "You miss me today, Babycakes?" He leans in and nuzzles the side of my face.

"Gah! Don't call me that. It's gross."

"Okay, Baby." He displays his crooked smile—the one he thinks gets him whatever he wants but irritates me to no end.

"That either." He finds my ear lobe and sucks it between his teeth to nibble. I push him back, and his teeth scrape my ear as he goes. "Go home, Cully. I don't want to be around you right now."

He drops me to my feet, putting his hands up like he's innocent. "Okay, but let me know if you change your mind."

Yeah, our quarters have an adjoining wall. Our gathering room is opposite Cully's bedroom, and just a quick rap with my knuckles would call him back. But I won't be doing that tonight. "Go away, Cully. I'm tired."

But he's oblivious and acts as if, instead of demanding his departure, I swooned and blew air kisses. Turning to leave, he imparts one final insult by smacking my backside and proclaiming, "Later, babe."

I whip around, ready to strike. But he's too fast and is out of my window and onto the landing outside. "I have a door!" I complain, but he merely smirks, then is gone.

My father's still downstairs with Lucan. The two men could be awake for hours discussing their tactics, so I take a moment and check on my mother. She's in her room and, per usual, is asleep, but only lightly. She stirs when I enter. "Meeting done?" she asks with a yawn.

"Yeah. You feeling okay?"

"I am. A little less sluggish today."

I crouch and brush my hand across her cheek before pushing hair from her forehead. Her skin is tight and clammy, but touching her smooth skin does something to my insides. "That feels nice," she says, and I hear the sleepiness in her voice. A tear runs the length of my face, stopping at my upper lip, which Cully calls pouty. I lick it off, anticipating another.

I don't know how to help her. I'd do anything—even

befriend Lord Endrack himself. Does he even have friends? Not for the first time, I consider the man from a giant light bubble who's obsessed with our little spot in the world. Regardless, becoming his friend doesn't seem a viable option to fix much of anything. I release a sigh just as my mother's breathing turns heavy with sleep, so I step out to give her the quiet she needs.

Back in my room, I'm changing into my nightclothes—my bottoms still on but bare from the waist up—when I spot a shadow at my window. Most lower-floor apartments have curtains, but the upper quarters don't unless they're bedrooms or have balconies—both of which apply to my home. No one likes a lurking shadow behind their thin cloth divide. Unfortunately, I know exactly who's on the other side.

I press my just-removed shirt to my chest and throw back my curtain. "Bredley Feck, you peeping pervert!"

Bredley's usually stern expression turns into one of surprise. He stumbles away from the opening, nearly tumbling over the railing. I'm unsure how I'd feel if he fell ten feet to the hard ground below, though I think I might like it—especially when his shock turns into an unrepentant grin.

That's it!

I tear through our living quarters to the main door, opening it just as Bredley huffs past. I reach for him and narrowly miss, my finger catching on his shirt briefly. He practically falls down the stairs, but his ungraceful feet meet every step.

"Run, Bredley, you sicko!" I yell from the top step. Deciding I haven't done enough to avenge myself, I race after him, still clutching my shirt to my front. He glances back, his brown hair falling across his eyes. He's at the edge of my building but pauses briefly before disappearing around the corner.

I'm in pursuit and turn the same corner only to discover what momentarily stopped him. Ronen is standing there watching Bredley run away. But the behemoth doesn't deter me. My chase continues as I shake my fist, yelling, "This isn't the end, Bredley! You do it one more time, just once more, and you're dead! I'll have my father chop you up for provisions. We'll pass you around as a rare steak, and the people will gobble up your sorry ass!"

Ronen's brows rise above his dark lenses. Even behind them, I can tell he's running his eyes up and down my unconventional appearance. In my defense, the west side of the Well backs up to the Hem, and the south side, where we are now, is against the river. There's usually no one here.

"Bells," he says, rubbing his tight beard before letting out a whistle. "Heard ye was bad, but tha' was somethin' else. Ne'er pegged ye as quite tha' evil."

I take a challenging step toward him. It's not simple to pull off—half-dressed and a third his size. Still, I let no one get the last word in over me. "Oh, what you've heard is true. I'm exactly... that... evil. Especially to perverts trying to glimpse things that aren't theirs to see."

"Chopped fer provisions, ye say?" Ronen chuckles, making little chopping motions with his giant hands.

"Gah!" I flip around in full retreat but call a final threat over my shoulder. "Watch yourself tomorrow, Big Scruff. I'm coming for you next."

"Excellent, lass," I hear as I stomp up the steps. "I'd make a lot o' provisions."

CHAPTER FIVE

I wake the following morning with a restless ache in my muscles. I need a release. I need to run.

Yesterday's reprieve from Nacole's chattering (crying, more like) was necessary for my sanity, but today, I search her out before the sun is up. I slip into her quarters and find her asleep in her bedroll. Nudging her shoulder, she rolls to face me. "You up for rung climbing?" I ask, and her morning grin, which I barely make out in the low light, is lazy but approving. "I'll wait outside," I say and slip out. On the dark transit path, I bend and stretch, feeling my legs loosen as I hold my pose.

Nacole appears, and we walk the short distance to our starting ladder. Her golden curls, gathered high on her head, bounce as she shivers in the cool morning air. I suppress a similar reaction to the cold, knowing we'll soon be hot and sweating. I focus my mind as I climb. Per usual, I'm in the lead, ascending the five floors. I keep my grip firm and my steps solid, pulling myself onto the roof when I reach the top. Without stopping, I cross the rooftop, reaching the irrigation flume spanning two of our buildings. Nacole stops next to me, already panting like I am.

"What's wrong?" she asks.

I look over the tops of our buildings, hearing the animals stir and observing the dark shadows of cool-weather crops. "It's just not very light. Maybe we should wait a few more minutes."

Nacole looks at me, tilting her head. "That's never stopped you before."

I laugh. "Maybe I value my life more today."

Only that's not true. I've always valued my life. I just always felt invincible, and this thing with the strangers, and Captain Malum, and Lord Endrack... well, I don't have a handle on all of it yet.

"We've crossed when it was darker," Nacole says, surprising me by taking the lead, stepping onto the narrow flume—barely two feet across—and taking quick steps to reach the other side. She's not wrong, so I follow—fifty feet in the air and giggling with exhilaration. Even the citizens who work up here cross on their bellies. No doubt, our parents would be sick if they knew what we were doing.

Thirty minutes later, we make our way down the ladder nearest Nacole's building, breathing heavily and feeling energized. It was exactly what I needed to start the day—better than any mental pep talk—and proves more than necessary when entering the Well for the reconvene. The atmosphere is tense. Lucan looks like the vein in his neck will explode, and Balee looks shocked, as if whatever's happening is beyond her comprehension.

"Maybe we should ask your father to join us today," Lucan says to the Dark brothers. After yesterday's avid avoidance of that scenario, the seriousness of what I've walked into is more apparent. Whatever the issue, it's not a minor trifle.

Or maybe it's simply these people being in a room together again.

"Our *father* is busy with your *son*," Geric says, and I'm reminded of how handsome he is, especially straight-backed and scowling. "As you're well aware, Captain Rhed's fielding ridiculously probing questions you've coached Cully into asking."

"I did no such thing."

"How many people in the guard? Where are they stationed? How far away?" Evans taunts. "What do you hope to learn with those details?"

"They're just idle questions from a curious young boy," my

father says from Lucan's side.

"A *boy*?" Evans blurts out.

My father's usually smarter—would typically consider the age comparison between the Dark brothers and Cully before making a statement sure to bother them. He talked with my mother late into the night, so I blame the error on lack of sleep. I'd never blame it on lack of judgment because my father has sound judgment ninety-nine times out of one hundred. (Although, even I must concede, this may be the one.)

Evans says nothing more because Laso puts up a guiding hand, gesturing us to the table. "We should sit," he says. "Let's take a step back and remember we're all interested in the health and safety of our people. *All* our people. There's no harm done, just issues that need to get resolved."

His voice is almost hypnotic, and before I know it, we're all in our familiar seats, silently facing tense and frustrated opponents with no idea where to begin. But Laso doesn't let the awkward environment deter him and maintains control of the meeting, saying, "With safety in mind, let's discuss our options."

"I'm glad you brought up options," Geric says, focusing his attention on Laso. "Because there's only one option for Harwell descendants. You and Vale are in danger and must leave this place." It sounds like an old argument, and Laso grumbles, reinforcing my theory. He's had this exchange before and doesn't appreciate being told what to do.

"Then they should go away and be safe," Lucan says, and we all hear the hope in his voice at being rid of them—not because it's safer for them, but because it's safer for us. He wants them gone. Period. (If you're interested, I'm on board with their departure and wish they'd take Tesha too.)

"What about your citizens? Did you tell them about their opportunity to go away and be safe?" Geric asks, referring to Captain Rhed's insistence on allowing each person the choice to stay or go. I appreciate the option, in theory, but dislike how the captain forced it on Lucan. Captain Rhed was especially unhappy Lucan relayed the situation to our people quietly—in small groups, behind closed doors—and not in an open forum. But Lucan didn't want the Coastals swaying decisions in their favor. He also believed it kept panic at a minimum.

Besides, who would want to leave Harwell on purpose? It's not as if the majority of us are in danger.

Lucan groans. "I told them, and some would like to take your offer."

Some of our citizens want to leave? My eyes widen. "How many?" I can't help asking.

"Approaching a third at last count."

A third. One thousand people want to leave. *How did I get that so wrong?*

"Did you tell them we'll reunite them with their departed?" Geric asks, and Lucan pauses a moment before slowly shaking his head.

"Whye'er not?" Ronen booms, his cavernous chest creating a sound that seems to reverberate within Lucan. Our leader looks at Big Scruff with newfound fear. Until now, he's been Cully's savior, but in an instant, he transforms before Lucan's eyes into a Coastal enforcer, arguing for what he believes is the correct course of action.

"We didn't want to invite unnecessary hope," Lucan finally gets out, followed by a tight swallow. His answer prompts mild grumbling from the Coastals and Goat Heads, but one response isn't mild in the least.

"Bells! There's lotsa hope ta be had!" Ronen slaps his hand on the table, and the legs wobble. I'm tempted to scoot backward and save my limbs in case it buckles. "Yer people in the bubbles know we're sharin' knowledge with ye. They're eager ta gather with loved ones."

They are? I didn't realize this was part of the brothers' plan, but Ronen's furrowed brow and accompanying words tell me it was an option all along. "Ye knew this," he says on a low growl. "We told ye how important 'twas ta tell yer people."

This doesn't affect me—not having any close relatives who've walked—but I'm still surprised Lucan held back the information. I want to believe he had the community's best interests at heart, but the only purpose I can determine for his silence was to prevent more people from leaving.

I hear a shaky breath released to my left before Balee asks, "You mean you'd help me find my mother?"

Ronen's stern expression softens. "Aye, lass."

Balee's face is a mix of shock and happiness. "I never let myself consider the possibility. I guess I thought you didn't know where they're located. Or you were unwilling. I thought, for sure, if it were an option, we'd have been told."

"We know where they *all* are," Ronen says, emphatically.

"You know where they are," my mentor repeats before the joy on her face is replaced by a scowl aimed directly at Lucan. She maintains the expression and her composure a second longer before falling onto the table in a heap of gasping sobs. "Mother," she mumbles.

Ronen lifts his double-sized hands, highlighting the stricken woman at my side as if she's all the proof needed to support his argument. Which, I guess, she is.

"Damn ye, man. 'Tis one o' the few good things ta come outta this mess." Ronen's cheeks are red with anger. But he's sniffing, and I wouldn't be surprised if those lenses are filling up like a water jug. The big guy is a sensitive container that spills over when it gets full. I look away until he gets it under control, but when I turn back, he's pointing a thick finger at Lucan. "Ye tell 'em, er I will. I've no problem yellin' it down yer paths."

Lucan doesn't speak, just stares at the brother who's always seemed the least likely to give him trouble. He's just now learning that's not the case. Ronen goes silent, thick arms crossed over his dense chest.

It's Laso who eventually gets us back on course, and we focus on logistics, exploring what an exodus of that magnitude would look like. It's exhausting, discussing how the people would travel, who would go with them, and where they would go. Vale gives insight into a bubble in the north called Wenzernot. It's bigger than ours, with open space, and within regular patrols for the Coastal guard—in short, a reasonable place to relocate many of our people. There's no more talk of reuniting families, though it's on everyone's mind.

I still can't believe we're considering abandoning our home. It's not in my personality to withdraw when facing a threat. I'd much rather resist until I get my way, and I can't help thinking we could resolve this situation similarly. Except, in this instance, to prevent the retreat from Harwell, we'd need to accept Lord Endrack's demands instead of resisting them.

"I have a thought," I say, breaking into Geric's harangue on all the ways Harwellians can be productive in their new home. I don't think anyone's sad to hear him go quiet. Even Vale, who always has that dazed look where he's concerned. She should have more self-respect.

"What is it, dear girl?" Lucan asks, not giving the slightest resistance to my interruption.

"Shouldn't we consider, or at least voice our reasons to discount, locating the items Lord Endrack seeks and turning them over to him?"

"You realize it's more than *objects* he's after, right? It's actual *people*," Evans says, trying to make me look insensitive. And I might sound callous, but that doesn't mean it's not a worthy discussion.

"Yes. I realize." I lick my lips, considering my words. "And maybe he'll take them away from here, just as you seem to expect. But isn't it possible that opening a dialogue with the man could reveal he's perfectly reasonable?"

"No, it's really not possible," Evans argues back.

"Gah! Just listen. What if we give him the objects he needs with a solemn vow that the people causing him unrest will cease to do so? Maybe he'll consider the matter appeased."

"Fer a man cravin' ta take, givin'll only create desire fer more takin'," Ronen answers.

"Maybe." I twist my lip, unable to discount his logic. "But isn't it worth a try?"

"We've *tried* for decades," Geric says.

"Maybe *you* have. But we haven't. Maybe he'll be reasonable to Harwell leadership if, in turn, we act reasonably."

Big Scruff's brows dip into his lenses. I assume he's considering my proposal until he says, "Mindless lass. How much'll ye let 'im take 'fore ye say 'tis 'nough?"

I straighten, spurred on by him calling me mindless. Again. "As it stands, he's taken very little—a crazy person and an old lady who had already departed from Harwell. By my estimation, Lord Endrack's hardly been greedy."

The minute the words are out, I know I shouldn't have said them. It's not that I don't stand by what I've said. It's that I didn't deliver the message in a diplomatic manner. No. Not diplomatic at all. I let my emotions take over, and as a reckoner, I must do better.

Vale gasps from across the table, her hand falling immediately onto that stupid wooden necklace, rubbing it furiously. She glares at me, then turns her look of disgust on her father. He's a few seats down, but he's got a hand up, placating her. I'm not sure why.

Ronen's sniffing again, and I swear daggers are protruding from Evans's lenses. Surely, they'd match the jeweled knife at his hip—the one that kills men.

I glance at my people. Lucan appears unbothered. My father's only tell is that he's biting his lip. And I've shocked Balee. I guess she hasn't seen this side of me.

Well, welcome to my show.

The room is filled with tempestuous emotions—they swirl around me. I like the taste of chaos. It's savory, like the stuff Ronen dumped into my soup. It gives life flavor. It's Laso, again, who brings the room to order. I don't know why he's so desperate to calm the emotional storm. My guess is he must like his life bland.

But then he surprises me.

"Let's explore Annibeth's line of thought," he says, and Vale gasps again—this time in pure astonishment. It's moderately satisfying, and Laso has my full attention. "Annibeth, your point is that we should save lives and curtail hardship by abiding two points of order. First, surrendering objects of interest to Lord Endrack. Second, giving up people of interest, as well. Is that correct?"

Hmm. I like his approach—less bickering and more factual debate.

"Yes. It's a simpler plan."

"Let's discuss the objects first?"

"Okay."

"Of which objects are you aware?" Laso asks.

It feels like he addressed the question to my side of the table, but Laso's only watching me. My brows dip into a scowl. "Captain Malum said Lord Endrack wants a necklace belonging to Vale." And there's no doubt it's not the ugly thing hanging around her neck. I didn't even need dead Captain Malum's clarification—which he gave to Lucan before he died—to deduce that. The thing's hideous and obviously without value.

"Yes," Lucan says. "We need to find that necklace." It seems a pointless statement, as if Lucan said it just to ensure he's still part of the conversation. I'm embarrassed for him because it only brings censure from the Dark brothers—I can see it in the set of their shoulders—but I ignore their reaction and keep my attention on Laso, who's nodding agreeably about finding the necklace. My frown deepens because this feels wrong. He's too patient. Too calculating. There's something I'm missing.

"The necklace is a family heirloom passed down through the Harwell line," Laso says. "It belongs to Vale and was mine before it was hers. Previously it was my mother's, my grandfather's, and so on for many generations of the Harwell line. Will any of you dispute the necklace belongs to our family?"

There's no dispute. It does. But that doesn't mean he shouldn't relinquish it to ensure our safety, but I don't voice that. I merely shake my head like the rest.

As if reading my mind, Laso asks, "You believe Vale and I should surrender to Endrack, take the necklace to him, and join my mother? You think this is the best way to ensure the safety of Harwell?"

"Yes. I believe it's at least worth a try."

"Would you concede these three may know more about dealing with Lord Endrack than we from Harwell do?" Laso points at the Dark brothers.

I press my pink lips together. "Yes, but we aren't sure of their motives. They may be the villains and Endrack, the hero."

Laso looks to the side, nodding his head. He doesn't argue. Even the brothers don't seem bothered I called them possible villains. "While we were away from Harwell," Laso says, "we explored documents in a place called Labrum that's to the north. We found a piece of paper that mentioned Vale's necklace."

"In another community?" my father asks, shocked like me that there are such things—papers about our home stored in other locations. It's an uncomfortable thought. It's violating that others know things about us we don't know.

"Yes. It described her necklace." Laso pauses. "This necklace, actually," he says, producing a sparkly item for us to see. I can't help it, I lean it for a better look, but it's at the other end of the table, and I can hardly take in the details. "The paper says this necklace belongs to the House of Harwell."

"Where's the paper?" Lucan asks.

Smoothly, Laso reaches to his side. "I have it here."

He holds it up, but not in a manner we can read it. Lucan reaches out, but instead of handing it over, Laso places it on the table in front of him and continues. "We were surprised to find another object described on the page, though in hindsight, we shouldn't have been."

Laso looks at a fidgeting Evans before saying, "A dagger, fourteen inches, curved tip, and jeweled hilt." Evans lays his dagger on the table, and I realize he wasn't fidgeting—he was retrieving the object.

I feel like I'm missing something, but I'm so caught up in their discovery, I don't dwell on the feeling for long.

"The page says the dagger belongs to the House of Dirby. Evans maintains that surname."

"Yay," Evans says, without an ounce of enthusiasm. He picks up the dagger, using the curved end to pull a chunk from the table's surface.

Lucan grunts next to me. Evans looks up and holds out his hands with the knife still in one. "What?"

"Stop, brotha," Ronen says, and when Evans looks over, the big guy gives him a headshake. Evans places the knife back on the table and, with a crooked mouth, tucks his hands between his legs where they'll do no harm.

"Back to Annibeth's proposal, it would make sense for Evans to turn himself into Endrack with his dagger."

"Yes. It's for the best," I say, unable to look at Evans—sure of the sneer that would grace his lips.

"The paper calls the objects regalia," Laso addresses the group. "And there are three of them."

"So, we just need to find the third," Lucan says, looking hopeful, and I'm glad I voiced this idea. It may be the better option after all.

"No need. We know where it is," Laso says.

We're all visibly excited. Even Balee scoots forward, sitting as far from Laso as possible and not wanting to miss a word.

"The third item is from the House of Dorian," Laso says, giving the first clue.

Lucan scowls. "We have no Dorians here."

"Bitha Dale's mother was a Dorian," Laso says next.

"Tesha." I blurt out. She must have the third regalia. For a brief second, I envision Tesha leaving Harwell with the Rennicks. Siman would watch her go. Nacole would help him through his loss, and they'd come back together. It's not that I'm excited about the romance of it. It's mostly seeing Tesha lose out and having Siman brought back to where he belongs that interests me.

But Laso shakes his head. "No. Bitha's mother didn't believe her daughter was stable enough to appreciate the item. Instead, she gave it to her other daughter—Bitha's divided twin and my late wife, Anny Rennick."

I, of course, know about this family history because of my father's position. Taboo topics have a way of not counting in our household—or Cully's—but next to me, Balee sucks in a breath because it's news to her.

"So, Vale has both," I conclude, looking at Laso's daughter, sitting serenely while her father explains this complicated situation.

"No. I don't," Vale answers.

"But, then—" my words fall away because I don't know what question to ask next. I look down my row. Balee's intrigued. Lucan's confused. My father purses his lips, staring at Laso, who isn't looking back.

No one's talking, which is bothersome because we're so close to figuring this out. Laso said he knows the location of the House of Dorian regalia, but he's waiting for us to decipher the answer, which is both intriguing and irritating. After a lengthy period, with no more conjecture, he continues, "The Dorian regalia left my household long ago. So long, I'd forgotten it existed. Anny gave it to a friend, and I had no objection—it was hers to do with as she pleased. Like the other regalia, it's made from a precious metal—yellow gold—and, like the others, it has an inscription."

"Inscription?" Balee asks, next to me.

"Yes. The necklace says, *Gemma Scientia*. The dagger says, *Ferrum Pax*. And the last item is an armband or bracelet with the words *Dives Sapientia*."

I shriek out loud. The noise causes Balee to jump at my side, and all the eyes in the room, at least the ones I can see, fall on me.

My arms are on the surface of the table. My hand nervously twists the bracelet around my left wrist, and my fingers run across the words inscribed there.

Dives Sapientia.

"Father?" I ask, turning toward him. "What is he saying?"

Marven Petters—Lucan's assistant—looks down at the object I'm holding onto fiercely. My father's pursed lips tighten, cheeks redden, and his eyes squint into slits. All this before he seethes, "Laso Rennick, you bastard. You did this on purpose!"

CHAPTER SIX

"You tricked us. You tricked *me!*" My father's hands fly wildly while I attempt to discover the trick Laso's perpetrated.

"I don't know what you mean," Laso says, eyes widening and lips tightening.

My father rises slowly from the table, leaning toward Vale's father. "You're aware I'm against this course of action. I'm outraged you would bring it up." But my father doesn't sound outraged. He sounds nervous, though it comes across as a bristling calm. His tone is more aligned with his usual intensity as opposed to the brief outburst we witnessed, but that doesn't mean the people in the room don't shrink. Well, at least, the ordinary people are affected. The Dark brothers remain firm, and Laso doesn't flinch but seems ready for a fight. Marven Petters is a man to be taken seriously—one of few people I respect. He's someone whose advice I follow and direction I take.

"What's going on?" I ask, pushing my chair back from the table and going straight to him—more to support his bad leg than anything else.

But both men ignore my question, and Laso continues to address my father, saying, "Bitha told."

"Told what?" I ask.

Father scoffs. "No one believes a thing Bitha Dale says," he argues.

"*Said*," Vale whispers, reminding us all Bitha no longer says anything, but Evans speaks over her. "Captain Malum believed it, and the members of his Six did too. Lord Endrack will have no reason to doubt."

"Doubt what?" I ask. "What are you talking about?" They all seem to possess knowledge, pertaining me, to which I'm not privy. I don't enjoy being on the outside, but they continue as if I haven't spoken.

"The bracelet isn't proof it's true," my father says, rubbing his bald head.

"Come out of hiding, little Harwellian," Evans taunts, standing to match his stance. "They won't need jewelry. They have something more exact." Evans picks up his dagger and pokes the tip of his finger with the curvy end, then leans toward us, dropping his hand to the tabletop. Sliding it across the surface, it leaves a perfect red line on the grooved wood. It's a crude gesture but effective. The line of blood leaves a sick feeling in my stomach. "That's all it takes. He knows I'm a member of the House of Dirby. He wants the dagger. He wants me dead. The end."

Evans straightens, stabbing the knife so it stands vertically in the table before lowering himself comfortably to his chair.

I drop my father's arm and take a step back. "What does this have to do with me?" My voice is shrill. They remain quiet, each person perusing their thoughts. "Explain what's going on!" I stomp my foot and immediately regret the childish gesture. (But I can't take it back, so in true Annibeth fashion, I own it.)

My father falls onto his seat and chokes out a sob. I've been frustrated and angry to this point, but this gives me my first feeling of unease. My father rarely cries, and never like this. It's as if someone he loves has died.

I'm even more startled when my mother enters the room. She watches my father—must have heard his raised voice. After all, it doesn't take much to listen to conversations between these floors. She's here for support, and no one complains about her arrival, but instead of going to her husband, she comes to me, linking her arm with mine.

Moisture brims her eyes, and the fear in them increases my unease. My mother's never afraid. Because Marven Petters can fix anything. And it's suddenly clear—his tears and her fear—whatever is going on is something they can't fix.

"Please tell her, Laso," my mother says, holding onto me with both hands, our arms still linked.

I look at Vale's father, and he nods. He seems calmer and not nearly as confident as before. "I want you to know I've only had this information for a few months. The day my mother walked into the Dark, in fact."

"Get on with it," my father says. At least, I'm pretty sure that's what he says—it's hard to make out. His arms are folded across the table, and he's lying face down, hidden. He's still crying.

On instinct, I want to wound the man causing distress to someone I love. I scowl at Laso Rennick. "I don't need embellishments. Just state the facts." I mean it to be hard-hitting, but Laso isn't fazed. He merely nods again and does exactly as I ask.

"Nineteen years ago, this upcoming April 14, Vale was born. My wife, Anny, was happier than I'd ever seen her. It was the most perfect time of my life. Until it wasn't. In August, she became withdrawn. She pulled away from Vale and me too. She became despondent. When I begged her to tell me the problem—to let me help—she became angry. And then, in September, she disappeared. The rumor was she fell into the river and floated into the Dark. But the truth is, one day, she was just gone, and I had no idea where she went."

Laso's eyes haven't left mine. It seems essential for him that I connect emotionally to his story, which seems improbable. I don't know Laso Rennick—except my father constantly argues with him—and I have no love for Vale. It's too bad they lost their wife and mother, but it means little to me.

"I recently learned she stayed in Harwell, living with friends who hid her in their quarters for six months. Her only visitor was Bitha Dale, who guessed Anny's secret and helped with her plan."

"Her secret?" I ask. My mother squeezes my hand and lays her cheek on my shoulder.

"Yes. Although we followed the, uh, required measures," Laso pauses and looks at Lucan before coming back to me, "it didn't work, and Anny was expecting our second child."

I freeze when the words are out of his mouth. An anxious flutter appears in my chest as I realize where he's taking this story. Still, I continue to listen because I don't know if I can do otherwise.

"If discovered, Vale would have been given away to be raised by another family in Harwell. Anny and I would have been punished for our indiscretion and sent into the Dark. Our unborn child would have shared our fate. Rather than burden me with that painful outcome, Anny approached her friends who didn't have a child."

Laso looks at my mother. She's straightened and is watching me. Her gaze feels like a burn on the side of my face.

"An accident in his youth left Marven Petters with a limp and—" Laso stops, and his eyes flash to my father, who hasn't moved from his grieving posture over the table.

My father sits up, waving a carefree hand at Laso. "You can say it. It affected my ability to have children."

Laso gives a brief nod and looks back at me. "So, they formed a plan. The Petters took care of Anny in secret. Clayre pretended to be with child and on bed rest." Laso pauses, looking at me again. "After you were born, Anny stayed long enough to recover some strength. And then, on a night with no moon, she left the Petters' home and entered the Dark."

After I was born.

To Anny Rennick.

I clutch my chest while my parents stare at me with concern and sadness. I don't know what to say or ask.

I look nothing like my parents and often wondered if I was a twin—one of the taboo separated at birth—but none are close to my age, so I gave up the idea. I never figured I was born outside the law. Faced with this new reality, I was right to question my background, but the findings are heartbreaking because I love my parents. I don't want anyone else.

"Was that factual enough?" Vale asks, snapping me out of my thoughts. Her mouth tight and eyes, glaring. "It's only the most painful event of my father's life. Not that you'd consider that. Just so long as he left out any *embellishment*. Are you satisfied, *Sister*?"

Sister? Sister!

There's too much to comprehend, and stupidly, that hadn't penetrated. Yes, I'd grasped I was born to different parents, but I hadn't considered the other familial connections—like a sister.

I blink.

Vale Rennick is my sister.

And now Laso, my *other* father, is reprimanding her. "Vale, it's a lot to take in," he says, patting her arm.

He's *defending* me. I don't need him defending me. I have my own father to do that! But Vale speaks before I get my opinion out.

"Yeah! I realize it's a lot to take in. I *remember*. It's only been two days since I found out myself!"

"It doesn't get better after two months," Laso says. "It's still a shock."

Geric pulls Vale into a hug. She goes reluctantly, and Laso stares as if he wishes he were close enough to be the one embracing her. I'm suddenly curious about their family dynamic, something I've never felt for the Rennicks because I had no reason to. He continues, "I thought you were okay with telling her."

Vale stays in Geric's arms. "Of course, *logically*, I knew we must. She's in danger. But, emotionally, well, I'd rather... I don't know! I just don't want her to act like such a brat about it! She always acts like everything is about her. She has no consideration for other people's feelings!"

Vale yells each sentence, and it gets my hackles up. I point my finger at her and start yelling back. "Maybe I'm acting like this is about me because... oh, I don't know... it *actually* is about me! You might be five percent of the story, but ninety-five percent belongs to me. I'm the one who just had everything she's ever known turned upside down!"

Vale pulls away from Geric and knocks back her chair as she stands. "Five percent! Growing up without a mother gives me five percent? Ha!" She puts a hand on her hip. "How do you figure?"

I pull away from my mother and round the table to face Vale. "You have a mother. Her name's Milany. Just like I have one. Her name's Clayre. We were both raised by someone other than the woman who gave birth to us. So, get over it."

Some of Vale's anger wanes. "Get over it? It's that easy for you to dismiss her?"

I open my mouth, but no words come out. I shake my head. No, it's not easy. I still haven't grasped all this revelation entails, but I'm not about to lose my edge by getting flustered.

Suddenly, Laso's at our side. "Let's take a minute and calm down." He's got one hand on my arm and one on Vale's. I stare at him—Laso, the happy father, standing here with his two daughters. It's a right joyful reunion in his mind. Well, not for me.

"You need a minute?" I shrug, breaking his hold on me. "Fine by me. I'll be back when you've had time to gather your wits."

Of course, it's all bluster. I'm the one who's utterly erratic by this turn of events. Someone says my name, but I don't make eye contact or stop as I find my way out the main entrance of the Well. The last thing I hear as I cross through the doorway is Laso Rennick, insisting the discussion cease until I return. I don't know if I'm grateful or angry.

I make my way to the river's edge, descending the slope to the platform where we get water. There's a large rock I often sit on to think—usually much more pleasant thoughts, but it will serve my purpose today.

"Rennick," I say, unable to hear the name over the sound of the river. My voice, being wholly swallowed by the noise, is freeing, and I let it all out. "Nope. I'm not interested in being a Rennick or getting to know my birth family." I shake my head profusely. (Adamantly.) I can't believe I'm related to them —Vale and Laso. They mean nothing to me. (Zilch.) "I hope they're not intent on having any sort of relationship," I say, disgusted by the thought. (Repulsed.) What if they push for that? Well, I'll push right back. It's nothing I want.

"And Tesha!" I blurt out, following up her name with a shiver. She's my cousin. *How appalling.*

The people across the water on the Common go about their daily business—no one noticing me. What will this revelation mean for my standing in the community?

I know what it means. I'll be no better than the Dale witches when this is all done. Cousin to the witch and daughter of the story keeper—when this gets out, it will put me on their level. I'll lose any respect I've gained all these years. I'll be like the rodents who come to us from the Dark—a mouse with too little meat to be of any worth.

I'm just grateful Cully wasn't there to witness my fall, though it's only a matter of time before he and the rest of the community hear it.

My mother always insisted that being adored and respected by relevant people and being feared by insignificant people would keep me in command of my destiny. Considering what I've learned today, those lessons suddenly make a lot more sense. This revelation has the potential to get out of control, and control is the key to survival.

I don't hear a sound but look up because the sun was shining on me, and now I'm cast under an enormous shadow. "What are you doing here?" I yell over the water.

"Checkin' on ye." It's a good thing I can see his face, or it would be tricky to understand him—his voice is almost the same tone as the rushing water.

"Again, with the short stick." I kick a small rock, and it bounces into the river.

"Nah. Told 'em I was stretchin' my legs. Really, just lookin' fer ye."

"What for?" I ask because I'm curious. We're not friends, and our interactions have never been pleasant.

"Felt bad fer ye," he says, descending the slope and leaning against the wall of rock, dirt, and weeds, towering above where I'm seated on my rock.

"Pitying the spoiled Harwellian?" I ask, mostly to shock him.

"Aye. Ye look pitiful."

I squint, looking for signs he's joking and realize he's not. "Wow. You really tell it how you see it."

"Been accused o' tha'."

"So, I look pitiful, and you feel sorry for me?"

"Spoiled too. But ye dunna deserve ta have yer world shook so hard."

"Well, since we're being honest, I find you annoying and prefer the inquisition in there to you telling me I'm pathetic."

I shove from the rock, step past him, and rush up the incline. It was a clean getaway until I run into the two people I want to see the very least. They're blocking my path—not intentionally, but still, it sets me off.

"Hey, *Cousin*," I say to the frizzy redhead, inserting as much poison into the word as possible.

"You know," Siman says, tucking his thumb into his pocket nervously, and I laugh out loud, realizing they knew the details before me. Of course, they did. Siman's leadership material and nothing says leader like being informed about secrets.

"Get out of my way." I could go around them, but I don't change course for anyone. People move to accommodate me. Tesha steps to the side, but Siman holds his ground.

"This could be a good thing," he says, stepping toward me. "Put aside your pride and consider the amazing connections you've just discovered."

"I don't listen to betrayers or heartbreakers," I say, breaking my rule by stepping around him because I don't want to listen anymore.

But Siman's not done and takes my arm to keep me in place. He leans in. "Don't be an idiot. Few of us in Harwell get to experience having an extended family. Even grandparents are rare. And you have a grandmother."

I turn on him and scowl. "Yeah, and I handed her over to Captain Malum. How well do you think that reunion will go?"

"She'll forgive you." He shakes his head, and I think he's changed his mind about the declaration, but then he says, "She's already forgiven you. Even when it was happening, she understood your reasons."

I huff out a laugh. "No one's that good."

"Ennette Rennick is. Give it a chance, Anni."

Anni. The same name as my birth mother, Anny Rennick. No wonder my *actual* mother never wanted me to use it.

"Let me go."

He does, but not before telling me, "I can see you're going to be stupid about this—churlish even. You're mad at me, but I still consider you one of my best friends. I'll help you however you'll let me."

"Gah!" I roll my eyes and push past him, quickening my feet to reach the Well.

I'm annoyed with Siman for so many reasons. For telling me reasonable things, though I'll never admit I feel that way. For being kind to me when I don't want him to be. And for hurting my friend and being with Tesha.

I'm also annoyed by the people just beyond the Well door. They're readying themselves with questions and explanations. Plans and schemes. I don't want to be a part of it, and right now, I'm at the center of it.

And I'm especially annoyed by the big guy, whose heavy footsteps I can hear behind me. It's as if he's laying each step down hard so I don't forget he's there. He said nothing while Siman preached to me, but I felt his silent presence, and he heard every word.

He's watching and judging me. Seeing and hearing too much.

And there's nothing I detest more.

CHAPTER SEVEN

Big Scruff follows me inside.

"Where are my parents?" I ask after a quick scan of the room.

"The shrew returns," Evans says with a devious grin, folding his muscled arms.

I squint, consider a rebuttal, decide he's not worth the effort, and ask again, "My parents?"

"In your quarters," Lucan says, making his way to me. "The excitement tired your mother."

My mother.

Without thought, I take a step, intending to go to her, but Ronen puts his thick hand on my shoulder, holding me back. "I'll go."

I'm so startled by the offer it delays my refusal. With his long legs, he's already across the room. It's ridiculous to allow him but pointless to stop him. He'll be at the top of the stairs by the time I catch up. I imagine him taking the steps three at a time. Involuntarily, I look at the ceiling and hope the structure can hold his weight. Then I wonder if the building might topple like Fifty-Three did in the storm. Logically, Ronen can't weigh more than two men. I tilt my head, possibly three. The floor's handled that before in the form of separate bodies. It should be fine. (Right?)

I've just decided it will hold when he reappears. He's uncommonly fast for his size and carries himself well—tall and proud, not rounded and loping like Harbert tends to be. No one in Harwell is fat, but Harbert's the closest you'll find with his thick chest and mini-paunch from his lousy posture. I consider the big guy again. It would be a challenge to find excess fat anywhere on Ronen. He's muscle all the way through —muscle and hair, I note when trying to find his mouth through his beard.

"They'll be down," he says in his usual clipped manner. No detail, just the situation as it stands. I'm all about presenting the facts, but even I sometimes like a little more.

"How long?"

"Na long." And then he's walking back to his brothers, and I'm left alone with Lucan.

"Let's take our seats," Lucan says. I'm tired of sitting, but I do as he says. I'm scooting under the table when Father appears.

"Where's Mother?"

"Upstairs resting. I had to force her to stay. This is all too much." He shakes his head, the worry clear.

I look across the table at Vale Rennick. She's watching me again, and suddenly, her look from earlier makes sense. She was watching me from a familial perspective. I'm doing the same to her now, comparing my blue eyes to her green ones and my blond hair to her black. We look nothing alike. I glance at Laso with his wavy black hair and green eyes—there she is. Ennette Rennick had their coloring too. Which means I must look like Anny.

A shiver runs through me that's cut short when Lucan addresses the group. "I will lead this discussion because Laso and Marven have broken my trust. Harwell's laws state we should banish the perpetrators, and—"

"Banish!" Vale blurts out, then laughs. "To where? The Dark? Because we can survive in there. You remember that, right? It's not the punishment it used to be. And besides, the entire purpose of banishment is to keep our numbers at exactly three thousand because of limited space. If you haven't noticed, our world just opened up."

Lucan puts up his hand. "Yes, Vale, I understand what you're saying. Now, if you'll listen—"

But this time, it's not Vale who interrupts. It's my father—the, uh, one I've known my whole life.

"Why couldn't you stay quiet?" he hisses the question at Laso. "You said you would!" He glares at Laso, waving his arms in the air—and while he's prone to gesticulating, it's worse when he's angry.

"The situation changed," Laso says. "We endangered her by staying quiet. She needed an accurate perspective to make informed decisions."

"That's a false story! You did it because you want to know her."

Laso looks at me. "The danger isn't false, but I indeed want to know you."

"You wanted to tell her from the moment you found out. You begged me every time we met!"

"Yes. I begged. I wanted you, Vale, and Milany to know about our connection." Laso's still looking at me, and I'm embarrassed by his attention. "But I respected your father's wishes until it was impossible to do so. I'm glad you know, for selfish reasons, but you had to know because staying silent was no longer an option."

"Don't look at my daughter! Talk to me," my father says, and Laso does as he asks, removing his gaze.

"Stop!" Lucan says from beside me. "I've been interrupted twice, and I'll have my say. I am, after all, in charge here." When the room stays silent, Lucan continues, "It's true the law banishing citizens no longer has a purpose, and I abolish it as of this moment. What bothers me is I've worked closely with the Petters family for many years while they perpetrated a false story." Lucan rubs his neck, shaking his head. "But it happened eighteen years ago, and they've raised a wonderful young woman. The Petters and Rennick families have suffered enough, and no further punishment is necessary. That said, I insist knowledge about Annibeth's parentage be kept to this group."

Lucan turns his attention to the Dark brothers, looking right at Evans. "You berate me for our taboos, but it's not the only consideration with this decree. An extra layer of protection is never a bad thing. And, on a personal note, Annibeth's very dear to me. Until she's ready to acknowledge this new family, in whatever way she deems fit, I don't want idle gossip on the paths of Harwell."

Lucan turns to me. They trained me to look at him with stars in my eyes since I was a child. *Make him love you. Make him devoted.* But over the years, the feeling has become real. This man truly cares about me. And I care about him. "Thank you," I say, feeling my first moment of peace since this all came to light. Unfortunately, the moment doesn't last long.

"Aye. They're sound words, 'n we agree with yer decision," Ronen says while Evans grimaces. "But we're fergettin' the heart o' the issue."

"What would that be?" my father asks.

Laso takes over the discussion, not answering my father directly but making their point known. "Annibeth, do you still agree with your original argument? Do you believe the simplest path is to turn ourselves, and the objects in our possession, over to Endrack?"

Do I?

I hesitate. Since I had a ready answer before learning of my involvement, I'm sure they think I'm waffling out of fear. But this deeper introspection isn't a result of being afraid. I'm no coward, though Tesha accused me of that when I gave up Ennette Rennick to Captain Malum. She was wrong and so are they. Fear is not my driving force. Logic is.

I'll boldly stand before Endrack and be a voice for my

people, but the longer we've conversed in these meetings, the more I've realized the others would do the same. Vale's no coward. She blatantly expresses her thoughts to Lucan and argues with me if the situation calls for it. The Dark brothers aren't wimps either. I mean, Evans is irritating, but he's intrepid and outspoken.

No, bravery is not the issue. The truth is, their judgment may be sound—that Endrack isn't reasonable—and following my plan could have disastrous results. Siman accused me of being prideful, and there's some truth in that, but more so, I'm sensible, making me willing to talk through this issue from both sides.

I twist the bracelet on my arm, planning my thoughts. My father catches the movement, and the action gives him an idea that's like the sun rising behind his eyes. "Give the bracelet to Tesha," he says, tapping the table with his index finger. "She's leaving Harwell anyway and has the blood of the House of Dorian."

I grip my wrist, scowling at my father. The bracelet's mine. I've worn it for years and don't want to give it up. I drop my arm below the table, considering his idea. Would I give it away to divert attention to another target? To prevent my discovery? I'm not one to run from a situation, though this is beyond my ability to manage on my own.

"It won't matter," Laso answers. "Like my mother and me, whether Annibeth retains possession of the bracelet or not, she's a target. Everything we've learned points to one thing. Endrack doesn't want us for a conversation. He wants us dead."

Dead. A man I don't know, living far from my small home, wants me dead. It's sobering, and, fine, even though I'll not transfer the burden nor shirk it, I admit there's a clawing need to find an avenue of safety, knowing those words affect me personally.

"Then what do you suggest?" Lucan asks, appearing

cooperative for the first time since these talks began yesterday morning.

"Annibeth should go into hiding with Vale and Tesha until we resolve this," Laso answers.

"Hide?" I blurt out. "I don't *hide!*"

Nope. I'm not interested in leaving Harwell, guided by the Dark brothers—Big Scruff, Vale's Hot Little Number, and the Droll. And no doubt, they'll be accompanied by the Goat Heads —Vale and Laso. Add to that Siman the Heartbreaker and Tesha the Witch. No. I'm not even tempted. It can't be as bad as they say. My family can keep me safe. Lucan's a capable leader. I need to remain here to stay in control and be happy.

"Just until we figure this out," Laso adds.

"You just want her with you," my father accuses.

"No," Laso answers, and a second later, "I'm not going with them."

Hmm. One Goat Head down. Nope. Doesn't make a difference.

"Father!" Vale shrieks. "We talked about this. You promised you'd consider going with us."

"And I did, but it's better this way. I have things to do here."

"So do I!" Vale argues, but Laso sets his expression. He's not budging. It makes me a little uncomfortable that I instinctively understand the look. "So, you're not going to the Cliffs," she says morosely, and I'm confused by the word. I haven't heard them talk about it before, and from how the brothers fidget, they didn't mean for us to know about it either.

"We'll go over the details later," Laso whispers, and Vale's mouth drops open. Yeah, she just figured out her slip, but it's too late.

"So, the Cliffs," I say, crossing my arms and leaning back in my chair. "Tell us about *the Cliffs.*"

"'Tis a safe place," Ronen answers coolly in his breathy

voice.

"Where, exactly?"

"Few know. 'Tis wha' makes it safe," he continues, crossing his arms to match mine.

"I'm not going with a bunch of strangers to an undisclosed location."

"Vale's not a stranger," Laso interjects, and it feels like he's pushing.

"She practically is," I argue. Until the last few months, when we started bickering over Cully, I mostly ignored her.

"That's true. You surround yourself with strangers. I've often noted you have few friends," Evans drawls, examining the edge of his dagger.

I scoff at his baseless statement. "I have *plenty* of great friends, and I'd rather stay here with them."

"Don't you have any... oh, I don't know... self-preservation instincts?" Evans asks, incredulous.

"Yes. But I'm no scared quitter," I growl back.

"Scared quitter?" Vale laughs. "You think that's what we are? Scared quitters? Wait until Lord Endrack has someone you love... your mother, maybe. Wait until he's had her for months, and you're not sure if she's alive or dead. Is she being treated properly or barely fed? Oh! And the best part... how will you feel when I'm the one who turns her over to him? I'll give her away without a thought, like waste in the bin. Let's see how you react to that, and then, you might have the right to call me a scared quitter for going somewhere safe to figure out how to save the people I love. And save myself while I'm at it."

My cheeks flame red—not from the put-down but from the silence in the room. No one's jumping in to support me. (No surprise.) Not even me. (Okay, that's a surprise.) But Vale's right. If she did to my mother what I did to her grandmother,

I'd hate her. I'd hurt her by whatever method was most effective and never feel a bit of remorse.

"Now, now," Lucan says. "That's a bit harsh." He pats my hand, and I turn my glassy eyes on him.

Is it harsh, though?

I push back from the table and stand, walking to the back of the Well and the exit closest to the steps leading my home.

"Where are you going?" Lucan asks.

It's my father—the one who serves as Lucan's assistant and rarely challenges our leader—who answers, "Let her go. She's earned a break."

CHAPTER EIGHT

"**W**hat are you doing here?" I ask the person standing a few steps below me. I didn't make it inside my quarters. I climbed the stairs and stopped on the landing, sitting on the step and leaning my shoulder against the railing. I've been staring at the trees. I'm unsure how much time has passed.

"Your father sent me," Vale answers.

"Hah! Which one?" I ask with a pained laugh, never dreaming I'd say something like that in my lifetime.

Vale doesn't laugh with me, but says, "Marven." That she doesn't call him Lucan's assistant softens me a bit. "He said your mother wants to speak to us."

"My mother?" I push myself up, getting a sliver in my palm. Great. Just another thing to brighten my day. I pick at it while Vale follows me inside.

My mother's sitting at our kitchen table. She was supposed to be resting but looks more strung out than I've seen her in a while. She tries for a smile as she says, "Hello, girls. Take a seat."

I don't feel like sitting, but lowering her stress is more important than arguing a stupid point, so I sit down.

"I'm sure you have questions," she says while Vale settles beside me. I've never sat this close to her before. It's uncomfortable, and I'm tempted to scoot away, but I stay put. Again, for my mother.

"We can do this later," I say. "After you get some rest."

"Rest will elude me until it's done. Let's get through this so we can all move forward."

Forward? (Not possible.) But she looks so hopeful (and I

can't crush her dream), so I nod and open the conversation. "I look nothing like you or Father. I suspected something but wondered if I was a divided twin."

"My father says you look like my mother," Vale says, confirming my earlier thoughts while she frowns at me and pulls on her black locks. "Said once he found out about you, it seemed absurd he'd never noticed."

"Anny was stunning. You look like her. So much." My mother gazes at me with an abundance of love. I blink and run my hand across my nose, feigning an itch. "She wanted to name you Annybitha. I told her no because it was too obvious, but I also felt I couldn't completely disregard her wishes, so I named you Annibeth. She never knew. She was gone before your naming day."

"That's why you insist I don't shorten my name," I say. Though I figured it out earlier, I want to hear her confirm it.

She nods. "Vale looks so much like Ennette. I was grateful you ended up looking so different because I was terrified of being discovered. But—" she pauses and abruptly gets up, crossing the room to get one of the freshly cleaned handkerchiefs from my crying sessions with Nacole. "But I wanted you so much, Annibeth. We couldn't have children, and when Anny approached me, I couldn't say no. I knew what trouble her family was in, and she refused to let the punishment fall on them. It broke my heart. She was my dearest friend, and I had to let her go."

"Dearest friend? I never knew you were that close," Vale says, as shocked as I am.

"Oh, yes. Laso and Marven were friends too. We were together so much." She takes in our expressions and then frowns. "I see that surprises you."

"They don't exactly get along," Vale says about our fathers. The observation is direct and accurate.

"Marven was against taking Annibeth." Mother sits,

reaching out to grip my hand. "Not that he hasn't loved you the entire time, but it scared him. It took a lot of convincing. And I'm afraid we both changed. We adjusted our lives and even our personalities to battle our fear. And we changed you too."

"How were you different?" I ask. They're the parents I've always known, so I'm unsure how they're altered from their youth. A tear runs down my mother's cheek, and she brushes it away. Her hand is shaking, and she looks so tired. We should really stop, but I want to hear more, so I wait.

"We used to be happier. Kinder." The tears coat her lips, and she wipes her mouth with the handkerchief. "And you... well, you were very young, and I saw the two of you playing. You looked more alike back then. Annibeth's hair was always white-blond, but Vale's was lighter—not quite the deep black it is now. But I could see the similarities and got scared. So, I—" My mother jumps up and gets another handkerchief, throwing the used one into her room. I know the spot. It's in the corner where she stacks all her laundry. "Oh, Anny would be so ashamed," she says, biting her lip and looking at the ceiling before returning to us. She lets out a heavy breath. "I began coaching you, Annibeth. I told you we were better than the Rennicks and that you should never associate with Vale."

I always believed hating Vale stemmed from my own experiences. Sure, my parents trained me to act above the others in the community—not just Vale—but I thought my hatred was my own. It's strange to consider a lifetime of bias cultivated from childhood.

"Well, it worked," Vale says bitterly. "She associated with me very little. She made it clear she was better than me. And she was never nice."

My mother's face falls. I've never seen her more remorseful, but I can't have her wallowing in it. I need to understand the depths of my conditioning.

"What else did you do?" I ask, but my mother doesn't

answer right away. We all watch a yellow butterfly (my mother's favorite) enter the room through an open window. It flits up and down, landing on my arm. The innocent creature completely opposes my tone when I questioned my mother. I feel a stab of guilt, but I brush the feeling away. Just as easily, I shoo the bug from my arm and watch it fly back the way it came.

"We wanted Lucan to think well of you and pushed a relationship with Cully. If they ever discovered our secret, we hoped a connection with them would protect us."

I shake my head. "I already figured that out. What else?"

"The Dales," Vale says. "I'm positive your family perpetrated their reputation."

My mother's lips tighten, and she nods. "While I faked a difficult pregnancy, your mother actually had a hard time. I didn't know how to help her, and she convinced me to confide in her sister. Marven was furious when he learned Bitha knew. I never liked Bitha—she was odd—but she was trained as a clinician before she went into the Dark and came back even more strange. She had the skills to help Anny. I don't know what Bitha thought would happen after the baby was born. Maybe that Anny would return to her husband like nothing had happened, but she didn't expect her to walk into the Dark."

"Why didn't she return to my father?" Vale asks, her voice small. The reckoner in me dissects the situation, but I don't have to say a word because, with my mother's reckoner background, she has the same answers.

"We were at our perfect number when Anny gave birth. She didn't want to be responsible for another person walking. Additionally, we didn't know how leadership would react to her disappearing for months and then returning." Mother wipes the edge of her eye and looks at me. "Besides the logistics, Anny knew she'd always look at you differently. She knew she'd be found out, which would ruin us all." Her attention returns to Vale. "It broke Bitha up when her sister left, and her parents were never kind, so they weren't any help. She became increasingly depressed, mumbling about Anny walking into the Dark. Almost gave up the secret multiple times. I admit I was glad when she left."

Vale frowns while my mother wipes the handkerchief across her brow. "Don't misunderstand. I was sad about what happened to Bitha, but I was young and scared."

"Do you know what happened to Bitha in the Dark? Do you *really* know?" Vale asks.

My mother shakes her head. "When she came back, she wasn't capable of telling us."

"Yeah. That should tell you how well things went for her. Maybe you should be more than sad." Vale pushes her hands down the front of her legs, scowling at my mother. "But go ahead. Tell the rest. Tell us what happened when Bitha came back."

"Hey," I bark out. "Go easy." My mother looks ready to faint. I won't have Vale making this worse than it already is.

Vale releases a long breath and nods while my mother licks the tears from her upper lip, not bothering with the handkerchief. "When Bitha returned with Tesha, she would mumble things about Anny walking into the Dark and protecting a special daughter."

"So, you made Bitha seem crazy to the citizens," Vale says.

"We didn't have to do that," my mother argues. "She acted strange enough to cause a sensation in the community."

"And you encouraged it. You didn't help her, even though you knew she was telling the truth. You allowed the citizens to believe she was insane. And a witch."

"No!" My mother shakes her head. "Never. I didn't start the rumor she was a witch."

No. She didn't.

71

I did.

It was easy enough because the people hated Bitha. And, at the time, I thought it was funny. I bite my nail, wondering if Vale will accuse me next (and pondering if I'll concede or deflect), but Vale continues her attack on my mother instead. "Did you ever try to stop it?" Vale pushes. My mother shakes her head. "What about your husband? Did he try to keep them in Harwell? Or did he vote to send them away?"

Tears track down my mother's cheeks. "He encouraged Lucan to put them back into the Dark. It didn't seem like a terrible idea. We figured they had survived there before, so we knew they could again."

Vale stiffens next to me. "Are you joking? You can't possibly have believed that."

My mother wilts. "I don't know. I'm sorry. I feel awful their lives were hard. Maybe if I knew how things would have turned out, I would have done things differently."

"What a consolation. If I'm ever faced with a tough decision, I'll be sure to act selfishly and decide later if it was the right move. It's rather convenient to remove yourself from any responsibility now."

"Oh, Vale—" My mother's face is pale. This discussion is the worst thing for her, and I hate Vale for physically and mentally weakening my mother.

"This conversation is over," I say, standing and wrenching Vale to her feet. Pushing her toward the door, she moves readily—as done with me as I am with her.

"No! We can't leave this unfinished," my mother pleads.

"What more is there to say?" I almost yell.

"Ennette told Laso about Annibeth. Did he tell you what your grandmother said?" my mother asks Vale.

Vale remains by the door, uninterested in sitting again. "It was Bitha who told Gran that Annibeth was Anny's daughter.

It happened when I was ten, and Laso had already married Milany. Gran stayed quiet because she didn't want to disrupt our lives."

"I'm grateful to her. It's a hard secret to keep."

Vale nods. "My father was distraught when he found out. Then, of course, he wondered if Anny was still alive."

Anny, still alive? My eyes widen, and I have a hard time forming my words. "Is... that a... possibility?"

"Just wondering that, huh?" Vale asks with a tilt of her head.

I want to launch a sharp-tongued comeback, but the day has proved too much for me, and my mind can't keep up. I ponder my feelings about meeting my birth mother. What it would mean, or if it's something I'd even want to do. The disappointment when Vale shakes her head gives me my answer.

"When I entered the Dark, I learned about her death. She didn't make it to your first birthday."

My emotions are rocky, but it's my mother who bursts into tears. "Oh, Anny." She leans over the table, her shoulders bouncing with her sobs. "It was so horrible. I told her I couldn't watch her leave. That we needed to find another way. She woke up and snuck out in the night." She sits up and stares at me. "There was so much guilt. Suddenly, I was free to care for a brand-new baby. My beautiful, new girl that I could love as my very own, all while knowing Anny was giving up everyone she loved. And I was just a poor substitute because Annibeth's proper mother sacrificed everything for her child. How could I ever compare when my actions were entirely selfish?"

Her eyes break from me and go to Vale. "I'm so sorry, Vale. Your mother was the best kind of person. I'm sorry you missed out on knowing her. I'm sorry I've mistreated you. I'm sorry I didn't find a better way."

With each professed apology, my stomach drops, and I feel sicker.

Sorry. Sorry. Sorry.

Sorry, *Vale*.

I glare at Vale. Hating this situation. Hating the way my mother seems so weak. My eyes burn with anger.

"I know you two don't get along, but Annibeth's a wonderful daughter. She'd be a good sister if you gave it a chance." Vale and I snort in unison. "Girls. You're sisters—the children of my dearest friend—and I created the divide between you. Please be better than me and work to heal this rift."

I blow air between my lips. "That's not going to happen," I push out with a laugh.

"What she said," Vale replies with equal disdain.

"Please. Please. For me. Just try."

Try. I don't know if we're capable of that, but then Vale says, "Well, I can promise I won't break a rotten egg over her head." She's grinning, and I'm assaulted by memories of the day I did exactly that to Vale. I choke out a cough, hiding a laugh.

My mother smiles. Vale watches her, and I realize she's doing this for my mother. Regardless of what happens when we leave this room, we can make her feel better right now.

"And I promise not to steal your boyfriend," I say, pushing my hair over my shoulder.

"As if you could," Vale says with a smirk, turning for the door.

"As if I'd want him." I'm trying to maintain the friendly banter, but our words turn more bitter with each volleying remark.

"Don't you?" Vale twists around, piercing me with her gaze. "After all, he is a *hot little number*," she says with loads of sass.

"I said that *once!*" I complain, but apparently, it was enough to get back to her. And Geric, I realize with a groan. *Lucky me*, I think as Vale grins in triumph before spinning and exiting the room.

CHAPTER NINE

"Do you hate me for keeping this from you?" my mother asks.

My parents did what was necessary to survive, saving me from a horrible fate. "No. I understand why you did it. You don't need to feel bad about that."

My mother tilts her head. "What do I need to feel bad about?"

I squeeze my bottom lip, unsure if I should bring this up now. But when would it be any better? "You told Vale you're sorry. Repeatedly. But you haven't even apologized to me."

Mother leans her elbows on the table, taking the weight from her shoulders. "I guess I should have. But with you, I wouldn't change a thing, so it makes an apology feel hollow. Am I sorry you found out? No. I anticipated this day. Am I sorry we didn't tell you when you were young? No. You didn't need the pressure. Am I sorry you didn't know Anny? As wonderful as she was, my answer's still no. I'm selfish. I'd want you even though it meant losing my best friend. I'd go through all the fear and sadness again. You were worth every tear and tremble. But I'd have preferred to tell you in a less dramatic manner."

I smile. It was quite a scene. Her explanation isn't the pleading apology Vale received, but she tailored her words perfectly for the two of us—raw and honest. My mother looks ready to drop, and I need to keep this short, but there are still a few things to say. "So, you planned to tell me?"

"On your birthday," she says, and I wonder how it would have gone. Would I have felt more settled with only my two parents explaining my connection to the Rennicks? I doubt it. The chaos of the day made the revelation easier to manage. I'm glad for the drama.

"You know, it's pretty unreasonable to want Vale and I to be friends. We hate each other—something you encouraged. You coached me to stay away from her, convincing me she wasn't worthy of my attention."

"It will be a struggle, I'm sure, but you'll both benefit from it. She's very much like Anny."

"And I'm like you?" I ask, needing to feel a connection to Clayre Petters more than ever.

"You are. Together, we were the best of friends. Together, we were unstoppable."

Maybe. But I can't see that happening between Vale and me. I'm glad she's gone. I'm glad it's just my mother and me. Watching them interact was frustrating, and the way my mother acted was out of character. "It was hard watching you apologize—beg for her understanding. It was a weak tactic."

"Not all of life is tactics and the upper hand."

I laugh. "That's not how you raised me."

"This situation is different. Can't you see it? Vale lost her mother, and I gained something precious in the exchange. If there was ever a time to show humility, this is it. Vale deserves our remorse."

"Remorse?" Who is this person in my mother's body? "I don't show remorse. I only demand respect. Again, you taught me that."

My mother sighs. "I'm sorry I drilled it into you so hard. I felt I had to."

"Finally. Something you're sorry for," I say bitterly.

My mother grabs my hand. Her grasp is weak, and her palm is cold and clammy. "Now's the time for new lessons. Better ones. The ones I was too afraid to give you. Please, just try to see her side."

I doubt that will ever happen, but I'm done talking about

it. I drop back into the chair, breaking our connection. "What now?" I ask, feeling as defeated as the question sounds.

Mother frowns, her chin dropping to her chest. "You need to pack so you can leave."

My defeated slouch lasts as long as it takes to register her sentence, and then I'm sitting straight, scowling at my mother —stiff and ready for a fight. "I'm not going anywhere."

"Annibeth, I heard it between the floors. We need to focus on keeping you safe."

"You want me to go with them? I can't leave you!"

"You can." She reaches out and grabs my hand. Her fingers are so frail. "Staying here won't help me."

"How can you say that? All your errands. The work you have me do."

"Lucan can find me an assistant. It's always been an option. I just ask you because I enjoy working together." She squeezes my fingers. "Besides, who says we'll be here much longer."

"You'll leave with Captain Rhed?"

"Probably not at first. I'll do whatever Lucan and your father do. But it could happen."

"I won't go. Not unless you come with me."

"Annibeth. Your father can't manage that kind of travel with his leg. And whatever's going on with me—" She pauses, running a weary hand over her face. "I don't have the energy."

"But you just said you'd go with Captain Rhed."

"I may feel better by then," she says, but I see the truth. She's not planning to go with him. She'll stay here, in Harwell, regardless.

"Father will never agree to let me go with the Dark brothers," I argue. He doesn't like or trust them. He's made that clear.

"He will. We've spent our entire lives making hard choices

to keep you safe. *Every hard choice.* And if your best option is going with the Coastals, he'll support it."

The yellow butterfly is back. I don't allow it to land this time before waving my hand and batting it away. I push up from my chair. "I won't go!" I lean over her, asserting my position. She looks so tired. I almost feel guilty. Almost.

She rises too, her eyes slowly blinking. "I understand your reluctance. We'll drop it for now and discuss it with your father."

"There's no point," I say, remaining firm.

She pats my arm, just a weak tap. "As you say."

The fight is gone from her, so I relax my stubborn stance. Our argument ends, but what comes after is almost worse. I'd rather be fighting than watching my mother wilt before me. I take her arm to steady her and get her into her room. After she's settled in bed, I go to my room and drop onto mine.

What a horrible day.

I don't know if I want to lie here and think or go somewhere and talk some more. I consider finding Nacole, but recounting the entire situation sounds exhausting. She'll ask stupid questions I won't want to answer, providing little insight.

I consider knocking on Cully's wall. He knows more about the situation, though I'll still need to reveal my new family connection. I shake my head, hating the idea. Besides, Cully will have his own agenda. He'll want to talk about what happened with Captain Rhed today. He'll flirt and tease with his own end in mind. Sometimes there are no good solutions, so I don't seek out anyone. I just sit in my room, staring at my wall, until I hear voices.

"Evans, go up there and see if she needs help. She might have questions." It's Geric, and since they're right outside my window, I figure it's me they're talking about.

"Do I have to?" the Droll whines. It's a mystery how they don't punch him every time he opens his mouth.

"I'll go," I hear in Ronen's signature deep voice, sounding as if he's speaking into a hollow log. By the time the words get out, you can barely detect them.

I push up from the floor and walk to my window, tossing the curtain aside and leaning on the sill to look out. Ronen's ascending the stairs—two at a time—perfectly aware I'm watching him. "Hey," he says before he's even halfway up, his black longcoat swaying behind him.

"Stalking my house, are you?" I ask. His brothers are gone. They pressured Ronen into the task, then abandoned him to do the deed. That I can scare the others off is rather gratifying. It's nearly the highlight of my day.

"Been stalkin' yer house fer close ta fifteen years."

Huh. I hadn't realized he'd been watching over Harwell for so long.

"You know what happened to the last boy who hovered outside my window."

Ronen chuckles. "Aye. Ye chased 'im without a shirt." He grins.

"You look too pleased about that," I say, drawing my arms tighter around me.

"Wasna a bad outcome." The grin remains.

"Well, that's not creepy or anything," I say, hopping onto the window frame and spinning my legs outside. Ronen's on the landing now and stops when he's standing before me. My friends typically lean on the railing and get comfy. Ronen's a bit big for that. I try to work out the logistics, deciding there'd be one of two outcomes. He'd either get a catch in his back from bending over so far. Or, more likely, he'd topple over the railing (possibly breaking it) and fall to the ground. Both could be entertaining.

"Nah. I'm innocent. Ne'er once moved a curtain."

I can't help my laugh, but I run my hand over my mouth to hide it. "Got the short stick again?"

Ronen shakes his head. "Volunteered." Unlike the boys in Harwell, the boys in the Dark keep their hair short. The hair making up his brown beard is the same length as what's on his head—about an inch long all around—so when he moves, it stays in place.

"Yeah. I heard. Just didn't think you'd admit it." He shrugs, his hefty shoulder lifting and dropping. It reminds me of when they fell lumber trees. I almost expect a crash. "So, what's your purpose in seeking me out?" I ask, swinging my legs and nearly kicking him each time my feet fly forward.

"See if ye need help."

"Or have questions. Yeah, yeah. Help with what?"

"Packin' ta leave."

I chuckle. "Ah. You're under that misguided delusion as well. Let me set you straight—*I'm not going anywhere.*"

"Yer father says ye are."

"Laso has no say in what I do. He hasn't for almost eighteen years."

"'Twas not Laso."

Dammit. The Dark brothers have gotten their plan into my father's head. "I won't do anything until I talk to him myself."

"Fine." Ronen nods. "Ye still can ask questions if ye have any."

"Where do you plan for us to go?" I ask with a smirk, knowing it's something he won't answer.

"Lass," he scolds with a groan.

"Even if my parents want me to go, it doesn't mean I will. I know places. I could hide from you all."

"Not fer long. Have ways o' findin' ye."

"How?" I ask, as both a challenge and out of curiosity.

Ronen puts his fingers in his mouth and releases a shrill sound. I've never seen such a thing. I put my hands in front of my ears just as he stops. I cautiously lower them, and then the platform Ronen's standing on is trembling like it will shake apart. A second later, the big brute's little brute is in front of me, lolling his tongue back and forth from one side of his mouth to the other.

"That thing?" I laugh, pointing at Ronen's dog. I've seen the animal around but never up close. I'd call him beautiful—all fluffy in mismatched black, brown, and white patterns—if not for the ridiculous lenses they have covering his eyes. They're different from the ones the brothers wear—larger and curved. And he's bigger than I thought he'd be. He's always by Ronen, and by comparison, he makes the animal look small.

"Aye. Can sniff ye out."

"Sniff? That's just weird." I wrinkle my nose, even though it enhances my freckles.

"Nah. Comes in handy." Ronen clears his throat. "Pack light, lass. Ye won't be hidin' from me."

"What is it I'm packing for again?" I ask, just to be a pain. I don't want him to think I'll ever be anything but.

"Leavin'," he says without pause. "Ye tell 'er, Yip." The dog barks, and I flinch because I wasn't expecting it.

"Is that his name? Yip?" The dog barks again.

"Aye. He'll answer each time ye say it."

"Yip." *Bark*. I giggle and reach out toward him. "Yip." *Bark*. He leans in and sniffs my hand, then licks me. "What the—" I hold up my wet fingers while Ronen chuckles.

"He likes ye."

I grin, wiping the wet hand down my pant leg. "Well, that's one of you," I say with a nod.

"Ye're not an easy one ta like, but we'll figure it out. Plus, ye're stuck with us."

"If you say so," I say, twisting in my window and landing in my room. Yip hops on his back feet, resting the front ones where I was just sitting while gazing in at me.

"Pack only yer absolutes," Ronen says through the opening, the thin curtain scrunched to one side.

"Sure. I'll do it tomorrow," I say, waving him off.

"Nah, t'night," Ronen says, and he's lost some of his relaxed tone.

"Fine." I'm not sure I'll do it but agree so I don't get lectured.

"Ye know, lass, how this goes is up ta ye. Question is, what'll ye do?"

"Go with you, I guess. Isn't that what I'm being *forced* to do?"

Ronen shakes his head. "I mean, how will ye let the changes affect ye? Will it make ye realize all ye could have or turn ye more sour?"

"More sour?" I ask with wide eyes. Did he really say that?

"Aye." He chuckles. "Ye know ye're sour. Dunna deny it."

I release a breath and cross my arms over my chest. Fine. I won't deny it. But maybe I'll show him how sour I can be. He takes in my stance, and that slight grin hidden in his beard turns into a full toothy smile. I almost lose my cool because it's so startling (and startlingly pleasant), but I keep it together.

"Be an interestin' trip, fer sure." Ronen tips his head and slaps his leg. "Yip!" *Bark.* "Oh, Bethy. Would ye like me ta take the bracelet fer safe keepin'?"

Bethy? Where did he get the idea he could call me Bethy? I scowl as he holds out his big hand. I imagine my little bracelet in his palm, and it seems as if it could be a ring for his large fingers. I shake my head. "No. It stays with me. I have somewhere safe to put it."

"Aye," he says with a nod. "Let's go, dog." Yip takes off. I hear every loping step as he descends the steps while Ronen, whose size is much more significant, is silent and steady.

I drop my hands from my chest and put them on my hips. Bossy, bossy brothers from the Dark. And bossy, bossy parents too. They may all get their wish in getting me to leave Harwell, but one thing is for sure, and I think on it with a smile. If they get me to go with them, they'll regret every second.

CHAPTER TEN

I doubt I'll ever fall asleep, but my emotionally charged day proves a perfect catalyst. My eyes get heavy, falling closed, and I exchange the glow of the moon for sunshine in my sleep. Ronen's animal is in my dream world, making noise, finding me with his mouth, and swiping his tongue on my cheek. It's too real to discount.

My eyes jerk open to find the goggled dog, standing over me and highlighted by the moon shining directly into my bedroom window.

"Get up, Bethy." I barely make out Ronen's shape in the shadows. I fly up in bed, and the motion causes Yip to stir, but then he settles, sitting beside me. The dog seems happy and calm, but I know this visit is anything but.

"What's happened?"

"Endrack's lamlight-wearin' cogs are 'ere. Guard's holdin' 'em off. Willna be long."

I push off my bed covers and stand. "I need to talk to my parents."

"Yer father's with Lucan 'n Geric downstairs."

"I'll get my mother."

I take a step forward, but Ronen puts up a staying hand. "Wha's tha' ye're wearin'?"

"My nightclothes." I look down, "Pajamas," I clarify. "What's the problem?"

"We're runnin'. 'Tis inappropriate attire."

"I'll change."

"No doin'. They're on our heels. Barely have a lead."

"I can't go in this!" I throw out my arms to show off my

clothes.

"No avoidin' it now. Ye pack a bag like ye promised?" he asks, ignoring my protest.

"I never promised," I argue, then point to the corner. "But, yes." I almost didn't—out of spite—and I'm unsure why I finally caved. Probably, I was too tired to fight. But now I'm glad I did it.

"Annibeth!" my mother calls from my door. "What's all that noise? Do you hear it?" she asks, stumbling into my room. She hasn't even noticed the man and dog in my bedroom. She's tired, scared, and singularly focused.

"I hear it. Ronen says it's Endrack's soldiers. Father's with Lucan and Geric downstairs."

"Aye. Bethy needs ta leave," Ronen rumbles.

My mother jumps back, clutching her chest. "Oh! Ronen. I didn't see you there." Typically, he's impossible to miss, but right now, he's one with the shadows. Still, the oversight is largely my mother's state of mind—she has yet to notice Yip, and he's in the bright moonlight, sitting quietly at my side as if commanded to do so.

"They're in the orchard. Havena crossed the bridge."

Mother's shock wears off quickly, and she's got my hand, pulling me forward. "You need to go!"

I hold firm and pull her toward me. "I don't want to leave you."

My mother drags me into her arms, pulling the long braid I wove before sleeping. "We'll be together soon. Like none of this ever happened."

"Oh, Mother. We both know that's unlikely."

"Maybe not. But let's pretend." She tugs the braid. "I'll miss you, but you must know this is the right thing."

Yesterday morning, tearing me from my room, kicking and screaming, would have been necessary to make me leave my parents and friends in Harwell. But after all the talk, I know this is the best way to not only stay safe myself but to keep them safe. I let out a resigned breath. "It is."

"Aye. 'Tis. We gotta go," Ronen breaks into the moment. He's not doing it to be mean. (That's what Evans would do.) Or to be bossy. (That would be Geric.) Or to make sure the attention was solely on him. (Cully.) Ronen just states the situation, simply and truthfully. "Grab yer bag," he says as I release my mother.

She sweeps in to place a last kiss on my cheek and pushes me toward my things. I have them in my grasp, and a second later, I'm flying in the air as Ronen swoops me into his arms.

"What are you doing?" I demand fiercely.

"Quieter if I carry ye," he says, squeezing our two bodies through the bedroom doorway. It would have been tight with just him. With two of us, my leg scrapes the side, and his head bumps the top.

"Put me down," I growl.

"Also, quieter if ye dunna yell at me." I open my mouth to complain, but Ronen's goggled dog licks my hand like a plea to comply with his master, and it takes the angry words right from my mouth.

I take one last look at my mother. She's smiling at me but also crying. Ronen's going through the outer door, and I keep my eyes on her as long as possible. He stops on the landing. "I promise ye'll see 'er again. I'll be sure o' it."

I can only nod before leaning into him to hide the tear trailing down my cheek. It's not the time for such an observation, but I consider the smooth texture of his longcoat. It's in stark contrast to the rough cotton we wear in Harwell, making me jealous, which only adds to my mixed emotions.

We make no sound as we descend the stairs, but when we reach the bottom, I regain my composure, shove his shoulder, and demand, "Put me down. *Now*."

"Aye, Bethy. Ye're down. Ye're down." Ronen leans over but doesn't let go until my feet hit the dirt. "Most people are grumpy when wakin', but ye're like a little storm, chirpin' away like an angry cricket."

"That's because I'm scared."

"Are ye? Dunna speak like someone scared."

"Yes! I'm scared. Out of my mind!" The noises coming from the Dark make my heart thump at an unprecedented rate. "What time is it? It feels like the middle of the night."

"Closer ta morn than nightfall," Ronen says, and I'm not sure it's an answer.

He relieves me of my bag—my belongings look like a little knapsack when attached to him—and he finds my hand, pulling me through the night. From my bedroom, I had an unobstructed view of the moon. From the ground, the milky light pushes through the slim gaps between the trees, flashing on the ground as we hurry to the back entrance of the Well.

We pass a window, and I see a small group gathered around the flickering fire—my father, Lucan, and Geric. Ronen tugs my arm so we can enter, but I resist. "I can't go in there in my nightclothes," I say with a scowl, pulling my hair over my shoulder because I'm sure it's a disaster too. Ronen looks back at me, then tugs again.

"Hey!" I pull my hand from his. "How would you feel if I carried you from your home in nothing but your pajamas?"

"'Twould ne'er happen. Yer arms'd ne'er manage it." He chuckles, and I scowl. "Truly, dunna sleep in pee-jamas."

"What do you sleep in?"

"Day clothes, o' course. Always ready ta move. Dunna wanna get caught runnin' with na drawers."

"That's just weird."

"'Tis not. Now, ferget yer clothes, Cricket. We're losin'

time." He pushes the door wider, exclaiming, "Yip!" to which his dog trots into the room, and Ronen follows. Then he drops the door. In my face. I push it open with a huff, and all eyes are on me.

"Daughter," my father says, taking unsteady steps toward me. "You're in your nightclothes."

"Established. Apparently, we're short on time," I say blandly, but my father isn't too concerned about my attire. He pulls me into a hug—a parting hug—knowing we'll not see each other for a while. Reluctantly, I've come to terms with it. "I love you, Annibeth. I hope these people keep you safe as they promise, but stay alert. And be smart. You've got a brilliant mind. Use it to help them."

"Yes, Father." He leans back and taps my cheek with his hand.

"I'm sorry to interrupt," Lucan says, breaking into our last moment. "Have you seen my son?"

"Cully's missing?" I ask, and the noises outside get louder —the shouting and the clash of metal booming in my ears. Whether it's that one of us is unaccounted for or the noise of battle, the desire to flee is overwhelming.

"How much time?" Ronen asks though I don't understand the question.

"Ten minutes," Geric answers, but he's shaking his head like he's unsure. He paces the room, his dark blue longcoat flapping while he clutches a bow.

Ronen taps his leg and walks to the steps leading to the Clarcs' quarters. "Lucan. Need a shirt the lad's worn."

Realization strikes. He's going to have Yip sniff him out. The dog can find Cully. Lucan doesn't question Ronen's strange request but rushes up the steps, disappearing upstairs. Ronen doesn't follow but asks Geric, "Where're the horses?"

"Northern Hem near Fifty-Three," Geric answers. Fifty-

Three is where Vale and Siman used to live, but it's just rubble now—one of the community buildings that fell during a recent storm.

"Take 'er with ye. I'm not there in ten, leave Clod 'n go."

"Take me?" He's sending me away? With Geric! I stomp my feet as I converge on Ronen, insisting, "I'm not going anywhere without you." For all of Geric's scowly hotness, I don't want to go with him.

Ronen tilts his head, staring at me through those vexatious lenses. His tense posture settles, and he turns to face me, a grin appearing in his beard. "Dinna know I'd made such an impression on ye, Bethy."

I step back, clear my throat, and calmly explain, "All I'm saying is, I don't feel comfortable with him." I forcefully thrust my thumb in Geric's direction. "I'd rather wait and go with you."

Geric chuckles behind me just as Lucan reappears. I take in his worried expression and add, "Besides, I'd rather wait and know Cully's okay."

Taking the shirt from Lucan, Ronen holds it in front of Yip's face. The dog leans in as if he'll eat it, but moves his wiggling nose over the surface, pulls back, and barks.

Ronen makes a clicking sound, and Yip runs to the door. Turning to me, he drops my clothing bag at my feet. "Wait or go, 'tis up ta ye." A second later, he's striding to the door, his long legs taking him there in the space of a breath and with less noise than one.

I'm unsure if he was upset by my declaration or resigned to it. But what I conclude, since having more interaction with Ronen, is that he's focused on the issue at hand, and I'm left to my own devices.

I can deal with that.

"When did you last see Cully?" Lucan asks, and I scoop up

my bag, facing him.

"Not at all yesterday. It was after you asked me to talk to him the night before."

"Did he seem okay?" Lucan wrings his hands, pacing in front of the fire. "Do you think he was out with Harbert and was found by the invaders?" As Lucan voices his question, we hear a loud, bellowing scream. Not a fearful run-away noise, but a charged I'm-going-to-get-you sound.

Geric drops his bow on the table and runs through the main door toward the chaos while my instinct is to slink upstairs. I've never been so scared, and with nothing to protect myself, I'm ready to hide like the coward I always insist I'm not.

"What's happening out there?" Lucan asks while I shake my head, equally perplexed by this development. My father steps behind me, guarding my back, and I can't help wishing Big Scruff was here. Though I'm glad I'm not alone, I'd feel safer with him around. A moment later, Geric's back in the room, his sword discolored. The sight turns my stomach, and I look away.

Geric chuckles darkly. "You surprise me, Annibeth. I heard you like violence."

I frown while his comment stirs a memory. I was taunting Vale (one of many times), and my purpose was two-fold: To warn her away from Cully and to remind her I was better than her. It seems ridiculous now, while we expect a death-minded cog to charge into the room at any moment.

I'm grateful Geric was here to handle whatever happened outside that door, but isn't he supposed to leave? Not that I want him to. No, I definitely want him to stay, so it's obviously stupid of me to ask, "Aren't they waiting for you by the horses?"

"So eager to die?" He laughs again.

I gulp down a swallow. *No. I just have a stubborn mouth.*

"Don't worry." He picks up Cully's shirt, the one Yip sniffed, and wipes it across the blade, cleaning away the blood. "I'll leave soon enough."

"How long's he been gone?" I ask, forgetting to be angry. Or choosing not to. I'm so on edge it could be either.

"We're close to time," Geric bites out, and I think he's angry at the situation, not my question. Geric's answer is not what I wanted to hear. I release a stuttering breath and twist the knot on my bag—at this rate, I'll never get it open again.

What if Ronen doesn't make it back? Should I leave now with Geric? Would that be the safer thing for all of us? I'm about to ask Geric when the main door flies open with a bang. I jerk in place. Lucan and my father join me in my startled state.

"Looks like ye had some trouble, Brass," Ronen says as Yip bounds into the room with a happy trot. "Found some trouble o' my own." He moves inside with Cully held by the neck, then shoves him to the floor. Cully skids to a halt in front of us.

"What'd you do to him?" Lucan bellows, rushing to his son's aid. I remain frozen, having never seen this side of Ronen.

"Less'n he deserved, but found 'im fer ye." Ronen flings the door shut, strides across the room, and throws sheets of wadded paper onto Cully's back before announcing, "Also learned the foolish git's our traitor."

CHAPTER ELEVEN

I drop my bag and step forward to help Cully up, but Lucan beats me to it, grunting as he leans over to pull his son off the floor. "What's this all about?" Lucan asks, scowling while he brushes debris from Cully's clothes.

"Ask yer boy wha' he was doin' out," Ronen says, walking to the long gathering table and lifting it as if it's as light as a provisions box. Carrying it to the main door of the Well, he drops it in place with ease, blocking the entry.

"I could ask you the same," Cully bites back, blowing the hair from his face with a huff. My boyfriend—always one of the biggest things in Harwell—appears excessively small in a room with Ronen. The glower he sends the big guy proves very ineffective, as Ronen's not bothered by it in the slightest but moves to take a protective stance by the back door.

"Dunna owe ye explanations."

"I could say the same," Cully returns, repeating the comeback. He's usually much better in an argument. I've never seen him so ruffled nor sounding so incapable.

Cully glances around the room, getting his bearings, and spots me. "Annibeth? What are you doing here?" he asks, then looks me up and down. "And what are you wearing?"

I release an exasperated sigh. I mean, where to begin? And is now really the time? Havoc and death are right outside the door. (Both doors, apparently!) I should have left with the Dark brothers ten minutes ago, but now accusations are flying. No, it's not the time to discuss clothing.

Geric steps up, scooping the papers from the floor. "How about we ignore Annibeth and look at what these might be."

Well, other than the part about ignoring me, I agree. Even

amid the unrest outside, I'm curious about what Ronen thinks he found. Geric peruses the two pages, leaning them toward the firelight and flipping them over to check both sides. "Didn't peg you as the one. Thought it was one of these two," he says, pointing at my father and Lucan while still holding the papers. "But you were in the room when Malum warned Tesha about who not to trust."

I shake my head, confused why they'd believe anything Malum had to say.

"I'm sure there's an explanation, no matter what the situation looks like," Lucan challenges, holding out his hand to take the pages. Geric smoothly passes over the crinkled documents.

"Situation is yer boy's up ta no good."

"Yep. That's what it looks like," Geric supports.

"And it looks like *ye're* stealing my girl away in the middle of the night," Cully mocks with a scowl, pointing at my bag.

"Aye. Tha' appears ta be the way o' it, 'n we need ta get goin'. Lucan, tell me ye'll handle this. Yer boy's just added trouble ta our journey." Lucan's still reading, rubbing his forehead and sighing in frustration.

"What do they say?" I ask, stepping forward to look over Lucan's shoulder.

"It's information for Captain Malum," Cully answers, straightening and facing the brothers.

"Malum? But he's dead," I say, looking at their faces for an answer.

"It seems the name has more value than the man," Cully says with a shrug, then winces and rubs his shoulder—his floor landing appears to have left a mark.

"One o' 'is Six took over," Ronen concludes.

"Maybe more than one," Geric adds. "They could share both aliases—Malum and Geminus—and with his dealings in the east, he could have more names."

Malum was a busy man, but I'm more concerned about Cully and his actions. "I don't understand. Why would you do that?" Communicating with those men makes no sense. "They captured you, and Captain Malum held a knife to your throat. He threw you in the river." I remember how panicked I was when the man had him.

"He wasn't supposed to throw me in the river," Cully mumbles.

"But ye planned the rest," Ronen says in his deep rumble.

"You provided safety for him while he waited for Bitha Dale," Geric says, taking a step toward Cully. "What did he give you in return? What was the price for betraying your people?"

"I didn't betray them. I helped them. Malum said he'd leave Harwell alone—leave it to my father and me to run. He just wanted the story keepers and the scientist."

"It wasn't real?" I ask, perplexed, and then my anger takes over. "You faked it! I thought you were in terrible danger. I was so afraid for you, and I blamed the Rennicks for what happened. But you planned it?" I squeeze my fingers into fists as his actions sink in further. "It's bad enough you enabled Malum, but worse, you were false with me. You repeatedly told me it was Tesha working with Malum to ruin Harwell, but all along, it was you."

"Babycakes, I did it for us. For Harwell."

I ignore the pet name I abhor. "Oh, Cully," I draw out, feeling his betrayal deeply, but it's barely heard over the other comments in the room.

"You believe Malum or any of his Six have the power to honor a promise like that?" Geric asks with a laugh.

"No one's makin' deals 'cept Endrack, 'n 'is only deal is death," Ronen says with a decisive shake of his head.

A cold chill runs through my body. "What did you tell

them?" I ask, pulling the notes from Lucan's fingers without asking, though he gives no resistance.

"That Vale and Tesha are here and leaving for the Cliffs," Geric says before I read it for myself.

The Cliffs! Cully told them our destination. The Dark brothers insist few know the actual location, but what if they're wrong? What if Lord Endrack knows the place and Cully just gave it up?

"Why are there two?" I ask—two *identical* notes. "You didn't deliver them yet," I realize, and let out a relieved breath.

Cully tilts his head at me, then shakes it. "No. I always put out four."

Always. It's true—he's a repeat offender.

Four. Two of them are already out there.

"Ye'll get the others back 'n destroy 'em," Ronen states.

"I will not," Cully responds defiantly.

"Lucan," Ronen growls and our leader nods in agreement.

"What's going on here?" Cully asks, looking between his father and Ronen.

"You must get them back, Son."

"No way," Cully argues. Lucan can get on top of this—force Cully to do what's needed—but he doesn't get a chance.

"Forget these," Geric says, tearing the notes from my hands and throwing them into the fire. "We need to know what else you've told them."

"I'm not telling you a thing."

"Son, we need to hear it."

"Father, what's gotten into you? Are you going to let these fools from the Dark bully you?"

"Lucan," Ronen says again, his patience at an end. He takes a step forward in warning, and our leader licks his lips nervously, nodding to confirm he'll take care of things, but he doesn't take action fast enough, and Ronen exclaims, "Bells! We're outta time. Last chance." Dropping his hands to his waist, he checks his weapons.

What's he going to do with his weapons?

"Cully, as your father and leader of Harwell, I demand you tell us what other information you've relayed."

"No. I won't. I'm not afraid of—"

Quicker than I've seen anyone move, Ronen's behind Cully, gripping his arm, twisting it behind his back, and lifting until his shoulder strains—no weapons required.

"Ahh!" Cully cries out. "Get off!"

"Tell us, er it's the tippies fer ya," Ronen says. Cully struggles, and it's hard to watch, but, we need the information. Ronen keeps his arm twisted while holding his shoulder steady, but Cully says nothing. "Tippies it is," Ronen says after he's done waiting, lifting Cully until his toes barely touch the ground.

"The necklace," Cully squeaks out. "And the dagger," he releases on a breath before Ronen lowers him.

Lucan shakes his head. "Not possible. You weren't in the meetings, and I didn't tell you about them."

"I listened through the floor," Cully admits with a grin, feeling proud for putting one over on all of us.

With the admission, my father, a silent observer until now, steps up to the boy he's always considered a son. His eyes are on fire, and his hands, which generally fly about when he's worked up, are fisted resolutely at his side. Even his limp is diminished. "What about Annibeth?" he asks, with unveiled anger.

Cully looks confused. "What about her?" he asks, looking directly at me.

"What did you tell them about her?" my father yells.

Cully jerks back. "Nothing." He pulls his head back, looking among us. "Why would I say anything about Annibeth?"

"Apparently, you didn't eavesdrop long enough," Geric says.

"Long enough for what?" Cully asks, and all their eyes fall on me.

I dreaded Cully learning about my connection to the Rennicks and Dales. I was sure it would lessen me in his eyes. But with this new information—knowing what he's done—I straighten my spine, angry and ready for a fight.

"You didn't eavesdrop long enough to learn that one of the people Lord Endrack is looking for is me," I spit out. "To find out, I'm going with them to the Cliffs, where it's safer. Or at least, it was *supposed* to be safer." I let out a breath, still hating to say these words. "And because I learned yesterday that Vale Rennick is my sister."

Cully sinks into Ronen, who's still holding his arm, though loosely now. But after my revelation, Ronen releases him and returns to the door. It's not as noisy outside, and I'm not sure what that means. We've been in this room for a long time. Even now, the new Captain Malum could approach the door to the Well with his freshly appointed Six to take me as his prize.

"I didn't know," Cully whispers, staring at me aghast. "I'll get the other notes. I would never put you in harm's way."

"But you did," I say factually, feeling a wall go up between us and wondering if I'll ever want to take that wall down. "It's done, and we'll adjust. Is there anything else you've done to put me in danger?"

"Baby, I'm sorry," he says, shaking his head. "There's nothing else."

"You know I hate it when you call me Baby. At least there's no reason for you ever to do it again." Maybe I say it for shock value. Maybe I say it to prove I'm in charge of our relationship. (Ex-relationship.) Whatever the reason, the moment the words leave my lips, I know I mean them. I'll feel sad tomorrow—Cully's been a part of my life for a long time— but right now, all I feel is a sense of rightness. (Well, rightness and indignation.)

"Annibeth! No. You can't mean that."

"Oh, I mean it! You bet I do," I yell while walking to Ronen. "What's there to finalize so we can leave?" I ask the big guy.

"You can't seriously leave with them!" Cully follows me.

"I hate doing it, but this group is my best chance of staying safe and, more importantly, keeping my parents safe. It is what it is. So, yes, I'm going with them." I turn back to Ronen. "What's left to do? I know we're in a hurry."

"Ye're takin' charge, huh?" Ronen asks. He's smiling, and I swear that dog of his, sitting obediently beside him, is smiling too. My change in attitude amuses him—no longer the girl they're pressuring to get on board. He acts like he's won something, and I can't have that.

"Don't look so happy," I snap, pushing his chest, and Ronen actually takes a step back as if my meager shove influenced him. I point straight at his lenses. "You'll regret every second I'm with you. That I can guarantee."

"Na doubt." He grins.

Lucan looks at me in shock. The man rarely sees anything but my sweet side. I've closed his eyes to my true self— a self the rest of the people in the room know well—but it's my father who complains about my behavior. "Annibeth!" he admonishes. "You might ease up a bit. Don't deter them from taking you before you're even out the door."

"What?" I put up my hands. "They know what they're getting. I'm difficult under the best of circumstances. And that's with people I respect." I briefly glance at Cully, and my stomach turns. That list has gotten shorter today.

"Let's go before I change my mind," I snarl, pulling my father in for a last hug. "Take care of Mother," I say, then turn and walk away from them all.

Cully steps up to block my path. "Annibeth," he says with

repentant eyes. He's sincerely sorry—I see it—and only wanted what was best for Harwell, but he sort of messed it up. Sort of a lot. His intentions were good, in a sense, but it's a betrayal, nonetheless.

His eyes beg me to understand—to know that he never intended to make my situation more troublesome and dangerous than it already is. But I ignore his plea. I consider checking him with my shoulder as I pass, but I divert around him without a touch or a word.

"Annibeth," he says again. This time, my name isn't a plea —it's a dejected loss. No crooked smiles are fixing this, and he knows it.

I stand by the door with Ronen and his dog, waiting for Geric, who's talking to Lucan. I don't process a thing he's saying. In a moment, I'll leave this room and enter the transit paths to maneuver the threats existing there. I should focus my mind on that, but I don't. I'm thinking about Cully, who's staring at me. It was shocking to learn he'd turn Vale over so readily—I thought they were sort of friends. Sure, he was frustrated with her, but I didn't know he was that kind of person.

I didn't know he was like me.

Because what he's done isn't very dissimilar from what I did to Ennette Rennick. Turning Vale's grandmother over to Captain Malum seemed like the right thing to do. That the action injured my rival only made it better. Why I'm second-guessing it now is bothersome. Is it because I've become one of the hunted? Is it because Vale's grandmother is suddenly my grandmother? Or is it because I have a new perspective and things aren't as clear as they seemed back then? I'm not sure.

My perfect life in Harwell is over. And now I'm leaving the people I love to enter the Dark with strangers. I sense there's a lot of second-guessing in my future. I just hope, when I get to the other side, I've chosen the best path.

CHAPTER TWELVE

G eric exits the Well. Thirty seconds later, we hear a whistle and know it's safe to leave. I go next, followed by Ronen and Yip. We hurry along the backside of the Well, then slink along the north side until we can see the Lower River Bridge leading to the Common. Water surrounds the Well and neighboring buildings, so crossing a bridge is our only way off. But bodies in motion block the bridge, swinging swords and flying fists. The moon is bright, so it's easy to see that none of them are Harwellians. It's all Rhed's guard and Endrack's army. I easily identify the guard members because of their lens-covered faces.

"Should we take the Bath House Bridge?" Geric asks. It's smaller—barely a foot across—but could work if it doesn't buckle under Ronen's weight.

Ronen shakes his head. "Fightin' tha' way too. 'Sides, 'tis the wrong direction. Need ta go north."

Geric sighs, pushing his hands through his short golden hair. "What do you think, Fuzz?"

When he says *Fuzz*, I don't believe he means me, but my life is at stake, and I have the solution. "I know a way," I answer and step in front of Geric. Endrack's soldiers have yet to cross the Lower River Bridge, so I feel confident when I step out from the shadow of the Well and scurry toward it.

"Thought it was clear this isn't a safe way to cross," Geric yells over the clang of metal. I glance back to see his head flying side to side, watching for any immediate threat, but I motion him forward. When we reach the bridge, I veer left and race down the steep incline to our watering platform.

The others follow, but once we're gathered, I have second

thoughts with Yip in tow. Then I remember the dog jumping into the river to rescue Cully. (Who shouldn't have needed rescuing if he hadn't allowed Captain Malum to fake-capture him.) But I focus on our task and walk the narrow dirt path under the bridge.

I stop, reaching for the first handhold, then take a step and find the rock, only a few inches below the water. It's trickier at night, and the moon's glare on the water's surface doesn't help, but this is a trusted route. The rocks in the water and the handholds under the bridge are precise—my friends and I made sure of it when we put it in place for our amusement.

"Just follow my lead," I say, stepping and reaching for the next hold. I do it a few more times, and I'm in the middle of the river, the water sliding over my feet, I look back, and in their dark longcoats, it's hard to make them out, but I see their outlines behind me and continue forward.

The second to last rock is the trickiest. We didn't get it lined up as well as the rest. I take a dramatic step-jump to the right, landing slightly off from where I should. I twist a bit, but my hold on the bridge stays firm, and I right myself.

Looking behind me, both brothers are watching. Geric nods, understanding it's a place to be careful. I step onto the last rock, and before moving to solid ground, I notice Yip is already on land, shaking water from his fur and pacing with a happy step—impatient for us to join him.

This side of the water is trickier because there's only one spot to exit the riverbank to higher ground. I lead the brothers thirty feet from the Common, toward the Dark, and stop. "This is the best place to go up," I say with little confidence. I've never managed the climb myself. It's about twelve feet up, with sharp rocks for handholds and a ledge that juts out.

Ronen surveys the surface, testing a few places before starting up. He moves his arms and feet only a few times before conquering the steep incline, standing above us and looking down. I stare in awe at his ability to manage the climb so easily.

"Yip next," he says, and the dog barks, breaking me out of my stupor.

"Here, boy," Geric says, tapping his chest. Yip leaps, and Geric grabs him around the bottom. How he manages is a mystery, but he lifts the furry ball high enough to find footing, and the dog scrambles up to Ronen, who's got him by the back of the neck.

"I'm soaked," Geric laughs, looking down at his saturated shirt.

"Furry too," I say, wrinkling the freckles on my nose.

"Yeah," Geric says while lifting off a chunk and flicking it into the river.

"Bethy, ye're up," Ronen says, sitting on the rocky ledge.

Geric shapes his hands like a cradle. "Grab my shoulders and step up." I do as he says, teetering as I go into the air. I grab onto the rocks as I straighten, and then Ronen's there. He puts his hands under my armpits, lifting and pulling me into his chest. Then he cradles my back and turns me to the side, so I sit next to him, wrapped in his hairy arms on our cliff-side bench.

"Ye okay?" he asks while I'm enveloped by him, feeling the words echo in his chest.

"Never better," I say, which hardly fits the tone of us running for our lives. Ronen chuckles and releases me, putting a hand down for Geric. When we're all on level ground, I start down the path that borders the Lower River, heading toward Building Seven.

"Where ye goin'?" Ronen asks, and I glance back to see he hasn't moved but stands with a curious tilt to his head with Yip by his side.

"To the Shore, of course. It's the quickest way to Fifty-Three." There's no way to make it through the transit paths tonight, even with the moon up. It's at the wrong angle, and the buildings block all the light.

"Fer ye, maybe," Ronen says, tapping his lenses.

He's got to be kidding.

Ronen turns to face the gap between Buildings Eight and Nine, and I remind myself that we're different. It's not the lenses that allow him to see down the pitch-black alley—it's his natural eyes.

I give in and walk back to Ronen because his logic is sound. The transit paths are the safer route since members of Endrack's army have eyes like mine, and the lamlight only adjusts our ability to see in the Dark. If it's nighttime and there's no moon or fire, we still have limited sight even when using lamlight. Whereas the Dark brothers have advanced vision, enabling them to traverse a darkened path in a light bubble.

"Anyway, who do you think's in charge here?" Geric asks though it doesn't sound like a complaint—more of an observation about my instinct to jump into action and lead. But I don't answer because my eyes catch on a bright orange light in the sky, shining over Building Five. I take a few steps to peer around the edge of the building, and my jaw drops when I see our lumber trees engulfed in flames.

"They're burning our resources!" I scream, distraught at seeing years of labor and sacrifice being destroyed.

"Quiet, Bethy," Ronen hisses just as one soldier on the Common turns toward us and begins a brisk pace in our direction. He's without lenses and wears a metal hoop around his neck.

"Oh, no," I breathe out.

"Incoming!" Ronen yells, scooping me up while his brother runs toward the cog. Over Big Scruff's shoulder, Geric rounds the corner with his weapon drawn while we've already covered quite a distance in the opposite direction.

"I'm sorry. That was so stupid," I say, smacking his arm in frustration and irritated I put us in danger like that.

"Aye." Ronen doesn't spare me any sympathy.

"Will he be okay?" He's not my biggest fan—and I'm not his —but I still don't want him injured on my account. Or dead.

"Brass'll be fine." Ronen's not even struggling for breath, and we're going fast. We've already passed Building Twenty-Four, going the wrong direction on a one-way path, though it doesn't really matter. The citizens are all tucked into their quarters, as they should be. They're keeping safe. My brows furrow. Yeah, they're safe unless they bring the fire to this side of the river. I tense at the thought.

"Wha's wrong, Cricket?" Ronen asks, not breaking stride.

"What if they burn our homes?"

Ronen grumbles low in his throat before saying, "Likely the plan."

My grip tightens on Ronen and my bag, and I suppress a shiver. "We need to do something. We can't let the people remain in their homes, not knowing what could happen."

"Dunna fret. I'll take care o' it," Ronen says.

His confidence to manage the situation instantly relieves me, so I do what I'm best at when feeling gratitude toward someone. I destroy the moment.

"I hate when you carry me," I say while clinging to him, though I don't have it in me to struggle or insist he put me down.

"I dunna find it so bad," he says, and I'd almost think he's teasing me, but his voice has a far-off sound. He's concentrating on our surroundings—keeping us safe—and my stubborn pride distracts him from his most important task, so I stay quiet.

I wonder where Geric is and consider asking Ronen if he

should go back for him, but the big guy knows his business. He'll do what's needed to keep us safe.

He stops at the edge of Building Forty-Four, looking toward the Shore. I try to look too, and my hand drops, hanging in the air to keep balanced. I see nothing, but a second later, Yip swipes my hand with his tongue.

"Your dog just licked me again," I complain in a whisper, wiping my wet hand across Ronen's shoulder.

"Bethy's fine, Yip," Ronen says, watching my fingers slide over his black longcoat. "Dog knows ye're nervous."

I bite my lip, uncomfortable that the creature senses my weakness. It didn't bother me before—I even admitted to Ronen I was scared—but one lick and suddenly, I feel exposed. I hold my arms close to my chest so he can't lick me again.

"Ye're gettin' yer wish," Ronen says. His words barely register before he puts me down. I squeeze my bag close to my chest while Ronen takes the sword from his side. I can barely see him. The moon has entered the area where the Dark becomes nebulous with the sky, and it's putting off minimal light, but the sky has turned from black to dark blue. The sun is coming. Another hour and it will be up. Until then, I can only make out shadows staring out from the edge of our buildings.

"Bethy, stay close. Yip, take the rear."

Ronen takes a step, and I lurch forward to keep close but end up running into him. "Sorry," I mumble, feeling like a stumbling fool.

"Na harm," he says and continues without a hitch. I hear Yip breathing from behind.

I grip my bag with one hand and the back of Ronen's longcoat with the other. It allows me to take in my surroundings—tall buildings to the right, living quarters for our citizens, and at the left, the Shore, a long stretch of sand and saltwater. But even in low light, I can tell there's something different about the Shore. Scattered across the sand are dark mounds. We get close to a few, and it registers they are bodies —motionless, except when the water comes ashore and jostles them.

Ronen is careful to steer us away whenever he can, but sometimes it can't be helped. We reach one spot where a group of the dead is gathered, and Ronen lifts me over someone's feet. (I'm not a squeamish person, but this is getting to me.)

"Are they yours or Endrack's?" I ask as he puts me down.

"Mostly theirs."

"Are any of them citizens?"

"None I've seen."

We're south of where Fifty-Three used to stand, getting close to where we'll meet the others. I open my mouth to ask about our next move since the shoreline is blocked near the toppled building, but Yip rushes past me, bumping my leg and plowing into someone standing fifteen feet in front of us.

At first, I think it's a threat and dip into a pointless crouch —I guess, just preparing to run—but then I hear the dog bark and recognize his merry sound. The person is a friend.

"Glad it's just you and your mutt, Ronen. You had me spooked for a minute."

"Hey, Biv. Got a Harwellian with me."

"Annibeth," I say, walking toward her.

"Hey," she says, bobbing her head, but I can't make out her details in the dark.

"Ye got a report?" Ronen asks.

"Captain Rhed has the main surge under control, but we're trying to handle the ones that slipped through. As you can see, a sizeable group broke our line and came up the Shore. We were puttin' out fires where they advanced. Literal fires. The guard went shoulder-to-shoulder to create a barrier between the cogs and the buildings. We targeted the ones carrying fire and took out the main threat. Things would have been awful if they'd gotten to the buildings."

I'm swamped by relief and also a considerable amount of shame. Only a day ago, I argued that Endrack might be fair, yet he'd sent in his army—his cogs—intending to burn down Harwell and the people in it. Instantly, the man has made an enemy of me. I may be a sheltered girl from Harwell, untrained in warfare, but no one wants Annibeth Petters as an enemy.

"Thanks, lass, fer keepin' the citizens safe. We gotta get movin'," Ronen says, turning back to check I'm ready to go.

"Hey, Ronen. Before you go, there's one more thing." Biv was so bold when she gave her report, but not anymore. Her voice is small.

"Aye?" Ronen asks, going still.

Biv takes a few steps and crouches down by the nearest dark mound. Leaning over, she pushes back long lengths of water-logged hair. The color is indistinguishable in the low light and covered in sand. "Got split up in the fight. I came back to reconnect and found her."

"Bells! No!" Ronen stumbles forward, dropping to his knees in the wet sand. "No. 'Tis na true," he groans, his huge hand landing on the woman's petite shoulder. "Na Zanny." Ronen's shoulders shake, and his head falls. His beard brushes his chest as he throws his head back and forth in denial over the loss of someone very important to this brave man.

The situation humbles me and prompts me to do something I rarely do. I stay quiet.

CHAPTER THIRTEEN

"**W**hat took you so long?" Geric asks Ronen when we reach the Northern Hem beyond the stacked remnants of Fifty-Three. That our companion under the bridge made it to the meeting spot before us—apparently, well before us—highlights our slow progress. Admittedly, I was part of the delay, but Biv was the more significant culprit.

But Ronen stays quiet, not answering the question. He's still stunned by the dead woman in the sand. I don't know who she is, and Ronen's not ready to talk about her. I can feel Geric's judging eyes on me behind the lenses, but I refuse to take the brunt of the blame.

"Someone named Biv held us up," I say, and Ronen's shoulders tense. "She reported on the guard's actions and the threat of Endrack's cogs burning down our buildings," I finish, and Ronen's posture eases slightly.

"We saw the smoke in the sky," Evans says, and I'm surprised he's here. I didn't see him, but it's hard to make out much in this light. "Did they already ignite some?" he asks Ronen.

The big guy is still caught up in his thoughts, so I continue talking until he can pull himself together. "They haven't. It's the lumber trees that are burning." I step forward, in front of Ronen, facing Evans and Geric. "What now? Where are we going?"

"We told you. To the Cliffs," Evans says.

I shake my head. "Cully gave away the location. What's our secondary plan?"

"Geric already filled us in on the traitor's doings. We're still for the Cliffs."

"But they'll find us!"

"Cully doesn't know what he's talking about, and neither do you," Evans barks out. "You ever been there?"

Of course, I haven't. It's stupid even to ask, and he's only doing it to highlight my inexperience.

"Brother," Geric says, stopping Evans's verbal attack, then turning to me before continuing, "The Cliffs make up a large area. It's easy to hide there, and no one knows the precise location of where we're staying. We barely do. Malum insists it's where we'll be safe."

"Malum?" I choke out. "Dead Malum? We're putting our trust in *him*? He tried to kill Siman two days ago." Not that Siman's my friend right now. Still, it doesn't mean I approve of Malum's methods, and this is the second time they've mentioned his intel guiding them.

"Yeah, he did," Siman says, and I'm surprised to see him appear. What's not a surprise is to see one of his thumbs tucked inside a pocket. Or to see he has Tesha in tow. They're both wearing Coastal longcoats—Tesha's has a fur-lined hood, but it's hard to make out much more in the dark. I've barely seen them separated since their return to Harwell. (I'd appreciate borrowing Ronen's lenses to block them from my sight.) "But we have reasons for trusting him about this. We all feel good about it."

"Since you brought up *feelings*," Evans starts, "how does your voodoo rate what we've planned?" It's light enough I can make out their smiling faces—except Ronen, who's still in his understandable funk—but I don't get the reference.

Siman shakes his head, his black hair swishing, while Tesha giggles and says, "We should talk about *your* feelings-s, Evans. For Biv."

"Nothing going on there, Songbird, and now's not the time

to tease," Evans says, just as Vale appears, stepping up to Geric. She doesn't have a longcoat but wears a jacket that ends at her waist. It's definitely a product of the Dark—nothing in Harwell looks that precise—and I suddenly feel very out of place in my rough cotton pajamas.

"You know I love your positive outlook," Vale tells Tesha. "But Evans is right—there's no room for teasing today. We passed the Wilsen wife on our way here."

"Passed her?" Tesha asks, clutching her throat and looking between Evans and Vale, who must have traveled together to reach the Northern Hem.

Vale nods. "She's dead."

The pronouncement silences us, and the crackle of fire and clash of metal sounds in the distance. I bite my lip, looking back in the direction we came.

"Which leads me back to my original question, Siman," Evans says somberly. "What do you think?"

Siman hums thoughtfully, but when he doesn't answer, I ask, "What are you talking about?" Dragging out the question, I look from one face to the next, trying to decide who I want to answer.

Vale's the one to take on my question. "Oh, you know, Siman's freaky intuition."

Intuition? "What intuition?"

Siman steps up, clapping a hand on my shoulder. I almost pull out of the friendly gesture, but I'm too curious. "No worries, Anni. I never talked to Cully's Crew about it. And no, Evans, I'm not feeling anything amiss."

I disregard the last remark and strike on what really confuses me. "Cully's Crew?" I ask, wondering about the label I've never heard used before.

"Yeah. Me, you, Cully, Melton, Nacole, and Harbert. These two labeled the group Cully's Crew."

I scowl, looking over Vale and Tesha. "Why was it Cully's? Why wasn't it Annibeth's Crew?"

"Uh," Siman hesitates. "Because Cully was the leader."

"Gah! No, he wasn't. I was," I say, but they all stay quiet. "I was!" I insist while Siman, Tesha, and Vale shake their heads.

"Keep dreamin', Padded Princess," Evans says with a sneer.

I open my mouth for a rebuttal, but Geric stops our fight with a hand and then his words. "Shut it, Evans," he says, then turns to me. "We don't have time for bickering, Annibeth. We'll answer your questions later." I'm in complete agreement with postponing this discussion, so I bite down on my scathing retort, though it itches to be released from my tongue.

"Excellent. Stick to the plan, and we'll all make it safely to Durus," Geric says, and I purse my lips to keep from demanding answers regarding another unfamiliar name. A second later, the urge leaves as I feel movement behind me.

"Bethy, ye're with Yip 'n me," Ronen says, the first words he's spoken since leaving the Shore, and he bends to pick up my bag.

"With you?" I ask, unsure of what he's saying.

"Splittin' up," he clarifies. "Better tha' way."

"What?" I ask, stepping in front of him, but he walks around me, so I turn and go with him. "Excuse me! Don't I get any say in what happens to me? In how I get to where I'm being forced to go?" Ronen just stares. I get he's having a tough day, but so am I. I'm in no mood to be ignored, so I stomp my feet until I'm inches from him, fiercely staring up into his face. "Gah! Answer me!"

Ronen watches me like I'm a mosquito on his sleeve—one he's prepared to flick off before I irritate further. "Dunna hurt yerself," he says, though his words don't hold their usual mirth. Again, he walks away from me—I spin to watch the retreat—going to Geric and announcing, "I'm takin' the

Tenebris route."

"That's not the plan," Geric says with a scowl. He's not arguing the point as much as trying to understand the change. As am I. "Vale wants to see our home with the circlight."

"Sorry, lass," Ronen says to Vale, then turns back to his brother. "'Tis a new plan. It must be me."

"It's a longer route," Evans says, sounding argumentative. "You want to drag her along even a day longer than necessary?" he asks, nodding in my direction.

"Hey—" I start, feeling the comment is quite unfair.

"Dammit, Kid," Ronen interrupts, lifting the edge of his lens to wipe an eye. "Zanny. She—"

Evans's mouth drops. Even with the lenses and in minimal light, I can see his expression wither with understanding, and my mind returns to the dead girl on the beach.

"What's going on?" Vale whispers to Geric.

"Sazanne," he says, shaking his head. "I take it she fell in the battle."

Fell? It sounds so trivial. Like she tripped, dropping to the ground with a stubbed toe. No, it was much more gruesome. I'll never forget her staring eyes, lined with sand, which someone filled with life would eagerly brush from their face. The proximity of the scratchy material to her sensitive eye, without so much as a blink, was a glaring sign the girl was dead.

Vale pulls in a breath at the discovery. She must have known Sazanne.

Geric nods his head, his mouth set in a sad line. "Of course, you must go to Tenebris. Give Kally our best, and warn our ma."

Ronen doesn't speak, simply nods and walks into the Dark.

Uh? Wasn't I supposed to go with him?

I'm left standing without a clue of how to proceed. Should I follow him? Is he so preoccupied he forgot me? There are many possibilities here, and I'm not sure what to think. The only sign he's coming back is his dog, who appears suddenly at my side.

Siman steps up next, carrying a metal ring in his hand, which I recognize is one of the circlights. It's so like him to take control. There are a lot of those personalities in this gathering. It's probably good we're splitting up because I don't know how we'd work anything out.

"They're not fragile, per se, but if you break the glass, the liquid lamlight will drain out, and you won't be able to see anymore," he tells me, then shows me how the latch works. I keep my personal opinions out of the discussion, deciding that learning vital information is more important than giving Siman another put-down. He instructs me to tuck away the circlight until Ronen says it's safe to use. Endrack's cogs—with eyes like mine—are in the surrounding woods, and we'll have a better chance of slipping away undetected with the circlight out of sight. I slide it into my knotted bag through a small gap just large enough for the hoop.

"You nervous?" Siman asks.

"About which part?" I return sarcastically. The comment affirms I'm apprehensive about pretty much everything: Leaving my family. Abandoning Harwell. Going into the Dark for the first time. Traveling with strangers. That Endrack wants me dead. That Cully betrayed our destination. That we're still going there. Take your pick.

"At least you get to go into the Dark with the ability to see," Vale says, sounding envious and also like she's delivering a jab.

"Except, apparently, I'm not," I say, recalling Siman's instructions. Then I notice Ronen return from the Dark, appearing piece by piece from the flat surface.

"It won't be for long," Vale says with a wave of her hand. "I spent weeks without my sight. You lot are spoiled. Soft." Tesha giggles while Siman backs up to stand beside her. Then Vale releases a little laugh.

Are they making fun of me?

"Soft?" I ask, straightening and stepping up to Vale. "I'm equally capable of being brave if the situation calls for it."

The cheerful expression drops from her face. "That's not what—"

"I just left my family to go off with a group of people who hate me. That act alone is proof I'm not weak."

Vale shakes her head. "Annibeth, I wasn't—"

"I don't want to hear it. Just leave me alone." I hold my bundle tighter and walk to the veil. I feel silly with my meager belongings and wearing my nightclothes. The black barrier hangs over my shoulder like an ominous prediction of the direction my life is heading.

The Dark brothers watched our brief altercation. It's hard to tell their thoughts with their eyes covered, but I can guess Ronen's from the small frown hidden in his beard. He approaches, standing silently by my side.

"Good luck to you, brother," Evans says to Ronen. I guess it's his farewell, and I wonder if that's what's commonly said on these types of occasions. I'm not accustomed to such things, having never left anyone behind—having never stepped outside of Harwell. Evans grabs Ronen's arm and squeezes, then lets go before glancing at me. "You're gonna need it. She's—" But he stops, leaving the sentence unfinished.

"What? What am I?" I grip my bag tighter, urging Evans to finish his thought. Fighting is more satisfying than thinking about reality, so I push again for an answer. "Tell me!"

"Crazy, if you must know. My brother will need all sorts of luck to deal with your type of crazy."

"Gah!" I charge into Evans's space. "Don't call me that!"

"Stop." The big guy moves in, stepping between us.

Confronting Ronen is like challenging the stone walls of the Well, and my anger deflates. "Quit yer tantrum, Cricket," he whispers to me. "Ye're only provin' 'is words."

"See you soon, Fuzz," Geric says, throwing his brother a wave. Ronen breaks away from me, stepping close to his two brothers and pulling them in for a hug. Evans and Geric each tap a meaty shoulder belonging to my keeper.

"Stay alert," Ronen says, a valid caution with all that's happening.

The group divides, and they all enter the Dark except for Ronen and me.

"Put the light on," Ronen says, nodding at my bag.

My brows turn in. "But Siman said—"

"Do it, Bethy. Gotta get goin'."

I do as he says, pulling the hoop from my bag and clasping it around my neck as Siman taught me. When I'm done, Ronen leans over, scooping me up. It's a shock, so I scramble to hold my bag as I'm lifted into the air.

"You're carrying me again," I comment, trying to understand the reason.

"Aye," Ronen says, merely agreeing.

"Why?" I ask because I'm learning I have to tell, or in this case ask, Ronen precisely what's on my mind.

"No way ye're gettin' on Clod without help." Ronen's on the move, taking long strides into the Dark.

Clod? I don't have time to ask about the name because we reach the barrier. Ronen doesn't pause or give me a warning (or an encouraging talk, which I might have appreciated) but continues forward. I blink and duck, reacting the same to entering the Dark as I would if someone were pouring water over my head. But there's no need. Nothing comes crashing down on me, and with the circlight around my neck, it feels like a not-as-bright continuation of Harwell.

"Aren't you concerned about the light?" I ask, putting my hand over the glass section, blocking the illumination until I see nothing. Not one... single... thing. It's startling, and I drop my hand, eager for a return of my sight, minimal as it may be.

"Nah. We can handle whate'er comes our way, Cricket," Ronen says, and I'm grateful to be allowed to use it. He looks down at me with a sad grin—the death of the woman still on his mind—before saying, "We cross any trouble, I'll stomp 'em down, 'n ye can slay 'em with yer tongue."

CHAPTER FOURTEEN

Ronen carries me fifty feet into the Dark. The entire way, I'm mesmerized by two things—the beam from the circlight gives light for an amazingly far distance, and the size of the beast we're approaching. When we're right next to the animal, Ronen lifts me high.

"Leg up," he says, and when I lift my right leg, he puts it over the animal's back and lowers me so I have one on each side. Ronen relieves me of my bag, and I hold perfectly still, unsure what to do astride the creature.

"The hors-ses are beautiful, aren't they?" It's the Witch asking, guiding her animal next to ours—only hers is two heads shorter.

"This-s is Knickknack," she says, reaching forward and rubbing the velvety side of the horse's neck. "Vale is riding Buttercup. I'm not sure what Ronen calls his horse. This is the first time I've seen him."

"I think his name is Clod," I say, my tongue finally loosening.

My sister, the Goat Head, moves next to her witchy friend. "I often wondered what sort of horse Ronen rode," Vale says thoughtfully. "I imagined an animal the size of Buttercup bearing his weight, poor thing. But that monster and Ronen... well, they're a perfect duo."

Clod bobs his head and makes a chortling sound. I hold out my hands, unsure if I did something or what exactly is happening.

"I think he agrees," Vale says with a giggle, but she aims her comment at Tesha. Not me.

"Look at his-s feet!" Tesha says, pointing low. I can't help but be curious and lean to see what's got her so excited. "They're furry." Sure enough, the bottom of Clod's legs are covered with long black hair that matches his black and gray mottled body. I quickly take in Knickknack and Buttercup, who have smooth legs all the way to the ground.

"Clod's a Percheron, is all. Different breed," the Droll says, drawing up close on his horse. The girls don't bother telling me this one's name because Evans asks, "You ready?" Again, he's ignoring me, addressing only Vale and Tesha with his comment and question. Vale turns her horse and nudges the animal forward toward Geric.

Tesha maneuvers toward Siman the Heartbreaker but lifts her pale, freckled hand to wave. "See you s-soon, Annibeth. S-safe travels."

I sort of nod, too stunned by Tesha acting so friendly toward me. Did she lose a bet?

The others are on the move while I sit alone on horseback. I notice vaguely that Vale's wearing a circlight, as is Siman, but not Tesha. That's odd, isn't it? I think about it as they fade into the distance. Then Ronen appears and pulls himself onto Clod, settling behind me.

"Clod's wide," he says. "Yer legs'll tire, but ye can sit sideways. Jus' lemme know."

And then we're off.

"What did Evans mean about Siman's intuition?" I ask, watching the Heartbreaker's back as he moves away from us.

"He feels things," Ronen says. "Future things."

Yeah. Not something Siman ever revealed to *Annibeth's Crew*. "How does it work?"

"Dunno. Ye can ask 'im in a few days." I bounce my foot in the air, thinking I'd almost rather not know than meet up with him again to ask.

As we move farther from my home, I notice the Border

Guard Trail circling Harwell. It feels strange to think of them watching us all this time. But I don't observe it for long because, ignoring what Ronen told me, I tuck the circlight under my shirt, giving up my sight. It feels safer, and it's not long before I discover an exciting advantage. In total darkness, I can see our enemies wearing lamlight. Ronen doesn't have the same ability, so I point them out, and he makes adjustments to avoid the cogs, making our escape from Harwell go without a hitch.

Ronen's prediction about riding on Clod quickly comes to pass. We pause long enough for me to rotate so my legs hang on one side, and then continue loping along to Clod's steady clomp.

When I eventually uncover the circlight, I make a game of watching Yip, who's trailing behind us. He disappears for a while, then reappears in my area of sight, usually sniffing the ground. Ronen stored away his lenses hours ago, and I've noted his eyes have color, though I'm unsure of the shade since the lamlight lends a strange tint to everything. But they're not white like many of the Dark animals, and I wonder what makes the difference. I'll ask sometime, but not now. In the few glances I've stolen of his face—which is too close, riding the way we are—I've picked up on his overwhelming sense of sadness. He's not in the mood for questions.

Indeed, our ride is quiet. Ronen's not big on words (though he's big everywhere else to make up for it), and sitting in someone's company all day with barely a word is new for me. I wonder if the silence is unusual for him too and that today's different because he's consumed with thoughts of Zanny. I guess in the coming days, I'll find out.

But I don't mind the reflection time because I have my own things to think about. Like how pathetic I am, getting chased from Harwell and putting my life into the hands of this behemoth. It hits me hard that I've left my family behind. If something were to happen and I got separated from the others,

I wouldn't even know my way back. I'm worthless in the Dark, and I'm questioning all the sureties I felt during the chaos.

Biv assured Ronen they had most of the disruption put down, but what if she was wrong? What if my family got caught in the turmoil? Injured? Burned? Dead?

It's hard enough to be away from them, but not knowing if they're safe is torture. And Lord Endrack doesn't seem like someone who would give up easily. My bet is his cogs will be back soon. Will Rhed's guard keep everyone safe? Will my parents be okay?

"Calm down, Bethy," Ronen says, the first words I've heard in hours.

"What?" I ask, pulling from my hypnotic thoughts, my shoulders sore from holding them tensely.

"Gave ye a promise. Ye'll see 'em again."

Did I speak my worries out loud? No. Ronen's just adept at judging my mood. But didn't I similarly detect his emotions regarding Zanny? I guess we're both very obvious, riding silently while dwelling on our individual pain.

I need something to cling to, and his promise is as good as anything, so I nod. Then we sway in methodical silence until our ride ends, finishing our day as it began, quietly. Curling into my bedding, I'm eager to leave my troubled world and soon fall into deep dreams.

"Sun's up. Need ta move."

Sun's up? I can barely see my surroundings. The circlight worked significantly better yesterday, and I can't figure out what's different, but something is, so I comment, "It still looks dark."

"Aye. Cloudy mornin', 'n we're campin' under trees."

I sit up and stretch, surprised by how well I slept. Ronen

spread out lovely-smelling branches under my bedding, which really helped. It was better than the hard floor in my quarters back home. When I get back there, I'll ask someone from the Dark to bring some of the same stuff into Harwell to put under my mother's bed. Maybe it would ease some of her tiredness.

I release a yawn, and a thought strikes me. "It's the new year," I say.

"Aye. Thrillin' start, runnin' from Endrack's cogs."

I chuckle, pulling the bedding back. My legs chill when my bare skin meets the air, and I suck in a quick breath that Yip hears. He rushes to me, pressing against my legs as if he knows precisely where I'm cold.

Ronen smiles, his big hand lifting a kettle from the fire. I recognize what he has and crave the warm liquid but hold in my excitement. Because I'm Annibeth, and I don't get excited about much, especially food provided by my watchman. But I had a sampling last night of what he's preparing, and I'm ready for more.

He pours some beverage for me—hot chocolate, he calls it —and I take one glorious sip before he ruins my mood.

"Ye broken up 'bout tha' Cully git?"

I lower the cup from my mouth, scowling. "Obviously," I growl, talking over my warm drink. "He's been my boyfriend for a long time."

"Was kissin' Vale a few months back. He yer boy then?" Ronen takes his own sip of the delicious concoction.

"I don't owe you an explanation, but we were going through a bumpy patch."

He tilts his head. "Seems ye're bumpy 'gain."

I bite the inside of my lip. "This is not a pleasant conversation after just waking up. In fact, it's not a pleasant conversation at any time. Talk about something else or, better yet, don't talk at all."

"Wha's yer ma do in Harwell?" Ronen asks, apparently not ready for quiet.

"You don't know? I thought you Coastals knew everything." Ronen just shrugs, and it sets me off. "*Ma's* the social director," I reply in a mocking tone. "And *Da's* the assistant to Lucan if *ye* hadn't noticed. I'll be a reckoner soon, and when this is all over, I plan to prosecute *ye*."

Ronen gives me a look—one I keenly feel—and I'm soon uncomfortable under his appraising gaze. "I see ye're serious 'bout na talkin'," he finally says. "So be it. I can be quiet fer two days if ye can."

"Gah! Two days?"

"Aye, Cricket. Two days 'til Tenebris." He stands, pouring the rest of his drink over the fire (such a shame) and gathering items for Clod's back. I take a little time to grab my bag, which I stuffed by my feet while I slept, and find a thick tree to stand behind to change out of my pajamas, which I've worn for approaching thirty-six hours.

Ronen secures my pack and lifts me onto Clod. Then, as part of his promise of silence, he takes the reins and leads the horse forward—choosing to walk rather than sit with me. And it's cold up here without Ronen and his longcoat to keep me warm.

There's constant shuffling from the horse and Ronen moving through the brush. The packs secured to the saddle make a thumping sound, and Yip races ahead, waiting for us to catch up before doing it again. That's how my day passes—on repeat—until two meals later when I can't stand it any longer.

"I wish I were back home," I mutter, then break off a chunk of carrot with my side teeth.

Snap! Crunch, crunch, chew, chew, chew.

"'Tis it so much better than 'ere?"

"Cully's father and my father are the most powerful in

Harwell. We get the newest and best things in the community. I even have a bedroom. People like me and listen to me. So, yeah, it was much better than here."

"Ye have yer own bed here," Ronen says with a deep chuckle.

"Not the same," I say, yanking my head back to break off a bite of jerky.

"Wha' was yer plan?"

"My plan?"

"Aye. Ye know... next three years, say."

"Marry Cully. Have a kid who would grow up to rule our community."

"Take more'n three years ta do all that, but sure, it'll do."

I roll my eyes. "I guess that's not happening anymore."

"'Tisn't?"

"Of course not. He betrayed me."

"Ah, Cricket. Ye'll fergive 'im. He didna know 'twas ye."

"Who says I'll forgive him? You don't know me well enough to presume such a thing. Besides, he didn't just betray me. He did it to Harwell."

Ronen's brow raises, and instantly, I know what he's about to say. "So did ye, as I recall. Turned Ennette over quick as ye could."

And there it is.

I sigh. "Yeah, well, we didn't know as much about the situation back then."

"Still. 'Twas 'bout when Cully started passin' notes."

"I guess. But I did it out in the open. I didn't sneak around making my plans without anyone else knowing."

"Aye, that ye did," he says with a chuckle, and my instinct is to retaliate. To pinch or smack his arm. But Ronen's sheer size makes me reconsider—his skin must be extraordinarily thick and likely wouldn't allow the sensation to penetrate.

It just isn't fair.

◆ ◆ ◆

The following morning, I want to ask something, but I'm not sure how Ronen will receive it, so I use my reckoner skills and start with something simple.

"It sure is prettier out here in the Dark than I thought it would be," I comment, looking around at the endless expanse of trees. Sometimes I wonder if we'll ever get a break from them. And sure, they're pretty, but not all that great. It's not a field of flowers. Daisies. That's what I'd like to see—an unbroken field of daisies. But that's not the point. I'm just greasing the stone to wear him down—like we do to turn grain into flour back in Harwell. "Yep. Really pretty."

"Wha's on yer mind, Cricket?"

I purse my lips and wrinkle my freckled nose, clicking my tongue in thought. It took little for him to be onto me, and calling me Cricket is never a good sign. I release a breath. "Fine. I was wondering if you'd tell me who Sazanne is," I say. "Uh. Er... *was*," I correct, blushing over my error. Not much makes me blush, but offending a person over the death of someone they care about will do it.

"A friend," he says after a moment, giving me no insight.

I rub my lip, thinking, then blurt out, "Who's Kally?" hoping he'll appreciate the direct approach, but the results aren't much better when he responds, "Closer friend."

Okay.

"What were they to each other?"

"Sisters."

That response has me frowning. One sister's dead, and he's taking the message to the other sister. That can't be a comfortable visit, but it's one he insisted on making. No wonder his mood's been so prickly. Well, prickly for Ronen, which is like a soup pot on simmer—enough to move things around, but nothing's getting heated fast.

It might pay for me to be more sensitive until our visit to Tenebris is over. Of course, I'm never very good at that sort of thing, even when I intend to be. But I can try. Big Scruff's done little to offend me. At the very least, he deserves my best effort.

CHAPTER FIFTEEN

Tenebris is a place that overwhelms my senses—too much to see, hear, and smell. The people wear colorful clothing that looks nothing like what we have in Harwell. There's music—some instrument I can't identify—and singing. And there's the smell of food cooking in the air—robust with many savory scents.

Black posts with round balls on top line the streets. Ronen says the balls contain bulbs that will turn on at night to light the way. His words create a beautiful image I hope to see. On each post is a bar, and from it hangs a panel of material with an image—the same one pictured on the boots guard members wear. "What is that?" I ask as we ride by one of them.

"'Tis a banner with the Coastal emblem." The emblem is a blue wave over green mountains. "Helpful fer knowin' where people call home."

Ronen says about eight hundred people call Tenebris home, but other nearby cities have more. Sixteen hundred serve in the guard. Most are stationed here, but they don't count toward the population because they come and go. Adlumen's larger than Tenebris—though not bigger than the Coastal Territory—and has many more people.

The Coastals are aware of the lamlight and worry how it will affect them since the Dark keeps the light blind safe. It seems Tenebris and Harwell both face uncertain futures. We've also had very disparate pasts. Their buildings differ greatly from ours—with various shapes and dimensions—spreading across the city.

"What's that place for?" I ask, pointing at a building with an open front. I notice a slight reflection and realize it isn't open but made of glass. I've never seen such a large piece of glass before. It's amazing.

"It's a place to buy supplies."

"Buy?" I ask, and Ronen nods. I've heard of bartering before and learned about the monetary system that used to exist, but we have nothing like that in Harwell. We simply work, and our needs are met.

The people wave as we go through the central part of town. I don't wave back because they're waving at one of their own, not at me. But I can tell they're curious about me, especially when their eyes run over my clothing. I stand out, and they're whispering. I'm not sure there's anything rude in their stares or comments because they smile at me as they do it, so I do my best not to return their gaze unkindly.

We reach a cute building that Ronen reveals is his home. I've seen nothing like it before. The outside is green, I think. Maybe yellow. It's hard to be sure with the circlight tinting the colors. Regardless, I can't help but marvel at the frivolous structure. Who would ever color a building? Ours are just the color of the wood—or rock where the Well is concerned—but here, they color everything. Around the doors and windows, there are thick sections of white. And the door is bright blue. Blue! Of all things. I shake my head.

The windows have curtains, like mine at home, but I can see the glass there to keep the weather out and the family sounds in. It's magnificent. Ronen's family must have the best of everything. His father is the leader, after all.

"What do regular people's houses look like?" I ask, imagining them stacked together like the family quarters in Harwell.

"Regular people?" Ronen asks, repeating my words.

"Yeah. Those not part of Captain Rhed's family."

He gazes up at the glorious structure. "Much like this," he says, then twists and drops off Clod's back.

"You've got to be kidding." I stare at the beautiful angles. It's not boxy like the buildings at home. And the roof is tilted—not flat to grow plants or house animals. "How many families share this space?"

"Just ours. 'Tis mostly just Ma here, but there's room when we're visitin'." He takes in my incredulous expression and continues, "'Tis like tha' fer all the families. We have more room ta spread."

I thought I'd feel uncomfortable in Tenebris. I wanted nothing more than to return to Harwell and live like I was. But after seeing this, I'm not sure that's possible. The beauty and abundance here suit me. Most people would say that's because I'm a snob and always want the best things. And maybe there's some truth in that (more than I'll readily admit) because I don't know how I can live in broken-down Harwell when this place exists.

Of course, maybe the solution is for Harwell to get in on the bartering system. Then we can work to make my home as lovely as this place.

When I haven't moved, Ronen nudges my leg. "Let's get ye settled, Bethy."

I clumsily slide down Clod, and Yip nudges my hand when I touch the ground. Then he speeds after Ronen, who's already halfway up the steps. I count twelve, leading to the main door. Uh, doors, now that I look closer. I shake my head. Who needs two doors? But then Ronen stands in front of them, and I wonder if it's necessary so he can get inside. I hold back a grin.

I hop the steps two at a time. It's sort of fun. Ronen does it because it fits his size, but I do it to see if I can. And, yeah, I totally can. I reach his side, puffing with exertion.

"I'll introduce ye, bring in yer things, 'n then I'll be goin'."

I hold my breath, even though I need the air. "Going?" I push out. I grab his arm, intent on turning him to face me, but I can't budge him. Undeterred, I step in front of him, exclaiming,

"You can't leave me here!"

"Got somethin' ta do."

"No! I won't be dumped on another stranger." I've already been dumped on him. One dumping is enough in one week.

"'Tis no stranger. 'Tis Ma."

"I don't care! I demand you take me with you."

"Demand?" Ronen lifts a brow. Then he looks down at Clod and a small group of people passing by who've gathered near the animal to listen to our disagreement. "Bells, Cricket. I'll be back in a few hours," he mutters. "I swear, ye have rose thorns in yer spine 'n vinegar in yer veins." He shivers while I decide his comment was uncalled for and his reaction unfair. But I don't get to voice my displeasure because he twists a round knob on the door and enters, saying, "Let's get inside 'fore they think somethin' serious is happenin'. Poor folks ne'er seen nothin' like yer rabid temper."

I huff, but he's already inside. Entering the quarters for Ronen's family, I'm surprised to see the color continues inside, which allays my *rabid temper*. I don't know why I'm shocked by the sight. These people aim to make their surroundings cheery. The walls even have painted flowers on them. Well, from my waist up. Below that, they're just blue. But I soon discover that's only in this room. The next one, which turns out to be a kitchen, is a different color entirely. Light green walls and white cupboards. With doors.

"Enjoyin' yer sight?" Ronen asks, walking up behind a woman not much taller than me, though more filled out.

"Oh, Ronen! You startled me!" she exclaims, spinning around. She wears a circlight like me, and also, a giant smile. "Always so quiet, dear boy. Yes! I love it." She puts her hand at her throat. "So good to see all my friends in their homes. And without their lenses! I'm packed and almost ready to go. I thought your father was coming to get me." Ronen frowns. "What's wrong? Is he okay?"

"Cap'n's fine. Cogs arrived sooner'n expected. 'Twas stupid assumin' they'd take the light ta Adlumen. 'Stead, the army was waitin' a few days out."

"Your brothers?"

"Fine. But Ma, ye're na goin' ta Harwell."

She frowns. "Oh. I was looking forward to spending time with my husband and boys." She shrugs, and I can tell she's trying for a brave face. "But life with important men isn't simple. Where are you headed?"

"Takin' the hunted somewhere safe."

"The hunted?" she asks, looking around Ronen's shoulder at me.

"This is Beth... uh, Annibeth." My full name sounds funny on his tongue. Wrong in a way. "She's Vale's sister."

"Divided twins," she says, but when Ronen shakes his head, her eyes widen. "Anny had *two* children? In *Harwell*?"

"'Tis why their ma left. Had Bethy in secret 'n left ta avoid family punishment."

"Oh, that poor woman. If I'd only known." She takes a step toward me, and I get a better look at her features, deciding she looks most like Geric with her golden hair. "Welcome, Annibeth. I knew your mother for a few months. Remarkable woman. She had the most beautiful hair I'd ever seen. It looks like you got that from her."

I pull forward my loose hair, running the white-blond strands between my fingers. "Oh, well, thank you. But, uh, she's not really my mother. At least, I don't think of her that way. My mother's name is Clayre, and she's at home in Harwell. She's sick." I don't know why I feel the need to add the last part.

"I didn't mean to offend you," she says with a worried dip in her brow.

This woman doesn't know me. She has no preconceived ideas based on my reputation or gossip. I'm a complete unknown, meaning I can behave however I wish, and it won't feel anything but natural to her. It's freeing. So, I decide to experiment with being a different kind of person—someone she might want to like.

"You didn't. And I hope I didn't sound rude. I just… I miss my mother."

She pats my hand. "Hungry?" She's looking at me when she asks but turns to Ronen, and I feel the question is more for her son, who must require a lot of food to keep in operation.

"Na now." Ronen shakes his head. "We lost some o' the guard." He pauses. "Zanny." His mouth tightens, and I can no longer see his lips in his beard.

"Son." She wraps her hands around his waist, and it's as if the contact releases something in him. Big Scruff chokes, and I look away. "Take your time. I'll have dinner when you're ready."

He sniffs, and I glance back. He straightens, and his ma takes a step back. "Willna be long. Leavin' early fer the regroup." Ronen's mother nods, no doubt aware of how the boys operate. He places a swift kiss on her head and is out the door a moment later with barely a noise, Yip at his side.

"So, Annibeth, tell me about yourself," she says. Her voice is friendly, but I hear the pain from hearing the news. For a moment, I consider putting her off but decide she might need the distraction. But then, I don't know where to begin. What would interest a woman from Tenebris about a young girl from Harwell? But maybe, given the news about Zanny, the details don't matter.

"Well, I've finished my formal education. I know how to read because I'm apprenticing to be a reckoner, and I know all of Harwell's laws."

"Do you enjoy working toward becoming a reckoner?"

"No one's ever asked me that," I say with a laugh. How strange. "I actually do. It means that someday I could take over for my father. He assists Harwell's leader. Of course, things are changing, so maybe that's not even a thing anymore." The thought instantly alters my mood. I hate trying to understand all these developments, especially when I don't have enough information to grasp how my life will be impacted.

"Don't worry too much about it," she says with a smile, reading my bewilderment. "It's up to you to make the world what you want it to be. If you want to be someone who understands and enforces the law, find a situation where you can do it."

"You make it sound easy," I say, still feeling lost, though her words give me some hope.

"It might not be easy, but it's possible."

I stand beside Ronen's mother and help her prepare the night meal. Begrudgingly, I decide Ronen was right—he hasn't dumped me on a stranger. She's kind and welcoming, and while I enjoy my time with her, she makes me miss my family terribly.

Hours later, we're at the table, sipping a cold drink made of limes. We don't have limes in Harwell, and I decide I love them. The table is set for the meal. There are three plates made of glass with a floral design on the surface. (I've never even imagined such a thing.) There are three utensils next to each plate—sleek and made of metal. It's already evening, so the sun is gone, but electric wall fixtures perfectly light the room.

The food is in an oven where constant heat warms the dinner to perfection. At least, that's what Ma tells me. Yes, Ronen's mother has insisted I call her Ma. She says she's mothering me in my mother's absence, so she deserves the title. I don't mind.

We've talked a lot about the luxuries in Ma's home, comparing what I discover to what I'm used to back home. Consequently, my mind is focused on Harwell, thinking about the invaders and wondering if they burned everything down.

The horrific thought has me commenting, "The Adlumians must be a despicable group of people."

"Not really," Ma says readily. "Though 'despicable' could accurately describe their leader."

"You don't think the people are just as corrupt?"

"I know they're not."

I scowl, thinking of the eager cogs. "You understand the situation better than me, but I don't think I could sit down with one." I sniff, straightening my shoulders.

"Really?" Ma leans back in her chair, folding her arms and grinning at me. "Well, I'm sorry to tell you, but you're sitting with one now."

My hand freezes as I reach for my drink. "What?"

Ma chuckles. "It's true. Adlumen was my home. They're my people. But I feel that way about the Coastals, Southers, and Harwellians too. I don't mean to discount your opinions, but there's good to be found everywhere. Even Torquent, and trust me, that's quite a concession."

I nod, grateful she's not upset I inadvertently called her despicable. I take another drink of lime and look for a segue, deciding to ask about the framed picture on the wall I've been staring at for hours. "What kind of flower is that?"

"A rose," she says, turning to look at it. "They're my favorite."

"I've never seen one before. They seem very—" I pause, trying to find the right word for how it makes me feel. "Complex," is what I settle on. "The petals are in thick layers."

"Yes, though I've never thought about it before." Ma takes a sip. "Do you have a favorite flower?"

"Daisies," I answer without hesitation. "Do you have those here?"

"We do. But not this time of year." Hmm. That's a little disappointing. "They seem like a very uncomplicated flower in comparison."

"I guess they do." I grin. "Did an ancestor give you that picture?" In Harwell, some families have similar heirlooms passed down from generations back, though I've seen none this nice. It's so detailed I feel like I could reach inside the wooden enclosure and take it.

"Sort of." She laughs. "Ronen made it for me as a gift."

"Ronen? You're kidding." Not that I'm surprised he'd give a gift—he seems a generous sort of person—but that he made something so delicate. And feminine.

"I'm not." She smiles and shakes her head—she almost seems embarrassed. It's sweet that Ronen painted his mother's favorite flower and gifted it to her. He's a tough exterior with a soft center—such a strange combination. She finishes, "He has a genuine talent for making things with his hands."

I nod, agreeing he's talented, then hear a whining sound from the direction of the double front doors. It takes a moment to realize it's Yip.

"Oh! They're back. And just in time." Ma hops up and goes straight to the stove. I lower my glass to the tabletop and go into the blue room. The minute I enter, I find Yip and Ronen, though they're both hard to miss, wherever they go.

Ronen turns, and his eyes and nose are red. I frown, suddenly unsure of what to say. "Tough visit?" I finally ask, feeling sympathy for what he must have gone through, relaying such heartbreaking news.

"Aye. 'Twas."

Yip seems to sense our somber mood and jumps in to fix it. Literally, he jumps, and I catch his front paws before they land on my chest.

"Git down, dog," Ronen says, but Yip stays where he's at, eye-to-eye with me.

"He's fine," I say, leaning to ruffle his ears while I work to stay on my feet. "All this talk of flowers with your ma must be playing tricks on my mind. I swear Yip smells like them."

I giggle about my joke, but Ronen's face remains stoic. "'Tis Kal's perfume. Yip was lyin' in 'er lap."

Perfume that smells like flowers. Vale told me about perfume when we were kids. Not long after, I kept strands of grass in a small cloth and occasionally rubbed it on my skin so I'd smell, but it was never like this. And it turned my skin green. And when I got older, I told Vale perfume was a false story and accused her of wanting attention—one of many times I changed her truth to my falsehood.

And after that line of thinking, Ronen and I wear matching frowns. I stare at him, feeling sudden remorse about my destructive behavior in the past. My frown increases from the shame I feel. By the look on Ronen's face, I'm sure he thinks my expression is aimed at some fault in him. I'm just about to explain when Yip bounces down to greet Ma as she enters the room.

"Did you offer Annibeth some dinner?" she asks her son.

He shakes his head. "Ye're makin' it togetha. Thought ye'd take care o' the invites."

"Ronen. Manners," she chides, and he releases a low growl.

"No, Ma. Walked in. Cricket gave me one o' 'er sudden crusties, 'n I was too scared ta talk 'bout food."

I wince. As I suspected—he thought I was glaring at him.

"Ronen," his mother scolds. "You shouldn't speak that way about such a nice young lady."

I open my mouth to defend the big guy because he did nothing wrong except interpret the horrible look on my face to mean I was finding fault with him. Not the case, but still understandable from his perspective. But I don't get the chance to make things right.

"Wha'd ye do?" Ronen whispers, leaning in. "Steal Clod's

lenses 'n put 'em on Ma ta turn 'er blind ta ye?"

I shouldn't laugh. His words aren't nice, but my idiotic behavior hurt his feelings, and now he's sent a well-aimed punch right to my gut. I deserve what I'm getting, and I can't help it—a chuckle bursts free, and I grin up at him. He tilts his head, trying to figure me out.

"Would ye like ta share a meal with us, Bethy?" Ronen asks in a level voice, and his mother nods her approval—he's done right by her expectations.

I wipe the side of my mouth, smoothing out my laughter until it's just a small grin rounding my freckled cheeks. "I could never turn down such a gracious invitation," I answer, sweet as can be, and Ma twists to return to the kitchen. When she's out of hearing, I whisper, "Watch your back, Big Scruff. Vengeance is mine." But I bite back a grin.

Ronen growls low, but he can't fool me. I can see the smile hidden in his whiskers, and I think I'm forgiven.

We turn to enter the kitchen, and I'm ushered to a chair while Ronen helps his ma. A minute later, he appears at my side, puts a bowl before me, and leans in. "Watch yerself, Cricket. Who knows wha' I put in yer bowl, 'n ye wouldna wanna hurt Ma's feelin's by not eatin' 'er food."

He straightens, and I glare up at him. This time he's not hiding it—his white-toothed smile is out for all to see. But I'm not sure whether he's teasing, or if the threat is real—his brand of vengeance.

"That's nice," Ronen's sweet mother says, gazing at his smile while settling into her chair. "I like it much better when you two are getting along."

CHAPTER SIXTEEN

After the most restful sleep of my life, we prepare to depart Tenebris to begin our first day of travel. I'm sad to leave Ronen's beautiful home—warm meals, soft lighting, and comfortable beds—and decide Tenebris is a city built on miracles. I thought soft branches under our bedding was a dream, but they're nothing compared to the raised bed Ma guided me to last night. The experience was beyond compare. Harwell can never satisfy after this.

Ronen's ma wishes me well at the door (double doors), then shocks me to the core by presenting me with a gift.

"Who knows where you'll end up, and I don't want you to freeze," she says, guiding my hands into the flared sleeves of a longcoat. It's blue—lighter than the sky—with black embroidered butterflies flitting up the sleeves. Like Tesha's longcoat, it has a hood lined in fur, only black instead of white.

"I'll have Ronen get it back to you when we're done," I say, breathless with wonder as I run my hands over the smooth oilcloth. It's soft, beautiful, and functional—rumor has it, it's a better water barrier than almost anything we have in Harwell.

"It's yours to keep," she says, brushing my arms. "It was mine when I was a girl and no longer fits me." She chuckles.

Mine to keep.

Few things can be gifted in Harwell, and I tend to obsess over possessions. This is a grand gesture, and I struggle with my response. Pushing aside the temptation to self-indulge in ownership, I thank her with as much sincerity as I'm capable.

When we're on Clod riding away, Ronen clears his throat awkwardly and says, "Thanks fer yer kindness ta Ma."

"Sure," I say with outward calm, but inside, I'm a storm

of confusion because my treatment of her was natural—not the least bit crafted or challenging. Typically, gratitude and consideration take great effort, but not with Ma. There's something about her. It's unfortunate for Ronen that this type of subdued behavior doesn't come naturally with anyone else.

"Dare I ask where we're going?" I snap. The Dark brothers were vague in Harwell, and Ronen's not said more since. We're on the move now, and I'm hoping he'll give me some details.

"No point telling ye. Nowhere ye've been b'fore."

"Right," I say, not surprised by his answer but wondering if a secondary question might get a better result. "I get that. But what about giving me a general idea?"

Ronen nods and slaps his hip. Yip jumps in place, where he's sniffing flowers along the path, and runs to match Clod's gait. "We're travelin' toward Hamo, with Circes ta the north 'n Torquent ta the south. Tha' mean much ta ye?"

"Well, now you're just being rude," I tell him. And I would know. I'm the Queen of Rude. The Queen of Sudden Crusties too. And when we were splitting up, Evans called me the Padded Princess—a reference from when Tesha accused me of being sheltered from pain. I guess I'm just royalty all around.

Ronen shrugs.

"And you're sure it's safe there? Even though Lord Endrack knows it's where we're going?"

"Doesna know the exact spot. 'Sides, 'tis crazy fer 'is cogs ta go there. Plenty o' unsavories lyin' in wait fer 'em." Ronen chuckles.

"And they won't be lying in wait for us?"

"Eh." Ronen shrugs again. "Let 'em lie. Me 'n my brothas know a thing 'er two." He chuckles some more, thinking about those one or two clever things they know.

"Ronen?" I start, wanting to ask a question, but not sure I dare.

"Aye, Bethy?"

"Uh. Why is it you talk so different?" I've been around his brothers enough to know they don't talk like him. Not a bit. Captain Rhed doesn't either. And now, after meeting his mother, I can't help but wonder how he came to speak the way he does.

"Diff'rent?" he asks, and it sounds like a clarification, but it's also like he's testing the word—trying to understand my meaning.

"Yeah. Different," I repeat.

Ronen scowls but still answers. "Raider's a friend from the South T, 'n he calls me a land pirate."

While I recognize Raider's name from our time in the Well, in true Ronen fashion, his answer isn't an answer at all. (I know. I should be used to this by now.)

"What's a land pirate?"

"Well, now... I dunno." He rubs his thickly bearded chin and chuckles. "But I like the sound o' it."

I smile but want more, needing a better explanation. "It's just, the words you use aren't like my people or even your family."

"Ye think I talk wrong?" His frown is back.

"Not wrong, exactly."

"Ye think I'm not smart," he surmises.

Is that what I think? Not necessarily. He's distinctive. He thinks and speaks unusually with oddly formed sentences and strange words. But do I think he's unintelligent? No. I'm mentally preparing my answer, but I organize my thoughts too slowly, and the delay gives Ronen a false conclusion.

"I'm smart enough ta keep ye safe. Tha's all ye need be concerned with."

"I never said—"

"Cricket," he pauses, his thick hand rubbing at his neck with no small amount of impatience. "Stop yer chirpin'. We need ta stay alert. Best not waste our attention debatin' my flaws."

I would never call out flaws in this man. That he thinks it's what I'm doing makes me pause, but his negative use of that name gets me stirred up. "That nickname sure has stuck," I say with bite, ignoring his request for silence.

"Fits. Little bug makes a pretty noise but is ugly ta look at. Ye're the opposite—pretty as an angel, but the noise ye make is foul."

"Noise?" I bark out, turning to him with a scowl.

"Aye," he says, looking me right in the eyes. "Ye rarely open yer mouth 'cept ta cut someone down."

I open my mouth to do just that—cut him down—and the realization stops me.

"And yer eyes are mean," he adds, pursing his beard-framed lips and returning his focus to the path ahead.

I have mean eyes? I never considered there was such a thing.

Mean eyes.

I feel a buzz under my skin—a mixture of anger, hurt, and embarrassment. I will it to subside, but it stays with me for a good portion of the morning. Neither of us speaks again because it's likely whatever we have to say won't be well received by the other person. It's a rather miserable ride.

On the second day of our travels, contentions simmer some. We take a break to stretch after finishing our mid-day meal. The ground has a light dusting of snow I disrupt with every step, but the patterns don't remain long with Yip obliterating them as he runs circles around me.

I try to be uninteresting so he'll return to Ronen because my walk has a purpose—one that doesn't include a dog—but he's too engaged in what I'm doing, loping alongside me. For the second time, I stop, make him sit, and tell him to stay. But he won't listen.

"Yip!" I scold and then say lower, "I need to relieve myself."

"Dunna think he'll let ye alone," Ronen says, still back by Clod. Did he overhear me? My cheeks flame red under my freckles.

I move ten more feet, and Ronen's right—Yip follows. "Buddy," I tell the dog. "I don't want you with me for *that*." He looks up with his sparkling dog eyes, ignorant of my wishes. I release a long breath, at a loss for what to try next.

"Yip," Ronen calls, and the fluffy mass hesitates, then sits. I take a few tentative steps, and he lets me go this time, so I scurry away to take care of business.

When I return, Ronen's working on something with Yip at his side. I don't recognize the object or tool he's using, but everything seems fine—Ronen's whistling and Yip's tail is bobbing to the tune—until Ronen drops the tool with a curse.

"What's wrong?" I ask, sure Big Scruff hurt himself.

"Bells!" he groans, kicking the tool.

"What happened?"

He looks at me dejected. "Ah, Bethy! 'Tis my sour luck. I'm tryin' ta fix somethin', but one extra turn o' the screw, 'n I broke its ass." He groans again, putting frustrated fists on his hips.

I bite back a grin at his sudden and unusual outburst, seeing he's not always cool and collected.

Ronen kicks the tool once more—he calls it a screwdriver —while spitting out a companion swear word and walking toward Clod, sulking. I pick up the abandoned item, tucking it into the bag Ronen keeps on Clod's backside.

◆ ◆ ◆

Day three is overcast, but it never rains. Still, even in my longcoat, I'm more chilled than I've been, and I lean into Ronen's mass to keep warm as we ride. That night, I sit extra close to the fire. While I warm my hands, I ask Ronen a few moderate questions that he answers without issue, and then I graduate to something more profound.

"So, Captain Rhed isn't your birth father?" I ask, concentrating on my fingers suspended in front of the flame, flipping them periodically to warm both sides. I know as well as anyone that not being born to a person doesn't negate them as a parent, and I hope he understands my question isn't meant to diminish his relationship with the captain. I'm just curious, but I can't look at Ronen while I wait for his answer. I'm accustomed to barreling into situations fearlessly, but with this topic, I'm suddenly hesitant.

"Nope. Da died when I was a baby."

"How old are you?"

"Twenty-two." Ronen considers me a moment before telling me more without any prompting on my part. "Growin' up, Ma'd send me ta stay with my da's brotha, Pattrick Wynne. 'Tis where I picked up my lazy way o' speakin'. Patt called it an accent." Ronen chuckles. "Whate'er 'tis gives me an advantage."

I asked Ronen about his strange way of speaking two days ago, and he's finally disclosed the mystery. If all our conversations progress like this, I'll need to develop more patience—not an easy task for someone like me. The other option is to temper my curiosity about Big Scruff.

"How is it an advantage?" I ask, realizing I've made my decision. He's too intriguing, so I'll have to force patience on myself.

"People dunna expect much, 'n I catch 'em off guard. Works ta my benefit." He's so casual, like leaving that impression doesn't bother him when I know it does. He revealed as much when he asked if I thought he wasn't smart.

"How did that all come about?"

"What part, Bethy?"

I rub the corner of my mouth because I'm Bethy today. I've been Cricket the last two, when he's deigned to speak to me at all. I clear my throat, answering, "Living with your uncle, not your mother. I don't understand how things like that work in the Dark." I can't imagine my mother sending me away if something happened to my father. Growing up in Harwell, there was nowhere to be sent and no uncle to get sent to. "Maybe I'd understand better if you told me more about your background."

Ronen jabs the fire and ruffles Yip's head that's lying in his lap. "Ma married Erick Wynne 'n had me. Loved 'im a lot, 'n then he died. Nothing fancy er heroic 'bout 'is death, but 'twas honorable. Ma was sad 'n married Renny Dover."

"Sadness? That's all it took for her to marry again?"

"Tha' 'n Ma thought I needed a da. Renny looked good ta 'er, but he wasna a good fix fer sadness ner fatherin'. Cut out soon after Geric was born. Now he's tryin' ta mend things 'tween 'em. Not sure 'tis workin'."

"Why not?"

"Too late, I'd guess. Geric acts indiff'rent, but I wonder. Next, she married Rhed Dirby. Great man, 'n he's good fer Ma. Treats her how I want 'er treated. They had Evans, who's a pain, tho' we love 'im. Kid's swagger doesna bother me like it does Geric." He pauses, looking me over. "Or ye, lass," he adds with a chuckle. "So, us brothas have diff'rent last names. Can be confusin', but 'tis how 'tis. As fer stayin' with Patt, Ma needed help, but I liked stayin'. Felt like knowin' 'im was knowin' my da."

"Yeah." A week ago, I would have listened to this story with partial interest and zero insight. Discovering my complicated ancestry makes me consider family connections more. I'm not interested in seeking the information, but learning about Anny Rennick from Ronen's Ma was intriguing.

I lean back, putting my feet closer to the fire (yikes, that's toasty) and looking at my white-blond hair draped across my chest. Hair just like Anny's. I rub my face, needing a distraction from the Rennicks. "So, you grew up in Tenebris?" I ask, not sure he did, but figuring he'll correct me if I'm wrong.

"Aye. Lived, schooled, 'n trained."

"You went to school?"

"Can tell ye dunna believe it, but aye, Cricket, I went ta school."

I shake my head, frustrated I'm so quickly back to being Cricket. It's not that I don't believe him about school. Truthfully, I'm sort of jealous. "We didn't have school in Harwell," I explain. At least, not in the way I imagine his learning was conducted. "Did you like it?"

"Hated ev'ry minute. In the beginnin', my heart was in it, but my mind didna agree with learnin'. Soon, my heart didna agree neither, but 'twas all fer the fight."

"The fight?" I ask, turning my face from the heat of the fire and watching Ronen over the flame.

"Trainin' fer battle, scoutin' the hills, 'n studyin' weapons. I'm not the tracker Evans is, but Yip helps out. Not quick as Geric nor as accurate with a bow, but I'm stronger, 'n I'm stealthy."

I can't help it—I laugh. Once again, it's not that I don't believe him. He disappears into shadows. He descends stairs without a sound. No, I believe him. It's just that no one else would unless they'd seen it for themselves.

"'Tis true. I'm quiet as a mouse," he says, emphasizing his

point. He doesn't know my thoughts—that I'm without any doubt—and it's fun to tease him. So, I stay quiet, and after a moment, he declares, "I'll sneak up on ye sometime, 'n ye'll see."

Ronen nods his head, making his mental plan, and I do all I can to keep my voice level when I ask, "You mean sometime when I'm sleeping?"

He quietly considers me with a confused scowl. He's so serious, and I can't hold it in any longer. I giggle—a smile breaking out across my lips. And then it's Ronen working to fend off a grin. "Aye, Bethy. Best keep one eye open in yer sleep," he says before pressing his lips together, sealing them behind his bushy beard.

On day four, I wake to music and the scent of a freshly woken fire. The crackle of new branches sounds in the Dark, but I can't see the flames with the circlight tucked under my bedding. However, I can feel the heat and marvel that while I can't see any light from it, the evidence of it burns on the left side of my face.

I'm lying down, my sightless eyes facing the sky, not ready to move and start the day. A deep voice accompanies the pop and hiss of burning wood. It's Ronen, low and throaty, singing words warm as the flame, soft as the breeze.

He sings the song twice. It's unfamiliar, but I enjoy the rhythm, even if the meaning is elusive. He starts a third time, and I follow along, echoing him in a quiet voice.

The wind swirls low in Wicklewood,

blown bare the shadows, all regrets.

A young girl bows 'neath velvet hood,

shown bare her eyes, her full secrets.

The breezes dance,

where sycamores twist and slow.

The breezes chance,

to throw a strangled blow.

The heat from the fire increases, and I sit up, rubbing my freckled nose and reaching under the bedding for the circlight.

"Ye hungry?"

I nod, then pull my knee up and rest my cheek there. "You know, a few times you've commented on my chirping, but it appears you're the music maker among us. That's quite a song."

"Heard ye singin' with me, Bethy. Ye make a beautiful sound." I smile into my knee, where he can't see. "Ye know, yer musical voice is a better reason fer openin' yer mouth than yer usual application."

I straighten, glaring in his direction while he stirs his morning meal, not paying me any attention. Ronen has a gift for dousing my mood with one statement. What began as a compliment turned into a slight. I'm ready to complain, but Yip opens his mouth and howls. It's as if the animal misses the song. Or maybe he suspects Ronen and I are about to slay each other with words. Either way, the noise shuts me up, and I surge to my feet, stomping the ground while I clean up my bedding and get dressed for the day.

Day five begins, and my mood is sullen. Ronen watches me with wary eyes, and I bet more than ever he's cursing the short stick he's repeatedly drawn where I'm concerned, wishing it had gone to someone else. And while I should probably go easier on him, I'm incapable. I dread when we'll meet up with the group this evening, so I'm grumpy all morning and contrary all afternoon.

"Can anyone do right by ye?" Ronen asks after I dispense another slight on someone's character—this time, it's Siman.

"What do you mean?" I ask, though there's no mystery to his question. I'm just in the frame of mind to bicker.

"None o' us are e'er good enough. We all lack somethin' in yer eyes."

"My *mean eyes*."

He grasps my shoulders and twists me around so I'm looking straight at him, his gaze boring into mine. "Ye'll have a lonely life, Cricket."

"You think?" I snap.

"Aye." He shakes his head and releases me, and I spin forward again so I don't have to look at him. "I feel sorry for ye," he whispers, and his sympathy only worsens my mood.

"Don't bother," I bite out. "When we reach the others, they'll talk you out of any sympathy you have. You'll be back on their side in no time while I play the role of the shrewish outcast."

Ronen stiffens behind me, and I'm prepared for him to set me down with his deep, growly words. But he doesn't. He stays silent. (And in pure Annibeth form, I dig deeper.) "Don't bother denying it. You're mostly nice to me when it's just the two of us, but when we're all back together, any hint of a good opinion will disappear. But don't worry about it. I'm prepared. I've donned my thick skin."

Ronen releases a sigh. Of frustration? Of defeat? Of indifference?

Who knows?

But I won't let myself care. No. I don't care about anyone out here in the Dark. All that matters is I'm ready for a fight.

CHAPTER SEVENTEEN

"Look at all my fans," I say, deadpan, as we ride into camp. The group's all here, arriving before us because of our stop in Tenebris.

It's shocking to discover I liked the brothers better when they wore their lenses. It was an advantage not to see their eyes and the censure therein. The Harwellians aren't much better. Only Tesha looks happy to see me, and she's the one I like the least. Go figure.

"Hold your applause," I mumble sarcastically, my fissiparous tendencies out in full force.

"Relax, Bethy. Ye're fine, so just relax."

Relax. Right. Easy for him to say.

"I feel like King of Court," I say sarcastically, referencing the stupid social structure among the youth back in Harwell. "Everyone's clamoring for my endorsement and an invitation to the inner circle." My cynicism knows no bounds. But I don't want to be here—it's as simple as that. I eagerly anticipate the morrow when we'll split up again. I'll be with the only tolerable members of the group—Ronen and Yip, with Yip being even more endurable than Big Scruff. At least the dog doesn't talk back.

I jump off Clod's back before Ronen even dismounts. It's a long drop, and my ankle buckles slightly on the landing, but I push through the ache and go straight to the saddle, untying my bedding.

It's time for night meal, but I'm not hungry. I'm not afraid of these people but despise being around them. Outnumbered. And I'd rather sleep so we can all wake up and go our separate ways. I stand behind Clod, scouting a spot close enough to the fire to stay moderately warm but far enough to keep my distance from the group.

"Hi, Anni," Siman says, appearing out of nowhere and looking over my longcoat. I grunt in reply. I considered asking him about his intuition when next I saw him but decide I don't care. He feels future things. Great for him. I don't need to know more. However, I'm curious if he picked up on how awful Nacole would feel when he dumped her. The thing is, I didn't need intuition for that. I could have told him precisely how it would go, and then I got a front-row seat when it happened. And if he didn't have any inkling, it seems a worthless gift.

"How was your ride? Did you like Tenebris? I've yet to see it. Looks like Ronen got you a longcoat."

I look at him, a scowl furrowing my brow. What's his deal? What's with the nice-talk?

"You're laying out your bedding already? We haven't gotten that far yet. We're still preparing our night meal. Come join us."

"I'm good."

"What do you mean, you're good?"

"Not hungry," I answer and curl the corners of my bed in my fist.

"Well, just come visit then."

"I said, I'm good."

"Geez, Anni, you're like trying to encourage a stone wall."

I drop my pack with my bundled clothes, putting my fists on my hips. "What do you want me to say?"

"I want you to talk to your sister and your cousin. I want you to realize they're amazing people, and you'll like them if you give it a chance."

"And I want you to go back to Nacole, but we don't always get what we want. Do we?"

"Anni." Siman rubs his pale hand over his pale forehead

and down his black-stubbled cheek.

"Why were you so mean to her?"

"To who?"

"Gah! Nacole!" Every set of eyes surrounding the fire is on me now.

"I was never mean to her. And I was honest about my thoughts and feelings."

"But, you dumped Nacole. For... *her!*" I throw an accusing finger toward Tesha. The little witch bites her lip and ducks her head as if I could strike her from this distance.

"Yes, we broke up, but it was at least a month before I got with Tesha. And I was never unkind. Not getting your way in the world isn't cruelty. It's just life. Nacole's still my friend."

"You're more than that to her," I argue.

"I'm sorry about that. I should have broken it off sooner."

"You were never serious about her," I say, realizing she was more invested in the relationship than he was. Does it make her a sucker or him a tease?

He doesn't reply, and my frustration takes over. "Enjoy your life with the witch," I seethe. Putting both hands on his shoulders, I shove him backward. Either he's not expecting it, or I'm stronger than I realize. Siman goes down, landing with a thud—right in the middle of the only wet spot in the vicinity.

"Hey!" he complains as he squishes into the ground, mud molding around his pants and sliding under his gray longcoat.

I can't deal with him. Or with what I've just done. Or the accusing eyes of every single person I'm with. I aim for the trees—a respite from the crowd—and use a bathroom break to escape this hellish night, knowing I've only glanced through the heavy doors of hell. There are many spacious rooms left to explore.

Night meal is a chilly affair—one I planned to avoid until Yip found me in the trees, clamped onto my pant leg, and pulled me forward. I don't know where his insistence came from, but I take a seat on the empty log he stops by, and then, he lies down on my feet, so I'm unable to move. He wants me here. (Not everyone is in agreement.)

I get the cold shoulder from the rest. Even Ronen's giving me a disconcerting stare. When I can't take it anymore, I do what I'm good at. I strike with force, right to the heart of my issues.

"I suppose you all think it should be hers," I say. Half are mid-bite on their warm fish dinner. Others are mid-conversation. They take in my scowl, posture, and accusing nod toward Tesha.

"What are you talking about?" Vale asks, with an empty fork poised in the air—one she looks tempted to fling in my direction. I'm sure she imagines it, just like me, the prongs embedding in my skin and the handle protruding outward.

"The bracelet," I answer. "I've had it my whole life, but I suppose you think I should give it up."

Evans narrows his hazel eyes on me. "I suppose you're a nasty—"

"Kid," Ronen interjects in his deep tone, looking at the rest of the group, who dip their heads in submission. It's only Evans who doesn't cower.

"Who's ever asked that of you?" he asks, throwing his arms up in challenge.

I don't respond because Ronen speaks again. "Bells! Remember what we agreed."

Agreed? What agreement? I'm ready to fight, but the big guy's reminding them of some secret pact, and they're falling into line. But I don't have to. It's as if his size serves as a weight on their tongue, but mine is free to move.

"What are you talking about? Did you discuss me behind my back?"

"Annibeth," Tesha says, getting my attention. "The braccelet is-s where it belongs. I would never think of asking for it. I don't want it."

She barely looks at me—not even breaking rhythm with her knitting—but the rest look at me like I'm a fool. And I realize I am. I hadn't thought about the bracelet in days. Hadn't even considered it. I was searching for a fight—a way to assert my power because I have none here. Their camaraderie is undeniable. Their bonds are strong, and I have no ties of my own. My Harwell connections mean nothing to these people. What I say or do doesn't matter to them in the least.

As the meal continues, the environment reveals further how entrenched I am... on the outside. They don't engage me or even look at me. I could stand on my head, and I doubt they'd notice.

I wonder if confronting Lord Endrack might be preferable to being in the Dark with people who hate me. It's a ridiculous thought after everything his cogs did in Harwell, but it's there.

Vale stands to gather the dishes. "It's not fun to be the odd one out," she says in a low whisper when she reaches me. She's not boasting and doesn't say it with pity. It's more of an observation. My plate's primarily untouched, but she takes it and then moves on.

She's right. I'm an outsider in this group—a position I've never held. I'm always top rung. I don't know what to do or say, so I nudge Yip off my feet and stand to go. Vale sees me move and groans. "Annibeth, stay. I didn't mean anything by it. Not really."

I want to snap at her—say something rude—but that instinct and my harsh behavior are what put me in this spot. I don't trust my stubborn mouth enough to say the proper words, so I put up my hand, school my features against an aggressive look, and shake my head, walking away.

Yip follows, and as much as I want to gather him in for comfort, I don't feel I deserve it. But he doesn't allow my indifference. The minute I'm in my bedding, he doesn't just sit next to me but climbs on top, his belly spanning my knees.

I clutch his fur between my fingers, pull the covers over my head, and cry. In my small space, I miss my family and friends and wonder how my life has suddenly turned out so wrong.

I wake with goop caked around my blue eyes—my salty tears dried and nearly sealed my eyelids together. I push down the covers, take care of my morning business, and get my things together and onto Clod's back. Ronen's nowhere to be seen, but instead of asking about him directly, I inquire, "Where's Yip?"

"Fond of the dog?" Vale asks, a curious tilt to her head.

"Just wondering why I'm not being slobbered on."

"He's with Ronen."

"Well, obviously." There's rarely another place he'd be. I wait for Vale to explain more but get nothing. "And... where's Ronen?"

She shrugs. "Likely updating his brothers about visiting Kally. Geric and Evans are friends with her too and are concerned. I mean, it's not an ideal situation. Ronen's girl's hurting, and he's out here with us."

"Ronen's *girl*?"

"Yes. Kally is Ronen's girlfriend. Didn't you know?"

I shake my head and walk away. I no longer bother searching out Yip or Ronen. I climb on Clod's back, scooting forward on the saddle to wait. It's not long until he arrives and wordlessly swoops up behind me. And then we're off.

Being away from the others, I'm happier than I could ever

describe. Traveling with Ronen is more straightforward and doesn't have me second-guessing my every word or action. He doesn't incite my ire to the same degree nor prod me into barking out accusations and cruelties, though he does have his opinions.

"Ye should give 'em a chance."

"Ronen. They hate me. They *all* hate me."

"Some truth in tha'." His chest rumbles at my back. "Had a dog they hated, but they came 'round."

"A dog?" I laugh at him, comparing me to an animal. "And what happened with this dog of yours?"

Ronen chuckles, twisting his neck. "Aroun' 'ere somewhere."

"Yip?" I hear a bark in the distance. "No way. They didn't like Yip?" *Bark.*

"Said 'e was too noisy."

"They probably say the same thing about me."

Ronen doesn't deny it.

My thoughts keep me quiet for most of our ride. The mystery of Ronen is slowly unraveling. I understand why his visit to Tenebris was painful, and I connect why Yip arrived back at the house smelling like Kally's perfume. Ronen and Kally are involved, and Yip's an intelligent and devoted animal. I imagine man and dog distraught to leave her side. I imagine her begging them not to go.

But then he came back and had dinner with Ma and me. The following day, he woke to escort me to the Cliffs. Why didn't he put me with the others and make the trip to Tenebris alone? Why didn't he stay with Kally? Am I an obligation he couldn't get out of? Or does she need time to grieve on her own?

Eventually, my mind reaches a point where I have to say something—acknowledge Ronen's loss. And while I've mulled over the situation for hours, I haven't considered what I'll say about it. A second later, I throw myself into the conversation with no preparation.

"I'm sorry again about Zanny."

"Aye," he says, not sounding sad but maybe surprised I'd bring it up.

"It must have been hard to tell Kally what happened to her sister. I'm sorry you had to do that."

"I didna tell Kal."

I tilt my head, thinking. What's he talking about? Did someone else reach her with the news before he did? I try to turn, but I'm on Clod in such a way that I can't look into Ronen's eyes, so I ask, "If you didn't tell her, who did?"

Ronen never answers as a high-pitched whistle sounds in the air. The shrill noise has Yip bounding off through a field and Big Scruff pulling Clod to a stop.

"What is it?" I ask, leaning into Ronen without thinking.

He looks down at me. "A friend."

The friend moves closer while we remain in one place. He wears a green longcoat with gold patterns—diamonds and lines—and rides a horse that Yip runs circles around. Neither man dismounts but bring their horses side-by-side before clasping hands in a greeting.

"Good to see you, Ronen. How're your brothers?"

"Ye just missed 'em. Camped togetha last night. How are things since I last saw ye?"

I'm listening to what they're saying, but mostly I'm staring at the stranger. (A very intriguing stranger.) He has the most perfect face I've ever seen. All his features are in ideal proportion—nose, eyes, mouth, chin—and his manner is relaxed, though he seems a little sad. His hair's cut so short as to be almost bald, but a thin layer of black hair covers his head. His skin is the prettiest color I've ever seen, dark and smooth, not even a freckle. It's hard to take my eyes off him, so it's good he's focused on Ronen so I can look my fill.

"Okay. Busy." He releases a weighted breath. "I didn't want to leave Tenebris, but I'm scheduled to meet Dad in Ora, and he's yet to see the lamlight canisters. He'll either launch into full military mode or make me do it. Probably the latter. Every day, he's more ready for me to take over. With all this trouble with Casmo, I wonder if it's time." He shrugs, then turns to me. "I see you're wearin' some of our new jewelry. How you like it?"

I touch the circlight, then tell him, "It does the job."

He nods and reaches out, waiting for me to take his fingers in greeting, saying, "I'm Raider."

"You're the one who calls Ronen a land pirate," I say, shaking his hand and tilting my head toward the big guy.

Raider grins, releasing me. "I guess I do."

Ronen chuckles behind me before saying, "Raider, meet Annibeth Petters from Harwell."

"Ah. You're Vale's sister. You look nothing alike."

"You know about us?" I ask with wide eyes. It's one thing for gossip to travel fast between the Northern Hem and Orchard Path in Harwell. It's another for it to move so quickly among the occupants of the Dark—spaced days apart.

"I have excellent resources for acquiring information," Raider says, and Ronen chokes out a laugh that doesn't seem appropriate for the comment. I squint in confusion. "It's a pleasure to meet you, Annibeth," Raider continues, dipping his head and looking at me with a twinkle and a crooked grin. "I thought Vale was quite the looker, but you've got her beat."

My lips fall apart in shock, and he smirks at Ronen before winking at me. I straighten in my seat, staring at the unrepentant flirt.

"I guess it's not fair to make comparisons," he says, straightening to match me. "I'd appreciate it if you kept that opinion to yourself." He grins. "Especially don't tell Geric. I've been told my nose is too fine to break."

I don't know what to say. Raider's rendered me speechless, and I'm unsure how to react. He chuckles, turning back to his friend. With the move, there's a return of his initial sadness. They discuss a few more details—things I can't hear past the fuzz in my ears—and then he waves goodbye before pushing his horse into a full gallop.

"Got stars in yer eyes, Bethy," Ronen says when Raider's out of earshot, and it takes a minute to register the words.

"What?" I ask distractedly, then shake my head. "I mean, no."

"Aye. Ye do. All the lasses get tha' way fer Raider." Ronen chuckles. "He's a charmin' 'n handsome man."

I lick my dry lips, watching Raider's back as he disappears beyond the reach of the circlight. "You sound jealous."

Ronen clicks his tongue, and Clod takes us in the opposite direction of Raider before Ronen answers, "Nah. Too much work lookin' tha' way. Easier bein' me."

CHAPTER EIGHTEEN

We're meeting up with the group again tomorrow. Last time, I stirred myself into a frenzy over the prospect and was ready for a fight before they even brought one to me. This time, I vow to keep it together. I'll tuck my head and keep my opinions to myself. Unless they start something, and then I'll unleash my fury.

I'm slightly embarrassed by my behavior from before. The revelation that my parents encouraged me to be distant and unkind has made me consider how I act. During our long rides on Clod's back, I've thought about the things I've done and why, and it's led me to one conclusion.

"I'm not a nice person," I tell Ronen, sitting around the fire minutes from turning in for the night.

"Aye. Knew it the moment I met ye." He grins, teasing to soften the truth.

The capability to be nice is a valuable trait—one I don't have. I always thought being fierce made me strong and in control. I'm starting to wonder if kindness is a sort of control. While others may not do it for that purpose, it seems probable that it's easier to get your way in some situations by being sweet.

"Then why have you been nice to me? Geric and Evans aren't. Especially Evans. He's not nice to me. Not *ever*."

"Ye ever been nice ta 'im?"

I squint and wrinkle my freckled nose to the side. Does that question even require an answer?

Ronen wiggles in place, getting comfortable on the log he's leaning against. "Mean people need friends too," he says without putting much thought into it. Like it's the most obvious answer there is.

But I laugh because it's not true. Mean people don't need friends. I don't. Sure, on the outside, people think Nacole's my friend. Even I thought that back in Harwell. But I see now that it's not true. I never let her in. I never treated her how I've seen this group treat each other—laughing with each other instead of at someone and doing things without expecting something in return.

I'm still chuckling over the fallacy when I notice Ronen's expression has gone flat—he's pulling back again. Not physically, but seconds ago, his demeanor was open, and now it's closed off.

"Hey, no. Ronen," I say his name softly, waiting until he looks at me. "I'm not laughing at you. It's just... I like that you tell me how I am. I don't know why because I hate it from everyone else. Maybe because you know there's no point in trying to change me. And yet, even understanding that, you still try to... well, be my friend, for lack of a better way of putting it."

"Ye think ye canna change?"

I shrug. I'm sure I'm capable of change, but would I want to? I'm comfortable with the way things are. Well, most of the time.

Ronen relaxes after I explain my laughter wasn't at his expense, and he asks, "Do ye like bein' mean?"

What a strange question. It's even more unusual that I'm eager to answer it. "I didn't at first, but I suppose I grew accustomed to it. I wasn't born this way, you know—scowlin' and complainin' right from the womb."

Ronen chuckles at my use of his lazy words. I'm glad he knows I'm joking with him. "Why are ye mean if ye dunna wanna be?"

"Did I say I don't want to be?" He doesn't respond, and I

suppose my question is an answer in itself. (Rhetorical and all that.) "I used to think fierce grumpiness was my natural personality, but I recently discovered I was groomed to act this way."

"Groomed by who?"

I pick at my longcoat sleeve. "Well, I could tell you, but who did it isn't the point. Because even though they encouraged me, I could have chosen to be different. I might have learned to enjoy being nice instead."

"So ye really do like being mean," he concludes, circling back to his initial question.

I laugh out loud. "You look so surprised. It's easy to like when it gives you what you want. If I change, I could lose everything. Besides," I can't help the smile on my lips, "I'm superb at it."

I expect him to laugh, but after a long silence, I turn away, unwilling to see his disapproval. Ronen's so big and tough— exactly how I want to be perceived in my small body—and maybe that's why I don't want him to disapprove of me. Except for my parents, the only other people I sort of felt that way about were the Clarc men. Lucan because he adored me, and Cully because he was destined to want me. At least, that's what my mother told me. (Once a day and twice on Sundays.)

A prickle of unease climbs my neck when I consider I just told Big Scruff things I've never admitted to anyone else— not even my parents—and I squirm uncomfortably being so exposed. But the raw feeling in my chest subsides the minute Ronen starts talking.

"At home, Ma would send me out ta dig traps. Small traps fer food 'n big ones fer men who wandered onto our land unwelcome. I hated diggin'. 'Twas dirty, 'specially after a long rain. And when I started trainin' in the guard, I'd always get picked fer it 'cause I was biggest 'n strongest 'n could shovel fastest. It didna seem fair. I wanted ta walk the line o' camp er set the fires." He rubs his bristly chin while I try to figure out where he's going with this.

"But I ne'er got picked fer any o' tha'. 'Twas always the traps. Thing was, I did it so long, I got real good. I'd come back filthy from bein' in the pits, 'n the lasses would run away, screamin' I was a bear. Ma would scold, sayin' I couldna come near our house 'til I cleaned." He chuckles, looking up at the trees while the memories pour over him, and I finally get an inkling of where he's taking this story.

"At some point, found I didna hate diggin'. I've dug all over. Caught more than one person who got off course." He grins at me. "I like it all—weary muscles, giant hole in the ground, wearin' the knees outta my pants, sweatin', thirstin', and, dependin' on the weather, gettin' coated in dirt or mud. But most o' all, I liked comin' home a muck o' a mess."

He leans in, resting his elbows on his knees. "Guess I'm sayin', Bethy, I can see how doin' somethin' fer long enough —even somethin' distasteful ye're good at—can become somethin' ye like. Most'll ne'er understand the draw. Most'll always see what ye're doin' as a muck o' a mess."

I smile at his attempt to relate, though I'm not sure it's sound. Learning to manipulate people emotionally isn't quite the same as learning to dig holes. But Ronen put forth an effort to find common ground, and for that alone, I'm appreciative.

"Thanks for understanding," I say, and for the second time tonight, my words come out gently. He nods and starts working his lips in a way I've become accustomed to—his beard sort of folds around them until they disappear, and I can't see what they're doing.

It's nice conversing in this lonely place. I decide Ronen's a pleasant companion—I like his stories, and his words make me feel better. I'm suddenly calmer about meeting up with the others tomorrow, and I might actually get some sleep tonight.

I grin as a question comes to me. "Did the girls really run

from you?" I ask, tilting my head, curious how he'll answer.

"Tha' they did," he chuckles, his lips reappearing. "Made fer a great game o' kissin' tag."

"Kissing tag?" I giggle, pulling my knees up to my chest. Yip notices me move and gets up from his place near Ronen to curl beside me. I drop my hand on his back and thread my fingers through his fur.

"Aye, did ye ne'er play tha' game? Runnin' after boys ta catch 'em 'n kiss 'em?"

"No," I say, my throat dry, while my mind tries to figure out what kind of place Tenebris is to grow up in.

At my look, he laughs again, low. "Honestly, Bethy, I've ne'er played kissin' tag. Evans has tho'."

I can believe that. Easily.

Ronen smiles and his eyes twinkle. "But we can agree, t'would be a funny sight. Me, with my big ol' body, jumpin' around, tryin' ta capture a pretty lass ta kiss."

I chuckle, pointing and unpointing my toes, so I rock backward and forth where I'm sitting. "It would be interesting to watch."

I think back on all I've told him. I'm indeed good at being mean, but there's something else I want him to know.

"Ronen?"

"Aye?" He seems to pick up on my change in tone—that I'm returning to something more serious than chasing people down for a kiss.

"Sometimes, it does bother me. I mean, that being cruel is so easy. I've wondered what it'd be like if I were different, but, like I said, I'm not sure I want to change. But it doesn't seem... right, I guess... to be so good at it." I shrug. I don't even know what I'm saying. Not really.

"Well, that's somethin', Bethy. Ye're soft somewhere in there," he says. I wish I could see his face, but he stands up and has his back to me, gathering his things to go to bed, but I imagine disapproval with a trace of hope in the expression I conjure.

We're back with the others, and I'm sticking to my plan, greeting them briefly upon our arrival and afterward, not allowing a single word to leave my mouth. Ronen tells them about crossing paths with Raider. With how Tesha perks up at the man's name, I can tell she's met him. Raider leaves an impression, that's for sure.

Poor Siman, I think and smother a laugh.

"Endrack's a confident leader," Geric says. They're discussing ideas for making it safe for us to live regular lives again and how to liberate Vale's grandmother. My grandmother too, I guess, though I've barely thought on it. Surprisingly, not one accusatory look comes my way, and I wonder if they've made their own plan regarding how they'll interact with me.

"He'll use Adlumen law to his advantage," Geric continues, scrunching his eyes in thought. Since I've mostly seen him with lenses or from a distance, it's the first I've noticed they're blue—just like his mother's.

"So, what we need is an expert in Adlumen law," Evans spouts, brushing a hand over his spiky brown hair. "I'm sure there's someone like that in every town in the Dark. We just need to ask."

"Shut it, Kid," Geric barks. "No need for sarcasm. We realize finding someone with that knowledge outside of Adlumen is nearly impossible." I rub my chin, thinking about Ma. She's from Adlumen. Obviously, they know this, so the information they need must be outside the realm of a regular citizen.

"So, we go there and find someone," Siman says.

"You're joking." Geric laughs.

"No, no." Evans holds up a hand. "Let Number Six speak. Maybe his voodoo is telling him something." It takes a moment to understand Number Six is Siman, though I don't know how he came by the nomenclature.

"It's not my *voodoo*." Siman sounds ornery, but he's also smiling. "I'm just exploring our options."

"Well, that option's out," Geric says with finality. I admit this discussion has intrigued me. While they usually speak about boring things when we gather, talking about the laws of an unknown place piques my interest. "Remember," Geric continues, looking right at Siman. "Endrack is smart and conniving. He's not bumbling and foolhardy like what you're used to."

The bristles rise on my neck. I try to ignore them, but they poke and prod. Vows be damned, I surge to my feet. "How dare —"

"Now, Cricket!" Ronen says, jumping into the conversation for the first time. Like, literally. He charges in front of me, his large hands up, warding off my attack. "*Lucan.* He's talkin' 'bout Lucan, Bethy, not yer da."

My chest rises and falls with anger. I admit I took the comment personally, aimed toward a family member. I've always considered my father an equal contributor to Harwell's leadership. That Geric didn't mean him softens the blow, but only a bit. I care about Lucan too.

I take a breath, close my eyes, and exhale through my mouth. I can't keep quiet, but I can explain my perspective rationally. Calmly. Like a reckoner would do.

Opening my eyes, I grab Ronen's wrist, giving him a slight squeeze to let him know I'm in control. He nods and steps back, breaking the connection, and everyone's attention falls on me.

I look right at Geric. "What you say has merit. Endrack

has vast experience, and Harwell barely has a foot outside the door. But for what we had to work with, Lucan and my father served the people well." I step forward, my only sign of aggression. "I've been to Tenebris and seen the wonders there. If we'd had such advantages, I daresay we'd be less bumbling and foolhardy in your eyes. Remember where we're starting from and have some compassion."

I realize it's unexpected for me to speak of compassion, but the word is out before I can draw it back.

Without a word from them, I leave the group and go to bed, knowing they won't miss me. Yip follows. I'm not sure if it was his choice or if Ronen sent him, but I'm glad either way. He curls up next to my head, muffling the sound of any further plans they're making.

◆ ◆ ◆

I wake to an argument. "You should be the one to go," Geric says in a heated tone. "It's past time to take on your responsibilities."

"You're better at it, is all," Evans replies without his normal animated tone.

I feel around for Yip, but he's not here to block out their noise. I lean up in bed and see that everyone else is up, their bedding put away.

How did that happen?

I jump quickly from my covers, eager to get going for many reasons. One, I don't want their argument to turn on me, accusing me of slowing our progress. And two, I'm happy to get back to just Ronen and me. Oh, and Yip. Yes, very happy about that.

"Brother, you can do this. We'll help you," Geric says while I've already rushed behind some bushes to get changed from my pajamas. Or pee-jamas, as Ronen would say. I can't help smiling when I think about that.

"Brother?" Evans laughs. "Not *Kid*? You think changing what you've called me all these years will make a difference? I'll suddenly feel ready for all this because you're willing to let me grow up?"

In the length of Evans's diatribe, I've changed clothes. I hustle to my bedding and start rolling it up.

"It's not just the name. For years, I've treated you as incapable because I'm the older brother, and it's expected I'll haze you. But you've started to believe the teasing, and I won't do it anymore."

I strap my clothing bag and bedding onto Clod's left flank, then run a comb through my hair. I hope we're near a place to bathe soon. This really is the last day my hair will look semi-presentable in a tail.

I spot Ronen quietly listening to his brothers and hop to his side, still completing the tie around my hair. All the Dark brothers turn to look at me.

"Morning," I say. Not chipper, but not sour either. All their brows drop into a scowl I'm unwilling to address. "I'm ready," I tell Ronen. "Whenever you want to head out." I grin and point both thumbs over my shoulder in the direction I think we're going. Geric's and Evans's brows battle over which can dip the farthest while I note one side of Ronen's beard lifts.

"'Twill be a minute. Waitin' on Vale."

"Vale?" I ask, premonition dropping heavy in my gut.

"Aye, Bethy. She's comin' with us."

CHAPTER NINETEEN

We're on the horses. Vale has her own, while I still ride on Clod with Ronen. The Dark brothers felt they were making decisions based on old data, so Geric left to connect with Captain Rhed's guard and get the latest. For the groups to be even, Vale is traveling with us. It's only for a few days, but I'm still disappointed.

Vale's presence irritates, but it's nothing I can't handle. I just stay quiet.

Not many days ago, I teased Ronen about being jealous of Raider, something he calmly denied. But there's no denying how I feel about having Vale with us. Ronen's a different person around her. They joke and laugh. They're happy and at ease. And Yip does everything in his power to get her to notice him when I'm right here and would lavish all kinds of attention on the ungrateful dog. Vale is more concerned with her horse than Yip, and it would tempt me to feel sorry for the little furry mound, except for his complete disregard for me. He's getting exactly what he deserves.

Little traitor.

On our second day of traveling together, I want to spit as Ronen helps Vale onto her horse—something she's perfectly capable of doing herself. Something he hasn't done for me since our first day together. Of course, that may stem from my reaction to such treatment. Like when I yelled at him never to do it again. I bite the inside of my cheek, annoyed with the situation I put myself in.

But, as much as I dislike Ronen's attention on Vale, it's even worse when her attention lands on me. "I hated Geric going off alone, but I'm glad to spend some time with you."

Automatically, I'm on alert. My brows furrow, and I try to figure out her game. "Why?"

"Well, we are family," she says, swaying to the rhythm of her horse. We don't sway as much. Maybe it's because Clod is bigger. Or Ronen. It could definitely be his size keeping the horse steady. "I figured we should clear the air, so we can at least act like we tolerate each other."

"What have I done to make you upset with me?" I ask with a mild level of snark. (Hey, I'm trying.) I have a few ideas about what I've done, but I want to hear her complaints since she's the one who wants to resolve them.

"Quite a few things. The real question is, what did I ever do to you?" Vale snaps back.

"Cully," I answer with a steady gaze aimed toward her.

"You still upset about that?" No doubt she's learned of Cully's recent betrayal.

"Maybe not at this very moment, but yeah, I was pretty upset about you trying to take my boyfriend."

"I never wanted Cully. And he only paid attention to me to get information. Oh, and to irritate you."

I grumble, figuring that was one of his goals. It frustrates me he was playing games with me, and I wonder how far it went. "Did you kiss him?" Ronen said she did, but I want to hear it from her, and I lean forward to see her face past his arm. The fire in her green eyes dims, and I know the answer.

"He kissed me," she says, removing herself from any responsibility.

"Right. So, if Geric kissed me, your issue would be with him not me?"

"Yes!" Vale yells, and both horses start. Even Yip lets out a little whine from below. "And Geric would never kiss you."

I grip Clod's mane, trying to block out her meaning—that I'm the one who had a boyfriend out kissing other girls.

Out looking for something else. "So, you're blameless?" I ask through tight lips. "How convenient."

"Lasses," Ronen rumbles in a soothing voice. "Simmer's fine, but dunna start ta boil."

Vale calms her tone, continuing, "Is Cully your excuse for stalking me, threatening me, and treating me like a disease from childhood?"

"You know what happened when we were kids, and I don't get why you're still harping on about that. You got your apology."

"What are you talking about?"

"My mother. She apologized. To *you*. It's more than I got, so I can't help but wonder, what more do you want?"

"What more? I want my mother back. *Our* mother back," she sneers. "It's because of you she's gone. Thanks for that."

"You're seriously blaming that on me?"

"Ugh! No!" Vale throws her hands up, and they land on her thighs. Again, her horse jerks. "I know that's not your fault. You just can be... really frustrating. But, no, that's not your fault. I'm sorry for saying it. It's been a rough few months."

I've had a rough few weeks, so I grumble in agreement, saying, "Tell me about it."

I lose some of my fire since we have a common complaint, and in the sudden calm, I bring up something I've been curious about. "I don't understand why you trusted these guys so readily." I point a thumb at the person caging me with both arms on horseback. I feel him chuckle against my back, relieved he didn't take the comment personally. "I mean, one of them killed Mort, and while the guy was a creep, he hardly deserved death. Now we're entrusting them our lives. Is that the best idea?"

With that comment, Ronen's chuckle turns into a grumble, and I wonder if I took it too far. But it's a valid question. Vale tilts her head—her black hair sliding forward—and frowns at me. "You didn't even like Mort."

It's true. Indeed, I accused Vale of consorting with crazy people, Mort being one of them. But that's not the point I'm making. "I'm not debating my like or dislike of someone. I'm just saying one of them is a murderer. It's as simple as that."

"There's nothing simple about it."

"You don't think they did it then?" I ask, surprised she's not defending them more.

"Oh, I know he did," she reveals with confidence.

"*He*," I repeat. "You know who it was?"

Vale nods. "It was Evans."

My heart beats double-time, hearing confirmation that Evans killed Mort. He took a man's life, and they treat him like a happy prankster. "You're not afraid he'll do the same to you?"

Ronen tenses behind me, pulling Clod to a stop. Vale stops Buttercup too, and it's a stare-off between us until Ronen says, "Ye need ta tell 'er."

"I know." Vale bites her lip and squeezes her eyes closed. "The day of Gran's Farewell Feast when you saw me talking to him on the Common—" She pauses, opening her eyes. "He followed me home. He was waiting for me down one of the transit paths where I couldn't see him."

My eyes widen. I always felt uncomfortable around Mort —I thought he was odd with his strange patch of hair on his mostly bald head—but I figured it was a vain prejudice based on his looks. (Well, prejudice and my recalcitrant disposition.) But with the direction this story is heading, he was more despicable than I imagined.

"He incapacitated me—hit my head a few times and gagged me. Then he took my blood."

"Your blood?" I breathe out, not meaning to interrupt but connecting the comment to the presentation in the Well, when

Evans drug his bloody finger across the tabletop.

"Yes. Lucan and your father know about it. They went with us to Mort's house, where we learned he was trying to locate people using blood technology. Mort correctly guessed I was one of those people because I was a story keeper." Vale swallows and takes a moment before she continues, "But they don't know that Mort threatened to do more—to kill my family and me. The brothers heard. Evans took Mort's life, but it wasn't without reason. He did it to save my family."

"Oh," I say, letting it sink in, but Vale still looks unsure, so I add, "I get it." And I do. I'll soon be a reckoner, and such deeds shouldn't go unpunished. The Dark brothers witnessed the crime and took care of the perpetrator in the only way they could. They saved Vale's life and took away her fear and humiliation. It's clear why she was never afraid of them. Indeed, it's obvious why she's devoted.

Vale relaxes after securing my understanding, and the rest of the story spills from her. "I was so scared and felt so alone. My grandmother was gone. My father had just learned about you and was dealing with it in silence. He shut us all out, ignoring our family. And Milany was working so much, but we don't have the kind of relationship to discuss such things, anyway."

"Do you blame me for that too? For him ignoring you?"

"I did when I first found out. But you didn't create the situation, and he should have acted better."

"I can relate to feeling alone," I admit, not sure why I'm opening up to more conversation when we've reached a point to shut it down.

"Because you don't feel a part of our group?" Vale asks, and I shrug. It's definitely part of what I mean. "It's not an easy thing to fix. I mean, you hate being stuck with us. And you must admit, we have plenty of reasons not to trust you. Foremost, you turned our grandmother over to the bad guy."

I open my mouth to argue, but she puts up a hand to stop me. "Look, that's another thing I no longer blame you for. Gran would have gone regardless. I'm still sad you'd do something like that, but it would have happened anyway. Let's put it behind us and consider this an opportunity to work together for the first time. We'll keep each other safe and do everything possible to reunite you with your family." And in case I don't understand who she means, she adds, "The Petters."

I put on a barely there smile and nod.

She returns it with a full grin. "And who knows? Maybe, during our time in the Cliffs, we'll find some methods for connecting in positive ways."

It seems like a lot to hope for, but I won't discount the possibility.

The third day together is different. As Vale hoped, it feels like we cleared some of the air. Though nothing is fixed between us, and I doubt it ever will be, we are cordial and speak on incidental matters. She's not a friend and doesn't feel like family, but I think I have one less enemy in the group, and I'm surprised by how much that means to me.

The journey's pleasant—the area's warm and dry for January. Sometimes the longcoat feels like too much, but I keep it on.

We turn onto an official-looking path not too far from our destination. Ronen calls it a road and says the surface is pavement. It's mostly flat, except in parts where it's broken and dirt shows through. Then there are other areas where trees and other plants have taken over, but it's wide enough we maneuver to unbroken parts and continue forward.

I enjoy traveling on the road because I know exactly what to expect. It's a perfect indicator of where we're going, so I don't need to ask.

Before I know it, we reach the Cliffs, which are not as expected. I pictured rock bluffs and more opportunities for camping but, it turns out, the Cliffs are buildings. Enormous buildings. They're taller and wider than anything in Harwell and farther apart, with the road going right through the middle. The separation makes them feel even more significant.

They're not made of wood, either, but metal and glass. Lots of glass—much of which is broken, especially on the lower levels. It's staggering, the things we could do with these materials—items not even being used.

"What is this place?"

"It used to be called the Glass Cliffs, until the residents shortened the name. It's just remnants of a big city. Ruins mostly, though there are squatters and cliff dwellers, so we must be watchful," Vale says, and it's strange to hear her speak so officially as if she knows what's going on. Admittedly, the inroads she's made with the Dark brothers make it so she knows quite a bit.

"What are squatters?"

"People passin' through," Ronen says. "Na perm'nent."

"And cliff dwellers?"

"Perm'nent. Some helpful. Some na."

"What are our chances of running into either kind?"

"Almost guaranteed," he replies, and my stomach twists into a knot.

Great. I was feeling safer, knowing we were almost at our destination. It gave me hope for a reprieve from the constant vigilance of watching our surroundings, but now I have to worry about squatters and cliff dwellers.

"I'll put in my request now for the helpful ones," I say blandly, and Vale chuckles, nodding in agreement.

But it's not five minutes later when Ronen mumbles,

"Bells." Then he clears his throat in a particular way—one that has me instantly on alert. And it doesn't take long to gather his meaning. Straight ahead, on our broad path, are five people intent on gaining our attention. Ronen and Vale keep their same pace on the horses. Yip's motions are even subdued, taking his place a few feet from Clod.

"Real casual," Ronen whispers, "Tuck yer lights in yer shirts. Bethy first."

I reach back and pull the ribbon from my hair. My white-blond strands fall down my back. I pull forward a section, draping over Ronen's arm, and feign brushing through the knots. Then I slide the circlight under the neck of my shirt. I straighten and pull another batch of hair over my left shoulder.

"Sorta goes ev'rywhere, dunnit?" Ronen asks, making a smacking sound. I turn enough to see my hair catch in his beard. For a second, the five people aren't on my mind as I pull the strand stuck to his face.

"Sorry," I say with a laugh, and Ronen grins back at me. When he's free of my hair, I twist to find Vale watching us curiously. I ignore the look and notice she's adjusted her light to be under her shirt while it still gives off a faint beam, as does mine. We can see in our vicinity, maybe ten feet, but no farther.

Ronen pulls Clod to a stop when the people are in front of us. Vale does the same with Buttercup. With no instruction, Yip sits and tilts his head to the side, his tongue falling from his mouth in a steady pant.

Their eyes move over us rapidly, taking in our clothing and not comprehending two people before them have light sight.

"You're a big one, aren't you?" the one in the middle asks after his perusal. He looks older than us, but not by much, and he's skinny. It would take four of him to make Ronen, maybe more. I wonder if that's why his first move is to show weakness, for that's all his comment is.

"Seen bigger," Ronen replies, and I want to laugh out loud. When's he ever come across someone bigger than himself? I surely haven't. The comment seems incredulous. Indeed, I glance at Vale, and she's holding back laughter.

"We govern the Cliffs."

"Cap'n Rhed governs the Cliffs as part o' the Coastal T."

"Technically. But we're so close to Casmo's land, the Coastal Territory doesn't care about things out here. Only we care about these parts." The man goes quiet, looking over our horses and Yip before taking a step forward and looking up at us. He narrows his eyes on me, saying, "You don't seem like you belong with this group."

"Me?" I glance at the others before focusing back on him. I'm unsure of his purpose, so I try for a bland response as I straighten my shoulders and ask, "In what way do I stand out?"

"In every way. So, ditch them and come with me," he says, raising his brows and grinning.

I take in the expression with a dose of disgust. "Maybe I don't belong with them, but I *definitely* don't belong with you."

"Eh. You might change your mind. I'm here if you want me." The man chuckles as I shake my head in denial, then looks back at Ronen, asking, "Where you from?"

"Tenebris, but stayin' 'ere a bit."

"Running from Captain Rhed?" Ronen shakes his head. "Good. We don't need that kind of attention around here. Mostly get left alone unless the wrong type of people drop by. You the wrong type?"

"Depends on the day," Ronen says and pauses. It's deliberate as he takes in their expressions. I don't know what he sees, but he adds, "We're aimin' ta keep things quiet."

The man nods and grunts—a sound nothing like Ronen's rumble for the same type of response. "They call me Spratt. You got a name?"

"Fuzz," Ronen answers, and I might imagine it, but it feels like their formation tightens. As if all five of them move at once, pulling their line together an inch or two.

"You need accommodations, Fuzz? We can set you up for a fair price."

"Got a place," Ronen says, relaxing behind me with his hand on his hip. Only, I know it's no casual gesture. His weapon is there—one of them—and he's prepared to use it. Maybe their uneasy response wasn't just in my head. Then Ronen surprises me by declaring, "Guests o' Cap'n Malum."

Dead Captain Malum? Is Ronen serious right now? I suppose he's using the name for intimidation, but who says it will work? I'm sure at any moment, Spratt and his group will pull out weapons, and it will be Ronen against the five of them. I'm not sure Vale and I would bring much to the fight except a nasty temper and a willingness to be helpful. (I'll let you prescribe the correct trait to whichever of us you choose.)

"You say you're aimin' for quiet. Why do I doubt that?" Spratt looks away from Ronen and right at me. His gaze is probing, and if I were in Harwell, I'd tell him what to do with his look. But here in the Dark, at the Cliffs, well... I keep my mouth shut. Yay for me.

A second later, his gaze goes to Vale, perusing her similarly before looking back at Ronen.

"You need anything—food or supplies—come to us. Don't search the buildings. Against Cliff code."

Wow. The Captain Malum thing worked. We should be grateful to the members of his Six who've kept his demise unknown.

"Aye."

"You can find us at Ellagio." Ronen nods like he knows where that is. Though, I guess he probably does.

The group of five divides to let us through. Yip darts out

in front of the horses, leading the way as if his freedom's in question and he can't get away fast enough. As we pass, I look down at Spratt's blond head. Not only is he skinny, but his head looks too small for his body, and his nose too small for his face. It's a disturbing combination, and I force myself to turn away so I don't stare.

When we're out of earshot, I turn to Ronen but speak in a whisper. "I'm still not sure. Were they the helpful kind or not?"

His lips twist in his beard. "Helpful fer now. Incentive might make 'em not."

"What kind of incentive?"

"Money. Power. Lord Endrack has alotta tha'." He shakes his head and grumbles. "Unfortunate they saw us, but couldna be helped."

We continue down the road between the towering buildings. We see no more people, including our own, and I wonder if we're the first ones here. I'm tired of riding and ready to get down and stretch my legs. It's too bad these buildings don't have irrigation systems on top. I could use some rung climbing about now.

"Ye're fidgetin', Bethy. Dunna worry. Almost there."

"Well, thank goodness for small favors," I say, reaching to rub my lower back and elbowing Ronen in the stomach.

"I think I see it," Vale says.

"See what?" I look left and right at the tall structures. No point in looking forward because all I see is Clod's giant head. Ronen's horse exhibits a lot of confidence for an animal. He trots along tall and proud, even with the weight of us on his back.

"The plinth," Vale replies, pointing straight in front of us where I can't see a thing.

"What's a plinth?" I ask while trying to see for myself, leaning to the side and squinting into the distance.

"It's a platform or a pedestal, placed to be viewed from many angles, usually to display an artistic or historical statue."

Huh. Leave it to Vale to turn a simple question into a history lesson, boasting all her knowledge from years of training as a story keeper. But I'm too tired to comment on it. Instead, I continue to watch for the plinth as we get closer.

It turns out it's circular, with five steps leading to the platform.

The *empty* platform.

I straighten in my seat. "I think you missed a detail in class," I say to Vale with a smirk. "Apparently, they don't all have statues." Vale scowls and opens her mouth to reply, but she's too late.

"Cool yer toes, Cricket," Ronen rumbles from behind. "The statue's in Adlumen. Took it decades ago."

Questions and complaints crowd my mind. I don't know what to focus on first. Why would Adlumen take a statue from this place? Why is Ronen siding with Vale? And how was that deserving of him calling me Cricket? But Ronen keeps going, "Quit yer chirpin' fer a bit. Need ta enter Durus cautious 'n quiet. Ye open tha' mouth, ye'll be attractin' ev'ry squatter 'n dweller in the Cliffs."

"Gah!" I throw my arms across my chest and glare at him over my shoulder, but I do exactly as he says and keep everything I want to convey inside.

Ronen brushes a rogue strand of hair from my cheek that's still free after meeting with Spratt. Then he puts his giant hand in the same spot and gently caresses my face. "Thank ye, Bethy, fer calmin'," he says, and all my anger melts away. Every trace is gone, and I stare back at him in shock, trying to figure out how he did it.

My anger is a source of power. I use it when I have no other defense, and he took it from me like it wasn't an obstacle. Like it wasn't even difficult.

"Now, I need yer help," he continues. "Keep an eye out fer anythin' lookin' wrong."

Wrong?

Oh, I've discovered something wrong. Very wrong. And I don't need to monitor our surroundings to find it. It's right here with me, sitting on the back of Clod—a person capable of obliterating every last vestige of my fight.

Yes, I've discovered something quite troublesome indeed.

CHAPTER TWENTY

The threat of danger is low, and the promise of simplicity is high in our quest to find Durus. Ronen discovers the entrance exactly where he expects it—due west of the plinth. We enter a tall building through a large metal door—horses and all—and after traveling two hundred feet, we go through another door.

We leave the horses and descend three flights of metal stairs with holes in the treads so I can see all the way down. We're well underground now—how very strange. I briefly wonder why we never did that in Harwell—made space below our buildings—but then I remember the cellars where we keep some of our produce. We must watch the items for rot because the water table is high with the river and Shore so near. There's no danger of that in the Cliffs.

I tap the smooth walls at the bottom of the stairs—hard like rock. "Cement," Vale says, and I nod, though I don't comprehend the substance. Meanwhile, Ronen inspects the door, and the attached sign: **DANGER. Keep Out. Storage of Hazardous Materials.** He checks the knob—it's locked—before pulling out a tool I recognize. Only days ago, he kicked it, and I retrieved it. He uses the screwdriver to remove metal screws from the two bottom corners of the sign, giving them to Vale to hold. A moment later, he lifts the sign on hinges. Behind it is a shiny black square surrounded by metal—eight inches tall and six wide.

"'Tis the place," Ronen says with a bearded grin.

"Great. So, how do we get in?" I ask.

"Like this." Ronen lifts his great hand and taps the metal surface with his knuckles, sending an echo up through the stairwell. Retrieving the screws from Vale, he reinserts them.

"You think Tesha's already here?" Vale asks just as the door opens, and a gap-toothed redhead pokes her head out.

"Hi!" Tesha says, pulling the door wide. "We barely beat you! We've been here twenty minutes-s," she continues, whistling her words. We file in after her, and Ronen pushes the door closed behind him.

"How did you get in?" I ask as Tesha guides us down a long hallway—more cement. I'm sandwiched between Ronen and Yip, with Vale and Tesha in the lead.

Tesha keeps pace but lifts her hand and wiggles her fingers. "This-s was my father's plac-ce. He told me my blood would open it."

Tesha's blood. This must be the blood technology they talked about in Harwell. "How does it work?" I ask, momentarily forgetting I hate Tesha—curiosity outweighing vehemence.

"Under the s-sign, there's a plate I put my hand on. It pricks-s my skin and checks-s my blood."

How strange and amazing. "So, can I get in here too, since we share ancestry?"

"Only Tesha," Ronen answers. "Ye share Dale blood, not Abbadon."

"Abbadon?"

"Malum's true name," Ronen says.

"Not to worry. We found keys-s!" Tesha wiggles a metal object in the air.

"Ye see anyone 'fore ye got 'ere?" Ronen asks, and Tesha lowers the key.

"In the Cliffs-s?" she asks, twisting to see Ronen nod his answer before she shakes her head. "No. You?"

"Aye. Guy called Spratt. Need our stories ta match if we see 'im 'gain."

We exit the long hallway into an impressive space. There are twenty-foot ceilings with metal pipes and lights running in stripes. The room's not pretty like Ma's house, but it's extra bright with no unlit corners. The floor is cement, but unlike the other areas, it's shiny. Along one wall are enclosed cupboards with a polished metal countertop running the same length. There's a separate counter a few feet away from the main one with unusual things I can't identify sitting on the surface. In the room are three brown couches—all the same size—arranged to make three sides of a square with a short round table in the center. The couches are huge. I daresay Ronen could lie down without touching either end.

Beyond the sitting area is a massive table with benches on each side and a chair on both ends—enough to fit a dozen or more. Next to it is another rectangular table, though no chairs are around it. The top is bluish-green, but the blue tint could come from the circlights we're wearing. There are white lines on it and a strange divider made of intersecting yarn, sitting vertically through the middle and rising about eight inches. "Evans s-says this is-s a ping-pong table," Tesha says, shrugging and touching it.

Around the perimeter of the room, I count five doors. Tesha guides us to each one, and we inspect what's inside. Since we've yet to see Siman or Evans, I expect them to appear behind each one. The first room is filled with beds on top of beds. It's bizarre but efficient. At least ten people could sleep in here. The next room is an indoor relief house, reminding me of the one I saw in Tenebris but sectioned off so more than one person could go. Similarly, there are multiple showers—another discovery in Tenebris—but no tubs. It's not as frilly as Ma's—everything is sleek, smooth, and bright.

We reach the third door, but Tesha doesn't open it. There's another panel on the front, like outside, but a sign doesn't cover it. "We're not sure what's-s in here. It took my blood but didn't open," Tesha says.

What's inside? And why would Captain Malum have a room he couldn't open? I reach out and try the knob. (It's not in my nature to trust—I always test things for myself.) It doesn't budge.

While the third door is a mystery, the fourth door blows all thoughts of it from my mind. We step into a room and my jaw hangs open in amazement. The ceiling and floors are the same, but it's enormous—three times the size of the rest. Around the perimeter is metal fencing, sectioned off into squares. And inside three of them are the horses.

I look at the ceiling again, perplexed at how they got in here. We're below ground, and there's no way they came down the stairwell or fit through the cement hallway. I'm trying to discover the solution when I get my answer.

A humming noise, followed by a loud clink, heralds the opening of two humongous metal doors flat with the wall. They slide open, revealing Evans with a skittish Clod. The animal appears undecided about whether to bolt from the metal box or stay inside.

"Your damn horse," Evans says. "It's almost too big for this thing." He walks out with his usual swagger, Clod in tow, before reaching Ronen and slugging the big guy in the arm. "Brought Danger and Riot down together, but there was no way of getting Buttercup in there with Clod."

"Thank ye, brotha," Ronen says, tapping Evans's arm. The younger man teeters, then glances at me.

"You're still with us, eh?"

"Seems so," I say, squinting and straightening my back.

"Huh." Evans shrugs like our conversation bores him, and his hazel gaze drops away. He spins around and helps Vale get Clod into his little fenced area. She's eager to get her horse to join the rest, and apparently, Siman's up top waiting to load the animal.

Vale's trying to get Clod to enter the gate when Tesha pops into my vision. She looks chipper today—as if it's the best day of her life—and I want to smother her happiness. I have a surplus of anger ripe for the job.

"Should we continue the tour?" she asks, looking from me to Ronen. Her eyes stay on Ronen. Smart move because I'll cut her down with my glare. I open my mouth, unsure what will come out, but Tesha's the target, and she'll be in ribbons when I'm done. But Ronen steps in front of me, holding out an arm and pointing the way we came.

"We'll follow ye, lass," he says, waiting for Tesha to walk before dropping his hand. Then he turns and gives me an icy stare—an unusual expression on Ronen's face—before following her. An uncomfortable chill runs up my back. I don't enjoy getting scolded in such a quiet manner. I'm more accustomed to yelled complaints, but all it took from Ronen was a look. It said everything. I take a few cleansing breaths and hurry after them.

Though I'd never admit it, I'm glad he stopped me—I was after a fight, but it would only make things more impossible in this place. The real question is, how did Ronen know I needed stopping? I rub my cheek, wondering if I'm that transparent. If I am, I can't help but wonder why Tesha doesn't keep her distance.

And why did my temper escalate so quickly? That's not common. Have I lost control of my emotions to where they're controlling me? That's a disturbing thought. I bet it's this situation—trapped in Durus with people who despise me. I'm sure my temper would be in check if I were back in Harwell.

We reach the fifth door, and Tesha swings it open, flipping on the light. It's another bedroom, only this one has just one bed, right in the middle of the wall. It looks big enough for four people, and it's raised, like all the other beds I've seen in the Dark—well, except for the bedding we use when camping.

"We dec-cided this room should be yours," Tesha says.

"*We* decided?" I ask, curious about the statement. Truthfully, I can't imagine Evans supporting that decision.

"Well, technically, this place is mine. So, yeah, it was my choic-ce. I told them I wanted you to have it. I know this s-situation isn't eas-sy for you. I thought you could us-se the extra spac-ce." The corner of my pink lips turns up in a wry grin—more like they could use the space *from* me.

There's pity in Tesha's tone. Some people find issue with being pitied, but it makes no difference to me. It doesn't make me weak. On the contrary, it only benefits me. Let them pile in that room like storage in the commodities building. I'll stay here... spread out... and get some peace and quiet. Thank you, pity.

We've been in Durus for a week when Geric returns. He says a quick hello, gives a brief update, then pulls Vale away to who-knows-where to do who-knows-what.

Well, I have an idea of *what*.

Regardless of their activities, the news Geric brings is mostly good. Captain Rhed is uninjured after the battle in Harwell, and he's working to secure a safe situation for our return. So far, it's involved planned attacks against pockets of cogs, capturing lamlight canisters and circlights. Taking sight from the cogs is the quickest way for Harwell to get back to normal—precisely what Lucan and Cully want—but I'm no longer interested in returning to the old ways. I'd rather work out an agreement with Adlumen because life back in tiny Harwell seems oppressive now I've experienced more.

Under Captain Rhed's protection, the citizens haven't had to defend themselves against more attacks from the cogs. In fact, half the citizens have left—more than the third who originally planned to go. But the leadership remains, including my parents, and Geric brought news of them. It wasn't much, but they're safe, and my mother sent a personal message—that she loves me and to be assured her health has improved some. He also told Vale that Laso's still in Harwell and working in the repository but has had no luck with their end goal.

And so, I wonder, what's the repository, and what's the goal they're working toward?

Overall, it's decided our escape was a success. The cogs are looking for us but haven't come in this direction. Geric evaded them twice on his return by backtracking and hiding. And while they haven't given up, they're looking in the wrong area. But if just one of Cully's messages made it through, there's no doubt we'll have an insurgence of cogs in the Cliffs.

It's been two days since Geric returned, and Vale has spent every minute with the man. She never leaves his side—as if he'll get away. Even Siman and Tesha are more likely to be divided.

Evans constantly makes fun of them while I do my best not to laugh—because I can't let Evans know I agree with every word from his mouth on the subject. But, yeah, they're disgusting.

But there is a positive. Yip has given up on Vale and showers all his attention on me.

I haven't been outdoors in two weeks. The Dark brothers are preparing for long-term lockdown. As such, Ronen coordinated the acquisition of supplies with Spratt and went to Ellagio three times. The second time, I nearly asked to go —feeling so confined by the stark white walls of Durus—but

Vale beat me to it, and he turned her down, so I kept quiet. But because of his errands, the stables are stocked with hay, and the kitchen is packed with food—enough to spill into the gathering room.

Today, Ronen made his third and final visit to Spratt. After his return, I discover a large picture on my bedroom wall. I take in the green grassy hills, the vibrant flowers in a riot of colors, and the clear blue lake. It transforms my space and improves my mood, so I sit on the edge of the bed and stare. I've never seen such a place—not a structure in sight—and I couldn't have imagined it even if I wanted to. I envision sitting on the water's edge with the wind in my hair, the sun on my face, and a floral fragrance on the warm breeze.

"Ye like it, Bethy?" I hear from behind, but I don't turn, not wanting to break the illusion.

"I most definitely do."

"Come help me?" Ronen asks, popping his head into my bedroom sanctuary.

"Where we going?" After two weeks (plus a few days) of confinement, I can't keep the eagerness from my tone.

"Ta muck stalls."

My mouth wrinkles. That doesn't sound fun. At all. It was Tesha's job with the goats back in Harwell, so my first instinct is to inquire why she's not doing it. But Durus is her place, so she has the privilege of dictating who does what, and I suppose they've relegated me to the demeaning jobs.

But when I enter the room, I'm shocked to find them all here—each taking care of their own animal.

"Clod's twice the work o' these li'l bits," Ronen says, pointing at the moderate-sized horses, comparing them to his behemoth. "Was wonderin' if ye'd help with Yip." He points to a corner where, sure enough, Yip has left his business.

"I've never done this before," I confess, staring at the pile. When we traveled, Yip did this job whenever and wherever the need struck. I suddenly appreciate the lack of requirement for cleanup.

"'Tis easy. Ye use tha'." He points to a tool with a long handle and a wide, flat end. "Then ye put the poop in tha'." An open, angled container with a wheel and handles.

"Got it," I mumble, shuffling across the floor.

It only takes a minute to remove Yip's deposits. Then Ronen instructs me to throw out more hay in the same spot, and he gives me a container of white powder to sprinkle over the top. "'Twill smell betta."

I'm already finished—while the others continue to circle their animals, brushing their short, silky coats—so I start back to my room. "Hey, Bethy!" Ronen calls out, and I turn, expecting another assignment, but he puts two fingers to his forehead and then points them at me. "Thank ye."

I nod and sort of smile, then push through the door. A second later, Yip appears at my side, running his wet nose along my fingers. I look down and shake my head at him. "You have no idea what I just did for you," I say, and his head flops to the side along with his tongue. "You tell anyone, and I'll deny it. You hear?"

Yip barks and takes off toward my room, though it's becoming *our* room since he's with me most of the time now. I let out a soft giggle no one hears and follow him inside.

Days pass, and it's more of the same. I spend time in the gathering area when it's time to eat, using the same fascinating kitchen luxuries Ma has in Tenebris—a refrigerator, stove, and indoor water. Occasionally, I sit on the couch and listen to the others talk. Ronen doesn't say much but watches me—waiting for me to lash out, so he can step in and de-escalate.

In our hole in the ground, we keep irregular hours—there's no point rising or resting by a sun we can't see—and they've taken to spending *hours* at the green table with white stripes. Ping-pong is played using white, hollow-sounding balls and paddles. Sometimes two of them play. Sometimes four. They've asked me to join a few times, but I haven't. Games aren't really my thing. At least, not physical games—mind games are another matter. But it's usually fun to watch—something different to do—at least in the beginning.

I've noticed recently how often I get hit by stray balls. It rarely happens to the others. And it mostly happens when Evans is behind the paddle. He smiles and tells me he's sorry. I'm unsure if his antics fool the rest, but I have no doubt about what's happening. I haven't revealed I'm onto him. I let him play his pranks because the balls don't hurt, and I'm making plans. I can't help but grin when I think about them.

I'm doing something wonderful—folding my clean, warm clothes. Soon after arriving in Durus, I became aware of another Dark miracle. There's a cabinet here with two electric machines inside—one washes, and the other dries. There's no lugging stuff to Building Seven and scrubbing it in frigid water. There's no sopping material hanging around our quarters to dry. It's as simple as washing, drying, and putting away—the machines do all the work!

The warmth is my favorite part. I want to wrap in the heat and take a nap.

I fold my last shirt and lift the pile to take to my room, then pause. It's a courtesy for the last person who uses the drier to inspect the washing machine for wet items—leaving them in for too long makes them stink. I hate being told what to do, but

I don't dare ignore their instructions—they might make me handwash my clothes.

A quick check reveals articles needing to be dried, so I put down my stuff and transfer items from one compartment to the other, and a smile forms on my mouth. As luck would have it, this load belongs to Evans.

An intense ping-pong game distracts the group, so I quickly detour into the stables before returning to start the drier. No one even notices my absence. Then I retire to my room.

I enjoy my space. I'm not sure if I'm happy or sad the others don't act jealous I have a room all to myself. I spend so much time here, I've memorized the room. The walls are the same stark white as every other area in Durus, except I have my picture. Plus, I have a wall made up of wooden cabinets full of marvelous things. (More about that later.)

The ceiling is low and cozy—not towering like the gathering area or the stalls—and besides the bed, the only other pieces of furniture are a large chair that's so soft I could sit in it forever and a little side table. It's my own little haven.

And when pondering my many comforts, I can't leave out the relief room. I don't have to share with the others because I have my own. There's a countertop with two basins, each with running water—hot and cold. There's a large tub—so very different from wading into the bathhouse coves in the Harwell river. But the shower is my favorite—it's exotic, and I enjoy filling the enclosure with steam. I've encouraged the others to use it because I don't want them to change their minds and take my room from me. They tell me they have their own showers, but I'm still willing to share—not a standard thing for me.

The most curious thing, though—and let me say, it takes a lot to outdo indoor, heated water—is the largest mirror I've ever seen. It's above the bathroom counter, and I've spent so much time in front of that thing—looking at the entirety of my form and inspecting my body from every angle. It's still so strange to see what I look like. And I don't hate what I see. I'm kind of nice to look at.

◆ ◆ ◆

It's almost the first of February—my birthday—and I can't believe I'll spend the day I turn eighteen in this hidey-hole with a bunch of people who hate me.

Well, that's not entirely true—my relationships with them have evolved.

Yip's the only one I'd actually call a friend. He spends every minute with me, shadowing my moves, and I return the favor as best I can—scooping his poop and not even complaining. Ronen tolerates me more than the others—at least, he's the first to defend me in an argument. (Also, the first to scold me if I get feisty.)

Vale's cordial, less of a Goat Head, while Geric mostly ignores me—not that he's rude, but he doesn't engage. It works for me.

The Droll is the opposite. Evans engages whenever possible —for the smallest of reasons—and I think I've figured out why. I'm sure the others would disagree, but I've discovered we're very much alike. We hold grudges and enjoy conflict, especially if we create it. The difference is, Evans does it with a smile. So, it's a strange development when I discover I almost don't mind him anymore. That said, I'm still waiting on my payback for the ping-pongs. It should be any day now.

Siman's the one I still can't face, which is odd since he's the one—not long ago—that was a close acquaintance of mine. But I can't get past the heartbreak he caused Nacole. When I see him, I get angry and turn the other way. He's tried talking to me a few times, but I'm not ready to forgive him.

And Tesha. Well, she's perfectly nice to me—all the time. Whenever I see her, there's a smile on her face and a kind word whistling from her lips. But the little witch hasn't put any spell on me. Nope.

I still can't stand her.

I'm relaxing in my room, lounging on the chair in the corner, my legs dangling over the armrest. It wasn't long after being assigned this room that I explored the cabinets on the wall, and what I discovered inside were books—hundreds, maybe thousands, of books—all machine-created printed pages bound on the edge with official covers. I never saw a book in Harwell—heard about them, sure—but it wasn't until I held one in my hand and explored its contents that I understood their value.

They're magical! I'm more grateful than ever I can read because they take me to places without ever leaving this room in Durus. And so, I'm grateful to the villainous Captain Malum for stocking his hideaway with literature to keep me occupied and help me understand the wider world those of us in Harwell were hidden away from.

Yes, they give me a lot of insight, but some things are still confusing, like the volume I'm reading now. It's a collection of short stories, which I like because they're so quick, but this story's called *The Yellow Wall Paper*, and it's freaking me out, if I'm honest.

Yesterday, I read a book about a crocodile that ate a clock. Early on, I discovered a well-worn book called a dictionary that explains the meaning of every word I can think of, so I used it to read about crocodiles. Turns out, they're like alligators, which gave me pause. Some months ago, I accused Vale of spreading false stories when she talked about alligators, and now I find evidence of them in these books. But I still wonder if I'm right to question their reality. After all, children can fly in the book with the crocodile and clock. So how much should

I be expected to believe? And when I checked the dictionary for flying children using pixie dust, I found no clarification either way.

While I've become obsessed with the content of the books, they also make me feel like more of an outsider. I read about close relationships between families and friends, but the examples on those pages aren't a representation of how I operate. Not at all. For the first time, I wonder if I've done something genuinely detrimental by distancing myself from others.

I finish *The Yellow Wall Paper* and put it back on the shelf. While perusing the volumes for less disturbing entertainment, I hear a terrific screech.

Ahh... the sound of torment.

Accompanying the noise is a string of profanities, which can only be attributed to Evans. A grin spreads across my face, and I leave my bedroom to find him dancing around the gathering room in a jerky, agitated jig. "What in the light?" he bellows, stripping off his shirt and flinging it across the room. His dark brown hair sticks up at every angle as he swears some more, rubbing his bare chest while red welts rise on the skin under each scrape.

The others appear—coming from whatever area they were holed up in—while Evans peels off his pants. Next off are his socks. I should avert my eyes—he's down to his undershorts—but I can't help enjoy his discomfort, and I bite my lip to hide a smile.

In no time, Ronen arrives at my side. "Wha'd ye do, Cricket?" he asks, attributing the chaos to me and accurately addressing my alias—the one he associates with mischief and revenge.

"I've just been reading," I reply, pointing toward my room and purposely misunderstanding his question. "What you been up to?"

"Readin', eh?" he asks with a glance back at his brother, who's ready to strip off the remnants of his clothing.

"Yep." I fold my arms and lean against the door frame. "You can learn a lot by reading. For example, wallpaper's scary, crocodiles eat clocks, and children fly." I tap my lips and full-on grin. "Oh, and I learned something else."

I pause because he's going to have to ask.

"Wha'd ye learn, Cricket?" His voice is a low rumble, and he's still calling me Cricket, which I guess I deserve.

"Oh, just little details most people ignore. Like, you know that powder you have me put on Yip's hay? It keeps the stink away, but if you get it on your skin, it can be rather... bothersome."

"Bothersome," he repeats.

"Yep. I'm grateful I can read." I reach up and tap Ronen's sturdy chest with my small hand. "You might want to tell Evans to rewash his laundry."

I step back, intending to ensconce in my room, but pause to give Ronen a pleasant smile. (One I've practiced in front of the mirror and categorize as disarming.) Then I say, "And please, be a dear. Tell him not to hit me with any more ping-pong balls."

CHAPTER TWENTY-ONE

I wake in bed to discover I'm surrounded on three sides—Tesha's to my left, Vale's to my right, and Yip's at my feet. Well, he's on my feet. In fact, they're all sitting on my bed.

"Morning," Tesha says.

"Time to get up," Vale adds.

I sit up, looking from one to the other. "Gah! Seriously? What time is it? And what am I missing? Is someone attacking Durus? Do I have an important appointment in the stables?" I yawn and release a little squeak at the end. "Oh, right. Nothing ever happens here. So why are you waking me up?"

"It's your birthday," Vale says like I'm an idiot. "Just because you hate where you are and who you're with doesn't mean you shouldn't celebrate your birthday!"

"Oh." I look between them.

"So, happy birthday!" Vale throws her hands in the air and little sparkly pieces float down on my bed and me.

"What's this?"

"Geric calls it confetti. I guess it's a thing." Vale twists her lips, eyes wide.

"It's weird, right?" I ask because it's really strange. And also, I'm deflecting while I come to terms with what's happening at this moment.

"I agree," Vale says with a nod. "It seems like another mess to clean up, but whatever."

Vale shrugs and turns to Tesha. The redhead places a square, colorful object on her side of the bed. "We had Geric get this-s when the boys were s-stocking Durus," Tesha says. "The wrapping paper and what's ins-side."

"What is inside?" I ask, reaching out to feel the smooth surface of the bright paper.

"We can't tell you that! It's the whole point. Wrapped presents are a birthday tradition outside of Harwell." Vale hops off the bed. A second later, Tesha slides off too, grabbing Yip by the back of his neck.

"Have a shower, or do whatever makes-s you happy, and then meet us-s in the kitchen," Tesha says, tugging Yip off the bed. "Jus-st make sure you open it before you come out."

With that, they file out of my room, shutting the door behind them and leaving me more than a little confused—I mean, they want to celebrate my birthday. I told Vale the date back in the Well before all this craziness started. I was sure it was a trick, but she remembered for all these weeks and planned something. I bite my lip, recalling Laso mentioned Vale's birth date, but I didn't think to remember it.

Before it bothers me too much, I hop out of bed and decide on the shower they suggested. No doubt, after nineteen days in Durus and eighteen years of life, there's no better way to celebrate—outside of being with my family—than starting the day with a marvelous shower. But first, I grab the package and carefully open the end, held closed by a transparent strip that's sticky on one side. I reach inside and pull out the prettiest thing I've ever seen. (And I've seen a lot of beauty since being in the Dark.)

I shower faster than ever before. I dry my hair with as much patience as I can muster, which means it's still damp when I comb it out, then go back to my present—a dress and a pair of shoes.

The dress is light blue and prettier than the color of the sky. On it are images of yellow butterflies and little white daisies—favorites of my mother and me. I slide into it, thinking about how much I miss her and how excited she'd be to see me in these clothes.

It hangs just past my knee with a white and ruffly trim piece around the bottom. The neckline is square, with two inches of the same blue material going over each shoulder, and the sleeves are the same material as the skirt's trim. Three silver daisy buttons are attached to the front. They serve no purpose I can detect except to look pretty.

I slip my feet into the shoes. They have flat, sturdy bottoms and thin white straps across my feet and around the back of my ankle to hold them on. My toes peek out the front but don't slide out of the shoe when I walk. I stand before the mirror, twisting to look at the front, back, and side. I'm there long enough my hair is dry when I finally leave my room.

I'm excited and nervous when I enter the gathering area. They're all there with their attention on me, and I hold up my hand with the birthday paper between my fingers. "I didn't know what to do with this."

Geric takes it from me, wadding it into a ball while the Harwellians gasp. "We can burn it later," he says, like he didn't just commit a crime.

"Happy birthday, Anni," Siman says, stepping up and forcing me into a hug—his black hair rubbing my cheek. "I hope you have a great day." I'm shocked by the moment and simply nod.

"Yeah, what Sir Cuddles said," Evans says with a grimace. "I hope your year doesn't suck too bad and that someone only puts itchy powder into your laundry once." Evans grins. "Preferably me."

I let out a brief laugh. I mean, really, I couldn't hope for more from him. "Thanks, Evans," I say, barely averting from calling him Droll.

"Oh!" he says, walking into the kitchen. "And you don't look horrible in that dress they got you." I look down, running my hands over the material across my stomach, then over the tops of my legs.

"Evans, quit being an idiot. That dress is amazing!" Vale says, laughing and throwing confetti in his direction.

"Oh, Girlie, you love me," Evans parries while Tesha ignores them, bouncing and declaring, "And the shoes-s! I picked the shoes-s."

"You did a magnificent job with the shoes," Vale says, and for a moment, the attention is off of me. They're blathering over who made the better decision—each giving the other credit. With the other boys mulling around the kitchen, Ronen walks over to me. He's said nothing yet, merely inspecting the shoes Tesha picked out. Yip trots behind him, reaching me and pushing into my side.

"Yip, git," Ronen says, and the dog gets a solemn look before loping to the other side of the room. I frown as he goes because it's not like Ronen to chide Yip like that. Ronen's face looks serious, and I expect bad news until he loses the gruff tone he used with his dog and says, "Ye look captivatin', Bethy, 'n tha' dress does amazin' things ta yer blue eyes."

He was staring at my shoes, but when he mentions my eyes, his lock with mine. Ronen's usually not this elaborate with words. I'm accustomed to him just laying things out as truthfully as possible—not using flowery language, flattering statements, or long sentences.

But then I search his face, and I consider something else. Nothing he's said is embellished, frivolous flattery—he's simply conveyed what he thinks and feels at this moment, and I hold my breath as I process the idea.

Ronen continues to watch me, and I'm overwhelmed by the power of his gaze, pulling me into a secret world only he knows. But I'm not moving at all. Indeed, he's coming toward me.

The scruff on his face brushes against my freckled cheek right before his soft lips land in a gentle kiss. Then he straightens and speaks to me like nothing is amiss. As if the world didn't just slip out from under my feet. Like my heart didn't stop, or my hearing go cloudy. He's entirely unaware of my inability to move after losing all feeling in my limbs.

Ronen just watches me with a tilt of his head. Waiting.

"Wha— What did you say?" I choke out.

He grins, his eyes going soft. I frequently waver on this opinion, but today, I'm glad he doesn't wear the lenses. It's nice to see his expressive eyes.

"Said happy birthday, 'n told ye I have a gift fer ye," he says, reaching for my hand and placing a wrapped package on my open palm. This one's long and slender. "Dunna have ta open it now." He shakes his head, and I swear his cheeks, which I can barely see behind the bristle, have gone pink.

"What if I want to?"

Ronen takes a small step back and clears his throat. "Up ta ye."

"Then, I'll open it now." I'm not careful with the paper this time, after seeing what Geric did with it. I tear into the package and remove the objects inside. At first, I'm not sure what to make of it until Ronen helps me.

He holds the little square vase, carved from wood, while I place three flowers into the container—daisies of varying heights and created from the same wood.

"You made this?" I ask, inspecting it closely, careful not to damage the delicate objects. The grain shows in each petal, leaf, and stem, and the center of each flower is textured with tiny bumps.

"Aye."

"I told your ma daisies are my favorite. Did she tell you?"

"Overheard."

"Did you tell the others?" I ask, running my hand over the dress. Ronen nods. "It's beautiful work. I've never seen anything like it," I say, looking over the simple beauty of my favorite flower represented in wood.

"Look closer," he says, nodding toward his artwork and reaching in to help me find what he wants me to see. Observing his gigantic hands, I'm surprised he could handle the delicate wood pieces without breaking them apart. But that's the thing about Ronen—he's large but also largely gentle.

Ronen twists one flower around, and on the backside is something particular to me. It's a little cricket. He's perfectly carved his interpretation of the tiny insect clinging to a daisy petal.

"Well, I guess there's no question it's mine," I say, a blush rising on my cheek.

"Aye. 'Tis yers." It's a strange sensation to own things—not just borrow or use them—especially such beautiful things.

"Come down here so I can hug you," I say, and Ronen's mouth twitches before he bends. I put my arm around his neck, and easy as lifting an apple from the ground, I'm off my feet. I giggle and squeeze his neck. Then I surprise us both by placing a kiss on his bristly cheek. I pull back to find Ronen staring at me. I stare back. His mouth parts and I think he'll say something, but he slowly lowers me back to the floor while we watch each other, my neck getting increasingly warmer.

"I'm next!" Tesha declares, but my mind's in a stupor. Next for what? Getting picked up by Ronen? But then she's rushing to the bunkroom, returning with another wrapped gift.

"Here, I'll take that," she says, retrieving Ronen's daisies from my hands. "Wow, Ronen. These are as-stounding! I can't believe the detail." Then she's back to me. "Go on. Open it. I'm too exc-cited!"

I rip into the paper and discover a sweater. Tesha knits, and it's obvious she made this for me, but the craftsmanship is better than anything produced by the people back in Harwell. All that aside, the most unusual thing is it's blue.

"The boys-s are helping me experiment with dyes-s," she says without me even commenting on the color. "We all knew you'd look great in blue, but I hoped it would turn out lighter." She shrugs.

"Uh, thanks," I say, having trouble with my words. This is too much. I don't know how to handle an outpouring of kindness. Mean is so much easier to manage and respond to. "That was nice of you," I finish in what I hope isn't a weak comment, but I can't gauge the appropriate level of enthusiasm, and I refuse to bounce around like Tesha. (She reminds me of Yip.) However, I try to act sincerely. I mean, I am sincere. It was nice of Tesha, even though I don't like her.

And now my cheeks flush because I'm embarrassed. Evans pops over just as the situation gets awkward. "By the way, I didn't get you a gift. Figured it was better that way, is all."

I release the breath I was holding, feeling sure of myself now that Evans is here to argue with me. "I'm sure you're right." I can only imagine what type of gift Evans would get me. Dog poop in a can comes to mind. And then, I consider using the idea for *his* birthday.

"Whatever! He helped with the nex-xt part." Tesha shoves Evans's shoulder.

"Hey, Songbird. Quit making me look good. Cuddles will get jealous."

"All of you! Be quiet and get Annibeth over here," Vale calls from the kitchen.

"I'll put your s-stuff in your room," Tesha says, relieving me of the sweater, and taking it, along with the daisy vase, to my room. Evans leads the way with unrestrained swagger, and Ronen walks with me into the kitchen, standing beside me as they present the next surprise.

"I made you a birthday cake! For morning meal!" Vale laughs, turning the cake nervously so I can see every side. "Well, morning meal for us. Technically, the time outside

Durus is closer to night meal, but whatever."

"Birthday cake?" It's a strange shape with a slanted top and a mostly circular body.

"It's another Tenebris thing," Vale says with a grin.

"It's an *everywhere* thing," Geric interjects, smiling at Vale. It's the first time I've seen him smile—his front teeth overlapping slightly. It only lasts a moment before the expression drops, and he looks at me slightly guilty. That Geric declares it an everywhere thing when it's not a Harwell thing remains unspoken.

"Whatever," Vale continues, waving a hand at him. "It's like bread on the inside, but soft and sweet, and the outside is frosting. It's the best. I hope I did it right."

I touch the outside, and the frosting indents, so there's a little divot where my finger was. "It looks interesting."

"It's Ma's recipe. She was in Labrum visiting family during part of our time there, and I helped her make it once. Of course, mine isn't as pretty as hers, but I hope it tastes great! And we all should thank Geric for packing the ingredients back from Tenebris." There's a round of thank yous, but the words don't come from my mouth. I'm too focused on something else.

"From Tenebris?" I ask, taken aback. Geric left for Tenebris days before we arrived in Durus. "You were planning this way back then?"

"Of course," Vale says, making it sound like I'm daft to think otherwise.

I take in the faces surrounding my cake, waiting for my response. I was positive my birthday would suck. I prepared myself to be in a horrible and hostile mood. And now look at what they've done!

Tears well in my eyes.

Weak, weak tears!

And I can't hide them.

"Annibeth?" Vale asks, leaning forward, the counter separating us. "What's wrong?"

I shake my head, needing her to stay back. "I don't understand this. Any of this. Why did you do it?" I sound angry, practically yelling the question.

Vale's concerned expression turns into a smile. She leans on the counter and takes my hand, even though she knows I don't want to be touched. She grips me tight and doesn't let go. "Because we *want* to like you. We *want* to be your friend. Someday we'll leave this place, and who knows where we'll end up, but I'd like to have a relationship with my sister. One where we're not on the cusp of a fight or retaliation. We all want that with you to some degree."

"Yeah! No more itchy powder," Evans chimes in, pointing at me while he laughs good-naturedly.

I bite my lip because what they're asking is impossible. "I don't know how to do that," I say flatly.

"Yes. You do," she encourages.

"No, Vale. I'm telling you. *I really don't.* I don't have friends like that. All this nice stuff makes me uncomfortable. It makes me mad. I'm ready to rip your heads off for baking me a cake."

"She's gonna hate what's coming next," Evans mumbles, but Vale shushes him, then says, "It's not as hard as you think. We'll help."

"Ha! How are you going to help?" I tug my hand, but Vale won't let go. I tense, preparing for what's sure to be an uninspiring and didactic lecture.

"Well, for starters, we'll be nice to you. And then, you can try to be nice back. See? Easy."

"That's not helpful," I draw out. "I, uh, already do that." Yeah. They have no idea how much I'm holding back.

"No problem," Vale says quickly. "If you act mean, we'll tell you you're a bitch, and that's your cue to stop." She smiles.

"You'll get the hang of it."

"That's absurd!" I shake my hand in her iron grip. I can't tell if she's serious or trying to get back at me. "If you call me a bitch, I'll call you one back. Or worse."

"Lesson one, Annibeth," Evans says, leaning in. "That comment was borderline bitchy."

"Gah! I can't deal with you." I shove him with my shoulder because I don't have my hand. He chuckles, and I scowl.

"But I'll let your indiscretion slide on one condition," Evans continues. "We stop all the warm, fuzzy stuff and get the real party started. Because I'm hungry, and I want to get to the food part of this shindig."

Evans winks at me, and my scowl softens because I'm grateful. To Evans! How strange is that? His expression is playful, but he understands where my head is. I'm uncomfortable. I feel pressured. And I'm incapable of doing what Vale asks. I needed her to stop talking—to stop being warm and fuzzy, as he put it—and he made it happen. Again, I'm struck by how much we're alike. In some twisted way, the Droll gets me.

"I like the idea of food," I say, giving him a nod. He replies with a tight grin. Then I'm caught off guard because Vale drops my hand, and the group disperses from the kitchen. "Hey! I thought we were eating the cake," I say, and some of them shake their heads.

"Not yet," Vale says. "It's time for your last surprise."

CHAPTER TWENTY-TWO

T he last surprise may be my favorite. As much as I love the dress, shoes, sweater, cake, and delicate daisies, this is something I need. Desperately. They have everything packed up, and we're going outside.

For an evening picnic!

I'm so excited to get out of Durus, I can barely stand it. I delay the others long enough to change my clothes—not wanting to get my dress or shoes dirty—slipping on my old stuff I don't care about and pulling my white-blond hair into a tail with a ribbon. Back in the gathering room, the Coastals are wearing their longcoats, hiding their weapons underneath—all except Geric's bow, which is over his shoulder.

"It's cold out with the sun low in the sky," Vale says, scrutinizing my outfit. She wears the clothes she got from the Dark—fitted pants and an oilskin jacket—but Siman and Tesha are in their Harwellian clothes, wearing Tesha's sweaters.

"It's easier to stay hidden in the evening shadows," Evans adds.

"You should wear the s-sweater I made you," Tesha says. "It's not raining, s-so it should keep you warm enough."

"I didn't want to get it dirty."

Tesha waves her hand. "It'll wash."

I get the sweater, and before we leave the safety of Durus, Geric gives instructions. Namely, the Dark brothers scouted an area ideal for our outing, but we need to be quiet getting there. Even upon reaching our destination, we need to keep from being noticed. For that reason, Yip is staying behind, and my heart breaks for him.

Taking my first step outdoors, I want to shout for joy. I

don't, of course, but I smile, feeling the mild heat of the sun on my face. It's still strange that the combination of sunlight and circlight makes it possible to see everything around me for hundreds of feet, but I can't see the sun itself—only feel its warmth. At first, I thought lamlight was like the long-burning oil we have back in Harwell, but I was wrong. Any flame or electric light must work in tandem with the lamlight to give sight in the Dark.

The lamlight is quite impressive, and sometimes I enjoy testing it, covering the circlight to get an idea of my vision without it. It's not a precise test since Siman and Vale are wearing theirs. But Tesha, like usual, doesn't wear one. It strikes me again how strange it is that she relies on our circlights, and I wonder if maybe they don't have enough to go around.

Geric leads the way, with Ronen in the rear. I can't hear the big guy back there and turn around a few times to make sure he's still with us. It's a short walk, under five minutes, and we reach an area of trees and tall grass. Vale throws down blankets near one of the larger trees while Tesha puts the food basket in the middle and Evans gingerly places the cake next to it. The boys each sit on a corner, with the girls in between.

Tesha opens the basket and starts passing around the food. They have meat on bread, freshly made by Vale, and yam slices that are crunchy and sweet. And they have apples which I always enjoy.

We've yet to say a word. We can talk if we're quiet, but we all seem content to enjoy the silence. And it seems safer just to be still and eat. Besides, we're enjoying the fresh air and sunlight, and what could we ever say to match that?

It doesn't take long for me to consume what I'm given. With only a few yam slices left, I turn and lay on my back to enjoy the trees, wind, and birds. It won't be long before we return, probably after having some cake.

I close my eyes to relish the moment when Ronen breaks our silence. "Ye hear tha'?" he whispers deeply, so it's almost a breath.

Both my eyes fly open.

"Northwest," Geric says.

"Aye."

"Hide the circlights," Geric commands. "Could be cogs."

Vale grabs the thick cloth bag that held our apples, and we unhook our circlights, dropping them inside. It's not enough to tuck them under our shirts because, if it's cogs, they'll see even the faintest glow. Sealing them in the bag, we're thrown into darkness. I try to envision my companions surrounding me, but it's difficult. I try to stay calm, but this isn't me testing the lamlight. This is scary, and I hate being without my sight.

"I don't see anything," Vale remarks. I want to lash out —because, of course, we can't see without the lamlight— but then her comment registers. Just like the cogs could see our circlights, we'd be able to see theirs. And what she says is correct—there isn't even a glimmer of light in this vast darkness.

"What's your voodoo say?" Evans asks, and we all know who the question is for, but Siman doesn't make a sound, meaning his answer is non-verbal because Evans responds, "Well, then, maybe it's nothing."

It's too bad Siman's intuition isn't more honed—something he could use like a weapon rather than waiting for it to surface, like a fish in the river. The initial fear of a possible threat wanes, and I start to relax until Geric says, "But maybe it's not." And then I'm instantly back on alert.

The Dark brothers have mentioned other dangers in the area besides cogs. I've heard them discussed enough times to memorize them, and I tick through the possibilities in my head.

There's Spratt's group, who've been accommodating but should never be fully trusted, and other cliff dwellers, who would be interested in our supply cache and even the clothes on our backs. (Though likely not the Harwellian cotton I'm wearing.) But it's assumed none would act unless provoked. Then there are the squatters, taking up temporary residence, and opportunists, who are just passing through. All of them are light blind, like the brothers, and most, according to Geric, we should approach cautiously but not be out-right afraid of.

None of those possibilities are comforting, though I'd rather face any of them than have Endrack's cogs find us.

"Bells. Tha's na good," Ronen rumbles, and his tone sends a chill through me. I'm not sure what's caught his attention, but his brothers are in agreement and fly into action.

"Evans! Tesha!" Geric commands in a forced whisper. "Take them and hide in the woods. Ronen and I will let you know when it's safe."

Everything happens fast, and I barely have time to grasp the situation before I'm taken by the arm and whisked away.

"We didn't scout the woods," Evans says. "I don't know the best direction to go, but hopefully, we'll find a suitable spot and keep hidden until this is resolved."

"Do you think we're in danger?" Vale asks.

Evans doesn't answer right away. The ground changes under my feet, and I'd guess we've hit the underbrush. "Can't know for sure, but experience tells me we should take it seriously."

"I'm sorry I put us in this situation," I blurt out the rare apology.

"Why's it your fault?" Evans asks.

"Because of my birthday," I explain, tripping over a stick but righting myself with Evans's grip on my arm.

It appears we're all acting contrary because Evans is

uncommonly kind when he says, "We were all feeling cagey, and your birthday was a good excuse. Besides, the girls were excited to give you something. Though, in retrospect, we should have been hardasses and kept everyone inside."

How disappointing that he's probably right. Our pleasant outing could well be considered the most reckless thing we've done since leaving Harwell. Evans turns us sharply to the right, and I stub my toe. A second later, he releases me, and I drop to the ground.

"Sorry, Bethy!" he calls amid sounds of hurried movement. Briefly, I'm shocked by Evans calling me by Ronen's nickname, but it passes with a startled scream from Tesha.

"Your hand!" she yells, smacking my shoulder. It's a moment before I understand her meaning and throw my hand into the air for her to take.

"How did you find me?" I ask, shocked by how easily she located me. All the while, I hear grunts and bangs—metal hitting metal. I duck away from the noise.

"I'm a beacon," Tesha says, pulling me to my feet. A second later, her momentum increases, and with another scream, she flies backward. With my hand in hers, I go with her, and we tumble to the ground, rolling over each other as we travel down a steep slope before coming to a stop.

"Tesha!" Siman yells, sounding like he's above us.

"Evans! There's a s-second one!" Tesha whistles as she pushes onto her feet. "Siman! Duck!" I make out the sound of her feet digging into the ground as she makes her way back up to the others, leaving me down here. Alone.

I don't know what's happening, but Tesha clearly does. I don't know what a beacon is, but I'd guess it has something to do with having the ability to see inside the Dark. Unfortunately, I don't have that skill, and for now, I'm alone while Tesha helps the others up top. I pull myself up, leaning back against the hillside, as much for support as to disappear into my surroundings.

The fighting sounds are muffled down here. I can barely make them out and don't hear any voices either. I want to help defend our group, but without my sight, I'm useless. If I were with Vale, I'd demand she retrieve my circlight from the apple bag. It's clear our pursuers aren't cogs, and I'm hopeless without my sight. At least Siman and Vale had some practice living without theirs.

My musing stops when I hear a noise to my left. Footsteps.

"Shh," I hear in a low voice. Evans. He taps my shoulder and takes my hand, pulling me up and grabbing my arm so we can move silently.

I'm entirely disoriented at this point. I knew the direction from Durus to our picnic area and was aware of the woods from where we picnicked. But since then, everything's gotten turned around. It feels like we're going toward the clearing, but the endless brush underfoot makes me think otherwise.

I want to ask, but Evans's instruction to stay quiet is still in my ears. I don't want to do anything stupid and give away our location. I assume we're circling to a meeting point known by the others, possibly at the edge of the buildings where the trees begin.

Our pace quickens, and I have a hard time keeping up. "Hurry!" Evans barks, his voice low and angry. It's no secret we don't like one another, but you'd think he'd be a tad more compassionate considering the circumstances. After all, I'm running at breakneck speed in the Dark without knowing how my feet will land.

We pull up and take cover behind a tree. My hands dig into the bark while I cling to it, trying to catch my breath. "Where are we? Where are the others?" I ask between puffs. Evans grunts, and I don't know if that's a sign to stay quiet or an answer—as in, he doesn't know.

It's not lost on me that he's taking on Ronen's traits—

grunting and calling me Bethy. He still has my arm, and from his grip alone, I sense he's eager to move, waiting for me to breathe regularly again or scouting the path ahead. Maybe both. A minute passes, and I'm feeling rested. I'm about to tell him we can go when something happens.

The wind shifts, whipping up out of nowhere and gusting straight at us. It's then I catch something unusual in the air. We've been doing our laundry in the machine in Durus for long enough I've memorized the scent of our soap. We all smell like it. It's unavoidable.

But the person holding my arm doesn't smell floral. No, I detect an odor similar to the machine that takes the horses to the surface—a bit of dirt and chemical. I stiffen as fear courses through my body, and then he laughs while his grip increases on my arm.

"Finally figured it out, did ya?" he asks in a mocking tone that sets me off.

I straighten my back. "Bit surprised it took me this long," I reply with a disgusted sniff, then I yank my arm back as hard as I can, hoping to break the connection. My captor follows the motion, leaning into me and laughing more.

"Too bad you figured me out. Was much easier when I dragged you along compliant."

He yanks me forward, and my shoulder pops. Nothing permanent, but it hurts nonetheless. "Ouch!" I scream.

"Quiet," he says, dragging me behind him. I try digging my feet in, but he pulls me along, my feet sliding across the ground. He may be strong, but I'm stubborn. And loud.

"Evans! Ronen!" I yell, getting as much volume as possible, making my throat hurt.

"Stop!" he says, yanking me forward. And then he does something I don't expect—he slaps my face. The sting remains long after the action ends, and I'm stunned into silence.

"That's better."

No one's ever slapped me before, but I'm not one to take such action and not respond. I step close to his side and lift my knee, bringing my foot down as hard as possible, right on top of his foot.

"Dammit!" he screams, pushing me back, but I go for him again, lifting my arms and reaching for his face. My unkept nails are in various lengths, and I use their jagged state to my advantage, digging them into the soft surface of the man's skin. The first thing I claw is his face, trailing down his neck.

He swears again and yanks my hand away before whipping me around and locking his arms around my upper body. "You'll regret that," he seethes, his cheek next to mine, the blood creating a slick between us that makes me smile.

Maybe I do like violence.

I continue to struggle, but he has a tight hold on me, and I can't get away, but a plan forms in my mind. I remember the lessons the other border guard gave us on the rooftop of Fifteen, and one comes to mind that fits my situation. I kick with my legs and try to escape. Each time, I slide further down in my captor's arms until I have him exactly where I need him.

He clamps his arms around my chest, keeping my arms at my sides. His chin is above my head, holding me in place. But the best part is that my knees are bent. I need one more thing before I take action.

"Do I know you?" I ask, suddenly going still.

"What?" he asks, probably confused by the question and wondering why I've stopped wiggling.

"Have I met you before?" I rephrase.

"I don't see what th—"

I strike, jumping straight up with all my strength, throwing my head into his chin, and hopefully catching his tongue in the act of speaking. His arms immediately fall away, and I lurch forward, landing on all fours.

"Ahh," he moans, and I think I got him good, but I don't wait around to be sure, scrambling away like Yip on all fours. With no clue where I'm going, I try to keep a straight line. At first, I hear him behind me—groaning, mostly—but not necessarily signs he's following. Soon the increased noise of running water blocks out most other sounds.

I meet up with the water and keep crouched, crawling along the river bank. Though my hands are raw from clambering over rocks and brush, I don't dare stand.

A sound from behind puts me on alert, and I scurry faster to escape it. That's when my foot catches on a branch, and I pitch over, landing on my back in the stream.

The cold water feels like knives piercing my skin, and I almost scream, but through some miracle, I keep the sound inside. My trembling fingers fumble along the shoreline until I find an area where the ground slopes, and I can crawl from the water. I reach dry ground, right next to a bushy plant. The foliage feels thick, and the leaves large, even in the colder months. I pull close to it, eager to hide while dripping dry. I hope I'm hidden behind the plant but could be completely exposed. There's just no way of knowing.

I sit and think, with my arms cocooned around my legs. I don't dare call out for my companions. What if that man, or someone else with him, finds me instead?

It's also possible Evans and the others got taken. Or Geric and Ronen had to do battle with a slew more. What if they didn't make it? The thought makes my head spin, and I feel sick. What if I'm stuck in the Dark forever with no way to see and no one to help me?

I shiver—more from fear than cold. The sun's still in the sky, and I can feel its effect on my wet clothing getting drier. But I also think the angle is lower. Indeed, I feel the passage of time through the loss of the sun, and I'm trapped in my spot for long enough it goes away completely. I'm still damp, though not drenched, and lying on the dirt to glean any remaining heat from the land. I tuck in close and hope it's good enough until help comes. Or until I feel safe enough to find help.

When will that be? There's no light. I don't dare make a noise. I'm cold and getting colder. I'm tired and don't know what to do. It feels like hours have passed, but it could be my impatient nature or fear corrupting my sense of time.

I hear a noise in the black and make myself as small as possible. Is it the man who had me? Or is it one of my people? Or an animal after a meal?

My thoughts wander, and I think about the hundreds of people from Harwell who walked into the Dark on their Departure Day. We put them in here with barely a thought. We were quiet and moody the day of the event, and then two weeks later, we had a meal. That was it.

What a load of crap! This place is terrifying.

How could we expect anyone to enter the Dark unprepared?

But Vale entered the Dark. How did she know what she was doing? Was it always about the brothers or something more? When did it start? And was she ever afraid?

I shiver again and curl into the dirt beneath me while I wonder what happened to my perfect life. I consider this and more until exhaustion, fear, and unanswered questions put me to sleep.

CHAPTER TWENTY-THREE

I'm only half awake when he scoops me up, his massive arms cradling my thin limbs. If he were a normal-sized man, I might've guessed it was any old stranger who'd found me in the Dark, but Ronen's unmistakable. Especially with his trimmed beard brushing my cheek, the faint campfire scent embedded in his black longcoat, and the muffled sound of Yip's feet on the dewy leaves as he trots behind us.

I shiver and lean into Ronen, clinging to him. Finding his wrist in the darkness, I wrap my fingers around as far as they'll go and start to cry.

"Shh, I got ye," he whispers, and his bass tone rumbles through his chest.

"He tricked me, but I got away. I was so scared." My voice cracks on the last word.

"Shh, ye're safe. Yip's a fine tracker 'n had no trouble findin' ye. Wish we'd gotten 'ere sooner ta ease yer fright, but I'll always come fer ye. Dunna doubt it."

"What if Yip's not around?" I ask into his shirt.

"Dunna fret, Bethy. I promised ye'd see yer parents again, 'n tha's only happenin' if ye're safe."

I nod against his neck, wanting to believe him, but the fear is so fresh. All I can do is pull him closer as he takes me back to Durus. But I can't contain my tears. I don't want to be out here, vulnerable and afraid. I don't want to be where I can't see. But more than anything, I don't want Ronen to let go of me. Not ever. They'll have to break my fingers to pry him from me.

Ronen's the strongest person I know. He's more capable than anyone in my acquaintance. And I never feel safer than when he's near. It's been that way from the beginning—back when I would have denied it.

I've always tried to display the confidence and power Ronen naturally shows. I frequently wished I knew his secret so I could mimic it. But right now, I don't want to possess those traits. I want to surround myself with them, using what he already has to make myself feel better.

So often, I would watch him, and he'd think I was discovering areas where I found him wanting, when in fact, it was quite the opposite as I envied his strength and character. Now those initial thoughts have grown into something more profound. Ronen is more than the others. More of everything —stronger, wiser, and kinder. And while he carries me, murmuring comforting words, he confirms something I've been avoiding. I care about him—more than I thought I would and in a different way than I ever imagined. I want to be with him. I don't want him ever to leave my side. And I want equally for Ronen to want to be with me.

But there are obstacles, and accepting them tears me up as nothing ever has before—not Cully's betrayal, not my mother's illness, and not leaving Harwell. Ronen's a dream and a desire I'll never realize.

Because there's Kally—the girl in Tenebris he changed course for—who left her perfumed scent on Ronen's skin, on Yip's fur, and in Ma's home. The girl's embedded in Ronen's life and heart.

But even more than Kally, there's a truth I've been hiding from myself. It was never Ronen who was wanting. It's always been me. I'm the one lacking in too many ways to acknowledge.

And so, my tears increase while Ronen comforts me, never knowing it's not the long night that makes me inconsolable. It's the knowledge I've lost something wonderful before ever having the chance to seize it.

◆ ◆ ◆

We enter Durus, and the girls gather around, talking faster than I can think.

"You found her!"

"Where was-s she?"

"I'm so glad you're safe!"

"I'm so s-sorry I left you. Can you ever forgive me?"

Ronen doesn't even stop. "I'll tell ye everythin'. First, gotta get Bethy warm."

He pushes through my bedroom door, forces Yip to stay outside, and takes the time to turn around and lock the handle. I guess he doesn't trust them to stay outside, though it feels awkward to be locked together after all the thoughts I'm having. I stare at his face, but he's not looking at me. He bends his upper body, releasing my legs and lowering my cold, stiff limbs until my feet touch the floor.

"Careful," he says, waiting until I get my balance. I grab the end of the bed and my dirt-encrusted hands mar the lovely cover. I can stand, though I'm still shivering, and each shuddering wave makes me wonder if my knees will buckle.

Ronen reunites me with the circlight, then disappears into the relief room. I hear the water turn on, and a moment later, he appears. "Water's warmin'. Ye need me ta call Vale ta help ye undress?"

I look down—everything I do feels slow—and my clothes are caked in mud like my hands. I shake my head, taking my first step toward the shower. The thought of warm water taking all this away encourages my feet.

"Bethy." Ronen stops me at the threshold with his hand on my shoulder. "Get warm, but dunna take long. I'm worried, 'n if ye're too long, I'll send someone in."

"Only you," I tell him, then after a moment, I try to go

forward, but his hand holds firm.

"I dunna understand," he says, his brows furrowing and his lips pressed tight, disappearing in his beard.

"If you're concerned, come check. But just you."

"Be-Bethy. I, uh—" Ronen stutters my name and then loses his ability to speak, staring at me as if I've asked him to climb a ladder to walk on the moon.

I rest my small, dirty hand on his large one. "I only want you, Ronen," I say, squeezing his fingers. "If you're worried, talk to me through the door."

"Bethy," he starts, but once again loses his words.

I've made things awkward between us. He's so attentive, and I'm asking things of him that aren't fair. They aren't right. Not with Kally. Not with me being the way I am.

I release his hand, and he lets me go. Stepping into the relief room, I close the door to shut Ronen out, but I don't lock it. I'm in a strange state right now—my mind and body—and Ronen's right to be confused.

I pull off my clothes as fast as I'm able and step into the spray. When my skin's red from heat instead of purple from cold, I get out and wrap in a heavy towel. (I love towels. We desperately need them in Harwell.) Ronen never speaks through the door but doesn't send anyone else either. When I leave the relief room, fresh clothes are on the bed—everything I need, underclothes included. Another of Tesha's sweaters sits on top—this one in multiple shades of blue and gray. I run my hand over the tight goat wool, again noting how soft Tesha's sweaters are. It's more finely woven than any others in Harwell.

I dress quickly, and minutes later, I enter the gathering area, combing my wet hair.

"Ye okay?" Ronen's at my side in seconds—Yip with him. Am I okay? I feel foolishly vulnerable, and I'm exhausted. Still,

I'm clean, so I nod minutely.

"I'll get you some water," Vale says, launching into action.

"Come this way," Ronen says, guiding me toward the couch. He plonks into the corner, putting his long legs out in front of him, then gets me positioned how he thinks is best—with my back to his chest, my head in the crook of his arm, and my legs spread out, taking up the sitting room on the couch. Then he throws a blanket over us, but mostly me. With this setup, my residual chill will be gone in no time. I've never been more grateful for short sticks or Ronen for drawing them.

"Ye're still cold." His hand appears, rubbing my arm down to my elbow. Up and down, he goes in a slow rhythm. Geric and Evans share a look, and I close my eyes when my cheeks burn. This is so wrong, and they know it.

I know it too, but I don't care.

"How long was I out there?" I ask, concentrating on something other than Ronen's hand and the looks his brothers are sending me.

"Two hours," Ronen rumbles.

"Fuzz and Brass were holdin' them off," Evans provides, and my eyes crack open to watch him smacking the side of his shoe while he talks. "But they had a good-sized group to contend with, and a couple got through. That's when I got separated from you. We subdued the threat, thanks mostly to Geric and his bow—"

"Hey," Ronen grumbles, adjusting on the couch.

"Let me finish! *And Ronen's sword*," Evans says, and Ronen nods, relaxing. "Anyway, I went looking for you while the others returned to Durus. I'm the best at tracking but lost your trail at the water, so I knew we needed Yip."

I should thank Evans for trying to find me and Ronen for returning with Yip. Instead, I say, "I missed the rest of my birthday."

"Aye, Bethy," Ronen says low. "Wha' can we do ta make it up ta ye?"

My mind can barely form words, let alone answer what seems like a highly complex question. It takes a minute before a logical answer comes to mind. "I'd like to try some of my cake," I say, remembering Vale's concoction. I glance into the kitchen and find her frozen in place and frowning.

"Yer cake got ruined in the fight."

"Ruined?" I ask, twisting to see Ronen's face. He looks so sad, as if the news has disappointed me beyond the point of recovery.

"Aye. I'm sorry, Bethy."

A spark of humor ignites in my stomach, but for now, I ask, "How'd it happen?"

"I, uh, think Geric threw it," Ronen says, and the spark builds.

"Geric?" I look over at Vale's guy and he grimaces.

"I'm sure he's sorry," Ronen assures me.

"Geric threw my cake?" I grin.

"Aye. Threw it at one o' the men he was fightin'. Right in the lad's face."

The spark ignites, and I lose it, laughter bursting from me. "In the face!" I bellow, tears accompanying my laughter, battling to see which can outdo the other. "Oh, my gosh!" I'm barely able to catch my breath, imagining their serious fight, sword against sword, arrows flying—cunning and strength battling for our safety and survival. And then my cake, flying through the air and landing in the face of Geric's opponent.

My laughter stops for a split second. Just enough for me to get out, "I wonder if he thought it tasted good." And then I can't stop. My face is red, and I feel like I will pass out.

"Are ye a'right?" Ronen asks, rotating me until my feet are on the floor.

"What's wrong with her?" Vale asks, and her concern has me doubling over, and I end up lying sideways on the couch while my stomach convulses with each hard laugh.

"Is-s she in shock?" Tesha asks next, and I roll over on my back, which makes the tears run down the side of my face and into my ears. I shiver, and Ronen leans over me, scowling in dismay, which only makes me laugh more.

"Maybe she's just happy," Evans adds, and I feel all their eyes on me.

"Have you ever seen her this happy?" Vale poses the question to Siman, who's shaking his head, eyes wide.

"Well, there's a first time for everything, Girlie." Evans stands by the couch, looking down like a clinician ready to give the verdict. "We should stuff food in her mouth. She'll either stop laughing and chew or choke on it and die."

"Evans!" Tesha complains while I stare at them, still grinning.

"What?" He throws up his arms. "Don't get mad at me, Songbird. Whatever happens, eat or die, it's ultimately her choice."

In the end, I eat but there's no stuffing required. And I don't consume much. It turns out, I'm more tired than anything, so after a few bites and a long drink of water, I crawl back into my blanket cocoon with Ronen. Getting warm is an excuse to be next to him and draw from his endless strength, so I'll do it while I can.

"Who were they?" I ask, thinking about the attackers I never saw.

The Dark brothers share a look, and Geric shrugs, sitting on the couch and propping his foot on the table. "We're not sure. They were light blind, so you could have kept your circlights," he says, though, in the moment, we couldn't take that chance.

"They had some fighting skill," Geric adds, rubbing the edge of his shoe.

"But not enough," Evans adds with a chuckle, then sobers, clearing his throat.

"Did you kill them?" I ask. Evans doesn't move, while Geric watches me.

"Aye," Ronen says, the confession vibrating through him. "'Twas them er us."

"How many?"

"Eight," Ronen answers while I consider the atmosphere and how taking eight lives barely phases them. But as Ronen said, it was them or us. After all, they didn't come by to share my birthday cake even though they got a taste. (I bite back a smile.)

"Was it just a random attack from a passing group?" I ask.

"If it wasn't random, they tried to make it seem that way," Geric says, and I get the feeling they believe the group was here for us. I absorb his theory and snuggle deeper into Ronen's side, and then I go quiet, preferring to watch and listen.

An hour later, I'm half asleep when Geric's mood turns unusually playful, saying to Evans, "Don't hurt yourself over there, Kid. We know if anyone in this room is going to do something stupid and end up unconscious, it'll be you."

Loving that they're picking on Evans, I chuckle sleepily. "What do you mean?"

"The day I met the brothers, Evans was unconscious," Vale answers. "We snuck into the Clinic, and I treated him."

"And when Malum came for my mother, Evans got knocked out on the Border Guard Trail," Tesha adds.

"Hey! Who is it that ended up with two sprained ankles?" Evans parries. "Oh, that would be you." He points at Tesha, but when his hand drops, the other moves to rub his neck, slightly embarrassed by their ribbing. How strange. And I can't help but add to it.

"Do you injure so easily because you're weak?" I ask, keeping a straight face. "Or do you enjoy vacating the world to dream?"

"Vacating the world," he says with a smirk. "Whenever the shrew is near."

The shrew. Ha!

He means me.

"Evans!" Tesha gasps.

But I'm not bothered. I take the put-down and prepare a volleying return. "I'm happy to help you vacate the world," I tell him. "Vale, would you hand me a cooking pan?"

"Ha. Ha. Lucky you're still in shock from earlier, or I'd have Vale introduce that pan to your backside."

"Evans!" Vale complains.

I giggle. It feels great to argue. "Am I five? You're going to have my sister spank me?" I laugh, and then my smile drops because I just called Vale my sister. It just came out like it wasn't a big deal. Like it was completely normal. I sputter briefly before I recover, clearing my throat and asking, "Why her? You afraid to do it yourself?" But I've lost some of my pomposity.

"Afraid you might like it," Evans says with an exaggerated shiver.

I roll my eyes. I'm still shaken (I called her my sister!), but no one else seems to have noticed, so I focus on the fact I'm having fun with Evans. Yes. It feels excellent to be in my combative element.

"Hey, Shrew, you've been comfortable long enough, all cozied up with Fuzz," Evans complains. "Get over here."

"Evans!" Ronen growls, but I'm already up, my mind pleasantly alert from our banter.

"What for?" I ask, walking toward the Droll, thinking one day I'll have to share with him his well-deserved nickname.

"I need your blood," he says like it's an everyday request, and I almost return to the couch. "We've decided to try everyone's ancestry on the mystery door. It was Sir Cuddles's idea, and I'm up for any of his voodoo."

"It's not voodoo! I just thought it would be good for all of us to check."

Not wanting to seem squeamish, I agree, and the others follow my lead, taking turns getting poked to bleed. But none of us pass the test... whatever the parameters are for the machine.

"No way I'm doing it again," Tesha says emphatically. "You've had me do it twic-ce, and I'm not up for a third time."

"Come on, Songbird. Just to be sure, is all," Evans prods, and she gives in and gets pricked a third time, but still no luck. Then she comes over and drops on the couch next to me, and we watch the boys gathered around the door, trying to decide on the next step to gain entry.

"What about breaking it down? Have Fuzz take a steady run at it?" Evans asks, looking at Ronen, but the big guy shakes his head.

"Too thick," he says. "'Twould break my arm." Then they look at it from all sides, even trying to get above it, but it's entirely made of cement and goes through the ceiling. Their ideas are dwindling, and gaining access appears hopeless.

I've rarely spent more than meal times with the group, and I have to admit, they're entertaining. I've built up a lot of questions and decide now's as good a time as any to ask them.

"Hey, Tesha," I say to get her attention. I can't help but notice she's not the only one who looks at me, though she's the only one that looks relaxed. Vale and Siman are expecting a scathing comment from me. They don't realize I can be civil when there's something I want. "Back in the woods, you told me you're a beacon. I wondered if you'd tell me more about that."

"Oh." Now she looks uncomfortable, glancing at Siman. "Yeah. Well, I can s-see in light bubbles-s and the Dark."

"I figured out that part. I'm wondering *why* you can see in both. And why don't Harwell's leaders know about it."

"It's-s not common, but my father was a beacon too, and I inherited it from him. As for why the leaders-s don't know— that's because it's a s-secret."

She tells me about a journal belonging to her dead relative, Derwood Dale, and how he not only created the Dark but created a counteractant to see in the Dark. Those from Harwell are guaranteed to have light sight because none of our ancestors took the counteractant. The Dark brothers have mixed parentage—both light blind and light sight—so it could have gone either way for them. Tesha's is mixed too, so clearly, ancestry isn't the only factor in determining the gift. But I quickly understand why she keeps it a secret because, in a place called Torquent, they capture and study beacons, trying to recreate the phenomenon.

"But Adlumen doesn't do that?" I ask.

"They don't, but they have their own quirks," Geric says.

"You mentioned on our way to Durus that Lord Endrack will use Adlumen law to his advantage. What does that mean?"

"Keine Endrack is a power-hungry and immoral leader," Evans answers, and his hazel eyes are grave. "As much as we disapprove of Lucan's tactics, there's goodness beneath his blunder. Endrack has none of that. He can act without reproach because the citizens of Adlumen have a deep-seated love of their land and unwavering respect for their laws. You might catch in a look or gesture that an Adlumian doesn't approve of Endrack, but they'd never rise against him. They believe too strongly in their long-standing system."

Evans is speaking my language. I love my job as a reckoner. It compliments my excellent memory, curiosity, and tendency to argue until I prove I'm right or until my adversary concedes. Based on his summary, my mind fills with questions I need answers to, so we can beat Endrack. When his cogs killed our people, burned our trees, and threatened our homes, he made an enemy of me, and I swore vengeance. It's time for me to do as my father said and use my skills to help this group defeat him.

"What details do you have about their laws?"

"Very little, and that's the problem," Geric says. "Some groups use storytelling to keep their culture or remember the past. Adlumians use it to preserve the law. It's over a hundred years old, and the adults teach it to the children, like bedtime stories. But they also revere them, almost religiously, and don't speak of things out in the open."

"What about your ma? She's from Adlumen, right?"

"She is," Geric answers, surprised I know. "But a Coastal adopted her when she was very young. She doesn't know the stories."

"There has to be a way to hear them," I say with a scowl, followed by a yawn. "We could capture someone and force them to tell us."

Ronen chuckles. "Workin' on it, Bethy."

"What else? I'm sure we can figure out an angle if we look at it the right way."

Geric raises an eyebrow, but Ronen shakes his head. "'Tis time fer sleepin' na sleuthin'. Save fixin' the world's problems fer t'morrow."

CHAPTER TWENTY-FOUR

We're in my room. Ronen's in the big comfy chair, reading, and I'm lounging on the big comfy bed with Yip stretched out beside me. I can't help watching him—my protector who's not abandoned his post in the nearly two months since we left Harwell. He glances up and catches me staring, then puts the book down.

"Did you decide who's going?" I ask.

Geric says it's time to check in with Captain Rhed since we've gone too long without information. We're cut off—blind in our little hole—and Ronen's volunteered to make the trip, saying it's his turn.

Panic rose in my chest at his announcement, and it felt like my heart was being strangled. It only calmed when Evans said he would go instead. Vale and Tesha shared a meaningful look while Siman straightened the kitchen, avoiding any involvement or reaction. The Dark brothers then took their conversation to the stables, and the Harwellians were left to guess what was happening.

The brothers raised their voices a few times, and we gleaned snippets of the discussion. Like when Geric said he could check on his legion—a portion of the guard he commands—but Ronen insisted they're in capable hands under Biv's leadership. Geric argued Evans should only go if it were for the right reason. Evans snapped, sure Geric would be glad he'd go for any reason. At that point, Vale came over and dropped a few tidbits in my ear—Evans doesn't always get along with his father, doesn't feel right taking over the guard or having the dagger's responsibility, and feels either of his brothers would do a better job.

The last point is quite obvious. Anyone can see it's

true, though I must concede, it was gutsy of Evans was to acknowledge his limitations. But Evans insisted he should be the one to go, explaining, "Hell, if Annibeth can try making things work with us, surely I can put forth an effort with our dad!"

Huh. Who knew I was such a role model?

After that, the argument ended, the boys dispersed, and none of the Harwellians heard the outcome. I'm sure Vale prefers for Geric not to go. I'd never breathe a word of my opinion, but I want Ronen to stay here. Evans seems a logical choice, and he did volunteer, so I wait with an anxious stomach and calm facade for Ronen to answer my question.

"Decided on waitin'. Cap'n promised an update by the eighth, 'n since the men in the woods werena cogs, we're waitin'."

February eighth. Six days away.

Ronen lifts his book and goes back to reading. It's one I finished last week and thought he might like. It's about a family stranded on an island, getting creative to survive. It reminded me a little of life in Harwell, except, instead of the Dark, water surrounds the book family. It also parallels my days in Durus with its cement walls, or being contained anywhere, really, where constant vigilance is required to maintain one's safety. It's comforting to read how others endure circumstances beyond their control and gives me my own survival ideas. It also makes me think about other things.

"Ronen?" I wait for him to lower the book again before asking, "What do you want out of life?"

"I dunno." He closes the cover and puts the book on the little table beside him. He thinks about my question for a minute and clears his throat before saying, "A good woman ta share quiet, starry nights. A lake home with a dog by my side, 'n lots o' kids ta teach ta fish 'n fight."

"Oh. So, you're not exactly sure," I say with a laugh. He

chuckles. "Well, it sounds like you know *exactly* what you're after."

"Aye." He purses his lips, and his grin disappears. "Sounds like a perfect life ta me. Wha' do ye want, Bethy?"

"Not lots of kids."

"Whye'er not? Ye're beautiful." He rubs his beard. "Be a shame ta deprive youngin's o' yer looks."

Heat rises up my neck. "Uh, I guess I've only ever considered having one." I lick my lips and look down at my lap. "I mean, there's a limit where I'm from. I hadn't thought until now it could be different."

"'Tis somethin' ye should change yer mind on." He drops his big hand on the book, tapping the top with his hairy-knuckled fingers. Is he going to read again?

I rotate until I'm lying on my stomach. Ronen's right across from me, waiting, but I hesitate. I don't know why. I'm not nervous to talk with anyone else, but Ronen makes it difficult sometimes. Maybe it's how he considers my words in silence before answering—my comments feel dissected before I ever receive a response.

Just do it. Say it!

I run my finger along the edge of the bedcovers, then clear my throat. "Ronen?" I look over, and his eyes are on me. Maybe they never left. "Do you think you'll make that life with Kally?"

"Tha' life?" he asks, tilting his head.

"Yeah. The one with the lake, and the dog, and the oodles of kids." I chew on my pink lips, waiting for him to answer.

"With Kally?"

Why does he keep repeating my words?

"Yes," I bark out, then tone it down. "I mean, she's your girlfriend, and I just wondered if you planned to make things permanent with her."

I rest my chin on my fist, my feet waving like the emblem banners in Tenebris while I wait for his answer. Yip adjusts on the bed, dropping his head on my back with a thunk that pushes air through my nose. I'd laugh if I weren't so attuned to what Ronen's answer will be.

"Why ye askin'?"

I shrug—not a natural motion while lying on my stomach. "Just curious."

He leans forward in the chair, resting his elbows on his knees. "Was datin' 'er, but things changed."

"Was?" I lean on my forearms, watching him. "What changed?"

"Kal's a lovely lass, but wasna meant fer me." He clears his throat and clasps his fingers in his lap. "A friend o' mine was showin' interest, 'n I noticed 'er reciprocatin', so I ended it fer us all."

Ended it? My mouth rounds as I process that, then ask, "Were you upset?"

"Nah. 'Twas how I knew 'twas right. Barely stirred my heart ta let 'er go."

Traveling to Durus, I felt bad Ronen had to give the news of Sazanne's death to her sister, but he said he wasn't the one to do it, though he never answered who did. "It was your friend who told Kally what happened to her sister, wasn't it?"

Ronen nods. "Better fer it ta be 'im. He can be there fer the tough times."

I try to find the right words of comfort, but I've never been good at this sort of thing. I'm almost relieved when there's a knock on the door. Ronen seems relieved too because the second Vale pops her head in to announce our night meal is almost ready, he's on his feet, placing the half-finished book back on the shelf.

"Hey," I say to catch Vale's attention before she ducks out, then I twist until I'm sitting on the edge of my bed, Yip staring at me, waiting to see if I'm staying or going. "After night meal, would you have some time to talk?"

"We can talk now if you want," Vale answers, stepping into the room.

"I'll leave ye," Ronen says, going for the door.

"We're having boar," Vale says before he leaves the room, and I wrinkle my nose because I hate boar. "Geric makes it with rosemary, and it's excellent," she adds, reading my expression. Ronen chuckles as he pulls the door shut.

"What was that about?" I ask when he's gone.

"Remember the boar party?" she asks, and I nod. We had an influx of animals wander into Harwell, and we had a big feast to celebrate. "They were the ones who sent them in."

"They did?"

Vale grins. "I escaped from you and Nacole into the Dark where Geric and Evans treated me to a meal, just the three of us. They kept a boar, and I liked the way they prepare it. Ronen's heard about it a time or two."

"So, that's how you got away from us?"

"Yeah. Sorry." Vale giggles, and it strikes me as funny when she apologizes for hiding when I planned to torment her. "Anyway, what did you want to talk about?" (Well, strange enough, she landed on the exact topic.)

I adjust on the bed, sitting on the corner. Yip stirs, sees I'm not leaving, then settles so his back is against me.

"Actually, about you entering the Dark. I saw you do it just the one time when I threatened to tell Cully." And ultimately did just that. There's no point in softening the situation. At the time, I was furious about it and wanted retribution. "But after we left Harwell, I heard things. It seems you often entered the Dark. Some of the others too, like Laso and Siman. I just don't understand. If you can't see in there, what were you doing?"

Vale stares at me hesitantly, and I don't know if she'll answer, but after a minute, she shuts the door and goes to the chair. "I can't believe I'm considering this," she says with a nervous laugh, her hand going to the pendant at her throat and her thumb moving rhythmically across the surface. "Annibeth, can you keep a secret? I mean, something you don't tell even your closest friends and family?"

"I know how to keep secrets."

"I mean it. Lucan and Cully can't know. Nacole can't. Your father and mother too. You only talk about this with me. Can I trust you that much?"

It's a big deal to keep silent where my parents are concerned, but I'll do it for answers. "You can. I'll stay quiet," I assure her.

Still, Vale hesitates. "In telling you this, I'm extending an excessive amount of trust. I'm willing to try because I think maybe we both need this. But after what you did to Gran, it seems incredible even considering it, though I think you've seen enough at this point to know the right side. But you must understand there could be detrimental consequences if it gets out."

There was a time I blamed the Rennicks and Dales for the uncertain changes in Harwell. Cully felt the same—his blame extending to the Coastals. I'm unsure if his mind is changed —it's strange not knowing his opinions after sharing them for so long—but mine has. The horrible events that befell my home are because of Lord Endrack and none else. He's the true enemy, and I need to assure Vale of my conviction. "I have no interest in supporting Endrack. I won't betray your trust."

After another brief silence, Vale leans forward—her black hair fanning over her shoulders—and she finally opens up. "By the lumber trees, a rock protrudes from the Dark. There's a cave inside where the story keepers maintain hundreds of written records. There's other stuff too. Gran went in all the time.

When she walked, she told my father about it, and I learned of its existence sometime later."

"How do you get inside?"

"You enter the Dark on the east side, keeping your hands on the rock. After about twenty feet, there's a slim crack. You shuffle in sideways, and when it opens up, there's an electrical switch for the lights."

"The leaders don't know?" Vale shakes her head. "Why keep it secret from them?"

"Besides the fact the story keepers have been entering the Dark for decades? You know the leaders aren't interested in the past. Until recently, you weren't either."

I nod, unable to dispute her claim. "Do you think there's information in there about Adlumen laws?"

"I found nothing about Adlumen law, but I found nothing about recorded music either, so—" She trails off with a huff.

"Recorded music?"

Vale waves her hand. "Yeah, it's a personal quest. Not important. Anyway, I'm hopeful the others will find something since I've spent less time in the repository than my father or Tesha."

The repository! I instantly recognize the name. Geric mentioned it when he arrived in Durus, saying Laso was there, working toward their end goal. Which means the end goal has to do with the records.

"Tesha?" I ask, curious about her involvement since she's not a story keeper.

"Yeah. She helped research after I had to leave Harwell and before Malum took her mother."

There's no point tackling that subject. We were on opposite sides, and it would only bring up bad feelings. "What are you all looking for?"

"We're trying to understand why Lord Endrack wants us

dead. That's why no one can know about the repository. If Endrack discovers it, he'll take it from us. And if we don't figure out his motivation, we can't find a way to change his mind, whether through persuasion or force." I lean in, liking the sound of that. "Gran said to search for governor lore —information about the governor's regalia and a Governor's Oath."

"The paper you brought to the Well listed the regalia," I say, making the connection.

"Yes, and the families they're associated with—Harwell, Dorian, and Dirby. But we found nothing about an oath. We think maybe our families were stewards for the regalia and worked for the governor." Vale shrugs. "Tesha also found a paper in the repository with strange words similar to what's engraved on our regalia, but we don't understand what it means."

"Sounds like it just led to more questions," I say with a frown. "I hate that."

"Yeah." Vale smiles and nods, her hand returning to the necklace at her throat.

"Say, what is that thing?" I ask, finally feeling like I can bring it up after all this time.

"Oh, this?" She holds it up so I can see, but it doesn't improve the look of it. "Gran gave me the regalia when I was young, and I lost it. My father made this one to make me feel better. I have a habit of rubbing it when I'm nervous or thinking. It's pretty worn, but I can't make myself take it off." She bites her lip, considering me before adding, "The chain is braided cloth from... one of our mother's old shirts."

"Oh." I don't know what else to say. While I appreciate it has sentimental value to her, it's still very ugly, but since I don't outright tell her that, I consider it a win for me.

She lets go, and it drops to her chest. "It feels strange to talk to you like this. I hope I don't regret it later because I really don't trust you yet."

After a pause, I nod and admit, "I can understand that."

And then we're both laughing. We have a long way to go before either of us feels content with the other, but she's revealed a lot to me today, so I guess I'll be the first to build confidence by keeping my promise.

"You know, our grandmother told me once that we're a lot alike."

"Really?" That seems odd. And it's strange for Vale to call Ennette Rennick *ours*.

"I didn't see it then, but besides struggling with trust, we both have difficulty telling people how we feel. Well, unless it's to express our dissatisfaction." She chuckles, biting her lip. "When Geric told me he loved me, I didn't say it back for a long time. It was stupid of me. We're in the middle of a conflict, and I've heard Captain Rhed comment more than once that there are no guarantees in life. Who knows what will happen tomorrow?"

Vale closes her eyes and takes in a long breath. "Wow, this is harder than I thought it would be." She shakes her head before her green eyes lock on me again. "Look, Annibeth, I like you. I never thought I would. In fact, I thought I'd walk into the Dark when I was old, or get tossed from Dead Men Tower, wishing you ill. But truly, I like you. I can't say I love you, or that you're like family, because it's totally not that, but I want you to know I have some regard for you." Vale pushes up from the chair. "Anyway. If something happened to either of us, and I never saw you again, I'd want you to know."

Huh. That was rather melodramatic, but my sister doesn't hate me. In fact, she likes me.

Who knew?

I have no response and Vale leaves. I stay in my room, feeling perplexed, while I gather my thoughts. (The most persistent of which is that my sister likes me.) It's ten minutes before Ronen pops in to ask, "Ye comin'?"

"Yes," I say but don't move.

Ronen steps in, shutting the door. "Wha's goin' on?"

"Just thinking." I pause, and the big guy waits for me to continue. "You heard about the injury that led to my father's limp," I say, and Ronen nods. "When I was little, I was fooling around on the back balcony and almost went down the stairs. He caught me, kept me from falling, and aggravated it in the process. He was in bed for weeks recovering." I reach over and find Yip's head, rubbing the soft fur between his ears. "My birth mother left Harwell to save her family. She gave me up to ensure I was safe. She provided a good life for me, but that doesn't mean my parents haven't sacrificed for me. They protect me constantly—not in one grand gesture, but in little ways, day after day."

"Ye dunna have ta keep some close 'n some far. Ye can care 'bout all of 'em."

All of them. *Both of my families.*

I let the advice linger, not responding.

"Open up yer world, Bethy. If ye dunna try, ye'll miss yer opportunities fer joy 'cause the world has more joy ta be had than sadness."

CHAPTER TWENTY-FIVE

February eighth comes and goes with no one representing Captain Rhed appearing in the area, though the Dark brothers don't see any cogs either. They're vocal about their unhappiness and unsure of how to proceed, but ignorance, in their opinion, doesn't foster success.

By the time the tenth arrives, their patience has expired. They're determined to take action and talk for hours around the gathering room table. After expressing the same ideas and concerns multiple times, I lose interest and retreat to my room. Eventually, the voices outside dwindle and the conversation breaks up.

I've just finished a book, and while perusing the shelf for a new one, I discover something. It's not like me to gather the group, but there's nothing else I can do. I open my bedroom door and immediately hear Tesha's whining voice. "I'm out of yarn," she moans. "What am I s-supposed to do now?" She holds up her empty needles as evidence of her plight.

As much as she grates on me, I imagine I'd feel the same if my books were gone. Without my main entertainment in Durus, I'm sure I'd cry. I might even be capable of matching the rate at which Tesha can produce tears—that's how much the books have become my sanity.

The brothers are no longer at the table. Evans is rummaging in the kitchen, Geric's on the couch with Vale (yeah, his posture's perfectly straight even when relaxing), and I'm unsure where Ronen is. There's tension in the air —which I'd usually feed off, but I refrain—and I wonder if part of Tesha's rant was her attempt to get them focused on something else. Fortunately, I have a more practical purpose for accomplishing the same thing.

"You all have a minute?" I ask, and Geric and the girls turn toward me. Evans snaps a cupboard door closed before looking up. "Where's Ronen?" I ask but Siman—who looks at me curiously, wondering why I'm gathering the group—opens his mouth too late.

"I'm here," the big guy says, strolling from the stables and stopping in the middle of the room. The brothers are evenly spaced throughout the large gathering area—a blatant sign of their current discord.

"I found something in one of the books," I announce, lifting the folded paper that fell from the pages of *Treasure Island*.

"Wha' is it, Bethy?" Ronen asks, stepping forward and taking it from me. He opens the page and reads quietly while I explain it to the others.

"The security doors can operate on voice command. Apparently, Malum didn't want to prick his finger every time he entered a room, and he didn't want to carry a key. His voice alone could open things, or anyone else if they know the master word."

"A master word!" Evans jumps from behind the counter, striding to the locked door. "Do you know what it is?"

I step closer so I'm next to Evans. "Winsome Warrior," I say, and the door clicks as the red light turns green.

"Brilliant!" Evans exclaims, giving my shoulder a happy shove before turning the handle. With a slight push, the door drifts open. "Winsome Warrior," he repeats with a laugh.

"Either Malum had a sense of humor, or he was vain," I say with a grin.

"He was-sn't very funny," Tesha says, appearing at my side and staring into the dark room. Evans switches on the light, and we all file in. It's a tight space, but we fit, though I don't understand any of what I see inside. The wall is full of black boxes with shiny glass fronts. Standing before them, I see a strange reflection of myself. They're not accurate, like the mirror, but blurry and dark.

"What are these?" Vale asks.

"My specialty!" Evans grins and drops onto one of two chairs before he pokes and prods different parts and pieces within the room.

"Geric," Ronen says from the corner. Geric moves to join him, with Vale and me tagging along. The object of Ronen's interest is apparent—a ladder extends through the ceiling and into a vertical cement shaft. Craning my neck, I can't make out much—it's too dark inside—but I'd bet it goes pretty far.

"What is it?"

"Secondary escape. Maybe a lookout," Ronen says with a shrug.

"Can we go see?" I've already stepped forward, placing my hands on the rungs. I can't help the feeling I get, reminiscing of Harwell and my time rung climbing with Nacole. I miss her and our times together.

"We probably should," Geric answers, and I immediately start climbing.

"I'll stay here," Vale's voice echoes from below.

I'm practiced at climbing, especially in low light, which is good since the circlight does very little in this small, dark space. It's not difficult—just a matter of securing your handholds before lifting your feet. My hands do most of the work, and my feet bear the weight.

It's longer than I imagined, and I keep my head slightly tucked so I don't hit anything I can't see. I get into a rhythm, and before I know it—with my arms and legs burning—I've reached the top. It's a flat ceiling, but I feel around and identify a latch. With a quick turn, it's undone, and I push it upward. It lets in enough light to see the brothers. Geric's right behind me, and Ronen's a little farther behind. We may have found one thing I'm more proficient at than Big Scruff. Of course, I have much less weight to take up with me. I climb out of the shaft and stand to the side, waiting on the others.

"Seems like you've done something like this before," Geric says, catching his breath as he enters the enclosed platform at the top of the ladder.

"Back home. I estimate we just climbed twelve floors." My assumption's based on how long it took, but I think I'm reasonably accurate.

Ronen pushes through the hole in the floor. "Bells, tha' 'twas a climb," he says, dropping the hatch. It's more comfortable, knowing none of us will trip and fall into the hundred-plus-foot shaft, plummeting to our death. Yes, a definite comfort.

I step to the edge and peer over the side of the safety wall. I can see the things in my immediate area, like the top of our building, but anything beyond fifty feet, the Dark shrouds entirely.

"Is it nighttime?" I ask.

"Evening. And cloudy," Geric answers.

"What can you see?"

"The entire city."

I look again. "Yeah, not so much." I chuckle, but the boys are too distracted by the view. It's rather boring up here, and I'm ready to head back down without them when something catches my eye. "Hey, what's that?"

"Where?" Geric asks, looking where I'm pointing at things flickering in and out of view. One moment I see a road, then it's gone. Then there's a storefront before it disappears.

"Someone's down there, and they have lamlight."

"I can't see them. They're staying hidden," Geric says with a scowl.

I see the shape of tree limbs, and then the light is gone. "Behind that tree." I point.

"I see the tree but nothing else."

"More than one area is flickering. I think there are two separate lamlight sources down there." I'm trying to discover if there's another, but I detect nothing. "They've stopped now. They aren't moving anymore."

A second later, Ronen jumps in front of me and drags me to the opposite side of the viewing platform. "What are you doing?" I complain.

"If ye can see their lights, they can see yers."

I gasp. "You think that's why they stopped?"

Ronen unhooks my circlight and tucks it into his thick sweater. Thrown into complete darkness, he guides me back to where Geric's still standing. I can see the lamlights even better now. "They're moving again. Continuing south."

"At least they're traveling away from us," Geric comments. "We should go back down and see if Evans has had any luck."

But I don't go anywhere until the circlight is back around my neck, though I stay away from the platform's edge. Again, I go first, and five minutes later, we're back in the little room, but it looks different from when we left. "What is all this?" I ask, slowly walking away from the ladder as I stare at the sight in front of me.

"Come look at this," Vale says, calling me over. The black boxes are glowing, and there's movement inside. "Malum has cameras all over in the Cliffs to watch people in the area."

Cameras. I've only heard the word a couple of times in my life. What a strange phenomenon. "There are sixteen views," she adds, and sure enough, there are sixteen of them, but I can only see movement in two. "Evans and Tesha can see things on all the screens, but Siman and I can only see them on these two." Vale points, and I can see evidence of the lamlight on the same two screens.

"We saw them up top," Geric says, stepping up behind Evans and giving a detailed description of what we saw, including the unfortunate fact that we think they saw my circlight.

The room is a valuable discovery. The Harwellians don't completely understand the technology, but we accept that it benefits our situation. And the Dark brothers' moods are improved because they're now in agreement—it's best to stay put. We know people with lamlight are searching the area. That can only mean Lord Endrack's cogs. And with that knowledge, we'll stay tucked away underground and wait for them to leave.

"Ye did good, Bethy," Ronen tells me later that night. "Gettin' in tha' room made a big difference."

I'm lying on my bed, wearing the pajamas the big guy carried me away in on the day we left Harwell. I'm reading a book to escape and not in the mood to socialize with the group. Ronen's only been here a few minutes, lounging in his chair with Yip at his feet.

"Ye okay?" he asks when I don't respond.

"Yeah," I say and lower my book. Ronen tilts his head as if he knows there's more. "I'm nervous about the people we saw. But mostly, I miss my family."

"Aye." Ronen presses his lips together until they disappear in his bristly beard. "The Dark is drainin' fer those from the light, tho' we all feel a bit o' sadness. I miss Ma somethin' terrible. She's a hugger 'n goin' too long without 'er arms feels wrong."

I grin and let the book close. Dropping it to the bed with a bounce, I snuggle back into the pillows. (I love pillows.) Staring at the ceiling, I think about Ronen's ma. She's a wonderful woman, and I can believe she's a great hugger. I've been in Ronen's arms a few times—not necessarily in a hug—but each time, I felt surrounded completely. If she taught him a portion of her skills, she'd be a top-notch hugger.

"Ma makes campin' potatoes," he says with a smile, and I try to figure out where he's going with this. "Wraps 'em ta drop in the fire. They're divine."

"Potatoes? Divine?" I snicker. Whoever heard of such a thing? Getting excited over potatoes?

"Ye can laugh, but I'm tellin' ye, they warm a person inside 'n out." I shake my head, but he continues, "Come, Cricket. Ye must have somethin' like tha' back home."

Cricket. Ronen's calling me out for being difficult. I bite back a grin that slowly disappears when I think about my life in Harwell. "Well," I pause, trying to ignore deep thoughts about my parents while simultaneously identifying a heartwarming moment involving food and family. "Okay, I've got one. My mother can do amazing things with rabbit. My father would ask Parrell Vacca—she's Sector Leader of Agriculture and Livestock—to skip our rotation until the next rabbit showed up."

"Ye dunna address yer people like the others."

"What do you mean?"

"Ye dunna call 'em Collins wife 'n Wendes husband. Ye say their names."

"That's how people talk in sector housing." I shrug, picking the skin on the edge of my nail. "The Collins wife is Sera. The Wendes husband is Den. That's what the Clarcs and my parents call them."

I've satisfied Ronen's curiosity, and he nods in understanding, but my thoughts haven't left my mother—her flitting around our cooking hearth, timing each step to prepare a perfect rabbit meal. She's fun that way, and it makes me smile. But then, a sad thought takes its place. She's not been the same since the tiredness came over her. And then another painful thought piles on top of the first one. "She's not really my mother," I say, burying my cheek in a pillow. "Learning that has opened a space inside of me, and I feel hollow as if she were taken away."

"Dunna think it, Bethy, 'cause nothin's gone from ye. Ye're separation's makin' ye feel hollow, but ye'll fill up when ye see 'er. Ye'll feel full again."

I nod, thinking over his advice. At first, I resisted, but the reality is I have two families. A mother and father who did a marvelous, yet flawed, job of raising me. Another father who feels cheated out of knowing me, another mother who is dead, and a sister willing to try if I will.

"When this is o'er, I'll snare ye a rabbit, 'n yer ma can prepare a proper dinner." He chuckles.

"You'll join us?" I keep my head down, afraid he'll see I want him there to eat rabbit with my family.

"Aye. Ma'll make 'er campin' potatoes."

"Okay," I say, hearing the aloof tone in my response. It's how I normally speak, but I suddenly don't like the sound of it. Not with Ronen. "That's good," I add, scooting up on the bed, so I'm not lying down, but never losing contact with his eyes.

Ronen smiles. His full lips spread between the thick hair of his beard. The ease and sincerity draw something from deep within me, and I smile back at him—broad and unguarded. His eyes widen, and his smile diminishes before he clears his throat. He speaks softly, his warm tone carrying across the room. "Ye've got an army in tha' smile, Bethy. Ye could slay a man just by showin' it ta 'im."

My eyes widen, and along with it, my smile disappears.

"Ahh, such concern for my life. I thank ye." Ronen chuckles.

"Tho', I'll tell ye a secret. I have a shield ta protect against the likes o' ye. So, smile all ye like. I can handle it. Just pricks at my heart a bit." He clutches his chest. "I kinda like tha' too."

What is happening? Is Ronen flirting with me?

A second later, he winks and confirms it's true.

My mouth slowly opens. My thoughts are scrambled, like my mother's eggs—she cooks really good eggs too. Maybe I should mention them to douse the sudden and uncomfortable silence, but Ronen pushes to his feet before talk of poultry commences.

"Seem ta have scared yer army away, so I'll leave ye ta sleep." He takes a few steps, and Yip moves too, jumping up and finding a place at the bottom of the bed to settle near my feet. Ronen shakes his head, grinning as he watches his animal. "Dog's an unlucky soul. Dinna even need yer smile ta get bewitched."

Ronen leaves the comment hanging in the air and goes to the door, leaving me speechless. I glance at my batch of wooden daisies, just able to see the edge of the cricket. I ruminate on the bug until Yip disturbs the moment. He mustn't like his spot and moves to be closer to me. He nuzzles my shoulder and then my cheek. I giggle before he curls in tight by my side, knowing his job well. I grab his fur and pull him against me, breathing in the earthy scent of his fur mixed with his natural dog smell.

I glance up, and Ronen's still watching from the doorway. "'Night, Bethy," he says, but pauses for a minute, watching us, before finally ducking away and leaving me to sleep.

Quickly, I discover it's not enough to have Yip lying next to me with thoughts and memories of my family making my heart ache. I need more from him tonight and scoot down to use his chest as a pillow. My ear rests over his beating heart, and my head lifts with each breath. It takes a minute, but Yip relaxes, accepting the position, and that's good because it's where I intend to stay for the rest of the night.

There are many difficult things about being in the Dark, but I've found wonderful things too. For one, I've learned to love this dog. And I have powerful feelings about someone else as well.

CHAPTER TWENTY-SIX

A few days later, I wake to an awful realization. It's Love You Day—the day when the people of my community express their love for each other. The problem is the two people I love most are in Harwell. The other problem is...

Well...

"I love you, S-Siman," Tesha says, and I want to gag. Siman chuckles, showing off the dimple in his left cheek, and he pulls her in for a hug—his red lips pressing against her freckled skin. Again, I want to gag. I roll my eyes, and Ronen catches it, then bites down on the grin hiding in his beard.

"I love—" Vale starts, but Geric raises his hand.

"*Please*," her man pleads. "Don't do this."

Thank you, Geric.

"What?" Vale asks, throwing up her shoulders. "I was just going to tell you I love it when you make my morning meal."

"Uh-huh." Geric shakes his head but doesn't look up. He's counting his arrows. I swear he does this every day, and I wonder if he thinks one of them will walk off. He keeps track of them like twelve wayward children who might disappear at any moment to make mischief.

"If you can stop pawing each other long enough, I have something important to say," Vale announces, looking at her two best friends.

"I don't know, Tesha, can we stop?" Siman asks, and Tesha giggles, pushing him away. Then we all gather around the countertop with Ronen hovering silently at my left—I didn't even hear him approach.

"I worked on something last night while everyone was

asleep." Vale leans over, opening the cupboard beneath her. "It's sort of for Love You Day, but mostly to make up for the one that got destroyed." She bends over, and when she straightens, a freshly baked cake is in her hands. She sets it on the counter, pushing it away from the edge. "Tah-dah!" she says, with her hands in the air.

"Yummy!" Evans leans over, finger poised to swipe the side.

"Stop!" Vale pushes him back.

"Yeah," I agree with a smile. "Don't let the Droll near it."

"Droll?" Evans asks, squinting his left eye.

"Yes. The Shrew has given you a nickname," I reply.

"Doesn't droll mean boring?"

I grin and shake my head. "Oh, no. It means you're a provider of foolish amusement."

"Are you serious?" His squint smooths out, and the corner of his mouth turns up. "That's... sorta cool."

"Gah! Evans, it means you're a buffoon," I argue, shaking my head. How does he not get that it's an insult?

"Eh. Under the right circumstances, it's a compliment. I like it," he returns with a happy smile, then turns to Vale. "Can we eat now, Girlie? The Droll's hungry."

He likes it! I can't even insult Evans properly. I grimace, deciding I'll need to try harder.

Evans leans over again to inspect the food, and Vale pushes him back. "You have to look at it first," she insists, staring at her creation, turning it a couple of inches every few seconds. Each new side looks precisely like the other. "It's better than the last one, don't ya think?" She bends down, eye level. "See how flat the top is? And the frosting is flawless."

I nod, agreeing the cake looks perfect—not a bump or divot to be found.

"Eh," Evans says with a disinterested shrug. "Doesn't

matter what it looks like, so much as how it tastes." He barely finishes his sentence before he mars the surface, stabbing a fork down the side and coming away with a large scoop.

Evans stuffs it into his mouth as Vale whimpers, "Look! Just look at what you did!"

"Had to be done," he mumbles around a mouthful of cake, then grins—his teeth outlined in frosting. "You're right, it's perfect," he says, spitting out a large piece of cake with the statement, then swallowing the rest.

"Gross," Vale says, curling her upper lip and pulling her cake away from him. The look on her face stops me in my tracks, and the tone of her voice echoes in my ears. I bite my lip, overcome, because she looks and sounds *exactly* like me. I glance at the others, expecting a reaction, but they're unchanged—it didn't even register with them.

"Clean that up," Vale orders, pointing at Evans while I focus on cake instead of the phenomenon of Vale Rennick feeling more like family than I ever expected. "Everyone else, get a plate, and I'll cut." She grins at me, and I grin back. If there's anything forced in my expression, she ignores it.

Evans does as he's told and cleans up his mess, bending at the waist and sticking his lips to the counter. He encompasses the stray square of cake and sucks it into his mouth, licking the counter to get the remnants of frosting.

"Evans! Ugh! Go—" Vale pauses, flustered to the point her words fail her. Throwing her arms in all directions, she finally gets out, "Sit on the couch or something! Just get out of my kitchen."

"*Your* kitchen?" Evans asks, leaning toward Vale.

"Shut it," Geric growls, and with a chuckle, Evans slinks away. I glance up at Ronen, who's watching me with a calm smile, and I wonder how much of my reaction he saw. I return my focus to the cake but soon feel awkward standing here, so I follow Evans to the couch, though we sit on opposite ends.

I've barely gotten comfortable when Siman appears with thumbs in pockets. He considers me a moment before sitting between Evans and me, though closer to me, so we're almost touching. "Hey," he says, sitting on the edge of the couch and glancing over his shoulder at me.

"Hey," I return, and the air between us gets uncomfortable when silence takes over. I'm unsure what's happening, but he seems hesitant. Evans inspects his shoes while the others stay around the food so no one's paying attention to us.

"Look. I don't know how to say it other than... well, just to say it," Siman begins. I'm trying to guess what he'll say—that I need to be nicer to Tesha is at the top of my list—but his words are unexpected. "Something's going to happen."

"Happen?"

"Yeah. You've heard mention of the impressions I get, and I have a very strong one... about you."

Well. That has my attention. I straighten and scoot forward to join the conversation officially. "What about me?"

His squinting black eyes, framed by his pale face, look especially serious as he answers, "You're the one who can fix this."

"Fix... what?"

"The danger we're facing from Endrack. You're the one who can solve it."

"Oh. Is that all? I'll get right on it." I flop into a slouched position on the couch, knowing that's the stupidest advice I've ever heard. *Siman thinks I'm going to fix things with Endrack?* When it comes to Adlumen, I know nothing. I'm the least effective person for resolving our issues.

Besides, Siman's worthless gift couldn't foretell I'd get kidnapped in the Dark and spend hours shivering alone in the woods. Instead of being saved, I get charged with changing our fate. Great fortune.

Or misfortune, rather, because what he's predicting is impossible.

"I realize what I'm saying is difficult to understand or even believe. Often, I don't figure things out in advance, but I know to trust what I feel because the promptings are never wrong."

He looks so sure, but I'm not convinced. "Well, what do you want me to do, Siman? Head into the Dark with a circlight and a knife and take out the cogs?" My voice raises, and the others look over, though I don't think they process my words.

Siman has the audacity to smile but keeps his voice low when he answers, "No. I want you to watch and listen. Sometimes opportunities are of our own making. It's up to you to turn a situation into what you want it to be." How can I take him seriously when he sounds just like Ronen's ma—a woman who claims no prevision? Siman finishes his advice with, "Act when it feels right, and do what you can to prepare."

"*Prepare*," I snort, imagining scenes of me with a knife moving without sound through the trees. But I'm no Ronen. "What do the others think about this?"

"They think nothing because I haven't told them. And I'm not going to." My eyes widen in surprise. Since when does he keep quiet about this stuff? "You shouldn't either. Keep this between us. It will make them tense, and instead of allowing you to focus, they'll pester you with questions."

Well, that's the first thing he's said I agreed with—they'd be relentless.

Siman goes quiet, and it's not long before Tesha appears. "Want s-some?" she asks, holding plates with slices of cake, one aimed at me.

"Sure," I say and take the offered food. Siman scoots closer to Evans, and the Droll greets him with one of his many nicknames—I'm pretty sure he says Lucky Charm, which is one I haven't heard before. The next thing I know, Tesha's taken the spot next to me.

I open my mouth and let the cake be my reason not to start a conversation, taking a bite and mumbling my appreciation. The flavor on my active tongue is also a reason to ignore what Siman told me. Tesha takes a few bites, and I decide she eats like she talks—small and timid. It's better if I don't watch her because it irritates me.

"I'm really s-sorry Nacole's s-sad," Tesha says in a whisper. Her voice trembles, but I concentrate on the cake because I'm not ready to hear this. "I never dreamed Siman could want to be with me."

Yeah. I wouldn't have dreamed it either. Evans is watching us, probably listening too, waiting for me to say something objectionable. He'll set me straight—likely call me a bitch as he promised.

I lick the frosting from my lips to stall, and it still takes a few attempts to gather my thoughts before saying, "I presumed you wanted Melton."

She tilts her frizzy head. "Did he tell you that?" I nod and take another bite. "Melton tells false s-stories," Tesha says in a very un-Tesha-like way—no hesitation, no cowering, and no wincing as if she's a disappointment for having an opinion. She owns the statement, and for the first time, I can respect something about her. I even agree with her—she's not telling me anything I don't know about Melton. Still, I'm confused by their situation.

"You seemed to like his attention when I saw you together."

Cully holding court on Fifteen seems like another life. It's been four months, but it feels longer. I miss the simplicity of that time, but there's something to be said about the Dark's complexity. I feel involved in important things and more excited about life in general.

"He was-s affectionate the firs-st day and then got mean. Things-s with Siman aren't that way. I'd do anything for Siman."

Anything. Very true, considering she killed her own father to preserve Siman's life. Sure, it wasn't her intention—and Captain Malum was by no means innocent and provoked his death—but she did it nonetheless.

"What I had briefly with Melton was-sn't real," Tesha adds.

Real. It's an unusual word to categorize a relationship. I can't help but ponder its opposite—fake. And I wonder if that's how all failed relationships turn out—an unreal situation you look back on with apathy. Is that what Siman thinks of his relationship with Nacole? I slowly take another bite of cake. Is that what I think of my time with Cully?

"I hope you'll forgive him," Tesha says, looking across the room at Siman. They've moved to the counter, and her boyfriend is messing with Evans, trying to push cake in his face, though I bet Evans started it. Tesha giggles, watching them, then gets serious again. "He mis-ses you."

I can tell that's hard for Tesha to understand—Siman missing me—and I can't blame her perspective. I won't defend myself, but I give her something for her effort. "You can tell him we're good. I'm over it."

Her eyes widen, and her mouth opens, revealing her gap-toothed smile. "Really?"

I'll never understand his choice, but I'm done thinking about it. "Yes," I say, returning to my cake, hoping she's not going to gush. I've seen her do it often, and I can't handle it. I'll react badly.

Luckily, she stays quiet, though I feel bad she's deprived Evans the joy of presenting me multiple awards for bitchiness.

◆ ◆ ◆

Finishing my cake, I go to my room, glad to be alone again. Memories invade my head—previous Love You Days I shared with Cully while largely ignoring my parents. It seems a waste since my connection to him is severed while I'm desperate to see my family.

I remember our flashy actions and public kisses. It was such a show—something I did for the benefit of others but never for me. Not even for Cully. At least, not in any genuine sense. I wonder if his public displays were for the same reasons. After all, we were rarely affectionate in private. He'd call me pet names he knew bothered me, and I was constantly pushing him away, demanding he leave me alone. The only time I wanted him around was to ensure everyone knew he was mine. It wasn't a sincere relationship by any standard. That word pops into my mind again—*fake*—and I close my eyes at the sting of it. It's no wonder Cully approached Vale. I would have done the same if there had been someone else, anyone else, I was curious about.

There's a knock on the door, and thoughts of Cully fall away as Yip bounces into the room, followed by Ronen.

"Sorry fer interruptin', Bethy," he says, looking prepared to duck out if I say the word.

"No. Come in," I say. I'm sitting in the plush chair, but I vacate it for Ronen because it's his space, even if he's never officially claimed it. I sit on the corner of the bed, and Ronen pushes the door closed. Yip's already on the bed, taking his favorite spot with his head on my lap so I can rub his ears.

"Down, Yip," Ronen says, and after a whimpered complaint, his animal hops to the floor, lying across my feet. Ronen surprises me by ignoring his chair and sitting on the bed, his hip brushing my thigh. "Ye're missin' yer family t'day," he says, watching me closely.

"Yes." I miss them daily, but they've been on my mind more because of the holiday. Maybe it's the same for him with those he cares about.

"Made ye somethin'." My eyes go wide, and I'm smiling. During my time in Durus, I've learned I love receiving gifts, and

I straighten in anticipation. "Dunna get excited. 'Tis not tha' good."

He lifts his hairy arm to reveal an object hidden behind his body (maybe he's got a person or two back there as well), laying a thick scroll of paper on the bed between us. I unroll it, discovering it's not very large—a foot on one side and not quite that on the other.

"You made this," I say because it's immediately obvious. It's different from the rose on Ma's wall in Tenebris, but also similar.

"Aye."

Sketched on the paper is an outdoor scene—a memory from our time in Durus. "It's my birthday," I say, taking in the details. The trees and grass. The buildings in the distance. Our group huddled on blankets enjoying the day. It's incredible all the things I experience by looking at it. Things he didn't capture in the drawing—like the sun on my face or the smell of the food.

"Dinna have a frame ner way ta color it," he says as if those things are flaws, harming the result.

"It's perfect."

"Coulda drawn us better. 'Tis hard so small," Ronen says, pointing out the tiny figures I can easily make out. He seems incapable of appreciating the wonderful creation he's made.

"I like it how it is," I say firmly. "It's exactly how I remember."

Ronen leans back, finally looking somewhat relaxed, though his brow furrows. "I'm hopin' 'tis na a bad memory."

I shake my head. "It was a crazy day, for sure, but not this part."

And then he relaxes fully, and I roll up my sketch, gently laying it on the bed so I don't bend it. Ronen leans forward and stands up. Yip moves, looking eager to join me on the bed again. "Dog," Ronen says, and Yip stays where he is, his tail brushing the floor.

"You're leaving?" I ask, sounding desperate—so very unlike me.

Ronen picks up on it, tilting his head to consider my question. "Can stay longer if ye like," he says, stepping toward the chair, but I grab his hand before he gets away.

"Stay with me," I say, and that's how, a minute later, my drawing's safely on the shelf with the books, and Ronen's on my large bed. I don't let him sit on the edge but make him lie back with pillows propping him up. I'm on the other side with crossed legs, facing him to watch him while we talk.

"I saw the rose you created for your ma. What else do you draw?"

"Lots 'o things," he says, chewing his lip. He's not looking at me but stiffly facing forward. I wish I could get him to unwind —he looks uncomfortable.

"Okay," I say, deciding how best to draw him out. "Do you have a favorite thing you've drawn?"

Ronen glances at me. "A meteor shower," he says, then he looks forward again. Toward the door. Is he that eager to escape?

"What makes a meteor shower your favorite?"

"'Tis when Ma fell in love with my da."

"Really?" I pull a spare pillow under my arm and lean toward him. "Do tell."

Ronen shrugs, watching me get comfortable. Maybe he'll figure out how it's done. "Da took 'er on a date, 'n they watched the sky. Ma says they counted fallin' stars with their kisses."

My heart swells, but it's not the story as much as the look on Ronen's face when he tells it. He's staring, searching for my reaction, but I barely dare move. I can't even draw in air. Ronen often gets sad when he talks about his father—someone he never knew who made his mother happy—but this seems a pleasant topic.

"Ma loves Cap'n Rhed, 'n I'm glad o' it, but she said tha' night with Da was the most romantic o' 'er life." Ronen takes a deep breath and turns his face to the door, and I can finally breathe again.

Something needs to be said, but I'm not sure what, so I ask, "Did it happen on Love You Day?"

"Nah. 'Twas August." Ronen pauses, and his eyes connect with mine. "'Sides, we dunna have Love You Day in Tenebris."

"You don't?"

He shakes his head but keeps our connection, and my stomach feels like warm sludge as he says, "We tell people we love 'em any time we feel like it. Dunna wait fer just one day."

I emerge from my room the next morning. My giant space is too quiet, and I need their noise. And yes, by *their*, I mean my companions in Durus. By some miracle, I've learned to enjoy their company... for periods of time... at my discretion. Increasingly, there are times I'd rather be among them than separate (it's a rather strange twist), so I'm disappointed as I enter an empty kitchen. I step up to the counter, leaning my hip against it, and a second later, Ronen appears from the stables, dressed in his black longcoat.

"Bethy!" he greets brightly, stepping up beside me. He bends at the waist, resting his thick arms on the counter until his head is level with mine. His bearded smile is curved pleasantly, and he tilts his head before asking, "Whatcha doin'?"

I rub the smooth countertop. "It's too quiet in my room," I say, finding his eyes. He's so close I almost lose my nerve to speak honestly—which makes me all the more frustrated and confused about the changes in me—but I dig deep and push out, "I came out to find you."

"Ah." His smile broadens until I see his white teeth, and the expression makes my stomach flutter. It's an odd sensation, and I wonder if I should throw up or enjoy it. "I came in 'ere ta find ye." Ronen moves his hand across the counter until our fingertips touch, and his movements are careful as he slides his palm under mine. The flutter turns into a thunderstorm.

"'Tis quiet up," Ronen says in a deep whisper that curls around me like his fingers curling around my hand, engulfing it in warmth and strength. "Horses are goin' crazy. Yip too. They need ta move," he continues. "There've been no cogs on the screens, so we're takin' 'em fer a run."

Horses. We're talking about horses. And a dog.

In his grip, it takes a moment to process his words. "You're going outside," I say, and besides his hand, something else warms me—a longing to see the sun. The thunderstorm in my belly slows to a light rain, and I feel in command of myself again, so I ask, "Can I go with you?"

"Sorry, sweet Bethy. Better if ye stay."

"Sweet?" I snort, getting stuck on the word more than the fact I don't get to go outside. "I've never been called that in my life. Don't let Evans hear. He'll debate you to the death."

Ronen chuckles. "Ye're right," he says, and I grin while we both think amusingly about Evans's arguing skills. But the lightness dissipates when Ronen's expression turns serious. He lifts my hand to his mouth, placing a soft bristly kiss on the back. My body freezes into position while I watch in anxious anticipation. "I'm right too," he says, never taking his eyes from me as he does it again—another swift brush of his lips on my skin—before concluding, "Ye are sweet, Cricket. Ta me, ye are."

The kiss—so gentle and heartfelt. The contradiction— calling me sweet and Cricket simultaneously. He layers words and actions, infusing acceptance of who I am and what I'm like. Everything about it has me stuck in my head, so when Ronen releases my hand, my mind's so bewildered I neglect to direct my body, and my hand falls to the countertop with a thunk. He either doesn't notice or doesn't acknowledge my stunned status, straightening to leave while I cradle my stinging hand and offer silent gratitude for his ignorance.

"Siman 'n the lasses are keepin' the horses calm up top, but they'll be down soon," he says, back to business. Even the tone of his voice has changed. "I've been ferryin' the animals on tha' clunky lift." He shakes his head while I try to focus on what he's saying. It's not easy until he adds, "'Fraid each shaky trip'll be the last."

"The last? What could happen?"

He rubs his bearded chin. "Could get stuck 'tween 'ere 'n there. Could fall ta the ground."

"You're not serious." I lean forward, gripping the edge of the counter.

"Na really." He shrugs, then smiles as he adds, "But ye ne'er know with Clod 'n me inside togetha."

"Maybe you shouldn't go," I say, approaching him, ready to set my hands on him and keep him down here with me.

"Dunna worry, Bethy," he says, looking down at me while his smile flattens in his tight beard. "'Tis wrong o' me ta tease. We're careful, 'n na coaxin' a bad end."

He's joking. But briefly, I imagine the world without him, and I don't like it. (Not one bit.) He watches me—waiting—and it takes longer than I'd like to recover, but I get it together. And in the spirit of teasing, I lift a brow and say, "I appreciate you letting me know what's going on. I would have freaked out if I'd discovered I was alone in Durus with no idea where you all went. Though, maybe that would be my dream come true— having this place all to myself with no one to pester me or call me unpleasant names."

"No one ta call ye Cricket," he says, leaning in playfully.

"I don't mind the nickname so much," I say, feeling uncommonly shy. "I guess you can stay, but the others need to go."

Ronen chuckles, and I could be wrong, but I swear the edges of his cheeks above his beard have turned pink. He hesitates as if he'll say more about us getting stuck in Durus together, but the moment passes, and his color returns to normal before he says, "See ye in a bit, Bethy."

I follow him to the stables, where he leads Clod into the box. As they go up, the lift makes the grinding sound the brothers keep mentioning with concern. But it continues to move, and they're soon out of sight, and I realize I've never been more upset I wasn't born an animal.

I head into the kitchen, grabbing a snack before returning to my room. I've cut off a slice of Love You cake (aka my replacement birthday cake) and am walking through the gathering room when I hear banging in the main hallway. I stop in my tracks and spin around, but instead of going in the direction of the noise, I walk back to the stables.

"Ronen?" I call out, but the room's empty—no surprise since he's on the surface with everyone else, but I wanted to confirm the box is still up top. Returning to the kitchen, I put my cake on the counter. The pounding hasn't stopped, so I make my way down the long walkway. By the time I reach the end, it's gone silent.

"Hello?" I say by the door, positive someone's on the other side, but I get no reply. With the lift not working to their expectations, they could be stuck out there. I reach for the knob, considering the situation. I'm sure they didn't take a key, and there's no vocal password set for the main door. But wouldn't Tesha just use her hand? I shake my head. Of course not. They don't have a screwdriver to remove the sign. Of that, I'm sure.

And while I stand here debating the situation, they're out there, trying to get back inside.

Twisting the knob, the door clicks, and I pull it open—just a bit. I'm surprised when there's no face on the other side to greet me. At least, none I can see through the little crack I've made. I open the door wider and confirm the space is empty.

They're probably regrouping to decide how to signal me since I didn't get here quick enough to open the door. I let out a small snort. I'm sure they think I'm holed up in my room with a book—the door closed, unable to hear their ruckus. They accuse me of it often enough—tell me I'm *hermitting*, which isn't even a word.

"Ronen?" I say, and the word grows, echoing up the stairwell. "Vale?" Again, the name gets repeated as if on a wave.

Nothing.

I hum as I consider my options. I look at the stairs once more before shutting and locking the door to Durus. I run to the lift and note it's still at ground level. Looking at the levers, I try a few buttons, but nothing happens, making me even more sure they're stuck topside.

I jog back through the kitchen, grab a quick bite of cake as I pass, and pluck a key for the main door from the wall. I tuck it in my pants and head outside. The Dark brothers have been watching the area, and Ronen said it's quiet today. I feel confident I can meet up with them with very little fuss. Since it will be a quick trip, I don't bother getting my sweater or longcoat.

Since our arrival, I've rarely left Durus, but I know if I take the stairs and keep to the south alley, I'll have a lot of cover. I can stay hidden and go straight to where they're holding the horses.

It's a good plan that seems even better when the stairs are perfectly quiet and the alley is predictably vacant. I speed alongside the towering buildings, but when I turn the corner, all certainty of my strategy disappears, as I hear, "Hello there."

I jerk to a stop, blurting out, "Spratt!" while I take in his too-small head and too-small nose. He's also cut his hair since I last saw him. I clutch my throat, catching my breath, as I declare, "You startled me."

"My apologies for surprising you," he says, performing a slight bow like entertainers on the Common stage after a performance. "I'm equally surprised to discover your lovely face outshines the memory I kept of you. How strange." He tilts his head. "But without fail, young woman, you never seem to be where or with whom you belong." I'm unsure how to respond to the observation, but there's no need, for Spratt twists to his left, addressing two men I didn't notice until now.

Two men wearing circlights.

Two cogs.

"Gentlemen," Spratt says with a grin. "This is who you're looking for."

CHAPTER TWENTY-SEVEN

Their hands are on me, dragging me down the alley. Away from the horses. Away from Durus. Away from Ronen.

The bigger man's thick arms are under my pits, holding me securely against him—one is bent, so his hand covers my mouth. My arms stick straight out in front of me while the second man ties my wrists, tightening the bands until I cry out, but the sound doesn't carry beyond the hand.

Spratt walks in front of us with a measured gait and a pleasant smile. After all, it's payday for him—whatever payment means for a man like him. They carry me through abandoned city streets, keeping close to the buildings. I recognize nothing until we reach the main road, and I catch sight of the empty plinth.

Due west! Durus is still within reach if I could get away.

I've never let up on my struggle, but I kick even more, thrashing in my captor's arms. The result is more hands on me and tying my feet together—then my knees—until the only movement I'm capable of is that of a worm.

But I'm not the worm in this scenario. (There's a first time for everything.) The contemptible one here is Spratt—he's Worm Number One. And the others can line up alphabetically to get their worm numbers.

After I'm incapacitated, they move faster, and we soon reach the edge of the trees. I'm trying to be brave. I'm trying to remember any small thing I've learned that could help because no one gets anything over on me. I'm a rock. I'm a force. I won't be pushed around.

No, I won't be pushed around, but when they stand me on

my two feet, tied at the knees and ankles, I wobble. My muscles burn with the need for action, making me weaker. I shake, trying to keep my balance, and Spratt watches with a grin, hoping I'll fall.

"Damn, girl. Get it together," says the man who carried me from the alley, putting two hands on my waist to keep me standing. "You're a frail little thing, aren't you?"

My spine stiffens. "Frail?" I shriek, realizing he's no longer covering my mouth. "I've never been accused as such in my entire life. I daresay, if you'd untie me, I could take you."

He looks me over. He has a short beard, plump lips, and close-together eyes, appearing cross-eyed while observing me so closely. "Tempting. But I'll keep you wrapped up." The other man and Spratt chuckle at the man's conclusion. They're distracted and don't notice movement in the distance—a recognizable shape.

"Yip!" I scream, and the dog turns his head toward me. I'm stunned, watching Yip's happy and somewhat dopey demeanor transform. He crouches, bares his teeth around a low growl, and launches like one of Geric's arrows.

The man holding me lurches backward, contemplating the dog's charge. He shoves me into the arms of another, commanding, "Take her, Dennie!"

"Yip!" I yell as the dog gets nearer, and new hands pull me away. Ronen's never far from his dog, and hope surges in my chest. But then I catch a shiny glint of metal—Yip's target holds a knife, prepared to defend against the sharp, snarly teeth intent on him.

"No! Don't hurt him!" I yank forward suddenly, and Dennie loses his hold on me, but I'm in no condition to act, tied up the way I am. As Yip reaches the cog, I drop straight to the ground, landing on my side—the key to Durus digging into my hip.

The key!

Oh, no! They can't get the key.

Dennie's arm encircles my waist, lifting me from the ground. My feet twist awkwardly, and I'm unable to stand. With my head aimed down, I see the shiny key in the dirt.

"Stand up!" he demands with a shake, pushing the breath from me.

"I can't!" I wheeze out, my hair hanging in tangles around my face. My left foot is flat while the right is angled and can't take my weight, the top of my foot facing the ground. Dennie throws another arm around me and lifts, righting my feet and setting me back down. My foot lands on top of the key, and I twist my toe into the soft dirt, pushing it down. He releases my waist and grabs my arms, sliding me backward. I keep pressure on the ground, dragging the fine dirt and gravel underfoot to cover the key, all but one tiny corner.

"Hell's beast, can we get out of here?" the man with the knife asks, walking toward us while cleaning his blade with a piece of cloth. He throws the material to the ground, stained with dirt and blood.

Yip's blood.

No. No! Not Ronen's dog. He's part of Ronen's dream.

I bite my lip, unable to hold in a sob for my friend—the first friend I made after being forced to go to Durus. My gaze, finding a crack between my messy hair, discovers Spratt kicking Yip with his toe. The beautiful ball of multi-colored fur doesn't even stir. My furry friend doesn't make a sound.

Oh, Yip.

Then he's blocked from my view as his killer approaches, opening his mouth to say something I refuse to hear. "You bastard!" I screech, my throat burning. I lunge from Dennie, throwing myself at the other man with my hands poised to claw his face. To take his blood. I want it. I want it for Yip.

He drops the knife and grabs my elbows, yanking me

closer. My fingers flex, searching for skin.

"Bastard? Well, that's what you think of me now," he says with a dark laugh. "But I'll get your opinion again in two weeks. By then, you may prefer me over the others."

"Endrack," I bite out.

"Yes. You'll prefer me over him too," he says slowly.

Endrack is responsible for all of this. Endrack's the reason I'm separated from my parents, who need me. Endrack's the reason we've hidden away for months. Endrack's why Yip's blood paints the ground. Endrack will pay. I'll ruin him for all he's done.

But he's not here now—it's only these men. My fingers contort to find whatever they can—an arm, a chest. But I'm immobilized and find nothing in my restricted reach to strike. Nothing to heal my heart that breaks for Yip. Nothing to reunite with Ronen. Nothing to liberate me.

I go limp, hoping they'll relax their hold on me, but it doesn't work. Then Dennie places something over my mouth, and I register the sweet smell briefly before crumpling forward, unconscious.

◆ ◆ ◆

"She's awake."

They're talking about me, though the statement's not entirely accurate. Sure, my eyes blinked open for a moment —long enough to see the ground moving beneath me—but I quickly closed them, nearly going under again. I'd hardly call my present state alert.

I don't need my eyes to know I'm lying across the back of a horse, my stomach digging into the saddle. My head aches from dangling in the air, bobbing to the horse's beat, and my fingers are asleep, trapped between my body and the horse. I turn my head with a groan, and everything spins. It seems inevitable I'll pitch off the horse and land on my neck, so I'm surprised when it doesn't happen.

"Let's stop and untie her," I hear in a voice I recognize too well—the voice of a murderer. Immediately, I make plans to inflict injury upon him, but all my extremities are numb, having been tied haphazardly to the horse itself with a rope crisscrossed over my backside to keep me on the animal.

They get me off the horse, and the blood in my body re-situates, leaving me lightheaded and queasy, along with persistent grogginess. I'm in no condition to fight, even with words. They cut the ropes at my knees and ankles, leaving the ones around my wrists. I have no energy to argue. Besides, I'm barely getting the feeling back into my fingers. Right now, it's just painful tingling.

I look around, trying to decide where we are and quickly determine we're no longer in the Cliffs. The flat surface we rode in on is nowhere to be seen, and instead of big buildings in my circlight's vicinity, it's dry grass and dirt.

"Saeva, you're riding with her."

"Sure thing, Hersh," Saeva says, and I take note of Yip's killer's name. Hersh seems to be the one in charge of this disreputable gang. I log the two crimes against him, putting him on my list of enemies for which I require retribution.

Dennie puts me on the horse, tying my hands to the horn, and Saeva comes forward. She's a pretty woman, probably a few years older than me. She's spry with an athletic haircut, ready and willing to rumble with any of them, but it's the glint in her eye that has me unnerved. I sense she's not all she appears.

She pulls herself up behind me and leans in. "Hello," she whispers into my ear.

"Hi," I return. Hersh taps his horse, and we're moving. They look different from the Coastals, dressed in jackets like Vale wears, not longcoats. There are four of them—Hersh and

Dennie were with Spratt. Now Spratt's gone, and they've joined Saeva and another guy.

Four captors. Ronen could easily take them.

Where is Ronen?

"People ever tell you you're pretty?" Saeva asks, and I don't know how to answer. Her question seems like a trick, so I stay quiet. It's not long before she prods me in the back a little too hard. "Well?" she presses.

"Yes," I say because what's the point of lying?

"We caught ourselves a beauty, though no one cares what you look like, only that we got you." A second later, I feel a slight tug on the top of my head and hear a quiet ping. I look down at Saeva's outstretched hand and discover a strand of my hair in her fingers. "Hmm. It's a pretty color."

And then she does it again.

"Ouch! What the hell?" I turn sideways and find her grinning.

"Quiet down, pretty girl." *Ping!* She pulls another one. I feel every spot where she's liberated a hair—each an individual, stinging ache—but with my hands tied to the horn, I can't soothe the areas. Anger stirs in my belly and bristles in my spine.

"No! I won't be quiet." I elbow her in the stomach, but my movement is limited, and she chuckles.

What's this girl's problem? I could see something off in her eyes, but this is more than I expected. The girl's a freak!

"Shh," she whispers. "Hersh will gag you to keep you quiet. Though I don't mind if you talk, so long as you keep it low."

Ping!

"That hurts. Please! Just stop." I'm complaining, but I've done as she asked and kept my voice low. I hate compliance (hate it!), but I don't see a way around it. I need her to stop.

"It does hurt, doesn't it?" She yanks another. "But look how pretty." She opens her hand, and half a dozen long strands of my hair are in her palm. Then she pulls another.

"Stop it!" I belt out, rearing back, my head connecting with her shoulder.

"Like I didn't see that coming," Saeva says, then hollers, "Hersh! I think we'll need that gag." She yanks again—this time is harder than the rest—and I'm sure she took more than one strand.

Hersh makes no move to stop or apply a gag, but he will if I put up any resistance. Then I'll be forced to suffer through her antics in silence. So, I decide to behave as if I'm already under those conditions—maintain my silence without the gag.

Ping!

I press my lips together, biting back my reaction and ignoring the sting of my scalp. I refuse to say a word. Saeva thrives off my responses, and maybe, if I stay quiet, she'll get bored and end her game.

"Ah, what a good girl," Saeva coos. She snuggles into my back, wraps her arms around me, and takes my tied hands in hers. "Lord Endrack wants to drain your blood," she whispers eagerly into my ear. "Right in the center of Harwell, where everyone can see." Saeva licks her lips and swallows. "I'm a good soldier and want to help him. Can you imagine how much better his show will be if you arrive bald?"

I gasp as she yanks another hair.

Saeva chuckles lightly behind me while a tear rolls down my cheek and hits my lip. *Tears!* I've always kept them at bay. I've never let them conquer me. Yet, here they are to defeat me.

And to this, I'm resigned—they're the first of many I'll shed under Saeva's hands.

CHAPTER TWENTY-EIGHT

I reflect on my perfect life back in Harwell, pondering what made it ideal. The answers I come up with are pathetic—the list I create is shallow.

Harwell was easy. That's the first thing I determine. The ease of my life made it seem perfect. Then there's the love of my parents—I had it, and their steadfast affection was all the tenderness I required. Last, I had power over the citizens, my boyfriend, and even Lucan at times.

But then danger drove me from Harwell, disrupting the perfection—ease, love, and power—and destroying everything I enjoyed about that life. I blamed the Dark brothers. I blamed the Rennick family. I blamed Endrack and his cogs. Anyone who had a part in my fate got a piece of my hatred.

Suddenly, things were difficult. My outlook was bleak, even when my new companions urged me to discover my place among them. And then, I spent time alone in the Dark next to a stream, and it felt like the worst kind of trial to endure.

I was a fool.

About all of it.

Saeva sits across from me. I'm miserably grateful for the distance, but it won't last. We'll be back on the horses soon, and she'll start another round of torment. She smiles at me with a thick clump of my hair in her hands—pulled from my head one strand at a time. She ties the end with a ribbon and licks the length to make it smooth. I squirm and look away.

"Beauty," she says, waiting for me to put my attention back on her. If I don't, she'll take it out on me later, so I slowly return my eyes to her face. She's done licking now, and she's braiding it. I know what happens next. She'll finish the braid, tie off the end, and put it on her head, tying it into her hair. Mine's longer, so it will hang past the edge of her tawny-colored locks, where it will reside along with the other four already swinging there.

I don't know if she does it on purpose, but each braid marks a day—five in all we've been gone from Durus. Five days I've spent with the cogs from Adlumen.

Five days with Saeva, who I believe is insane.

They took my circlight, but I can still see because they each wear one. However, theirs look different from mine, crafted after Malum collected the lamlight canisters from the Scientist's Box.

Is this what Siman envisioned when impressed by the course of my future? Is this the circumstance he believed would position me to save our lives? That I'd be at the mercy of an unhinged person and her fellow cogs who aren't concerned by her actions. A group whose end goal is to deliver me to Endrack for execution—a topic Saeva won't go a half day without mentioning.

No, after my days with the cogs, I can say with surety that what Siman believed was wrong. I can't save myself, so how could I ever save us all?

"Time to sleep?" Saeva asks, drawing my attention. The question's for Hersh, but she watches me—a reminder of the late hours we spend together, just she and I. The time when all I want is undisturbed sleep, but Saeva denies me rest, administering pain and reveling in it.

The first night, they kept my wrists tied during the night, but Saeva attached her own length of rope to my hands. "To keep her from running," she told Hersh, but she used the excuse for her purposes. Every time I'd go under, she'd pull—not a casual tug, but a yank, jerking me forward and jarring my shoulders. Then she'd grin over the flickering fire. Eventually, I kept my eyes open, staring at her until she finally fell asleep. But she woke in the night to do it again.

The next evening, I expected more of the same, but instead, she tied the long rope to one of the horses. It stretched my arms above my head, and every time the horse moved, I felt it. Until my arms were so numb I could barely feel a thing.

On the third night, they took off the ropes. "You'll die if you run. Not anyone near enough to save you," Hersh surmised with a shrug. But it wasn't good enough for Saeva. She tied the dinner pans to my feet. "You move an inch, and I'll hear it," she said. Then she left camp and was gone for an hour. The skin on my wrists was raw—red from friction—and I was grateful to have the ropes gone. Grateful to know I wouldn't be strained by a horse or yanked awake in the night. I felt almost relaxed.

Until Saeva returned.

"Not an inch," she warned, then curled over in her bed.

I fell asleep quicker and deeper than at any other time in my entire life. I barely registered the sound of pans clanging together when I rolled in my sleep, but I heard Saeva whisper. "Beauty. Beauty." My eyes flew open, and I found her right above me. "You moved," she said, dipping her fingers into a cup while I blinked the sleep away. A second later, she placed a squiggly worm across the bridge of my nose. Screaming, I threw it away and flew up from my bed, drawing my knees to my chest while the pans interrupted the quiet night.

"Hell's beast! What's going on?" Hersh yelled, flipping in his bed and laying an accusing stare on me.

"She—" I started but quickly came to my senses. Hersh didn't care what Saeva was doing. His concern was uninterrupted sleep. But then I considered Saeva was the worse of the two, and complaining to him might improve my situation, so I smoothed my features and sat up straighter. "She dropped a worm on my face, and I screamed," I said factually. Hersh nodded, throwing back his bedding and walking over to us.

"What did you do?" he asked Saeva with a frustrated growl.

I slumped in relief, seeing that Hersh would put a stop to it. My days of torment were over.

"I did this," Saeva replied, throwing another worm at me. This one smacked my chin and landed on my chest, dangerously close to going beneath my shirt. I screeched again and gathered it up, throwing it toward the fire.

The other cogs were awake now, watching the show, just in time to see the finale. Hersh leaned in, grasped my chin, and threw his right hand against my left cheek. The impact sent me flying to the dirt—the pans rattling as I went. "Carry on," he said to Saeva and lumbered back to his bed.

My cheek burned. My jaw ached. I shook as I pushed myself up from the ground, unable to hold back my sobs. I cracked open, showing Saeva all my weaknesses, and she laughed—full and hearty.

Laying a hand on my shoulder, she pushed me down. She straightened my legs, placing the pans an inch apart. "I think you understand now," she whispered before returning to bed. I didn't close my eyes for the rest of the night, remaining perfectly still, just as she'd asked.

In the morning, she sauntered over, untying the pans from my feet. "That wasn't as fun as I'd hoped," she said, then turned the cup over on my head. Spiders, crickets, ants, and worms—some dead and some still moving—rained down on me. Saeva laughed as I launched to my feet, beating my clothes and flinging my fingers through my hair. But I'd learned a lesson—I kept my mouth closed, not releasing a single sound the entire time.

Last night there was no preamble before bed, and I hoped her fun had run its course. After all, she still enjoyed her daytime pleasure of pulling out my hair. But Saeva's not without creativity in finding fresh methods of torment. I'd only been asleep for minutes when suddenly, I couldn't breathe. Lurching up, I coughed, expelling the water she'd poured into my nose.

My nose!

I spewed and sputtered to her delight until finally settling my lungs. But at least for this prank, I had a defense. I slept on my stomach for the rest of the night and finally got some sleep.

I long for a similar outcome tonight, though my hope is in vain because it's obvious her mind is already working on something new. I sometimes doubt Saeva's human—though I'm unsure what the alternative would be—because she doesn't seem reliant upon rest to power her body. No, she seems capable of operating just as well on persecution as sleep.

"I'm hungry," Hersh says, breaking me from my thoughts. It's an order for one of his underlings—Pinyon or Dennie. They're the bottom feeders in this group.

"Should've brought the dog," Pinyon replies. "Could've made a few meals, even if we only took the good parts."

My mouth drops open, and I'm lightheaded at the thought. I wouldn't have survived watching them eat Yip. It's hard enough to endure them as is, knowing what they did to my friend, but that would have destroyed me. Watching Yip die was horrible, but to eat him. My lip curls, and I struggle to swallow.

Hersh chuckles, watching me. "Lucky for you, I don't like dog." He turns back to Pinyon. "Get your lazy ass out there and find us something. It's your only purpose on this trip, so get to it."

"Dog," Saeva says, and like an idiot, I look over. She licks her fingers like they're remnants of a meal—a meaty bone she's just defleshed. "Yum." She pops a finger in her mouth, and I wince while she titters. Saeva's not a disruptor in a showy sense. She enjoys her quiet chaos (and not so quiet too), something Hersh seems to appreciate. She does a fine job keeping me in line, there's no doubt, though I'm always on the edge of losing my mind.

I don't care what Pinyon finds for them to eat because I'm not hungry in the least. They usually give me the scraps anyway, and tonight I'd rather not consume a thing. I lie down, curling up to make myself small, and watch them. They're normally a calm bunch, but tonight they're bickering. I think they're sick of one another, and it's something we have in common. I hate the sight of them.

Pulling the bedding over me, I turn onto my stomach. Saeva smiles at me over the fire. "Sleepy?" she asks in a voice so quiet she's practically mouthing the word. I don't move. I don't speak. I don't even blink but continue to stare at her.

She's wearing my circlight. She traded hers out this morning. It bothers me, which is precisely why she did it.

I want to punch her in the nose, rip it from her neck, and bash Hersh in the head with a pan Saeva tied to my feet the other night. Then hop on a horse and ride away—Pinyon and Dennie too dense to make chase. That's my fantasy. Instead, I lie here, haunted by sounds in the Dark. Last night, after the water incident, I thought I heard a dog in the distance, and I remembered Ronen's words. He assured me Yip could find anyone. But Yip's not around anymore to search me out.

"I'll always come fer ye. Dunna doubt it," Ronen had said.

Will he, though? It's already been five days. Maybe Hersh isn't a regular cog and possesses the ability to outmaneuver the Dark brothers—even Evans's excellent tracking skills. Or maybe Durus was compromised, and they have more significant problems than reclaiming the shrew.

I swear I hear the sound again—a mournful yowl. Even Saeva turns her head, but then she sneezes, and I decide I'm looking for signs where there are none.

It's a dream and a nightmare, thinking my furry little friend is close enough to hear while knowing he's not alive. And I begin to wonder if any of them are.

A tear runs down and drops off my nose. Saeva's eyes

follow it, and she smiles, still crouched next to the fire. What will she do to me tonight? Another tear falls—they come so easily now. Maybe she'll break me this time, and I'll fall upon her with all my rage. I've come close, but memories of Hersh hitting me have stopped me so far. I change my mindset to find peace, imagining the Dark brothers are okay. Imagining Ronen finding me before I lose all composure and do something to get myself killed, but it's hard to have hope, especially with Saeva watching like she does.

I drift off. I'm unsure how long I'm out before a sudden and searing pain wakes me. I yank my hand back with a whimper and sit up in bed while the bedding falls to my waist. I push my throbbing finger into my mouth and take in the surrounding faces. The boys all watch with interest—Hersh's gaze more aloof—while I rub my wet tongue over the raw tip of my index finger. Saeva sits among them, a long stick in her hand, the end black with char and glowing red with heat.

She burned me.

I stare at her while it sinks in.

She burned my skin!

What's next? My hair? My clothes? My bed and body?

I don't know what to do, but the results are invariable for any reaction. Saeva relishes any response, and Hersh will get angry, possibly hitting me again. Any retaliation will make my situation worse. My best choice is to let them think they've won, but I can't go on like this. I've got to find a way to escape.

I pull the bedding over me again, gingerly tucking my fingers between my legs where she can't find them. I shut my eyes, only I don't sleep. Behind my closed eyes, my brain works overtime. My father encouraged me to use my mind to help the Dark brothers, and I need to do as he instructed, only I must put the effort into helping myself. While my finger aches, I remind myself of a few things: I'm a reckoner. I'm a thinker.

And it's time I make a serious plan to get free from the cogs.

CHAPTER TWENTY-NINE

The fingers on my left hand are barely functional—red, swollen, and looking worse than any sunburn I've ever had. I have three blisters, and the one on my thumb is horrific.

It's Saeva's new joy in life, and she's been at it for days. Whenever I fall asleep, and there's a fire—meaning, every night —I'm woken by pain and the odor of burning flesh. Besides my fingers, there are red circles on my legs and burn lines on my arms. She's yet to mark my face, but I don't rule it out. Her hair has nine white-blond braids, so there's plenty of time to get to that. Still, her favorite spot is my fingers, and she sticks exclusively to one hand. I'm not sure why.

As much as I've come to loathe Saeva, I hate the others equally because they let her do it. Every day, I'm increasingly agitated by lack of sleep, minimal food, and the constant suffering I experience at her hands while they watch, entertained.

But waking this morning, I'm shocked to realize she gave me a reprieve last night. By some miracle, she granted a night of repose with no shocking or painful awakenings, and I can't help but be suspicious about why that would be.

I sit up in bed, hugging the bedding close to keep out the morning chill. Pinyon's poking the fire to stir the warm coals, but he keeps glancing my way with a weak grin, putting me on instant alert.

My nose is cold and starts to run. I reach to brush away the moisture when something catches my eye, and I watch a chunk of hair tumble down my bedding.

"What the—"

Reaching for it, another falls. Then another. I touch my scalp, and a piece comes off in my hands. *A section of my hair!* I drop my bedding and reach for the other side, where more clumps fall away.

I vaguely register Saeva's giggles as I look down at where my head was during the night and discover various lengths of my blond hair circling the spot.

"What did you do to me?" My fingers go to my head, searching out what's left. Some sections are untouched, while most are haphazardly cut in various lengths—some shorter than Ronen's beard. Nothing is standard.

"Thought you needed a trim," Saeva says in an even voice.

"My hair! Look what you did to it!"

"Oh, I'm looking." Saeva snorts. "Got tired of getting just a little at a time. Wasn't this more efficient?"

Efficient? I barely register the word.

"You cut my hair," I say in a daze. I love my hair.

Loved.

Everyone did. Mother often told me I was the prettiest girl in Harwell. Cully seemed to agree. And Lucan doted on me like I was his own. All of them complimented my hair. Ronen's ma called my hair the most beautiful she'd ever seen. And Ronen, he'd watch me brush it with a mesmerized look in his eyes. I couldn't do much with it on my own, but Nacole spent hours doing my hair—it was one of our favorite things to pass the time—and she had real talent. It was so much fun.

And now look at me! I've lost weight while with the cogs —I feel it in my face and clothes. I'm sleep-deprived, burned, and bruised. And now I'm sheered like the goats back home, though not in any organized manner. As much as I long to be back in Durus, I'm glad I'm not where there's a large mirror to show me how I look. (I'd hate the reflection enough to break the glass.)

"I didn't cut all of it," Saeva says in a soothing voice. "I considered it, but then Lord Endrack would have no idea how *beautiful* you are. I mean, *were*. This way, he can guess. If he looks hard enough."

"I hate you!" I yell, tightening my hands into fists and banging the ground. Once. Twice. But it's just not enough. "Argh!" I scream, jumping to my feet and throwing myself onto Saeva. I get one punch to connect with her face, but she turns, and it mostly deflects, ending up more of a shove. But she follows my momentum, and we go down until suddenly, I'm on the ground with her on top of me.

"Hold her down!" Saeva yells at Dennie. Her voice has no joy, which I admit is scarier than her familiar amused tone. Dennie just stands there chewing his cheeks, looking like the idiot he is. All the while, I struggle beneath her, all my attention on a clump of hair sticking to her shirt. *My hair!*

I try to get at her again, but she has the advantage and laughs at my attempt.

"Saeva, cut it out," Hersh says. "Let her up."

"Oh, Hersh, don't ruin my fun." Saeva settles over me, pressing my wrists into the rocks. Twisting until I wince. "Pinyon, get over here."

"Hell's beast! I said, let her up!" Hersh bellows, grabbing Saeva by the collar and hauling her to her feet. "We've got a few more days of this shit—"

"Five," Saeva interrupts with a grin while I tenderly sit up, brushing gravel from my skin.

"Three at most," Hersh growls. "If I have to drag your asses there sans sleep, we'll make it in three because I can't stand a day more." He pulls Saeva until they're face to face. "The girl's ready to crack, though I doubt you see it. I want some peace for the next few days."

"Peace?" Saeva's lips twist, repeating the word as if she

doesn't know the meaning.

"Yeah. Be original and do something nice. Maybe take our captive on a tour of the Dark. I don't care as long as you get out of my face and don't make her cry."

Saeva glares at me, disgusted, but then the expression morphs. "A tour sounds good," she says, holding her hand out for me. I don't respond, keeping my hands wrapped around my waist, careful of the fingers on the left.

Hersh eyes both her and the gesture with suspicion. "Pinyon, go with them," he barks out while Saeva nods compliantly. "I don't want to see any of you until Dennie has breakfast ready."

Moments later, Saeva's dragging me through the woods. Pinyon keeps up, hopping behind us, eager to see what Saeva has in mind. I wish I were as keen.

Abruptly, we stop in a strange clearing. Trees surround us, but it's grassy where we stand, with a couple dozen wood planks and logs sticking up from the ground.

"Lie down," Saeva says, pushing me in front of her so the strange objects surround me. I pause, afraid she'll get me in a vulnerable position and kick me. Or worse. There's always a worse, even if I can't determine what it is.

Saeva takes a step forward. "*Down*, I said." Slowly, I lower myself to the ground. The grass tickles my arm, but the dirt is solid under me. "Don't sit. *Lie down*."

I turn on my side and fold my elbow under my head. There's no way I'm lying on my back, and I'm grateful when Saeva doesn't complain about my position.

"Good. Now take a nap."

"A nap?" What is she talking about? I just woke up. And she just dragged me into the woods to lie down for a nap? What am I missing?

"Yes," she grins, crouching down so I can see her. "Take a

nap with the dead people. Because that's what you'll soon be."

"Dead people?" My body tenses.

"Yes, Beauty. You're lying in a graveyard." The word means nothing to me, and it doesn't take Saeva long to realize it. "A graveyard is a place where people in the Dark put the bodies of their dead. They're right below you."

I bolt upright, scrambling to my feet while Pinyon grins and Saeva laughs outright. "Didn't enjoy your dirt nap?" she asks, stalking toward me. It's not the worst thing she's done—not even close—but it was startling, and I'm upset at myself for reacting. I back up until I hit a tree, and it holds me in place while she stalks closer.

Pinyon is still off to the side about twenty feet away. He's not dumb-muscle like Dennie but is smaller and weaker. We're at least a hundred feet from camp, and it occurs to me this might be my chance to get away. Saeva's only feet away, and I whip around to the other side of the tree.

"Hiding from me?" She laughs and steps into view.

Immediately, I thrust my hands at her throat. I squeeze my left hand, making the blisters sting, and move the right to the back of her neck. She makes a gurgling sound, and her fingers come up to pull me off, but I continue pressing while fumbling with the latch on the circlight. I won't survive a minute out here without one. A second later, it's undone and dangling from her neck. I'd feel some success except for two things.

First, Pinyon asks, "What are you two doing back there?"

And second, Saeva's no longer struggling. Instead, she's watching me calmly while I clamp down on her throat. I'm about to take the circlight and push her away when I understand the change in her demeanor.

The pain is sharp and quick. I drop my hand, and Saeva gasps for breath while backing away from me. She's still holding the knife in front of her. It's short, only a few inches, and covered in my blood.

Gripping my side, the liquid flows freely.

"Pinyon! Get over here!" Saeva grinds out amid wheezes from her raspy throat. I'm slumped against the tree, covering my aching wound, when Pinyon appears. "Hold her," Saeva says, pacing before us while Pinyon grasps my arms.

"You're lucky we're so close to Harwell." Saeva points the knife at me but doesn't make eye contact. "You're lucky I can't kill you before we get there. Lucky, lucky, lucky that Lord Endrack wants the honor," she sings. I think she's saying these things for her benefit, talking herself out of taking further action. But I barely have the stamina to hear her while I list sideways in pain.

Saeva steps forward, lifting my chin and forcing my head from the tree I'm using as a pillow. "I hope you enjoyed my knife. It's good Endrack doesn't need you for long because I used it to gut dinner last night. I was feeling lazy and never cleaned it."

She drops my chin, and my head hits the tree with a thud. Pinyon's holding my arms from behind, though he doesn't have to do much to keep me in place. The ache is too extreme to concentrate on much else. Saeva takes one of my arms from him, and his hand moves to my shoulder.

She grips my blistered fingers, and I wince, biting back a response as she jerks my arm straight. "I told you to lie down, and you didn't obey. I don't like that," Saeva says, and in a quick swipe, she makes a shallow cut on the back of my arm. I gasp from the instant source of new pain.

"You ran from me." She slices again. I moan, trying to pull away, but she holds firm. I look down at the two parallel lines. "You choked me and tried to take my light."

Cut! Cut! Two more perfect lines.

"Stop! *Please!*"

Saeva holds the knife in front of my face. "I will stop." She wipes the blade on my shoulder to clean off my blood. "But only if you stop crying."

I'm crying?

Since when?

And then I feel them—the tears rolling freely now.

"You cry, I cut," Saeva says. "You talk, I cut. You disobey... well, you get the idea."

She secures the circlight back around her neck, making Pinyon clean the tears off my face before dragging me back to camp while she brings up the rear.

"You're all still alive," Hersh says, sounding almost disappointed as we appear from the trees.

"She's bleeding but not crying," Saeva tells him. "Considering she tried to escape, I did my best."

Hersh furrows his brow as he looks me over from a distance. "Avoid everything vital?"

"She'll live," Saeva replies, and like Hersh, she sounds disappointed. "Dennie should wrap her up, though."

With that, Pinyon drops me next to Dennie and goes for his morning meal. Saeva skips the food, scooping her horse's saddle and dropping it on his back. It's not long before I have a bandage on my side (already soaked through), and we're back on the horses. I wish I could ride with anyone except Saeva, but it's been this way from the beginning. The boys like their space, and Saeva enjoys her time with me. She enjoys it too much.

There's the packhorse, but I don't dare suggest they put me on it, though my extra weight shouldn't be a concern. I already looked scrawny before missing another meal this morning amid getting bandaged up. My stomach's become accustomed to the emptiness and doesn't even complain.

We're on the move. I hope the ride will be uneventful, but Saeva kills that dream, whispering in my ear. "I'll grow tired of cutting your arm. We both know it. But I think I'll try your tongue next." I hear the smile in her voice as she lays out her plans. "I'll do it in perfect little slits, like spider's legs. You'll sound like a snake when you talk." Saeva chuckles deeply.

I keep absolutely still. No reaction is the only safe choice. Any response will provoke her to act. Eventually, her giggles stop, and we continue forward to Harwell.

Cradled in Saeva's arms, I remember all the times I've been unkind, and there are many. People would call me cruel, and I thought it was funny, just like Saeva does.

The last months have changed me—my perception, outlook, and behavior—but nothing has molded me more than Saeva. It's a strange consequence of our time together, but I've decided I can forgive myself for my past behavior. Indeed, while I'm sorry for what I did and embarrassed by how I behaved, I don't find the prospect of making amends to be any hardship. I'm ready and willing to ask for forgiveness from those I've wronged. I'll beg for it and find no shame in doing so.

For in all the things I've done—and I was unkind, epically unkind to be sure—I was never cruel. No. At Saeva's hands, I've witnessed true cruelty, and it's nothing I've ever achieved. It's a relief to realize I wasn't as terrible as I always believed. And after my time with the cogs, it's something I can promise I'll never aspire to again.

CHAPTER THIRTY

We ride toward Harwell, and Saeva cuts me two more times, though I did nothing—no talking, moving, or disobeying. "Sometimes, you just annoy me," she says as her reason. "It's fun to count your indiscretions," she adds, touching each of the six lines on my arm. I note the third one is slightly longer and deeper. It's the one I got for choking her. Did she do it on purpose, or was it a simple miscalculation of pressure?

Saeva didn't wake me during the last two nights, which isn't surprising since we're getting minimal sleep. Hersh is pushing us hard, intending to make Harwell in one more day of travel, though he grumbles it will probably be a day and a half. And while Saeva didn't interrupt my sleep, she was still busy, which I note upon waking to discover my latest gift.

"You stink!" she says, yanking me to my feet. She'd been waiting for me to open my eyes to deliver the line.

Drawing a long breath through my nose, I look down at the horse shit smeared across my skin and clothes. I recall all the times I spread rumors about the Dale witches stinking. In a few days, I'll be home, reeking worse than they ever did, and I can't even be bothered to care. Why be concerned about the citizens' good opinions when I'll soon be dead? And, honestly, why did I ever care? It was a problem for a small place.

I shake my hand, and some poo flies to the ground. I didn't feel Saeva's touch in my sleep, and I'm positive I would have woken if I had. (I've become subconsciously attuned to nighttime disturbances.) She must have put it on my clothes and in my bed. My innocent movements while resting spread it everywhere else.

"I don't like people who stink," Saeva says, running her

knife across my arm to add another line—number seven. I bite my lip, knowing she'll make it eight if I say a word.

"Clean her up!" Hersh barks at Saeva while blood appears on the new line in my skin. Saeva only smiles, not worried in the least over his tone.

"No time. But I'll take care of it," she replies, leading me away.

It turns out taking care of it means I'm on the packhorse. (A blessing.) And I'm riding thirty feet behind the others, hands tied to the horn with my fingers tingling, and nearly out of range of the circlights, so it's hard to see. (Still a blessing.) But hell's beast, as Hersh would say, if I don't reek like a relief house and animal pen all in one.

I sway on the back of the horse, giggling deliriously, thinking Siman's intuition is seriously flawed. He should go to a clinician and get checked. Maybe they could give him a salve to get his mysticism working again—spread it over his brain to correct his false feelings. Then we can talk again and clear up the mistaken instructions he gave me. "Sorry," he'd say. "We're the ones who will fix this. Not you. Once you're with the cogs, we'll sort it out. And by the way, you, Anni, are going to die."

"And you, Siman, are unforgiven for providing false hope," I retaliate in our fake conversation. "In addition, you and Tesha both suck."

I giggle again, and my head falls forward, where I watch a trickle of blood run down my arm. The other lines are scabbed over, some puffy and red—infected. And they haven't checked my side since Dennie wrapped it up. I'm sure it's a mess. It hurts something awful, especially when riding on horseback.

The animal glances back every so often, snorting out a complaint. He, too, can smell me and doesn't appreciate my disturbing odor. "Live with it, Snorty," I say low enough only I can hear. I may be unable to exert any power over the cogs, but I'm not letting this animal think he's better than me.

We don't make camp again. Hersh keeps us moving all day and into the night. Sometimes I'm grateful to be tied to the horse—like when I nod off and pitch to the side, threatening to fall off. My hands are the only thing keeping me from toppling to the ground, though the possibility of getting trampled is likely preferable to meeting Endrack in Harwell. But even when I think of that man and my future, I can't help but wonder if anyone could be worse than Saeva.

◆ ◆ ◆

We arrive in Harwell just before sunrise, but there's enough light to see my once peaceful home.

As the horses cross over the Hem, my eyes widen as I take in the sight before me. Despondency sits stout in my chest as we follow the River Path, where the black skeletons of lumber trees send up tendrils of smoke. There's no open flame, though fire continues to consume our carefully cultivated resource. Traveling through the Dark has taught me there are more trees than I can count outside of Harwell, but the effort and sacrifice represented by those burned trees still make me sad.

Across the Upper River is the empty Common. The living quarters flanking the area have the same charred appearance as the trees. Building Six is completely gone, a pile of smoldering ash. I don't know what I expected upon my return, but this isn't it. There are no people bustling up and down the transit paths. No citizens pulling in fish from the river or lifting water to the tower to irrigate our rooftop crops. Indeed, the water tower no longer stands—the large barrel is in the river with the legs sticking up on the banks.

We reach Rocky Point, and I recognize a few of Harwell's citizens on the Orchard Bridge making repairs. "Not everyone is gone," I say to myself, wondering about my parents and friends. The Clarcs too. I'm so distracted I don't realize we're no longer moving until Saeva pulls me from the saddle. I dismount the snorty packhorse and narrowly avoid falling on my face, struggling to get my feet under me. Saeva shows no concern, dragging me while my feet work to find a rhythm.

I've barely gained my footing when we arrive at the Rocky Point shore. Saeva throws me in, and I land on my side. The water's shallow this time of year, but it nearly covers me. I keep my head above water long enough to get a good breath, and then I sink, water washing over me for the first time in nearly two weeks.

It's freezing, and I realize I no longer know the date. It might be March, but it's at least the end of February. January bathing is the most uncomfortable in Harwell—the water is frigid. By March, the water feels comparatively balmy. But nothing comes close to the wonders of a hot shower in Durus. Still, while this is unexpected, it solves a few of my problems.

My head pops above the surface. With stiff fingers, I roll in the shallows until I'm on my belly, and then I drink, taking in great gulps of water. I've been thirsty for so long but constantly fearful of saying something.

It's then I see her shadow on the water, appearing just as the sun peeks over the Dark. "You think I threw you in for your *comfort*?" Saeva asks. And while I should have expected it, I'm surprised when she seizes the back of my head and pushes it under, holding me there.

My arms flail above me, and I squirm to get free, but Saeva only pushes harder until my cheek digs into the rocks on the bottom of the river.

And then she lets go.

I push up, gasping air and sucking in water too.

"She'll smell fine enough now," Hersh says above us. "I know you're sad to lose your toy, but stop playin' and get up here."

"Hersh saves you again," Saeva says, and I release a breath

of relief. I can't handle much more without going mad. I glance up at her, hardly believing it's over, and the look in her eyes confirms my doubt, crushing my fragile belief. Her cheek goes up in a grin as she says, "Then again, maybe he doesn't."

Saeva slams into me hard. My hands bounce across the rocks, getting sliced as they go, and then we're both down. My head's back under, and she's on top of me. With a grunt, I breathe out all my excess air, and the desire for more burns my chest. I pound my fists, trying to reach her, but it's useless. My side hurts and my hands too. I've barely eaten or slept, and my muscles ache from dehydration and cold. I can't find the energy to fight anymore.

My hands stop their assault and float up, bobbing with the movement of the river.

Maybe this is where it ends. Maybe it's better if I stop fighting. I miss my family and want so desperately to see them again. And there's Nacole. I'll never get to tell her how sorry I am for not treating her better or becoming her true friend. But do I want any of them to see me like this? Not really. So maybe it's okay to give up.

Sure, I'll even miss the stupid people back in Durus—Harwellians and Coastals alike—though maybe not Tesha. And depending on the day, Evans.

But Ronen. I'll miss him most of all. And how shocking is that? The big, scruffy man who became my unlikely champion and burrowed beneath my prickle to reside in my affections. My muscles relax, thinking of him. Even my need to breathe diminishes.

Ronen promised I'd see my family again. He promised he'd always come for me. And he probably tried—he's a good man and would never go back on his word. He's just too late. Or maybe... he's dead.

Dead.

The idea is repulsive, and I choke out a sob—bubbles of air

float past my eyes. What little was left in my depleted lungs is gone. My body weakens even more and demands air. Without permission, my nose pulls in a stream of water. I convulse on the liquid, and my thoughts drift on nonsense. I smile, imagining it's Saeva drowning in Harwell's river instead of me.

I decide it's the method I'd choose. This is how I'd want Saeva to pay for her many sins—death in Harwell's river at my hands. If I could make it happen.

How could I make it happen?

My eyes flutter, and I accept the inevitable—I won't. Saeva won. Endrack too. Harwell used to be my haven—where ease, love, and power came together to perfect my life—but it's nothing like that now. I am nothing. This is it. I am done.

And now—when I've finally made peace with my fate—I fly to the surface.

"What the hell are you doing?" Hersh's stern voice rings in my ears. He smacks my back, and water pours from my mouth. It's not until it's gone that I can take in air. I barely register the racking, wheezing noise coming from my mouth as I struggle to restore life to my body.

The life Saeva almost drown out.

She's unrepentant, staring at Hersh with a pleased expression—self-assured in her actions. Confident he'll not punish her.

Well.

He won't.

Hersh bends over to check on me. "Keep breathing, girl," he says. "It's not your time yet."

No. Not yet. But it's coming soon. So, while we wait for my breathing to settle, I decide I'm not leaving this world without taking something with me.

I'm taking back my pride.

I'm taking back myself.

Hersh lifts my hunched shoulders, and I listen to the air moving through my nose and mouth. I end each inhale with a cough, still getting the water out. But each exhale gets steadier and more controlled. Saeva stands calf-high in the water, her arms crossed, wearing a flashy grin while her eyes bore into mine.

She doesn't see my clenched fist. (Tightening.) She doesn't expect a thing. (Foolish.)

I'm more than happy to surprise her for once.

I lunge forward and use every ounce of strength in my weakened muscles, swinging my fist at her face. I strike her cheekbone hard, transferring perfectly the force of my rage through my punch. I feel it in my hand, which throbs and bleeds. Something's broken—it feels like my middle finger—but I hear her painful cry, and it's gratifying but not enough. I need more. I want to watch Saeva bleed. More pain for me means more pain for her. I'll break all my fingers if I must.

She barely straightens—the shock of what I've done plain in her eyes—when I send my other fist. I hit her opposite cheek. It's my weaker arm, and my knuckles glance off, but I catch her nose with a satisfying crunch. This time she goes down, her butt landing in the water and her hands cradling her face.

I stand above her, staring at my hands, shaking and throbbing with pain. There's more blood—mine or hers, I can't be sure. Between my hands, her face stares up at me. It's only a moment before she recovers and bounces to her feet, blood and spit flying from her mouth as she comes at me. "I'll kill you!" she screams, and I notice one of her teeth is missing.

Hell's beast, I knocked out her tooth!

I feel nearly giddy.

Saeva surges forward, but Hersh throws out his hand, and with one hard shove, he puts her back in the water. "Not your job," he says, and I realize he's laughing. "No one can say you didn't deserve it. You've been an annoying little mosquito the last two weeks—picking and drawing blood where you can. So, take your lumps. I have to go find Lord Endrack."

"He'll be furious when he sees what she's done to me!" Saeva bellows, getting back on her feet but keeping her distance. My first hit's already blackening her eye. My vision narrows, and my lips curve into a satisfied grin I'm sure she notices.

"Furious? I'm sure he will be," Hersh says, glaring down at her. "But not necessarily at her. From here out, it's Lord Endrack's show. It's *his* prerogative what happens to her. *Not yours.* You keep out of it." He pokes her shoulder with his finger to drive home his point, then turns away with me in his grasp.

He walks me up the slope to the horses, the various lengths of my hair dripping or swaying as they're able. "You've been a regular pain, and I'm eager to be rid of you," he says, and there's nothing in his comment that's a surprise until he adds, "But watching you put Saeva on her ass made these weeks almost worth it."

CHAPTER THIRTY-ONE

"**W**e the first to return?" Hersh asks, leading me into the Well. I'm back in the place where I last saw my parents. I glance around, noting the room looks much like it always has. Maybe a little more cluttered with gear and supplies, but not destroyed like so much else. Attempting a casual glance, I look at the ceiling, wondering if my quarters fared as well—wondering who, if anyone, is up there.

"You're the first," a woman confirms, dropping her feet to the ground, which had been resting on the meeting table. Lucan would be furious.

She has short hair that's pulled back, but much of it rests shaggily over her forehead and around her face. Her nose is long. Her chin is too. She reminds me of my snorty packhorse I rode into Harwell today. Her hair's even the same color as the animal's coat. (If I factor out the blue tint of the lamlight.) "She one of 'em?" she asks, tilting her head at me, making her chin look extra long and wide.

"Yeah," Hersh says while I observe the room's only other occupants—a man and woman sitting off to the side, barely acknowledging the conversation. Dennie and Pinyon are gone. Hersh dismissed them before we crossed the Orchard Bridge, and they left with the gear and horses. He dismissed Saeva too, but she's still here, insisting she'll take her next orders from Endrack himself. Hersh had sighed, discontent, but ultimately allowed it. Clearly, he has no control over her, which makes my skin prickle nervously. "Still not sure what her crimes are," Hersh finishes with a shrug.

"You haven't asked her?" the horsey woman inquires, standing up and stepping closer to me.

"What's the point? She'd lie anyway."

Hersh is a smart man. Often dull and passive but not stupid.

It's disappointing none of these cogs know why I'm here. Saeva broadcast my death eagerly for someone so ignorant of its purpose. It really says something about her. Also, something about me—I'm not prepared to die without knowing the offense that brought it about. I'm owed an explanation, but it won't come from these myrmidons.

Horsey leans in to inspect me, and I look at my feet (my absurdly dirty feet) while her eyes take me in from mere inches away, her elongated snout in my periphery. "She doesn't look important. She looks moments away from perishing." She lifts a piece of white-blond hair from my forehead—one of the long ones. "Whatcha been doin' to her?"

Saeva snickers, tromping across the room and dropping onto a chair.

"Oh," Horsey says, raising her brows with a knowing look. Apparently, Saeva's antics aren't unknown. "Well, you should spruce her up in the Clinic if you want a *living* captive for Lord Endrack. He's not expected until tomorrow."

"I've no objection," Hersh says. "But I need to report in. Planned on getting her secured and giving my update."

"I'll take her," Saeva says, running her tongue through the bloody hole in her teeth.

Before the comment registers—and the accompanying terror—the woman snorts in disagreement. "Yeah. That'd guarantee her status." Saeva clicks her tongue and shrugs. "I can take her," the stranger tells Hersh. He doesn't reply verbally, merely pushes me forward and leaves. Just that easily, he's rid of me. How nice for him.

"I'm Eddy. Anything to prevent you from walking?"

"No."

"Good. Let's go." Eddy ushers me out the main door, and I glance back to see Saeva following like a hungry animal prowling for a fresh carcass. "Don't worry about her. I can't keep her from taggin' along, but I can keep her from finishing that hairdo."

Without thinking, I grab one strand. I don't know if Eddy's words should relieve or warn me. I don't trust any of these cogs, even those who proclaim nice things. So, I do what I've learned—keep quiet and remain maniacally alert for traps.

The sun is higher, and the status of Harwell can be more easily seen—charred buildings standing in stark contrast to the blue sky—but we're not outside for long. We reach Building Three, which houses our Clinic, and I take the stairs slowly —unable to expend much energy and careful not to further injure myself. Saeva's not happy with our speed and prods me from behind. Eddy doesn't notice, so with every step, Saeva repeats the action—harder each time. I'm ready to slug her again when we reach the top, but she stops her prodding and stands out of reach from me.

Usually, many citizens actively work in the Clinic. Today, it's empty except for one person sitting in the corner. I recognize her instantly.

"We need some help, nurse," Eddy says, and I frown at the antiquated term. We call our medical people clinicians—all of them, regardless of skill or knowledge.

"Of course," she says without a trace of cheer in her voice. She walks straight into an observation room, assuming we'll follow, and we do. "What's the issue?"

"Cuts and bruises, but I'm not sure what's underneath," Eddy answers. I don't look at Saeva, knowing the grin I'll find. "Likely needs food and water, but we'll take care of that after we leave here."

The clinician faces me and stops—her brows dropping as she observes my face with an inkling of recognition.

"Hello, Janny."

Her brows fly up as her small eyes pop open. "Annibeth Petters? Is that you?"

I nod, ready to say more—to ask about my family—but I don't get the chance.

"Ahh," Saeva coos. "Is that your name? Annibeth? So pretty." She runs a hand down my arm in a gentle stroke, then spits a wad of blood at my feet.

"Saeva!" Eddy takes a step back. "You're disgusting. Clean that up."

"No." Saeva leans into me, loudly sucking air through the blank space in her smile. Her tongue comes away red. "You took one from me. I'm taking two from you. Just need permission first. Since you're dying anyway, I don't believe there'll be any objections."

"Saeva! Out!" Eddy pushes her, and Saeva falls to the side, laughing.

"See you later, Beauty. We'll be reunited soon. So, so soon." She winks, grinning with bloody teeth. She's proud of her injury and loves showing me what I did, so I remember I'll receive worse. She's still staring at me when the door shuts on her face.

"Let's get this over with," Eddy says, irritated. "The sooner we get you patched up, the sooner I can get you secured, and we can both get some food."

Janny steps forward, a frown on her round face. "What did they do to you?" she asks, aghast. I'm once again glad there are no large mirrors in Harwell.

"No talking except to say what hurts," Eddy says.

Janny scowls, but I keep a blank expression. Her instructions aren't a surprise. Though Eddy's not insane like Saeva, she's still a cog, and I'm still a prisoner. I'd be more concerned if she approved of us talking.

"These cuts on your arm look awful," Janny says, observing my seven lines. Just wait until she sees the hidden one.

"Dirty knife," I say, keeping it brief but letting her know what she's dealing with. Her brow goes up, but she says nothing. She takes the cog seriously, as she should.

She treats my arm, cleaning the wounds and putting on a salve. She remarks that the infection isn't too bad and the openings should heal, though they'll scar. I don't tell her the plan is for me to die before that ever happens.

Next, she looks at the fingers on my left hand. "Are these burns?" she asks. The octave of her voice relays her horror.

"Yes." I keep my head bent, unable to look at Eddy—unsure what the cog will do if she sees me cry. "I have more on my arms and legs, though these are the worst." I pull up my pant leg, barely able to manage it in my weakened state, showing her the other spots. I'm grateful when she leaves them alone, deciding it's best to let them continue healing on their own.

I release a heavy sigh.

"I'm not sure she can wait," Janny says, and I realize she's addressing Eddy. "She needs food and water now." Janny leans down so I can see her face, her upturned nose still angled determinedly. "How long since you ate or drank?"

"I had a drink when we got to Harwell before Saeva almost drowned me," I say with an irrational giggle.

Janny's frown increases, and I find that funny too. "What about food?"

I try to think, but my mind won't work. (And honestly, a non-working mind is relaxing.) I feel almost happy with Saeva not here. I'm shut away in a little room with two women I don't consider a significant threat. I don't care about thinking, eating, or drinking. I don't care about getting bandaged up. I want to sleep. I wonder if Janny could prescribe that?

"Annibeth, when did you last eat?"

I shake my head, trying to recall. All the days have become one. "Uh. Before the cutting. After the pans."

Janny clears her throat. "These cuts are days old," she tells Eddy with an expectant expression.

Eddy doesn't immediately react, waiting for Janny to get back to treating me, but when the clinician doesn't move the cog releases a heavy breath. "Fine. I'll get her something," she says, pulling the door open and finding Saeva on the other side.

"You're still here," Eddy says, unable to hide her surprise. Meanwhile, I feel queasy at the sight of the unsavory cog, and I hear a sound I soon realize is a whimper, and it's coming from my mouth. Eddy looks back at me. "Don't worry. She won't bother you again."

"Hah!" I bark out with a laugh. "Heard that before." Eddy's brow lifts. Her eyes peruse me, from my shorn head to my blistered fingers. She lingers longest on the lines on my arm. "Those aren't the worst," I say, and Eddy's eyes snap to mine. I don't wait, yanking up my shirt and turning so my side faces Janny. "Go ahead. Take it off."

Janny gets to work, removing Dennie's wrap from days ago, and both women gasp at the sight underneath. I don't have the stomach to look. I keep my eyes focused on the wall.

"Oh, Annibeth," Janny pushes out the words with a breath, shaking her head in dismay. "What did they do?"

The compassion in her voice is too much. I bite my quivering lip, still looking at that stupid, flat wall, until I finally repeat my earlier words. "Dirty knife."

If Eddy leaves, Janny and I are no match for Saeva. No doubt, when Eddy returned with food, I'd be utterly incapable of eating because I'll be bloody and minus two teeth. Eddy seems to understand this because a second later, she says, "Saeva, go get her some food."

Instantly, my lip stops quivering, but when Eddy's

preposterous command registers, I laugh. Hazily, I realize I'm acting as unstable as Saeva. But, really? Like I'd eat anything Saeva brings! There would be bugs mixed in. Or it would be baked with rocks inside. And, considering how this day has gone, I can't rule out poison.

Eddy glances back at me, a scowl on her brow, which threatens to become permanent. She takes in my erratic state and adds, "And you'd better hurry. She's getting slap-happy."

"No. You do it," Saeva answers. Her refusal isn't wholly unexpected with all the times I've seen her contend with the other cogs. I expect Eddy to cave like last time—like the others usually do—but instead, she pulls the door closed until there's a small gap between them and us.

"You'll do as I say or be punished for insubordination," I hear Eddy's muffled voice through the door. I glance at Janny, wondering if she knows how much I love hearing that, but she's rummaging chaotically through the cupboards. I realize I'm still holding my shirt—still baring my wound—and decide to leave it exposed until Janny gets back to me. Eavesdropping, I lean toward the door to better hear the conversation. I plan to enjoy this moment—listening to Eddy put Saeva in her place.

But the horrors of these last weeks return in full force when Eddy says something to heighten my nightmares. "Though Lord Endrack is your uncle, I am your *superior*, and you will obey me."

Uncle!

And I knocked her tooth out. I'm in so much trouble! Not that I wasn't already, but I imagine they'll double my torture in light of this revelation.

Saeva huffs, and I envision her annoyed expression. She's only vaguely intimidated by Eddy's threat. But hearing footsteps, I consider I might have underestimated Eddy. Maybe she's capable of bringing Saeva into submission. It appears Saeva's off to fetch me a meal I'll never dare eat. I'm ready to tell

Janny that—or at least inquire how much longer I should hold my shirt up—when three things happen in succession.

Eddy reenters the room. Janny spins to face her, slamming a thick, wooden bowl against Eddy's head. Eddy's eyes roll, and she falls to the floor like a felled tree. Unconscious.

"What did you do?" I whisper, experiencing some shock over this latest turn of events while also slightly amazed by Janny. How many times have I tried to get one over on the cogs? She made it look so easy, and Eddy's a big girl.

"What I had to," Janny answers, gripping my hand and brushing a gentle finger down my cheek. "Because we need to get you out of here. *Right now.*"

CHAPTER THIRTY-TWO

"Where do you expect me to go?" I ask. Not that I'm not grateful. Not that I'm not leaving. But because I wonder if she has a plan.

"I don't know."

Okay. So, no plan.

"But they're going to kill you." And I realize Janny's better informed than I gave her credit for. "There's been constant talk of your capture and execution for weeks now, and you're not safe as long as you're in Harwell."

Leave Harwell? A few issues stand in the way of making that suggestion a reality.

"I'm exhausted," I say, even though the energy surge remains from watching Janny drop Eddy—it thrums beneath my skin but will be short-lived.

"You can take my meal." She taps a rather large knotted package on the countertop, but food only solves part of my impediment.

"My injury?" I point at my side. It's awful and needs tending.

She picks up the tied bundle. "I packed what you need. Keep it clean, wrap it up, and put on the crushed herbs. Other than applying stitches, which we don't have time for, it's all I could do for you anyway. Now, really, you must get out of here."

This brings me to my most significant issue.

"I don't have a circlight, and I'm stuck here until I do." I put a fist on my hip and wait to see what perfect solution she's arranged for this problem.

"Annibeth Petters! You act like I don't know you, but you're wrong. I've known you since childhood, girl. The Annibeth I know wouldn't let something as basic as obtaining a circlight keep her from achieving a goal. Now, are you the girl who can solve any problem, or are you not?"

My fist drops after her put-down turned pep-talk.

Because I am that girl. (And I'm disgusted because Saeva made me forget.)

"I'll find a circlight," I push out with conviction.

"Good." Janny pulls me from the table, helps me step over Eddy's body, and reaches for the door, but I put a hand on her arm to stop her.

"Have you seen my family?"

"No." She doesn't look at me but grasps the handle.

I put a hand on the door. "Are they still alive?"

"I'm not sure." She huffs, scrunching her small eyes. "There's no time for this discussion. Don't you understand? They're going to kill you. Lord Endrack's not someone to mess around with. He'll do what he says and not think twice about his unsavory actions."

"I understand very well. I've lived with the threat for months now." Though from the safety of Durus, it was difficult to believe the threat was real. These last weeks changed that. "Come with me, Janny. We'll escape Harwell together, and then I can ask you what I need to know."

"I have someone here who needs me. Now, go!"

"Just thirty seconds," I argue, and when Janny doesn't press, I push out, "When was the last time you saw my parents?"

"I haven't seen them since Captain Rhed was forced out."

"Is Captain Rhed still alive?"

"Last I saw."

"Did many people die?"

She talks fast, but I absorb the details. "Two hundred total, though most were Coastals. Sixty citizens died fighting back or in the fires. Five hundred of us are still in Harwell. The Clarcs tried for diplomacy. They're still here with other leadership families—the Vaccas and Ruprets. Others too—maybe even your parents—but I'm not sure. They keep us separated."

"You say the families are here and not just the parents?"

"Yes. And I know some of them are your friends, but be careful, Annibeth. Don't search them out. They're in survival mode, and I believe they'll hurt you before they'll help you."

The wave of happiness upon hearing about my friends morphs into frustration. Nacole, Cully, and Harbert are here, but Janny advises me not to contact them. I don't know how I feel about that.

"How did diplomacy work?" It was my suggestion, back when I was an apprentice reckoner trying to help my community.

Janny snorts. "It didn't. Not one bit. Now, I really must insist you go."

"Thank you, Janny." I pull her in for a hug, grimacing with the pain in my side. "Thanks so much." I hang on for a moment longer before adding, "And if I was ever unkind to you, I'm sorry."

She chuckles against me, and I lean back as she says, "You were always a terror, but I never minded. It was sort of fun to watch your reign of fear in our quiet little community."

I smile. What are the chances the first citizen I attempt to make amends with found enjoyment in my behavior? I'm not dense enough to think they all felt that way, but maybe restitution isn't impossible or always unpleasant.

Releasing Janny, I slip out the door, finally doing her bidding. I delayed my escape by a few minutes by demanding information. The knowledge draws a scary picture of what

Harwell's become. Still, it's good to have a basic idea of what to expect because outside the relative safety of the observation room, my stomach churns with nervousness. What if I run into Saeva? And where can I even go?

One thing's for sure—I can't stay in the Clinic.

Rushing to the stairs, I speed down each step, not seeing anyone along the way. My luck holds as I exit the Clinic doors facing west toward the Dark. I creep northwest to the corner of Building Four. The river is about ten feet away, and I peek around the corner. While fewer people walk Harwell these days, I still glance across the water to the living quarters and crane my head to glimpse the Common. I notice a few people, but they're far enough away I can't make out if they're citizens or cogs. That should mean they'll be equally incapable of making out who I am.

Too bad our Building Fifteen lessons from the Coastal guard didn't include tips on escaping captivity—that would be useful about now. And the only thing Ronen told me was to hide, and one of them would find me. Again, not helpful today. But I escaped Harwell once with the Dark brothers— and during a heated battle—so I figure with a bit of ingenuity, I can manage evasion again. It's up to me to decide my subsequent actions, and knowing my father expects me to think masterfully under pressure, I concentrate on making the best choices I can to make him proud.

With a temporary destination in mind, I sneak along the north side of Building Four, knowing I need to get away from this area before Saeva returns. At the northeast corner, I quickly check my surroundings before exiting my minimal cover. It looks safe enough. As safe as it will ever be. Without overthinking it, I step away from the building and approach the watering platform, about a thirty-foot walk. I take quick steps but resist breaking into a run that could draw attention.

Soon I'm on the dirt path sloping steeply to the water

below. I'm halfway down when I hear voices. I drop into a crouch (wincing at the pain in my side), but I'm low enough to be hidden from above. I can't determine who's nearby, but the voices get quieter. They're moving away.

Staying low, I continue to the platform, taking the narrow dirt path under the Lower River Bridge. From here, it would be difficult for anyone to see me tucked into the rocks like I am. I'm safe for a moment but not for long. Still, a quick break to eat some of Janny's food is warranted—a few bites, at least. I need it.

I pull the knot and open one side, finding salted fish and cucumbers. I devour half the fish before forcing myself to stop—I'll get sick if I take too much. I probably already have. Wrapping it up, I consider my next move.

The last time I was in this spot—escaping Harwell with Geric and Ronen—we crossed the rocks, went to the Northern Hem, and then into the Dark. It's not an option today. Not without a circlight. How I wish they were here to help with this decision. But they're not. Even more than wanting them here with me, I want them still to be alive. But I won't get their help or know the status today. I'm on my own and need to think and act smartly—like they'd do. Like I'm more than capable of doing.

A commotion near the Clinic interrupts my thoughts. They've undoubtedly discovered my absence, which is confirmed when I hear someone call out, "Get the dogs!"

They'll be back soon to look for me. A few cogs searching could find me in my current location. If they bring dogs, they'll find me in no time. I saw Yip at work enough to know that. But Ronen also told me of Yip's limitations in sniffing out a target —water, a vertical ascent, or a disrupted scent. I need to use all those things to have a chance of getting away.

I drop quietly into the river, hissing at the cold. The level reaches my waist, and after a brief shiver, I start forward, hugging to the side. The ground is carved out in this area where the water is deeper and the channel narrower. It makes hiding along the walls easier, but the farther I go, the more that will change. The water will get wide and shallow, exposing me on both sides by the time I reach Rocky Point, which is only halfway to where I need to be. I've got to hurry.

Pushing through the current, I make as little noise as possible though speed is the more important variable. I'm glad the water is low this time of year, and the current is not too swift. If I were doing this in late spring, it would be impossible.

I'm nearing Rocky Point, weighing my best options, when someone calls out, "You there! Stop!"

I freeze in place, not daring to move, while my eyes search for the voice's owner. It takes a moment, but I find him on the Common. I can only see from his shoulders up as he approaches another person—someone I recognize as a Harwell citizen, solely because of the clothing they're wearing. I hasten to the other side of the river—closer to the cog and Harwell offender—then get lower in the water to gain more cover. I try to keep my bundle above water, but it's useless and sinks below the surface, so I push it in front of me as I crawl along.

They argue above me. The cog is upset the person is on the Common at an inappropriate time of day. The citizen explains their logic but doesn't debate very hard. I understand why—cogs are anything but reasonable. The conversation gets quieter and then goes away entirely because of distance or because they disbanded. Either way, I'm happy I made it to the toppled water tower, which provides much-needed cover.

I climb behind the structure and reach the fishing platform near Building Twenty-Eight. I heave myself onto the surface, feeling a twinge in my side. Pulling my bundle with me, I squeeze it out. Watching the water drain from the contents, I question their value, but I'm not ready to abandon them, so I tuck the bag under my arm and race to the side of Building

Thirty-Six. I'm grateful it's not burned, and one of my favorite climbing ladders is in good condition. Before there's a chance of being seen, I race to the top with the bundle's knot between my teeth. Each rung highlights my injured body—my burned fingers and my wounded side. When I reach the roof, I nearly fall to the surface in pain and exhaustion, but I find a reserve of energy and keep going.

Glancing around, I don't see any movement, so I move to the side and drop my bundle in a corner. I worry they're patrolling the rooftops—they're convenient places to observe many things—but see no one as yet. With a tinge of regret, I realize one thing I didn't get from Janny was the number of cogs watching over the five hundred citizens. It's possible there are so many they're not concerned with rooftops. It's also possible, like for many of our people, that the height is unpleasant. It's equally likely they're too confident in their abilities. Whatever the reason, I'm glad it's empty, though I can't get reckless. I keep in a crouch as I run across the rooftop and crawl over the irrigation duct while monitoring the paths below, but there are no citizens or cogs in sight—Harwell is quiet.

I reach Building Thirty-Four. While most buildings in Harwell house people, this one is where they store and distribute provisions. They also keep surplus commodities on the upper floors, so I hope to get all I need in this one building. If not, I'll need to stop in Thirty-Five, where they keep most of the commodities.

I recheck the transit paths. The Provisions Path is clear —the one closest to my target—and I don't see anyone in the windows of the adjacent buildings. Ultimately, I feel safe enough to descend a few feet on a ladder and swing into the window of an upper storage room. I'm grateful that even with my injured side, I'm able to maintain a steady grip, entering the building with no issue. Once inside, I quickly search, relieved to find everything I need. Well, everything except a circlight—not that they've ever stored those in here.

Pulling off my clothes, I'm glad to get out of the filthy items I've worn for weeks that cling to me wetly. I put on two sets of underclothes, two shirts, and two pairs of pants. Then I add another shirt because I can tear it up to wrap my wounds. The only food items in the room are long-term storage—a few containers of jerky, boxes of potatoes, and a sack of yams. Since I prefer yams over potatoes, I load up on them and copious amounts of jerky.

Selecting a long-sleeved shirt, I knot a strip of fabric to close the bottom before loading my bounty through the neck. I hang the bundle on my back, wrapping the sleeves over one shoulder and under the opposite arm before tying it. With it secured, my hands are free to climb the rungs. I exit the way I came, climb to the roof, and return to Thirty-Six, where I stuff Janny's bundle into my pack. With the sun heating me from above, I consider my next move.

I can't stay up here forever. I need a place to hide—a location that provides shelter and gives me time to heal while I plan my escape from Harwell. I suppose I could approach Nacole or Harbert. Even Cully might be an option, though I'm unsure how any of them would react. Janny seems to think it's a bad idea, but I also hesitate because of the danger I'd put them in—their homes are likely the first place the cogs will look for me.

It's strange I wouldn't hesitate to ask Vale for help if she were here. Even Tesha, as much as I hate to admit it. Both of them would help me—our months in Durus showed me I could rely on them—yet Cully, who I used to go to for everything, is someone I'm not sure I can trust. What a perplexing turn of events.

I rub the triple layers of fabric on my arms, warming the skin beneath, and my thoughts wander to my history in Harwell. It's pathetic how I used to stalk Vale, chasing her through the community with Nacole. It was a slick move to step into the Dark to escape us. I was furious she disappeared, but now it makes me smile, but the expression doesn't last because I wish escaping could be that easy for me. It could be if I had a circlight. Without one, I'm stuck.

And sure, Vale didn't have one either, but she had the Dark brothers to watch out for her. And if she went in alone, it was only to enter the place with the records. What did she call it?

Wait a minute...

The repository!

My hands still on my arms, and I straighten in my seat. Vale swore me to secrecy about the repository, telling me that besides the story keepers and Tesha, no one in Harwell knows about it, and very few Coastals do, either. Meaning there's a chance Endrack's cogs haven't found it!

I jump to my feet, trying to recall every detail Vale gave me about the repository and knowing my basic destination is the lumber trees and the big rock jutting into Harwell.

I hurry down the ladder, keeping my eyes peeled for movement.

Which side did she enter from? Was it the east or the west? I know she told me.

I reach the edge of Thirty-Six and watch the Upper River Bridge. It's twenty feet away. Then it's another thirty to the cover of the trees—what little is left of them. The ones closest to me are stubs of what they used to be—short and black—so I'll have to keep low and stay extra cautious.

A few minutes pass while I try to remember east or west while simultaneously gathering the courage to cross into the open. It reaches a point where waiting any longer seems foolish, seeing as I could have covered the distance and then some without being seen if I'd just gone already.

Just go!

Still, I pause a few more seconds and take a last look around before I tear across the bridge. It makes a horrible sound as I do, my feet not quiet in the least. When I reach the other side, I don't pause but push on, throwing myself against the first tree and peeking around the edge, but everything seems quiet.

I take a moment to catch my breath—from nerves more than any real exertion—and wipe my face. Looking down, I discover the scorched tree marked my fingers. Anywhere that's touched the tree has turned black, including the front of my new clothes.

Well, at least I'll smell different from what the dogs are sniffing for. I push from the tree and scurry to the next one, weaving through them and feeling relieved when I reach a section still standing. I'm able to move upright through them while keeping hidden. Soon enough, I arrive at the rock. When Vale ran from us, she came from the Common. The west side is closest when walking from that direction. But I'm standing by the east side now. So, which should I try?

East or west?

Gah! Why can't I remember?

Because it wasn't a necessary detail at the time!

I bite my lip, contemplating. I have to pick one, and if it's wrong, I'll backtrack and try the other. Vale said it was like twenty feet in. Or was it fifty? Ugh! I don't know. But she said as long as you keep your hands on the rock, you can enter safely. Hopefully, those instructions apply regardless of the side I choose.

Eventually, I pick the east side since it's closest to me, and I'm too nervous to stay any longer in the light. Who knew there'd be a time when I'd feel safer in the Dark?

My mind made up, I rush past the Hem, pressing against the rock and stepping into the Dark. I may not have a circlight, but at least I can see if someone else in the vicinity is wearing one. So far, there's nothing. All I see is black. All I feel is rock. All that's underfoot is dirt. I smell the soot on my fingers and hear the slight breeze and faint sound of running water.

My steps are cautious but steady, hoping with every advancement I picked the right side. But it feels like I've been in here forever. (And that I chose poorly.) I'm ready to give up and go back when my hands run over a sharp ridge in the rock. I reach around, and it's clear there's a gap. This must be it!

I slide the pack from my back and maneuver until I'm inside, tugging my supplies behind me. It's a tight fit with rock in front and behind. I lift one arm and find the ceiling. Inching forward, I'm very aware of the narrow passage—afraid I'll hit my head or scrape my nose if I go too fast. I bet this is a tight squeeze for the others. I'm positive Ronen wouldn't fit.

The passage seems unending, and it feels like the world is closing in on me—a combination of the confined space and the surrounding Dark. I'm on the verge of panic—trapped in this endless tunnel—when I glimpse a sliver of light. My heart rate increases, and I bite my lip, bombarded by fear. Vale said there was electricity in the repository, and I imagined I'd be fumbling against the wall in search of the switch, but it's already lit.

Which means someone left the light on.

Or, more likely, there's someone inside right now.

CHAPTER THIRTY-THREE

I have two options. I can back out of the tunnel and find another place to hide. (Yeah, right.) Or I can quietly enter and peek inside. Resolved—because there's no other option—I move forward. Unfortunately, four feet from the opening something crunches underfoot.

"Who's there?" It's a man's voice—stern and demanding. Not freaked out, like me. And then, he adds, "Vale, please tell me that's you?"

Vale.

My head falls forward—only an inch in this cramped space—and my body relaxes. If it's someone relieved to see Vale, it's someone I'm not scared to approach. "Not Vale," I answer. "But I'm a friend of hers."

Well, kind of. Actually, I guess I'm family, but that's beside the point. That I'm not her enemy is our focus.

I continue forward, and the crunching starts again. Another step, and I kick something metal that clangs against the rock. What is all this? I contort and look down, finding scattered objects I'm betting are here to announce an intruder. Well, it worked.

Reaching the edge, the electric light steadies my nerves after walking through the oppressive Dark. However, I'm still slightly apprehensive about who's inside. I guess it's just the unknown. But I'll have my answer after one more foot.

Moving that last step into the cave, I drop my supplies on the floor and stare in shock at my birth father. "Laso?" I ask, blinking because the room is bright and because I'm a little stunned. No wonder he wasn't nervous about Vale approaching. She's his daughter!

And so am I—a fact that still doesn't seem real—so I guess he should feel nearly as calm about seeing me as her, though maybe not as excited. However, I wasn't very kind the last time we met—yelling at everyone and naming him Goat Head and such—so he'd be within his rights to feel some apprehension. But to my credit, at least I never said his nickname out loud.

"Annibeth? Is that you?" It's a telling question, revealing my ragged state when both Janny and Laso have a tough time recognizing me.

"Yes, it's me!" I exclaim, my voice full of frustration and sadness. The stress of the day and everything during the last two weeks overwhelms me. And with that, I dissolve into tears.

Laso approaches, gripping my shoulder. "Hey, you're okay. You're safe." Am I really, though? Somehow I doubt it, but I can't stop crying to argue with him. "What can I do? Do you need to sit?"

He draws me forward, getting me to the chair. He helps me onto it, but I just sort of drop. Then, squatting beside me, his hand grasps my knee, and he watches me lose it. So much has happened since I last saw him here in Harwell. Back when things were normal. When he was Vale's father, and I had no connection to him.

Laso runs his hand down my back while the sobs pound through me. My release is so hard my head throbs, and my ears feel foggy. "Shh," he says. "It's okay. You're safe."

I still don't believe it, but gradually, my crying slows. I don't move or make eye contact because I'm not ready to talk. He's not doing a terrible job in the fatherly role, but I don't know how to relate to him. And then I get the hiccups, and every few seconds, I jerk, which takes the situation to another level of awkwardness.

When there's no sign they'll go away anytime soon, Laso rises and walks to the shelf, rummaging around and bringing back a cup of water, which he forces me to drink. In actuality, it doesn't take much encouragement. I'm still thirsty. My dips in the river didn't do enough to quench my thirst. My hunger, too, is an unresolved issue that announces itself with a deep growl.

Apparently, my birth father is a fixer because a moment later, I have an apple in my hand.

"Are the others with you?" he asks after I've taken a few bites. There's a mixture of fear and hope in his voice. His green eyes look too much like Vale's, and I have to look away.

"Not that I'm aware of," I say as I chew.

"They attacked you in Durus?" he asks with a heavy swallow. Fear rules the question—fear for his daughter's safety.

I think back to the picnic they planned for my birthday. "We were once, but that was a month ago. The Dark brothers took care of it, and we were safe again."

"But you're alone now," he says, rubbing his neck and pressing his lips together before asking, "Did you leave them?"

I lower my apple and swallow the big chunks, scraping my throat.

When I learned Laso was my birth father, I hated the idea. But over time, I've softened some toward the situation, hoping he'd give me a fair trial—try to think well of me until he understood what I was about. But I was wrong. Of course, I was wrong. He's close to Vale, and there's no way he hadn't long ago formed an opinion about the Padded Princess of Harwell. He's kind but also aware of my character, figuring I might abandon them if the action suited my needs.

Once, I would have been furious about his implication, but he expresses too much truth to argue against—it was always a possibility. And Laso's just trying to figure out what happened to the person he loves most in the world. Just like I'd tried to do with Janny, asking about my parents. No, I'm not angry. But I'm ashamed of myself. I'm sad he has good reasons for the question to cross his mind.

He deserves an explanation and every detail I can remember. Hopefully, he can find some peace in my story even though I haven't.

"We made it to Durus and were doing well there. A few weeks back, the group took the horses out for exercise. I thought they'd gotten stuck outside because they were concerned about the lift used to go to the surface—it wasn't working properly. I exited the main door to help them get back in, but the cogs captured me. A man we met in the Cliffs was helping them."

"So, you don't know where the others are?"

I shake my head, licking the sticky apple flavor from my lips. "I had a key to get back into Durus," I say, looking down at my fingers and forcing a hard swallow.

"They got it?"

I glance up. "I don't think so. There was a struggle, and I hid it under some dirt. I don't think they found it. The group could still be safe in Durus. But—" I drop the apple on the table and rub my hands over my face. "They knocked on the door to Durus. They'd found us. I don't see how they could still be there. And then Yip heard me and came to help, but... but..."

My head drops to the table where my tears fall on the surface like pattering rain. "He was my friend," I whimper. "Ronen's dream," I moan, my shoulders shaking under the weight of sadness. Saeva made it impossible to grieve, but now, it's all coming out.

Laso's hand returns to my back, moving in circles. "I'm sorry, Annibeth." The comforting loops continue until I'm settled enough to sit up again. I notice the apple sitting sideways on the table. I can't eat anymore, but we can't waste anything.

"You can have the rest," I say, motioning to it. "I don't think my stomach can handle any more right now."

Laso picks it up and nods before taking a bite. He watches me for a moment, then asks in a subdued but disconcerted tone, "What did they do to you?"

"I'm sure you've noticed my hair," I say with a self-deprecating laugh, flipping some of the long strands. I guess I've developed a sense of humor about my awkward appearance—that's new. Though, with Saeva around, I couldn't afford anger or tears, so maybe laughter is the obvious next choice.

I sigh, feeling bone tired but knowing there's more to accomplish before I can relax. "I might as well give you the tour of my wounds, especially since I need your help."

I point out each scar and bruise—reminders of every unpleasant moment I endured over the last two weeks. Laso's sickened by my fingers, which is interesting because I thought the near-drowning would bother him more. (It did me, making the top of my list.) In addition, I've developed an overwhelming dislike of insects.

Saving the best for last, I reveal the knife wound in my side. This time I look at the injury and immediately wish I hadn't. The surrounding skin is dark, and the wound itself is a gaping hole draining liquids in multiple colors. I'm shocked I didn't detect it in the Clinic, but the smell is atrocious—putrid and pungent.

Laso retrieves Janny's bag, laying out the supplies so they can dry. Then he gets to work, making an herb poultice while he asks about my latest escape from the cogs. Laso's grateful for Janny's help and seems impressed by my actions in Harwell. A strange warmth surges through me at the pride on his face.

He uses the last of his water to clean the wound as best he can, then tears a strip of the extra shirt I got to wrap it up. When Laso's finished with me, I lie on the floor, exhausted, staring at the rocky ceiling. This place is no Durus, but I'm happy to be here. And I'm happy Laso's here.

Months ago, this man was introduced as my birth father, and I couldn't get away from him fast enough. But today, I'm grateful for him. He's been patient and calm, though I see the anger and frustration he conceals. I could have tended to my wounds, though not as efficiently, but he did the job without making a big thing of it. He took care of me, and I feel uncommonly comfortable with him. It's the last thought I have before falling asleep.

I wake hours later. It's impossible to tell the time in here, but Laso says it's the next day and morning. He helps me from the floor onto the chair, then brings out a comb for my hair. Only it doesn't work as intended.

"There are so many clumps," he says when his first pass gets stuck after sliding a few inches. I'm sure if I'd grown up with him instead of my adoptive parents, he would have helped me like this when I was little. It's a strange thought.

"It would be better to cut it," I say, resting my chin on my elbow. I'll be sad to lose my hair, but there's no point in hanging on to what's left.

"I was hoping you'd say that," he says, flashing a blade.

"Where did you get a knife?"

"It's Captain Rhed's. He left it with me for protection. And lucky us, it's capable of more than one job," he says, walking behind me and inspecting the mess he's attempting to fix.

"How did you end up hiding from Endrack in here? Or did you never leave your research?"

I was in the room when he insisted on staying in Harwell because he had *things to do.* Has he been here all this time searching the repository?

"It's stupid, really," Laso says, making his first cut. It's curious that this time, watching long strands of hair fall from my head is a relief rather than a shock. "I sent Milany to Tenebris. I planned to identify a few promising books and take them with me, following her a day or two later, but right before my time to leave, Lord Endrack arrived. Captain Rhed told me to hide here, intending to fight them off and retrieve me. But the cogs outnumbered the guard. It happened quickly. The Coastals were overcome and retreated, and the Adlumians took Harwell."

Laso steps close to tackle another side of my miserable hair. He sighs. "He said he'd come back when it's safe." His concern about Captain Rhed's safety is apparent in the statement.

"Janny said she saw him alive," I say, wanting to ease his worries while not knowing if her sighting was before or after he instructed Laso to ensconce here.

"I hope that still holds true. I just keep telling myself he's working to make it safe, and then he'll come get us."

"Yes," I say because my desire is the same. Separation from those I care about is a physical pain, but it's also what sustains me during the long hours in this tiny cave—the hope they're out there longing for me as I do for them.

CHAPTER THIRTY-FOUR

Time in the repository passes differently from Durus because, while I'm still cut off from the world, I'm aware of the hour. Laso squeezes through the gap at nighttime to replenish our water from a nearby spring. In the mornings, he changes my poultice, and each time the look on his face is the same—carefully concealed worry. In between, I argue—with myself more than him—that we should do more, but he tells me our job is to wait. He says my injuries need to heal before we can take any action, but it only seems like an excuse to delay. Still, I appreciate his quiet care. He doesn't push or fuss but helps where he can and gives me space—what little there is—when I need it most.

Too soon, the events of the day become monotonous. Faced with the stresses of my health and boredom in the repository, I revert to the activity that kept me occupied in hiding. I read.

I went from reading fun adventure stories in Durus to the serious histories about Harwell. It's not that I dislike them, but it's less of an escape. I also have frequent and uncomfortable revelations from all those times I accused Vale of telling false stories. I thought the facts she relayed were silly, and now, I'm pouring over the same stories with rapt interest. It embarrasses me, which I'm sure would delight her. The thought, strangely, makes me smile.

My parents kept us from one another, but I wish it hadn't been so. We would have been friends, but we never had the chance. Nacole would have liked her—probably more than me—and might have learned to defy me instead of always deferring to my wants. I grin at the prospect. (I also hate the idea.) It would have caused problems with my need for power, but maybe that drive wouldn't have been as strong without the constant pressure to be seen in a certain light.

Thoughts of Vale lead me to thoughts of the others. I miss them, and it hurts to think they might be held captive like I was, persecuted while bringing them back here for Endrack's inspection.

For Endrack's knife.

I long for nights curled up with Yip, reading while Ronen looks on. I didn't realize it at the time—separation from my family hid the possibility—but my time in Durus was one of the happiest of my life. And the two of them made it that way. I brush away a tear over my loss.

Laso harbors his own worries, and watches me battle mine, witnessing my sadness but not asking questions. And I never voice my sorrows, but I ask about my family. Even though it's awkward, Laso doesn't act bothered. He says my mother seemed less tired the last time he saw her. I learn Captain Rhed told my parents I met his wife in Tenebris, and my mother brightened upon hearing news of me. My father expressed gratitude for Ma's kindness. Then Endrack came, ending Laso's knowledge of their status or location.

I've hesitated to talk with him about Ennette Rennick, though I'm curious about her. I figured he'd be angry and refuse to speak—upset I got her taken away. And while I could argue many excuses—uninformed, scared, and arrogant—the truth is, I was vindictive. I'm ashamed I gave up an innocent woman—a woman who turned out to be family—to a crazy man, and it was all in retaliation against Vale for besting me.

But when I get the courage to bring her up, Laso's nice and doesn't judge, answering my questions. Ennette Rennick sounds like other great women I know—Ronen's mother, my birth mother, and the mother who raised me—all wise and kind.

"Another person for us to wonder and worry about," I say, thinking about Ennette Rennick's welfare, and Laso nods in agreement.

◆ ◆ ◆

When the tedium becomes too much, I explore the repository, finding many strange things. I look at them with an eye toward fixing our situation, doing as my father asked and using my reckoner's mind to help. Doing as Siman encouraged and staying aware and alert for opportunities.

It turns out there's a bag of spare circlights—of course, they'd get stored in the repository—though one of them is broken. Laso has his own, sitting unused on the shelf. He doesn't dare risk someone spotting our location. But I feel less cagey, knowing we have them in an emergency.

There's an arrow on the shelf. Laso thinks it's one of Geric's, though he doesn't know why it's here. And behind it are two wooden boxes. One's bigger than the other, each with unique carvings and stone inlay. One contains a necklace I instantly recognize as Vale's regalia, having the same writing as my bracelet. The other box is full. There are two rings, a comb and brush, and other curious items I don't recognize. Laso points out a gold piece of jewelry, telling me it's used to relay the time of day. There's also a picture of Tesha's mother and father when they were younger—both looking less insane than ever I saw them. There's a letter to Tesha which I don't read, and a dozen or so blue ribbons haphazardly stuffed on top.

I take out Tesha's brush, deciding it sounds comfortable to use on my short hair. I don't think she'd mind. Knowing her, I bet she'd give it to me before refusing me use of it—not that I'd ever ask that of her. (Though at one time, I might have.) These boxes and their contents tell Vale's and Tesha's stories. Observing their contents, I don't feel like an intruder. Indeed, I feel like a participant in these events. I'm part of their journey, and I suddenly want to commemorate that.

Without overthinking my actions, I retrieve one of Tesha's

blue ribbons. Finding the remnants of Laso's haircut, I select the longer strands and straighten them with my fingers, securing one end with a knotted ribbon. Then I braid. My stomach twists with memories of Saeva, but I push those thoughts away. She has no place in this room. This is for me. This is a reminder of my journey—my wins and losses.

I reach the end and make a loop of the braid, tying off the open end with the same blue ribbon so my hair makes a perfect circle—a bracelet, like my regalia. Laso looks on, observing the result of my efforts but not commenting. He seems to understand I'm not one to dwell on sentimentality. My creation is something I needed for myself—a symbol of strength and belonging. I'm not prepared to assign words to my task or explain its meaning to another person. That he gives me my moment without demanding answers makes me respect him more. He simply gives me a tight smile and goes back to his reading.

Approaching the shelves, I open Vale's box but lift the lid with too much force. It tips back, almost spilling the contents, but I catch it in time. Gently, I slide the box to the side, mindlessly putting my hair inside and closing the lid because it's not what's in Vale's box that holds my attention—it's what's under it.

I've read thick volumes of Harwell's history for days, but here I discover a relatively slim book with *Research and Creation of Lamlight* printed on the front.

This book belonged to Derwood Dale—the scientist who created the Dark that the group told me about in Durus—but it's not the journal they mentioned. This is something else.

I open the cover and find a folded map that's not part of the book. It's crinkled, dirty, and worn on the edges. I view it briefly before slipping it back inside and flipping through pages of drawings and calculations. I'm not great with numbers. But my reckoner's mind, which works in facts, knows this book would have outstanding value to Endrack. With it, he could create as much lamlight as he wanted, advancing easily into the Dark territories.

Laso sits on the floor with his back resting against the wall and a book on his lap, but unlike a moment ago, his eyes are closed, and his head is tilted to the side, resting against the shelf. Without causing him to stir, I take the book to the table. My comprehension is minimal, but the drawings are precise. A person with the right mind—someone like Harbert, who excels in mathematics—would have no problem understanding and following these instructions.

I turn every page, engrossed in Derwood Dale's process for making his creation and witnessing the origins of a scientific miracle. Reaching the end, there's a final entry, but it's in different handwriting than the rest of the book, and it's titled.

The Words of Garard Dale, Son of Derwood Dale.

I consider waking Laso to show him the scientist's son's entry, but he probably already studied this book in depth, so I let him sleep and begin reading.

Year Thirty-Four in the Dark.

It felt wrong to add my thoughts to my father's journals. I don't know that it's better to add them to his research book, but ultimately, I needed to put this somewhere, and I picked this one.

The counteractant transfers to the next generation. It's a blessing for those living in the Dark, but my father had hoped the ability to see in light bubbles would also be present in offspring, giving them dual sight. So far, it has not been the case. He would be so disappointed—in himself more than anything. I've yet to research the result of a child from mixed parentage. Another generation may pass before we know that answer as few interact between the light bubbles and the Dark. Still, he believed it was possible, and I will continue to inquire about the phenomenon my father called a beacon of hope for the future.

A young man named Kerk Harwell was responsible for our bioluminescence study. I accompanied my father occasionally to check in with Kerk's settlement in the south—what came to be known as Adlumen. I received unfortunate news of unrest in Adlumen, and accompanied by my eldest son, Dalles, we snuck in to meet with Kerk. Once there, we were told about a threat to Adlumen's leadership led by General Endrack, who served in the highest ranks of their military. I offered to help the leaders—Kerk Harwell, Linnus Dirby, and Shon Dorian—by guiding them through the Dark with the lamlight. I made it clear we'd use the resource to flee their home, but it would remain with me at the end of our journey, and they agreed.

So, with Dalles and I wearing lamlight collars, we helped them escape Adlumen, leading them to where my father found Kerk Harwell as a child. Kerk remembered it and recounted the time he carved his name into the surface of the rock building that's the only structure there.

A group of Adlumen's military and their families accompanied the leaders to start their new community. Upon arriving in their new home, there was some contention when a portion of them requested the counteractant to form a separate guard stationed in the Dark to protect the refugees in the new light bubble. The commotion came about because of the negative opinion held by some citizens of Adlumen regarding those who are light blind.

In the end, Linnus Dirby joined the Dark group as their leader. Back in Adlumen, he led their military, and the man felt some responsibility for his subordinate's success in de-seating them. Dirby's new guard vowed never to tell anyone the location of Dorian and Harwell. And those in the community swore to never look down on those who sacrificed their light sight to protect them. I wasn't privy to any additional governing choices as I left soon after, returning to secure my father's bunker.

Unexpectedly, I returned alone as Dalles became enamored of a young woman among them and stayed with the new settlement. My emotions are divided over his decision, but I promised to return with a few personal items for him to keep. I also left a lamlight collar with him. It went against my better judgement, but I couldn't bear leaving him without a way back to me if he needed it.

The world has gone crazy. Those in the Dark have threatened to administer the counteractant to those in the light, claiming superiority and demanding fealty. They became angry with me when I refused to give them more of the formula, but I couldn't be responsible for such reprehensible behavior, so I buried any remaining counteractant.

My interactions with those in the light are nearly as hostile. They feel it was my family who caused their troubles. My father would agree, though he'd dwell on the creation of the Dark, while they view the counteractant as the issue.

I'm one day from the light bubble where my other son Derak lives. I'll spend a few days, recapping my travel accomplishments, gathering what I need, and relaying Dalles's choice. The brothers are close, and I don't look forward to the conversation.

Then I'll leave to fulfill my promise to Dalles and secure my father's interests before returning permanently to Derak's light bubble. I've been on the move for too long, but I've nearly concluded my business, and I'm eager to remain in one place.

I hope the best for Harwell, Dorian, and Dirby. Not only because they're good people who've lost their home, trying to build a new one in that tiny light bubble, but because, it appears, my son's future is now linked to theirs.

But for now, it's up to the people—both light blind and with light sight—to make their way in the world. Success or failure is in their hands. For the next few hundred years, they'll have to figure it out for themselves until things change once again. The Dales have done all we can.

I'm full to the brim with questions and unwilling to wait for answers. Crouching down, I shake Laso awake. He leans up, rubbing his eyes. "Did I fall asleep?" he breathes out with a yawn.

"Yeah. I need you for something."

"Oh. Sure." He licks his lips and scoots until his back is straight against the wall. His eyes are still droopy when he asks, "What's on your mind?"

"I found this book under one of the wooden boxes."

"Oh, yeah. It's Derwood Dale's, outlining how to create lamlight."

"So, you've read his son's note at the end?" I ask. The wound on my side aches in this posture so I adjust to sit cross-legged instead.

Laso stills. "No, I haven't." I pass the book to him to read. He's quickly immersed in the text, his lips moving while he reads silently. (Strange. I do that too.) When he's done, he looks up. "Wow. Well, I guess that explains how the houses came to Harwell. We've been theorizing about that for some time."

"Sure. But did you catch the last section?" I lean in and point, reading the words to him. "*For the next few hundred years, they'll have to figure it out for themselves.*" Then I stress the vital part. "*Until things change once again.* Any guess what that means?"

"I don't have to guess. I know. Because Derwood Dale's journal explains it."

The one Tesha told me about. I tap my lips and ask, "Can I read that one?"

"I wish we both could read it," he says with a humorless laugh. "Malum took it. Thankfully, after Siman, Evans, and Tesha had read it. Nevertheless, Lord Endrack has it by now. They didn't tell you any of this in Durus?"

"They told me a few things but were just starting to trust me. Vale telling me the repository's location was one of her first exercises in trust."

"Ah. Well, I'm glad if she told you one thing, that was it."

"Me too, but now I want you to tell me about the journal."

"I guess the most important thing is that Derwood Dale erroneously made the Dark."

"Okay, I knew that. Tesha told me."

Laso nods. "His guilt drove him to develop the counteractant, which changes people's eyes so they're light blind and can see in the Dark. His experiments turned the eyes white on many of our game animals. He was successful in some ways but had hoped for more."

Fine. I know that part too. "He wanted to make people beacons, like Tesha," I say.

"You know Tesha's a beacon? Seems they extended more trust than you thought."

I give a non-committal shrug. "It was circumstantial. Keep going."

"Well, then he created the lamlight so those with light sight could see in the Dark, but he didn't trust the people to use it for the right reasons. Ultimately, he discovered all his efforts were temporary fixes anyway—well, temporary if you consider 200 to 400 years as fleeting. That's how long he estimated would pass before the Dark begins to abate."

Abate? Now, this information is new.

"Like, it will go away?" I ask to confirm my interpretation of the word.

"Yes."

My eyes widen at this astonishing news. To imagine a world with no Dark seems unbelievable. "How long since Derwood Dale created it?" I ask since it isn't clear in Garard's entry.

"About 150 years."

My mouth falls open, and then I blurt out, "That means it's getting close!" I can't help feeling excited over the prospect.

Laso chuckles. "Yes. Maybe in your lifetime, you'll see signs of abatement. Let's just hope it brings about good things and doesn't merely cause more trouble."

CHAPTER THIRTY-FIVE

I 've spent a week in the repository with my birth father. At first, I felt safely confined in this small space, but now I feel restless. I feel useless, which induces despondency. And I feel sick—like literally sick—and in pain. Not only my side where the cut isn't healing but my head throbs and muscles ache.

And there's nowhere to get help. If I returned to the Clinic, they'll capture me, and I'll be executed. Even if my condition deteriorates rapidly, my chances of a longer life are better if I stay here. Saeva didn't kill me in the river, but it seems plausible I could die in this room—at her hands, in a round-about way.

Our food supply is getting low. Laso stocked up before Endrack's occupation since he spent so much time here, and it was easier than coming and going throughout the day. But even with the items I brought from Building Thirty-Four, it's almost gone.

I need to get serious about acquiring more—make a plan for sneaking back to the provisions building—but I'm too tired. I can barely entertain the problem. (Can scarcely focus long enough to remember it's a problem.) Add in the fact I'm more thirsty than hungry, and it's probably a waste to go. Laso can eat my share. And, anyway, he's convinced neither of us should leave right now. He's sure something will change our fate soon, but I don't have that same hope.

I'm sprawled on the floor, reading another of the Harwell volumes. It's not captivating enough to keep my attention, and I wish for a Durus novel. But maybe it's just that I'm uncomfortable. I shift from one hip to the other and knock over my cup of water.

"No!" I shriek, getting Laso's attention. Not only is it the last of our water, but it's saturating the pages of the book I have open.

As a descendant of story keepers, my ancestors would skin me alive for the affront. I laugh at the thought while Laso looks on curiously, mopping up the spill with one of my spare shirts.

Only there's not much water to gather. Not nearly what there should be.

"Stop!" I command, and Laso stills while I lean closer to the floor, detecting a soft sound.

Dripping.

The repository floor is stone, covered with a fine layer of dirt gathered over the years. It's not like anyone kept up daily or even weekly cleaning in the place. I run my finger through the saturated ground, finding the space between two stones. I continue pushing my finger along the edge, digging deeper into the groove. Then suddenly, my finger punches through the gap, finding nothing but air beneath my fingertip.

As I suspected upon hearing the sound, there's an open cavity beneath the stone floor. I wrap my fingertips under the stone and pull, but it's too heavy. "Let me try," Laso says, and I scoot over so he has leverage. Within a minute, he's loosened it enough to lift the stone from the floor. Then we gaze inside the hole at another rock. This one's smaller and thinner, so Laso has no trouble removing it. We immediately realize this second stone serves as a lid for the contents inside a stone box.

And what's inside is a book.

An important book, I conclude, since someone made an effort to hide it away. A book that's worth is revealed as I brush the dust from the top and read the title: *Book of Adlumen Law - Governance and Guidance.*

"The Dark brothers have been looking for this information for months," I say in awe.

"As have I," Laso replies reverently.

"Guess it's good I'm clumsy."

Laso looks over at me with concern—the expression making him look so much like Vale it hurts—and says, "Except, we both know you're not."

No, I'm not. "Well, let's agree it was luck because I'm not giving Saeva credit, even inadvertently." Laso squints. He's seen my wounds, but I haven't told him about Saeva's part. He seems to sense that although I let the comment slip, it's something I don't want to talk about.

We settle on each side of the opening. "I'm almost afraid to touch it," I say, my mind going wild with what could be inside.

Laso chuckles—it's a real father-daughter moment—then says without shame, "I'm not." He lifts it out, blowing the fine residue from the surface before opening the cover. The pages are yellow and stiff. The cover's holding on with barely an inch of connection. I don't believe the book came to this condition under the floor but was placed inside this way, possibly after a harried escape from Adlumen.

The first thing we discover is a folded piece of paper not part of the bound pages. In my limited experience with books, it seems a common thing to tuck things inside. Laso opens it, finding a written message from Kerk Harwell. There's no date like Garard Dale's entry in his father's book, but based on the content, they wrote it around the same time.

My role in Adlumen as the Governor of Knowledge was documenting our history. I've already started keeping the stories of my people in our new community and will pass the responsibility to my offspring, training them in their duties.

Linnus Dirby, Governor of Peace, has taken the counteractant and started a Dark community. A portion of the military that accompanied us from Adlumen has joined him. We tried to talk Linnus out of this decision and begged him to reconsider, but he wouldn't be deterred. He wants to be in the larger world, not confined to such a small space, and he feels he can fulfill his duties better from the outside. Like me, he's promised to pass his responsibilities for protecting our community to the next generation.

Shon Dorian, Governor of Wisdom, stayed with me in the light. He's advised that we drop our titles of Lord and Governor to remove ourselves further from Adlumen. None of us feel the threat from that place is behind us. The only thing preserving our safety is the barrier of the Dark. Linnus will watch from that realm and notify us if a time comes to reclaim our Right to Rule. We hope it will happen someday, but we also know that living on unfulfilled hopes is an empty existence. With that in mind, Shon insists the rising generation should remain unaware of our history with Adlumen. If we are found and aren't in a position to reclaim what's ours, their naivete may be the only thing to protect our people from what would surely be a massacre.

The adults in the community and those joining Linnus in the Dark have made an oath of silence regarding our history in Adlumen. Linnus added his own vow—a promise to organize the guard, never to forsake their duty, and most painful of all, that they will make no more contact with us. He believes without suspending communication and living separately, our people will never fully break from Adlumen and the danger our old home presents.

I will miss my friend, but this is our life now.

I plan to hide this missive along with the laws of Adlumen during our time. Only Linnus's and my family will know of the location, hidden in a cave, uniquely straddling the Dark and the light bubble we call home.

I'll never forget Linnus's last words to me, which have become a theme for my new life here: We'll watch you from the Dark and keep the rogue forces of Adlumen from ever finding you.

It's our common goal. To that end, we will, as Linnus is prone to say, 'succeed or die with honor.'

"There were three governors, not one," Laso says after reading it several times. "All this time, we've been looking for one."

"I guess it makes sense because there are three regalia," I add. "Though it was confusing because the paper you got from Labrum talked about houses, not governors, when referencing the regalia."

"Maybe using the term houses was part of the governors' plans to distance themselves from Adlumen further."

"Well, why put the information on paper at all?"

Laso shrugs, running a hand through his wavy black hair. "Who knows? Maybe they weren't the ones who did it."

I look back at the book. "The Dark brothers were sure knowing Adlumen law would help us take down Endrack and get your mother back." My grandmother, though I still struggle to remember to call her that. "Do you believe this book has that much potential?"

Laso's quiet as he considers my question. Then, releasing a long breath, he says, "Well, we've got the information right here in our hands. Maybe we should find out."

He's right. There's no point in supposing. It's time to find our answers.

We spend hours turning pages together. It feels familial—shoulder to shoulder, sharing this discovery. It seems strange how comfortable I suddenly feel with this man. Maybe the ease stems from our shared investment in the book's contents, which connects us through purpose instead of ancestry, making it more meaningful and less forced.

The book is very formal. It's not handwritten but presented in the old way, like the books in Durus—a typed font made on a machine. We raise our eyebrows at shocking discoveries. We frown at disappointing news. One time I even gasp over a revelation. Adlumen, led by these governors, seemed a happy and secure place—somewhere I'd want to live. It's a system I'd happily be governed by, so I can't help but wonder what went wrong. How did the Endrack family so efficiently oust the three governors without a fight or their citizens even pushing back?

We read every page. The last ones are filled with official decrees, ceremonies, and leadership oaths, along with a Citizen's Allegiance Vow given by the people. And that vow is what I find most interesting. It explains the deep connection Adlumians have with their law. If their people believe in and uphold this vow, it's a powerful weapon indeed—more effective than any knife.

Laso tips the back cover, closing the book, and we stare at it.

"So, what do you think?" he asks, eventually.

"I think this could change everything," I reply, my voice sounding overly loud to my ears. I think Siman could be right —with this knowledge, I could be the one to alter our destinies. I'm letting the possibilities run wild in my head, and that's when I hear it.

A faint sound coming from outside the repository. Coming from the Dark. I hesitate a half-second before the sound turns meaningful (before recognition dawns), conjuring a truth I dare not believe.

I jump to my feet, Laso rising with me. I take a step, and he takes my arm, holding me in place. I pull again, needing release, but he keeps his grip. "Where are you going?" he asks with a shake of his head.

"Out there."

"Don't," he says, a plea more than a command, but he doesn't understand. There's *nothing* that could keep me from going outside.

CHAPTER THIRTY-SIX

My birth father doesn't relinquish my arm, but I hear the noise again and tug against his firm hold, saying, "I'll be back soon."

"Annibeth, what exactly do you expect to see out there?" He narrows his eyes, waiting for an explanation.

"Oh! You're right!" I spin away from the exit, and he finally releases me. Rushing to the shelf, I grab his circlight.

"That's not what I meant!" He throws his hands up, exasperated.

"I know." Grinning, I skirt past him, skipping to the entrance and slipping into the gap.

"Please! Don't go out there. It's the middle of the day!" he implores, but his words are muffled since I'm halfway down the channel. Only the fact I'm scaring him gives me pause.

"Only one person uses that signal," I call back with a massive, unstoppable grin. My heart leaps into my throat as I think about that one person. I no longer feel tired. I don't remember my injuries. I'm too happy for lethargy to possess my mind or pain to afflict my body.

I shimmy the rest of the way through the gap, ignoring the burn in my side and moving faster than I've ever gone before—even during late-night relief breaks after holding it for so long I thought I'd explode. I'm not cautious. I don't even pause. The minute I'm outside, I throw the circlight up, lighting the world to reveal the wonders around me.

And there he is.

Right in the middle of it all, looking big and safe and perfect.

So perfect.

"Ronen!" I scream before running full speed and launching myself. He doesn't even wobble as I slam into him. Instead, he scoops me right up, and I drop the circlight as my arms wrap around his neck and my legs go around his waist. His thick arms envelop me—one hand landing on the back of my head, holding me against his shoulder.

"Bethy! Ah, Bethy. Are ye real?" He smooths his hand over my butchered hair (greasy and gross), but he doesn't seem to care. "Didna think I'd e'er find ye."

I squeeze him tighter, knowing he can handle that pressure and more. "I knew you would," I mumble, snuggling into his neck, drawing strength from him, and feeling calm for the first time in ages.. Ronen's shaking hand runs down my back before bringing it back up behind my head.

"Ye cut yer hair," he comments, and I stiffen when memories of what happened with Saeva assault my mind.

But I don't want to think about her right now, so I push through my reply, simply saying, "Yes." I lean back, enjoying the feeling of his scratchy beard against my cheek. It's longer than before but smells like him—campfire and leather.

Ronen rubs the side of my head. "Ye're sorta lumpy."

"Gee, thanks." I chuckle, and we look into each other's eyes. He has beautiful eyes. "I see you've not broken your habit of saying whatever pops into your head."

But he doesn't acknowledge my teasing, asking, "Bethy, why'd ye cut yer hair?"

I break our stare, looking at a button on the top of his shirt. "Let's not talk about that right now."

He takes a minute to respond while I still inspect the button. "Need ta know," he says in his rumbly voice.

"I'll tell you, but does it have to be now?" I don't want to talk about Saeva. There are plans to make, and focusing on the horrors of my time with her won't bolster my energy for the critical job ahead. "Can't I just revel in happiness, knowing you're here and safe?"

He smiles, but the expression has minimal joy—too weighed down with concern. "Bethy?" Ronen asks, brushing the short bangs from my forehead. I let out a defeated breath, knowing he'll demand to get his way. But then he says it again. "Bethy." Only this time his tone is different—startled—and there's a look of shock on his face. "Bells! Ye're hot."

"Hah!" I giggle and grin. "I always knew you thought so."

"Nay, Cricket." Ronen's in no mood to joke. "Ye're burnin' up."

"Yeah." I tap his hand so he'll let me down. "Got a battle wound that's not playing nice."

"Wound?" The word squeaks from Ronen's lips, as much as any sound is capable of squeaking from Big Scruff. "Ye're hurt?" he groans out. "Did it happen same time as Yip?"

He still hasn't let me down, and I don't want to be this close when we talk about Yip. I tap his hand again, but he just holds me tighter.

"No. It was a little later. Ronen, please let me down."

This time he does as I ask, lowering me to the ground. When I'm on my feet, I take a breath and grab his arm, covered with his black longcoat. "Ronen, I'm so sorry about your dog. Yip was my friend too. I shouldn't have called out to him, but I was scared and did it without thinking. If I could go back, I'd stay quiet. And then... then he'd still be alive."

"Ah, Bethy." Ronen's large hand cups my cheek. His thumb gently wipes away a tear for Yip, moving slowly so he doesn't take out my eye. "Wouldna've mattered if ye were quiet. Yip's like me. Both us dogs'll do wha's necessary ta keep ye safe." He grins, trying to coax a smile from me, but it's impossible, and I look away. I loved that dog—was there to witness Hersh cut him down—and it will be a long time before I can smile when thinking about him. "Bethy," Ronen says, waiting for me to look at him before he continues, "Fact is, Yip's na dead."

"He's— what?"

"Yip's alive. Vale sewed 'im up 'n he's healin' fine."

"Alive," I repeat, and the massive weight of sadness I've carried the last few weeks falls away from me. "Oh, Ronen!" My head falls forward, and my shoulders shake with the power of my relief, tears dropping from my eyes like rain.

"Bethy," Ronen says, keeping me close. "Bethy, wha's all this?"

I lean back and look up at him, tears saturating my eyelids and trying to seal them shut. "Your dream," I start, but my lip quivers, and it's hard to get out the words. "I thought you'd lost your dream," I say, then bite my lip to prevent another round of sobs.

"My dream." Ronen stares at me with a revolving expression, changing from confusion to understanding, then sadness to relief. "Aye," he says, putting his cool hand on my warm cheek and holding me steady. "Suffered terrible days thinkin' I'd lost my dream too," he whispers.

Ronen's expression settles, going from many to one, but relief isn't the emotion that wins the battle. It's something else entirely, and it has my heart doubling its beat.

Suddenly, Ronen's dream comes to life in my mind: A starry night and a lake. A child playing by the shore, carrying a fish. Yip barking and trying to steal it while Ronen laughs, bringing in another catch. But the surprising part is the person entering the scene is a girl with white-blond hair, wearing a dress with butterflies and daisies. She's barefoot, wading in the water, scooping up lake moss, and sneaking up behind Ronen to put it down his shirt.

The picture fades, and I almost feel the wet plant in my

palm. "We need to put your dream back together."

"Workin' on it," he rumbles. "Loosin' sleep gettin' it back."

I see it now—the dark shadows around his eyes. "I missed Yip." And you.

"Soon as I can, I'll bring 'im ta ye."

"I'm content for now." More than. "But where is he?"

"Stayin' with Raider, gettin' fed treats, 'n turnin' fat."

I let the news settle, imagining the fluffy dog licking his lips in delight, and then I laugh. "Good for Yip. He deserves it."

"Dunno 'bout tha'. No use fer a fat, lazy dog," Ronen says, and I laugh again at the serious look on his face. "Now, tell me wha's wrong with ye," he says, and then I'm the one to turn serious, but before I can talk, Ronen glances behind me, and I turn to watch Laso squeeze from the gap.

"Don't mean to interrupt," he says, looking sheepish, then adding, "I, uh, didn't know you two knew each other so well."

He sounds like a meddling and embarrassed father. It puts my bristles up, which Ronen senses, and his hand lands on my shoulder to keep me from reacting. Then he pulls me into his side, wrapping his longcoat around my back, before saying, "Been togetha lots o' hours. Easy gettin' attached ta someone lovely as Bethy."

"Bethy?" Laso blinks, absorbing the nickname, taking in our proximity, and glancing from my eyes to Ronen's and then back to mine. I doubt my birth father could detect it in the lamlight, but my cheeks burn red, and it's not from fever. How mortifying—Annibeth Petters blushing over a boy. "I meant no disapproval," Laso says, stepping forward. "I don't see your friendship as anything other than good."

Friendship. Is it my imagination, or did Laso put a questioning emphasis on that word?

Ronen clears his throat. "Wouldna matter if ye felt diff'rent," he says, outlining his position like it's his prerogative to do so—as if we have some understanding between us. Laso's brows furrow, reemphasizing his over-protective father act. But then Ronen leans forward and offers his hand. Laso relaxes, and they shake like they've just agreed on some deal. (And the deal is me.)

I cross my arms, dissatisfied with their assumptions. I've not given Laso permission to act so fatherly, though he's clearly desperate to do so. And Ronen's not my boyfriend, though he fills the position more perfectly than anyone before him. Still, they act like something's settled when I've never agreed to or recognized such a connection with either of them.

They release each other, and I'm left confused. Still, I'm unwilling to neither validate nor destroy their assumed agreement, so I do what I'm good at and revert to being a reckoner. "While that was touching and a tad strange, we have more important things to discuss."

"Like yer wound," Ronen agrees with a nod.

"No," I say.

"Yes," Laso says. "You should know about all her injuries, but—"

"*All*?" Ronen bellows. "There's more'n one?"

"Later," I say, quiet and calm. After all, shouldn't we keep our voices low out here in the open?

"Now," Ronen insists and starts looking me over.

"Stop. You can catalog my body later," I tell him, stepping away.

Ronen and Laso share a look. Then Ronen tilts his head and chuckles while Laso looks at his feet. "Tha' sounds like a good deal, Bethy," Ronen says with a sideways grin in his beard. I sniff and tighten my arms over my chest, wincing when it disrupts my cut.

"Enough of that," Laso says, and Ronen clears his throat, losing his playful demeanor. "Annibeth's right. Most of her ailments, and the story behind them, can wait." I give Laso a grateful smile before he continues, "She has a horrific knife wound in her side that's heavily infected. She needs better treatment than we can give her. At the first logical moment, attending to her is a priority. But, for now, we need information. Namely, where are the others?"

Ronen groans, rubbing a hand over his eyes and down his beard before tugging on the end. "'Tis na good," he breathes out at last.

"Details," Laso prods.

"'Twas out runnin' the horses with my brothas. 'Twas an hour 'fore we knew ye'd been taken. Yip disappeared, as he does, 'n I went back ta Durus lookin' fer 'im. The girls 'n Siman were panicked, sayin' ye was gone 'n checkin' everywhere fer ye, includin' up the ladder, 'fore Tesha noticed a missin' key." Ronen frowns, then asks, "Why'd ye leave Durus?"

"After you left with Clod, there was a knock on the main door, and I thought you might be stuck up there."

"It wasna us."

"Well, I know that *now*," I say, biting my lip and looking away from him. "I tried the lift first and was careful when I checked outside the door, but they'd left by then. Anyway, I got a key because I was convinced you needed help. I planned to meet up with all of you, but they found me instead. And I dropped the key in the struggle. They didn't find it, did they?"

Ronen shakes his head. "No. But they didna need it. Found Durus solidly."

"Because of me?" I ask, feeling terrible about putting them in danger.

"Nah, Bethy. Not 'cause of ye," Ronen says, shaking his head firmly. "Wha' happened next?"

"They tied me up, and then I saw Yip. He ran for me and tried to help, but Hersh—" I bite my lip again, tearing into the

342

skin. "Anyway, they put something over my mouth, and I slept. Woke up with four cogs taking me back to Harwell." I shake my head, thinking of the despicable group, then remember another distasteful detail. "Spratt was helping them."

"Aye. Spratt," Ronen spits out between gritted teeth. "He's how Vale got taken."

"Vale!" Laso grabs Ronen's arm. "Taken?"

"Aye." Ronen gives Laso a sympathetic frown. "Cogs brought 'er ta Harwell t'day. Geric's with 'er."

"They're together," I whisper to myself—at least that's something. And they're here in Harwell. "Keep going with your story."

"Ye were gone, 'n didna take long ta discover Yip hurtin'. Got 'im with the others back in Durus 'n left straightway, trackin' ye. Were eight in the group. Cleared the Cliffs 'n the cogs' trail split—four one way 'n four the other. Studied the trail 'n made a guess." Ronen releases a weary breath. "Guessed wrong."

"But you tried," I say, attempting to remove the defeated look from his face.

"Made a promise ta ye, Bethy. Took it serious."

"And your promise held," I say, gripping his wrist. "You promised you'd come, and you did. Don't dwell on things beyond our control. Focus on telling me what happened."

"'Kay, Bethy." He takes my hand that's on his wrist, turning it until our palms meet and fingers curl together. Rubbing the back with his thumb, he continues, "Returnin' ta Durus, happened across a Souther friend who agreed ta take Yip ta Raider in Ora fer tendin'. Arrived ta tell the others I lost ye. They helped get Yip ready fer travelin', 'n when he was gone, I left ta come after ye."

I squeeze his hand, afraid of what comes next. The *Book of Adlumen Law* gave a lot of insight into our situation. I have an idea about how to proceed—I could almost call it a solid plan—but it hinges on key people, and Ronen has yet to reveal where they all ended up.

"'Twas a week later Evans caught up with bad news. The cogs broke inta Durus. Secured Geric 'n Vale first, Geric yellin' fer the others ta get out. Evans escaped with Tesha 'n Siman up the ladder but got ambushed by a large group o' cogs 'fore leavin' the Cliffs. Evans got away, ridin' hard 'n barely sleepin' ta reach me."

"Where are Tesha and Siman?" I ask, and Ronen shrugs.

They're an unknown but might not be key to my plan. "What about Evans? Is he here?" I ask, unable to hide my anticipation at the prospect of him being in Harwell.

"Aye. Hidin' 'n watchin' in one o' our spots."

I consider the situation, reviewing the details as if reckoning the law—only, in this instance, it's not the law of Harwell I'm balancing. "So, Evans and Vale are both in Harwell," I say, needing to confirm their vital presence.

"Aye."

"You're positive?" I ask, not meaning to pester, but I must be sure.

Ronen's lips purse until they're hidden in his beard. Then he licks his lips and says slowly, "Aye, Bethy. 'Tis a fact they're both 'ere."

"Well, that's just—" I pause, thinking.

"Bad luck. I know," Ronen supplies.

"No, Big Scruff," I say, and his brows rise. "Actually, it's *perfect*." I pull my hand from his, then rub my palms together like Evans does when he's excited about something. "What plans did you make with Evans?"

"Truly, ye're confusin' me," he says with a chuckle. "'Twas workin' ta understand the situation 'fore makin' plans, tho' he's expectin' me back in the hour. Tryin' ta get word ta Cap'n

Rhed, but we daren't wait ta act."

"You're right. We shouldn't wait, and I know exactly what to do. Will you help me with my plan?"

"O' course, Bethy," he answers like it's an insult I'd consider otherwise. It makes me smile, but the grin quickly wanes. I don't have the energy to keep it there and am already focused on what comes next.

"We need to go to the rooftop of Building Fifteen."

"So, nothin' diff'cult," Ronen says in an attempt at sarcasm, though his breathy voice doesn't do the delivery justice. I'd tell him to stick with stating the obvious—which is more fitting for his personality—but there's no time.

"Annibeth, I don't like you doing this," Laso says, wringing his shirt with his hands.

"You know this is how we fix things."

"Yes, but maybe I should go in your place." He glances at my injury, worried. It's a kind suggestion, but his thought process is faulty.

"That won't work. Sure, you have governor blood, but you're a spare—like Ennette, Tesha, and Captain Rhed. Lord Endrack will want you all eventually—because the titles revert to you—but you're inconsequential for what needs to happen today. Vale is Kerk Harwell's heir, Evans is Linnus Dirby's, and I'm Shon Dorian's. For this to work, all three heirs need to be together. That means Vale, Evans, and me. Not you."

Ronen looks on, confused by all the new information I'm spouting, while Laso groans, shaking his head. "I guess you're right."

"You *know* I'm right because we read the same book," I say with snark, stepping into his space. My lips twist in anticipation of breaking his heart or healing it—however he takes what I'm about to say. "Look, I appreciate your concern and want you to know something. You're not my father like

Marven Petters is, but you've been good to me this week. And I've decided I wouldn't hate knowing you better. We can figure that out later, but right now, you need to understand you have no say in what I do or don't do."

Laso surprises me by chuckling. "You sound just like your father."

I grin—it's all I can manage. "He has little say in my life, either. I'm rather independent and recalcitrant." Laso grasps my shoulders, holding me in place. Maybe he knows how depleted I am, or perhaps he just enjoys the connection.

"I appreciate your honesty. Now you get to hear my side." I nod, even though I don't know if I can handle it. "I'm worried about you. That cut's severe, and you need help I can't give you. Ronen, you need to watch out for her." He looks at the big guy, and whatever Ronen's expression, it softens Laso's.

"I've had more time adjusting to the idea, so it's probably easier for me, but I love you as my own. Besides, you look so much like my Anny. Milany's a good woman, and I love her, but Anny was my heart. I loved your mother more than anyone in my life." He brushes away a sudden flow of tears, stepping away from me before finishing with, "You're a lost piece of that love, and it's a privilege to have you in my life. I don't want to lose you."

I bite my lip, unsure of how to respond, but then his jaw hardens and his tone goes flat as he adds, "So, do what needs doing, and be extra alert."

He immediately turns away, walking to the gap in the rock while his shoulders shake with emotion.

And something inside of me breaks for this man.

He's scared for me. He loves me.

I follow him, putting my hand on his shoulder. The contact is too much, and he breaks into loud sobs. "Hey," I say, surprising myself when I pull him around to face me, bringing him into my arms and hugging him for the first time in my life. He clings to me like he'll be lost if I leave him, though we both know that's precisely what I'm going to do.

"We're okay. We're safe," I say, echoing his words of comfort from when I entered the repository, distraught over my experiences. "And it's going to stay that way. I'll protect Vale and the others." Laso nods against my shoulder, and then, because I can't reassure him without giving full disclosure, I add, "And when this is all over, she and I will resume our bickering, providing you all with some very excellent entertainment."

CHAPTER THIRTY-SEVEN

I follow Laso into the repository while Ronen waits outside. I was right—he's too big for the gap and says he hasn't seen the inside since he was a boy of ten. Opening the ivy box, I take out the only thing needed from this room to carry out my plan—Vale's regalia. I secure the heavy necklace around my neck. The weight is almost too much for my feeble strength.

"We'll come back for you when it's safe," I tell Laso at the gap.

"Heard that before." He shakes his head in dismay. "But I look forward to it, if I don't die of fear first." He means it sarcastically while sounding rather earnest.

"If fear were capable of that, I'd have been dead weeks ago," I say, thinking of my time with Saeva.

My last glimpse of Laso is of his worried but smiling face. His only task is to return the *Book of Adlumen Law* to its hiding place under the floor, and then he'll wait. I understand his frustration—waiting is the worst.

"Fifteen, then?" Ronen clarifies as we start toward Harwell. Endrack's cogs are headquartered between the Dark brothers' cabin and the Well. The most significant concentration is in that area or patrolling the Border Guard Trail. We're lucky the repository is so near the gully because the path makes a wide detour in this area.

"Yes. Fifteen." I recall the many times I've gathered there for happier reasons. However, the memories aren't as sweet now as I remember my constant struggle to control Cully and my friends. Maybe it's not a happy place after all.

It's unfortunate I didn't give my bracelet to Ronen when he asked for it. He would have put it in the repository with Vale's necklace, simplifying things. As it stands, my stubbornness is causing me trouble rather than sticking it to other people. I'm sure they'd say it serves me right. (And it probably does.)

We reach the border between the Dark and Harwell. Ronen pulls on his lenses, and I instantly miss his eyes—sometimes, all I need is his reassuring glance to renew my strength. But Ronen's intuitive and puts a calming hand on my back as we enter Harwell together.

We reverse the path I took during my escape, crouching through the burned trees and slipping over the Upper River Bridge. My tiny feet crunch rocks and kick sticks, even when I'm doing my best to prevent it, while Ronen is so quiet I don't even know he's behind me unless he chooses to break the silence. He excels at stealth, and I'm failing him with every slight noise.

We reach the nearest ladder without incident. I stand at the base, looking up, and Ronen's gaze follows as I tell him, "Now we go up."

Ronen takes my arm before I start. "Ye done this b'fore?"

"Sure. As kids, we'd dare each other. I'm one of few who'd do it." I grin. "More recently, I did it for exercise."

"'Tis safe then," he comments, looking up again.

I chuckle. "Yeah. Did you forget? I grew up here. I know what's safe and what's not."

He tilts his head. "Did ye forget, Cricket? I watched ye growin'. There's nothin' I dunna know."

"Well, that appears untrue. It seems you never spied me rung climbing. Just trust me," I say, and Ronen gives in. But five minutes later, he argues my plan again.

"Bells! We're walkin' 'cross tha'?" he asks, pointing an accusing finger while I stand at the edge of an irrigation flume spanning from one building to the next.

"It appears you drew the short stick again," I tease, but he doesn't laugh, so I add, in a slightly more serious tone, "You can walk or even crawl, but I like to run."

"'Twill ne'er hold me," he says, shaking his head. He paces the edge, chewing his lip so his mouth disappears in his beard.

"Joff's up here all the time, and he's never had a problem."

"Aye. Heard 'bout tha' man. Also heard I'm bigger."

"Don't chicken out now," I say with a jovial tap on his mighty arm.

Behind his lenses, I'm sure his look is pleading when he says, "Na chicken, Cricket. Just smarta than this."

I run at the structure, calling out, "Just don't think about it."

That's how I provoke him into action, but I admit—after we've crossed two flumes—I understand his concern. Ronen doesn't run nor crawl but walks the line at a steady pace with the old, wet boards groaning beneath him. The first time I hear a pop, I turn to ensure he's still with me. The second time, I reconsider my taunts. Before there's a third time, I admit my poor judgment.

"I think you were right about this. Maybe we should take our chances on the transit paths."

He shakes his head. "'Tis a solid plan, 'n I havena yet fallen ta my death."

"What if you wait here for me? I could hurry to Fifteen and come right back?"

"No doin'. Not leavin' ye, Bethy."

The most dangerous section is going from Twenty-Four to Eighteen, where the flume drops eight feet between buildings of differing heights. Ronen, who's always so sure on his feet, loses his footing and slides down the last section, ultimately jumping to the rooftop and rolling. If it were summer, the cabbages would be dead.

After crossing three more flumes, we reach Building

Fifteen. I rush to the northwest corner and lift a stack of broken and worn boards. They're old and brittle with barely any use left in them, but we discard nothing in Harwell. I dig six inches into the dirt and retrieve a folded cloth. Unwrapping it, I reveal my bracelet—the regalia for the Dorian governor.

"I know," I say, standing and brushing dirt from my hands. "If I had given you this for safekeeping, we could have avoided this errand."

"Aye, 'n missed out climbin' rickety rooftops togetha."

"What a shame that would have been." I slide the bracelet onto my arm beneath my sleeve and tuck the cloth into the waist of my pants. "And, lucky you, the adventure continues. There's no ladder down from Fifteen, so we must cross to Sixteen." Ronen voices an unenthusiastic cheer that makes me laugh.

We reach the top of the ladder on Sixteen, but Ronen blocks the way, asking, "Where next?"

"Vale's likely being kept in the Well. I thought we could get over there using the rocks under the bridge, like on the day we escaped Harwell together."

"Aye. Seems logical."

We scope the Tower Path below. It's empty—still a surreal sight in my community—and we descend. I near the bottom and jump to the ground, skipping the last rungs. We shuffle down the short unnamed path between Sixteen and Seventeen, and I peek east and west down Old Row to ensure the way is clear. It is, which makes it especially unfortunate I wasn't more cautious about what might be behind me.

"Annibeth?" I hear and whip around. Ronen moves closer—not tricky in the narrow path—and takes a protective stance. But it's unnecessary, and I rush toward the person unbidden.

"Nacole!" I'm shocked by how ecstatic I am to see her. Maybe our friendship was more real than I believed. It's been months, and I want to share everything with her, though now's not the time. Still, reaching her side, I pull her into a hug without asking, my fingers tangling in the golden curls hanging down her back. She stiffens, and I chuckle—we've never been hugging friends. I was around the Durus group for too long, and it's made me affectionate. I pull back, looking her over. She looks good.

"It is you," Nacole says, sounding unsure and confused after my uncharacteristic behavior. I let go of her and step back. Now it's her turn to look me over. She can't take her eyes off my hair, and I finger the jagged lengths. "They're looking for you everywhere. Where have you been?"

"Hiding," I say, leaving out the details. While I want to tell her of my experiences, I made promises about keeping the repository a secret. Besides, other topics seem more prudent.

Nacole squints and looks past me at Ronen. "With him?" she asks, nodding over my shoulder.

"No," I say, again giving a brief answer. Nicole peers back at me with unsure eyes. "I'm so glad to see you. We need information. Can you tell me where they're keeping Vale?"

Nacole pauses, then scowls. "Why should I?"

I tilt my head. *What's she playing at?*

"Because we're friends."

"Are we, though?" Nacole folds her arms across her chest, and I release a heavy breath. I understand why she would wonder that after all these months of separation. She's had time to reflect on our relationship as I have and likely came to similar conclusions. But I'm ready to put in the work. I've learned a lot about friendship in our time apart, and I'm ready to be one. At least I am until she says. "I don't think I'd be friends with someone who's taboo."

"Taboo," I choke out with a laugh. "What are you talking about?"

"Don't act false. I know all about it. Cully told me. *After you didn't.*"

"You mean what my parents did, secretly adopting me when my birth mother walked into the Dark? I barely learned of the situation before I was forced to leave. There wasn't time to tell you. And I'm not being false. I only laughed because who even cares about taboos now? Things like that don't matter anymore."

"Oh, they matter. Taboos are more important than ever to reinforce Harwell's standards. We don't want the wrong kind of people living here."

Those aren't Nacole's words. I know better than to think she'd say something like that. "Is that a general belief around Harwell or something specifically directed at me?"

Nacole clears her throat. "At you."

"By Cully," I surmise.

"Yes."

Which means Lucan—the Clarcs—have cut me loose. I was a member of their inner circle for my entire life, but that's no longer the case, making me wonder even more about the status of my parents. Were they persecuted in my absence?

"Bethy," Ronen says, touching my arm, his tone urgent. I'm lost in thought, and there's no time for that. Indeed, we don't have time for Nacole's taboo-driven animosity, either. My friend has erroneous ideas, and a pleasant reunion will have to occur later when she's gotten her head straightened out. I just need her to cooperate for now, so I revert to our old dynamic.

"Don't worry, Nacole. I'll get out of your hair. I just need information, and I need it now. Tell me where they're keeping Vale."

Nacole tilts her head. "No."

"Gah! Why are you being difficult?" I throw out my hands, wincing when my side pulls.

"Because I realized something while you were gone," she answers, uncrossing her arms and putting her hands on her hips. "I don't like you."

I knew this. Back when we'd sit in my room, she'd do my hair, and I'd catch a look, and I knew. Still, I scoff. "You can't mean that."

"Oh, I can, and I do. You bossed me around constantly and never cared how I felt. You talked bad about everyone, and yet everyone liked you most. I was afraid of you, but I'm not afraid anymore because now people listen to me. Like Cully. He's my friend and not yours."

And then I realize what I got wrong. I always felt like Nacole didn't like me. What I failed to understand is that she hates me.

"I'm sorry about how I treated you. I was wrong. I should never have acted that way, and I've always considered you my friend. You're my best friend."

"It's easy to scatter apologies since I'm on top now," she states with no sign of yielding.

"Nacole, it's not a competition."

"You're joking, right? It's always been a competition—you against everyone else. But now it's my game, and I'm winning."

"Don't make the same mistakes I did. There are more critical things to worry about, like the people taking over Harwell. We need to stop them."

Nacole shrugs. "Why? They're not so bad."

"Now, you're the one who must be joking!"

"I have a right to my opinion, though you never allowed me one before." She lifts her head high. "And when this is all resolved, things will return to normal. The little witch will be gone, and Siman will get back together with me."

"Gah! Well, that's just stupid." I jeer.

"Why?" She stomps her foot.

"Look, I should have been a better friend, and I'm not saying this to be mean, but believe me when I say Siman never loved you."

She bites her lip and sniffs her nose. "You're wrong. He loved me before, and he'll love me again."

"After you turn a blind eye and let his girlfriend get murdered?" I ask harshly.

"Don't be so dramatic. They're not going to kill her."

"Don't be so naïve. That's exactly what they're going to do."

"I'm not naïve!" Nacole yells, and there's no doubt people nearby could hear her. We need to get out of here. I take a retreating step, ready to abandon Nacole, but I'm surprised when her angry face turns calm. She glances behind us, and recognition shines from her brown eyes as she asks, "What took you so long?"

I spin around, and my worst nightmare stands before me— a group of cogs led by Saeva.

"Hello, Beauty. I missed you," she says while the cogs surround us. There are dozens of them. Even Ronen, with his size, couldn't fight off this many. Saeva looks at Nacole. "You were right, then?"

Nicole nods. "It was her crossing between the buildings on the irrigation flumes."

She turned me in. (Disgust fills my belly.) Janny was right about Nacole's loyalties. (I'm ashamed I doubted.) And she's working with Saeva. (Chummy with her.) It's almost enough to make me take back everything I said to Nacole and decide to hate her equally. Instead, I focus on Janny for a moment, understanding when I arrived back in my community how lucky I was to end up with one of the few remaining Harwellians with a conscience.

I'm frozen, unsure what to say or do, but Saeva reaches for me, grabbing my arm and yanking me against her. My side aches, and Nacole watches the pain on my face, not seeming bothered by it. Her reaction, or non-reaction, loosens my mouth.

"For months, I gave Siman shit about dumping you. I kept telling him what a fool he was to give you up. I insisted you were the better choice. But, you know what? I was *dead wrong*. He picked the better person, after all. Not that I think Tesha's all that great—in fact, she drives me crazy most of the time —but she didn't betray me. She never turned her back on me, even with all the bad things I did to her." I lift my hands and clap as Saeva passes me off to two cogs who drag me away, but my eyes never leave Nacole. "Bravo, Siman! Bravo for being smarter than me. Bravo for recognizing true *loyalty* when he found it."

Nacole's still in my sights, and I can't stop the words pouring from my mouth. "He loves her, you know? He actually tells her, and she doesn't have to wonder." We turn a corner. Nacole never moved, and though I can no longer see her, I still yell out, "I'm glad he'll die loving her, and you'll only be a faint memory for him!"

I take a breath and move my feet to keep up with the cogs pulling me along.

Getting captured isn't the worst thing. In fact, I told Ronen it would have to happen to carry out the plan, though making contact with Evans and knowing Vale's location first would have been helpful. Still, since it's part of what needs to happen, our moods aren't completely broken, which is evident when Ronen speaks to me cheerfully.

"Bells. Fergot 'bout tha' side o' ye, Cricket." Ronen whistles. "Ye sure can be scary."

"Scary? But it was such a lovely, scathing speech," Saeva says, hopping in front of me and walking backward. "I didn't know you had it in you." She leans close. "I hope you yell at me as passionately when we have our time together. I've already talked to Uncle E, and he's agreed you're mine." She straightens and makes sure I'm still looking at her. "After all, I owe you," she says, tapping her lips and giving me a wide grin, showing off her missing front tooth. A second later, she spins away, laughing loudly and tromping to the front of the group.

I glance at Ronen, who watches her with pressed lips and a furrowed brow. "'Twas Saeva who had ye," he says, making the connection as he turns to face me.

"Yes."

His mouth presses tighter, then it opens, and he lets out a few winning swear words. It makes me smile though he's not happy in the least.

"I take it you know her."

"Aye. Lass is evil. Evans calls 'er Bad Brains."

I snort. "She know that?"

Ronen shakes his head. "Nah. Kid wants ta live." I smile tightly, but Ronen doesn't lose his frown.

The cogs push us forward to stop our talking, but they don't have any luck maneuvering Ronen off course. They try nudging me in front of him, but he stays even with me, and the cogs appear perplexed by his ability to resist their herding. Because of that, we keep talking.

"Her smile's diff'rent since last I saw 'er," Ronen comments.

"My doing," I say proudly. "It's the least she deserved after everything she did to me."

"Everything she did—" Ronen's words cut off, and he expels a breath, practically emptying his lungs. "Bells, Bethy, 'tis no time ta talk 'bout tha'. I'll do somethin' foolish."

I tilt my head and trip over a rock, but the cogs have me. "Really? What would you do?"

"Rip the arms from the cogs 'n take all Saeva's teeth."

The cog—the one trying to wedge between Ronen and me

—opens his mouth in fear at the prospect and falls back a step.

Our conversation is a welcome distraction. I know what needs to be done, and I believe my plan could work, but executing it will require a delicate balance of knowing when to speak and when to stay silent—also, remembering the exact words I need to speak. Consequently, I'm nervous, but Ronen's reminding me I'm not alone. He's with me—supporting me— and it means more than he could ever understand. And so, as we're taken to meet our fate and witness the success or failure of my plan, I'm having fun joking with this handsome boy. I smile up at him and say, "Okay. You can have Saeva's teeth and all the cog arms. And while now's not the time to enact your revenge, please promise you'll do it later."

Ronen chuckles and shakes his head. "Ye're somethin' special, Cricket."

We enter the Common and reach the Lower River Bridge. It shouldn't surprise me—yet it does—to see Lucan and Cully standing on the other side.

"You're really here," Cully remarks, watching us approach —his dirty blond hair hanging over one eye. There's a mixture of sorrow, anger, and fear in his tone. "Nacole said so, but I—"

"Where are my parents?" I ask before he can say more. I only have a moment before we're past them, and the opportunity to inquire will be gone.

I glance up, and Lucan's bewildered gaze rests on me—as if he doesn't recognize me. Cully gets a better look too. I'm unsure if it's the scars on my body, my missing hair, or my dirty, haggard appearance that makes Cully's lip curl when he asks, "What happened to you?"

"Lord Endrack's niece," I answer, struggling against a cog wanting me to keep pace.

"Hey! The lass is talkin' ta 'er leader," Ronen says, shoving the guy off. The cog's fingers slip from my arm, and he doesn't look ready to put them back. I don't blame him, based on

Ronen's expression.

"Have you met Saeva?" I ask Cully. "She's doing her best to take my place here in Harwell. She's got Nacole on her side. Maybe she's got my ex-boyfriend too." I look him over, and when he doesn't reply, I add, "She's very thorough in her efforts to become me. She took my hair to wear—pulled it out a strand at a time—and promised to take my teeth. But I'm sure she'd settle for taking my life."

Lucan's eyes widen, but I'm done talking about Saeva and ask again, "Lucan, my family?"

His eyes run over my skinny body and sheared head before saying, "They're not in Harwell."

"But you're still here."

Lucan clears his throat. "We're hosting members of a fellow light bubble who need help with a problem."

"A problem." I laugh, having never before been labeled as a problem. "You can't seriously be supporting him."

Cully stays silent while Lucan says, "If there was a way to help you, I would, but there's no dissuading Lord Endrack." His words sound memorized like he's repeated them previously to convince himself.

"Is that why you degrade my family, telling the citizens we're not the kind of people you want living here? Because you want to help?"

Lucan swallows hard but has no response. I look at Cully. "I knew we'd never be a couple again, but I didn't think you'd support something like this. The last time I saw you, you swore you'd never put me in harm's way. What happened to your vow?" I ask, pointing at the cogs surrounding me. Cully's eyes fall to the ground, but his mouth stays closed. "Yeah. A Cully Clarc promise is only as good as what Cully Clarc will get in return." I shake my head, looking over both Clarc men. "I didn't expect this from either of you."

"We must protect our people," Lucan argues meekly, and I remember when I thought the same way—acted the same—but witnessing Endrack's ruthless determination has set us on different paths. It made the Clarcs shrink in their duties while it emboldened me.

"I'm one of your people!" I exclaim, thumping my chest with my fist. My lungs burn, and I'm breathing so hard my side hurts. "What Endrack has planned for us isn't justice. It's murder—plain and simple." I lower my voice, pain leaching from every word. "I used to be dear to you. You called me your daughter. I stood up for you. But the Coastals were right all along—the words of Lucan Clarc are worthless. And today, my death is on your hands."

Though, I don't plan to die.

But they don't know that, and I want them to feel it. Cully sniffs and wears an unbelieving expression, while Lucan's nose betrays the slightest twitch. Looking away from them, I discover Saeva walking toward me. Reaching me, she grabs my arm and jerks me into her side, saying, "You just don't quit."

And she's right. I don't.

"You're both cowards," I say to Cully and Lucan, accusing them but also feeling sorry for them. They don't have enough conviction or skill to stand up for what's right. All the respect I once had for them is gone. I never thought I'd feel that way about the Clarcs. Janny was right not to trust them. If I'd gone to them when I escaped, they would have handed me over.

Saeva laughs and yanks me forward. "Come on, big mouth. You're coming with me."

But today, no one's intentions are playing out as intended. Because one second, Saeva's digging her nails into my arm, and the next, I'm released, and she's on her knees with Ronen towering over her.

CHAPTER THIRTY-EIGHT

Ronen has his powerful hand on Saeva's elbow, and the other grips her fingers, stretching them backward. "Dunna touch 'er," Ronen growls, and Saeva wails in pain. When the other cogs step up to help her, Ronen growls at them too. They freeze and back off.

I don't know what to do. Ronen seems to have everything handled, so I stay back, but I'll jump into the fight if needed.

"Ye're the one tha' hurt my Bethy," Ronen grumbles, leaning into her. "Now yer fight's with me." Before I realize what's happening, I hear a snap. Saeva screams, and when Ronen releases her, her index finger hangs at an odd angle.

My jaw drops while the cogs jump into action, going for Ronen, but he steps away from her, putting his hairy-knuckled hands up and addressing the converging cogs. "I've no quarrel with ye," he says while Saeva whimpers below him. "If ye know Saeva, ye know 'tis a small portion o' wha' she's earned. Now, shall we be goin' without further fuss?"

The cogs wordlessly agree, surrounding and ushering us forward. Ronen gives no resistance but makes sure I'm by his side. I glance back at Saeva, who's still on the ground at the foot of the Lower River Bridge, clutching her hand while rocking back and forth.

"I can't believe you did that," I get out in an astonished whisper.

"Are ye angry?"

I look up, surprised by the concerned set of his mouth, wishing I could see his eyes. I shake my head. "No. I was shocked. And then really happy. And now I feel a bit guilty."

"Aye. Feelin' guilty myself. Not proud o' wha' I did."

"Did you… dislocate it?"

Ronen's head droops, and after a moment, he shakes it.

He broke her finger.

I reach over and take his hand, and we continue forward together.

They don't take us inside the Well, but we wait on the small grassy area in front. When the doors open, a smaller group of cogs emerge with our friends. Vale and Geric appear first, followed by Siman and Tesha. As much as I hate seeing them captive, I'm relieved they're safe and appear uninjured.

Their eyes go wide seeing me again. Vale smiles sadly, and my heart burns because I recognize something extraordinary in her expression—she's happy to see me. It's the reaction I expected from Nacole, and I'm unsure whether my friend's hatred is my fault or hers. Likely a bit of both, though I wonder if I'm mostly to blame because if Nacole's acting despicably, I'm the one who taught her to behave that way.

None of us are bound, but we're outnumbered. There's no sign of Evans, which could hinder my plan, though I'll attempt it even without him. It might be trickier to pull off, but I'd be happy if he's evaded capture. Then, if this all goes to crap, at least one of us got away.

Their cogs join ours, and we return to the Common—the best place for a group this size to gather. Cully and Lucan haven't moved, but Nacole's with them now.

They line us up in front of the Common stage, where so much has occurred over the years. I recall instances of Lucan addressing the community, Farewell Feasts where the departed's family ate on display, and countless afternoons sitting cross-legged in the dirt while others entertained us with a talent or acted out a story.

I'm glad the cogs don't put us on the raised stage because today's proceedings are for taking lives (Endrack's goal) or saving lives (my goal), not providing entertainment. I'm in no mood to act out a drama for Lucan, Cully, Nacole, or the rest of the gawkers. At least, not the show Endrack's prepared. If, however, I turn things my way—well, I'll happily unravel a mystery for an eager audience.

Vale's next to me, and we turn to stare at each other. Her hand is on the pendant our father made, hanging on our mother's old shirt. Her thumb moves steadily across the surface. While she appears the same as when I last saw her, she observes all my changes and tears pool in the depths of her eyes. She shakes her head, and I swear her thumb picks up speed as she says, "I'm so sorry."

I'm about to still her hand and take it in mine when a cog bellows, "Quiet!" and shoves Vale in the back. She throws out her arms for balance, and Geric scoops her into his side, glaring at the soldier.

Ronen steps closer to me, and feeling his heat, I lean into it. I look down the line at Tesha and Siman, sad because he's not standing casually with his thumbs resting in his pockets. Instead, he cradles a distraught Tesha, her face buried in his gray longcoat. But while comforting her, he watches me, and with my attention secured, his eyes widen. There's a question in them—one he encouraged me to think on and explore weeks ago—so I give him a brief nod because I found the answer we need. Siman visibly relaxes, putting all his attention on Tesha.

Another group of cogs appears on the Lower River Bridge with someone in the lead. It doesn't take an intelligent person to figure out who it is. He wears a deep green coat cut perfectly to fit his trim frame, and as he approaches, he puts light green eyes on us, which both observe and condemn. He oozes confidence, walking like someone without a care in the world. But maybe he's too confident (a shortcoming with which I have personal experience) and should proceed more carefully. It's possible things won't yet go his way.

He's an impressive figure, but I'm personally unimpressed.

Saeva shuffles after him, and when he stops in front of Siman and Tesha, she pushes past him until she's across from me. "This is the one that escaped!" she exclaims, pointing at me. "I told you I'd find her."

"You're Annibeth," he says, pressing together his thin lips and looking down his thin nose, observing me with interest.

I opened my mouth to answer, but Saeva beats me to it. "Yes, Uncle, it's Annibeth." Her eagerness is irritating, and I'm surprised when Endrack's expression betrays the same.

"Good, good," he says dismissively, waving her off. "Go get the other one."

The other one?

Saeva grins, putting me on edge even more, and then she's gone, traveling back over the bridge toward the Well.

"I'm Lord Keine Endrack, Governor of Adlumen. I won't ask for your names since I expect you'll lie. Besides, I'm not interested in names. An aphorism comes to mind: *It's what's inside that counts.* And where this group is concerned, the observation is sublimely accurate."

Endrack calls forward two cogs. One has a cut log they place vertically to make a tabletop, sitting three feet off the ground. The other carries a metal box which they set on top.

"Him first," Endrack says, pointing at Siman. My friend doesn't hesitate, peeling himself from Tesha's grip and walking forward. Like with the panels in Durus, they instruct Siman to put his palm on a flat surface that's part of the box. A second later, Siman pulls back his hand, rubbing his finger, pricked and bleeding.

Endrack hovers over the bloodletter. Moments pass before he declares, "Nothing." He looks at Siman. "Disappointing."

Siman watches me as he walks back to his place in line. He's expecting me to act, and I will, but this isn't the right time.

For all his intuition is worth, it's not a patient gift. Siman's a natural leader—accustomed to taking charge and pushing his ideas forward. But this is my bailiwick. I'm a reckoner—skilled at knowing when to watch and when to strike.

Endrack nods his head toward Tesha, and the cogs bring her forward. She puts her hand on the machine, and it's not long before Endrack declares, "*Magna Physicus*. And it looks like a bit more."

A bit more. The machine detects Shon Dorian ancestry from Bitha, just like Vale and I have Dorian ancestry from Anny. But Tesha won't have Kerk Harwell blood because it comes through our father. But, although she's a spare, she's still capable of destroying Endrack's reign.

"His Six told me quite a bit about you." He looks over Tesha. "It makes sense you're his with all that red hair. It's surprising such a calculating man had a child, but it's no surprise your biggest value to him was the cash he could earn. I'm disappointed he's dead, as he was a useful sort of man, but I'm glad to be saved the payday." He brushes his hand in the air, and the cog escorts Tesha back to the line.

I'm reluctantly impressed by Endrack's leadership abilities. He speaks with conviction and exhibits an assurance that all he does is correct and good. He has these cogs fooled. It will be my pleasure to enlighten them. Just not yet.

Geric's next. Rigid and tetchy, he puts his hand on the pad. Endrack doesn't seem surprised when there's nothing remarkable about him. "By the light, you boys are turning out to be real duds," he comments as they usher Vale forward.

"There's a strong family resemblance," Endrack mumbles, and I think of Ennette Rennick and her dark hair that matches Vale's. "I don't know that testing you is even necessary. Still, it's good to be thorough."

He takes Vale's blood, and when Endrack sees the results, his eyes widen, and he stumbles backward, staring at Vale.

"Well, well. Thoroughness is rewarded."

He expected an ancestor of Harwell—a story keeper—but not a Dorian too.

I'm next. I don't even wait for the cog to escort me but walk straight to the machine. Vale's still there, giving me a despondent look as she passes. I put my hand on the panel before Endrack's even ready, and he tilts his head at me curiously. He becomes more intrigued when he sees the results.

"You're practically twins," he comments.

"Sisters, actually," I correct, and his eyebrows raise, aware of the taboo in Harwell around such things. I'd probably receive a monologue on the topic if a commotion didn't call everyone's attention to the Orchard Bridge.

"Oh, no," Vale says behind me, and I glance where she's looking to find Evans struggling against three cogs. His longcoat whips behind him, and his longer brown hair—from months in Durus without a cut—flops with each jerky movement.

There's a chance he could get loose, but the possibility fades as they drag him across the bridge to the Common, gathering with the other cogs. There are too many of them for any of us to run and have a chance of surviving. But our best prospect for survival doesn't depend on running, so I smile because Evans has joined us, and the last piece needed is in place.

Ronen's at the machine. My arm brushes his as the cogs shuffle Vale and me back to the line. The big guy puts his hand on the panel. "Another negative," Endrack grumbles and looks at Evans. "Looks like you're the only one left."

The cogs release Evans, and he stretches his arms in the pretense of getting limber, taking on his Droll persona. I haven't called him that in weeks, but he's earning it now. He takes a few deep breaths and walks to the machine, dropping his palm on the panel. A second later, Evans yanks back his hand, staring at the dot of blood on his finger before pointing accusingly at Endrack and saying, "Prick."

Geric chuckles, and I glance beside me to see Ronen's beard hiding his smile.

"A mole." Endrack glares at Evans. "It's not a surprise this little asshole is my third problem," he says, referring to the fact that Evans is a Dirby—a descendant of the final governor. But Evans has other things in mind.

"If you have a little asshole and find it's a problem, maybe you should see a doctor instead of discussing it in large gatherings." Evans puts a fist to his mouth and coughs, *"Overshare!"*

A few cogs grin before Endrack yells, "Get him in line!"

They push Evans toward the row of the accused, placing him next to Ronen. Meanwhile, Endrack takes a stance in front of Vale and me. "I've learned a lot these last few months," he says, looking between us. Vale stiffens at the undefined reference to her beloved grandmother. I don't know Ennette well, so a different emotion fills me—remorse. He lowers his voice, continuing, "There are only a couple of fathers to track down, and I'll have you all."

The cogs behind him lean in, trying to hear his words. His insistence on concealing them has me thinking. *What's his motive for speaking so quietly? What's his reason for being so vague?*

"All who?" I ask loudly, testing him. "What exactly did our blood tell you?"

"That you're who I want."

"But why are we important?" I press, and Endrack rubs his lips.

He twists away from us and says in a booming voice, "I've waited long enough to punish these criminals. I won't wait any longer."

Endrack leaves my question unanswered, and, in so doing, reveals precisely what I wanted to know. The day Hersh brought me back to Harwell, he and Eddy wondered why Endrack wanted me. Similarly, these cogs are trying to understand what's happening. I'm reasonably sure they know nothing about our heritage—there was no one near Endrack to see the results of our tests. All they know is we've wronged their leader somehow, and he's ready to exact punishment. The realization makes me smile, and I look at Vale, who's watching me with a confused expression.

"He can leave, and those two as well," Endrack says, pointing out Siman, Geric, and Ronen in turn.

"I'm not leaving," Geric says, not moving an inch.

"I also prefer to die with my friends," Siman says, glancing at me impatiently.

Yes, Siman! It's time, and I'm ready. Just relax!

I attempt to relay the message to him with what I'm sure is a crazy look on my face. The gathered cogs look between the boys and Endrack, unsure whether to let them stay or follow their leader's order. It's then I notice one of them holding Evans's dagger. It's not with Evans, but it's in sight. It's the final detail, and although I'd feel better with it in his possession, I'll make it work.

"I refuse to leave as well," Evans blurts out, folding his arms and holding his ground. "The Droll's here to stay. After all, I'm the life of the party, and the man with the little asshole wouldn't know how to proceed in my absence."

"I never excused you!" Endrack snaps. "I pointed to the big one."

"Oh, excellent!" Evans exclaims, clutching his chest. "I wasn't ready to go. But you must admit, it was a logical mistake. Fuzz takes up lots of room, and I couldn't tell you were pointing at him, not me."

"Somebody shut him up!" Endrack yells, motioning a group of cogs in Evans's direction. "Or better yet, let's take care of him first."

"No!" I scream, jumping forward, but Ronen holds me back.

Endrack grumbles, looking at me and then at the big guy. "Just keep them secure for now," he instructs his cogs before turning to Ronen and asking, "What of you? You've yet to voice your preference in the culling."

"I'm stayin'," Ronen says, squeezing my shoulders with the hands he placed there moments ago.

"You ready to die with me, Big Scruff?" I whisper.

"Aye, Cricket," he whispers back. "But sorta hopin' ye have somethin' better in mind."

I do. And it appears the time to act is upon me. In another moment, Endrack will order the death of us all, which he confirms by responding to Ronen's decision to stay. "By all means, die together if that's your wish."

I glance at Nacole, and her eyes are wide with understanding—they're going to kill us, despite her firm belief otherwise. Siman, too, upon his request. But I don't have the time nor inclination to watch the truth settle over her. There's a critical job to be done. I'm the one to do it, and it requires all of my attention.

I'm exhausted, but people are relying on me. Lives are in the balance, and the pressure might wreck another person. But as a reckoner, I'm trained to survey the scene and wait for the ideal moment. It's what I do. It's who I am. I prepare. And I strike at the opportune time.

And that time is now.

I open my mouth.

"Lord Endrack," I call out, loud enough to get his attention. He spares me a glance before turning away to address a commotion on the Lower River Bridge.

"Saeva, you're back!" he exclaims, and the mention of her name throws me off track. He walks over to pace in front of us, and I watch only him, unwilling to spare a look at my torturer. "I'd forgotten," he says, watching me.

"Forgotten what?" I ask in a small, confused voice. When Endrack doesn't respond, I look up at Ronen. The big guy doesn't answer because Endrack steps into my space.

"I almost forgot a step. One made necessary by you."

"By me?" I squeak out while my hands shake. It's Saeva's promise. She'll get her way. Endrack will turn me over to her. She'll torture me until dead, pulling my teeth out and forcing my friends to watch.

The time to alter this course is now. If they remove me from the others, I can't save them. But my throat is clogged with fear, and nothing comes out.

"Bring her forward," Endrack says, and I expect hands to land on me at any moment, but instead, Saeva pushes a struggling Janny into my vision. I tilt my head in confusion. Janny's mouth is cloth-covered, partially over her upturned nose, but it's her small eyes that keep my attention—they're unusually large and wet with tears.

"This is for the trouble you caused by escaping," Endrack says, and a second later, he draws a knife and pierces Janny's breast.

I inhale a gasp.

There's a faint sound behind the cloth, and when Lord Endrack moves to the side, Saeva releases Janny, and the woman drops to the dirt, her eyes wide and vacant.

Tesha's scream pierces the silence, and she clings to Siman.

Lucan and Cully watch from the bridge with tight lips and blank expressions. I remember how Cully blamed the dangers our people faced on the Dark brothers and story keepers. I did the same. It was so easy back then to stay removed from any responsibility. But it's our job to watch out for each other, and today we let down one of our own.

"Janny," Vale says in a shocked whisper, shaking her head in disbelief.

I stare at Janny while my friends fall apart. Siman and Vale probably knew this woman better than I did, but she died because of me. She knew Endrack's determination to see this through. She knew what he'd do to me and that he'd complete the task without remorse. Janny was brave and followed her conscience to save my life, and it cost her own.

I can't take back what's done, but I can make the most of her courageous sacrifice.

So, I give Endrack what he expects after executing Janny in front of me, showcasing my tears, my sadness, and my fear. I visibly shake, turning to my friends to mourn, and only a tiny portion is a ruse to cover my true intentions because I'm sickened by what just happened. But we'll experience more of the same unless I keep it together. I pull Ronen down for a hug. "Be ready if this doesn't work," I whisper.

"Aye, Bethy," he says. And then, because he's in my arms, I turn my face into his chest for one steadying breath. Fueled by the scent of leather and campfire, I release him and go to Evans, pulling him into a hug.

"I didn't know you cared," Evans snarks, but I understand him now—his hazel eyes are sad, and the joke's purpose is to conceal his astonishment over Janny's execution.

"I have a plan."

"*You* do?" he asks, not sounding too sure about me drafting our survival.

"The cog in front of us and to the left has your dagger."

"We're fighting our way out?" he asks, his tone even more skeptical.

I shake my shoulders in exaggerated sorrow. "Not exactly. You'll know when you need it."

I let go of him. "Vale!" I wail and topple into my sister's arms, then whisper, "I'm going to cry louder. Comfort me and turn us so your back is toward them." I release another giant sob, and she does as instructed. "Janny helped me, and he killed her," I say loudly, then sort of choke because it's the truth, and while I hate using her death this way, it's not the time for inaction.

"Shh," Vale says. "She knew what she was doing. She was a wonderful woman and could never stand to see injustice."

I cling to Vale, glancing at Endrack between the strands of her hair. He's tired of the show. Any second now, he'll command they pry us apart.

"Quick. Rub my back and then take my right hand in yours."

She does as asked, finding the object waiting for her. The weight of it leaves my fingers a second later. "What's this for?" she whispers.

"I have a plan. Just be ready." Pulling back, Vale looks bewildered—likely a bit shocked I moved her necklace from the safety of the repository—but there's no time to explain, so I just say, "After all, we're neither of us scared quitters."

A ghost of a smile graces her lips as I remind her of something I accused her of months ago. At the time, we were at odds. Now we're in this together.

I return to Ronen and lean into his side. My wound aches. I'm tired and scared, but I breathe in his scent. His arm wraps around me, and I try to glean his energy for what comes next.

Tesha's still sobbing. If we make it through this, I must thank her for being such a noisy crier and making my conversations with Evans and Vale more private. But, for now, I wish she'd stop. One look at Endrack says he wants that too.

Soon enough, he calls forward his cogs and tells our group, "You may want to save your tears for your own lives."

I stare at my opponent, dressed in his fine green coat, knowing the time has come to take action, and a smile graces my lips. I consider the advice of wise leaders. Kerk Harwell, in his missive, declaring, "Succeed or die with honor." Captain Rhed, who believes there are no guarantees, encouraging us to speak while the opportunity is available. And finally, I think of my parents because the Petters family has a motto too: *Don't bring an issue to my door unless you're ready to be reckoned with.*

After all, we're a family of reckoners.

"Lord Endrack," I say, respectfully using his formal title when I'd much rather spit in his face. He turns to me, unsure of my calm demeanor since I was wailing inconsolably moments before. "Before you take our lives, I have one question for the citizens of Adlumen."

Endrack shakes his head in annoyance. "Whatever. Out with your question," he drawls, waving his hand impatiently.

I take a deep breath and step forward. Here it goes... our chance... our reckoning.

CHAPTER THIRTY-NINE

I t's time to fight—not with fists and feet like Evans taught us on Fifteen, but with words like my parents taught me to do since I was a child.

I've studied the law my entire life. If there's one thing I know, it's how to speak with the intent to influence. In the past, I used that talent as a show of power. Today, I'll use it to save our lives.

Hopefully.

I glance at Siman, and he nods back. He knows. His intuition, or voodoo, as Evans calls it, pointed to this moment. At the same time, I see Saeva. She watches me intently while I hope most cogs aren't like her.

"Are you going to say something?" Vale whispers when my silence goes on. In my head, the plan is simple. I'm about to call upon ancient laws, over a century old, and hope that somewhere in the minds of these cogs, there's a memory to bring forward—a spark of recognition and acceptance of revered truth.

"Your governors are before you," I say, addressing not Endrack but his army. Talking about multiple governors is news to the others—it's something I learned with Laso—but I don't spare them a look to see their reaction. Instead, I draw back my sleeve and hold my wrist high above my head. The bracelet from the Dorian family—my birth mother's family— slides down my slim arm. "Your ancestors upheld the law of three governors. Their heirs are here today, being put to death contrary to the laws of Adlumen."

"Stop this nonsense!" Endrack says, turning his back and walking away from us. "You!" he commands, pointing at a cog.

"Put a gag in that one so we can get on with it."

Before I can say anything more, Vale steps forward, lifting her regalia overhead so they can all see it. "I am an heir of the governors!" she shouts, loud and strong.

Endrack glances back with a huff. "Well! Gag her too," he orders, pointing at another cog. The two soldiers start toward us.

I peek at Evans, who returns my gaze warily. But, with a shake of his head, a second later, he calls out, "I'm also an heir of the governors."

He has no regalia to hold up since a nameless cog still possesses it. Evans wisely doesn't go for it—it's not the time— but he clutches his chest where the blade belongs.

Endrack turns on Evans, no amusement in his eyes as he storms across the Common. He gets right in Evans's face before saying, "You're a false heir. The Dirbys tried to steal the birthright of the Endracks, but it didn't work. We lead Adlumen, and you're nothing."

His voice is low, so none of the cogs hear the rebuttal, which is unfortunate since it contradicts his statement from moments ago when he called our claim nonsense. He even admitted knowledge of the Dirby family, though the details are off since, according to Garard Dale, it was the Endracks who stole from the Dirbys. It makes me wonder if Endrack's become so skilled at mixing truth and lies, even he can't separate them. Either way, it stirs something inside of me.

The cogs holding gags stall in their progress to quiet us, looking for clues from their leader on how to proceed. Saeva still watches with interest, stepping closer to hear her Uncle's words, though I doubt she picked up a thing. Meanwhile, I take advantage of the lull.

"Peace, Knowledge, and Wisdom stand before you," I tell the gathering, once again revealing more details unknown to my friends. I just need them to go along with me and not decide I'm crazy. "Will you do your duty and uphold their power?"

"Will you shut them up!" Endrack bellows.

"Will you uphold the rightful heirs or follow one man who seeks to destroy us in silence?" I point at Endrack.

"We won't listen to your lies." He motions the cogs forward again. Anxiety floods my body as they advance on us. The cogs aren't persuaded.

"If they're lies, let your people decide," I say in desperation. "We submit to a lawful tribunal in Adlumen where you can judge our claims and punish us if we're fake."

"They have no rights in Adlumen. Silence them. This idiocy ends now." Endrack's glare is meant to intimidate, but all it does is encourage me because I can tell the language in the *Book of Adlumen Law* is still in use today—their judicial system operates much the same.

I brush aside his comment about my idiocy and continue with a smile, "But we have rights because we're part of your history and laws. We're not fake—a fact Lord Endrack just now confirmed." I point at the blood technology machine.

At least half the cogs glance at it, pondering my claim— at least half are considering the possibility of our legitimacy. The cogs appear suddenly restless, looking at one another for direction. I'm just deciding this crazy plan might work when I hear Saeva's grating voice. "I'll shut her up!" she grunts out, ripping a gag from the hand of a cog before advancing on me.

She's feet away when Ronen steps forward, blocking her way. "Get yer worthless face outta my sight!" he booms. "I'll break more 'n a finger if ye go near Bethy."

Saeva stops in her tracks. Stunned, she drops the gag and takes a step back.

Ronen's shoulders relax, but his voice remains hard. "Ye're still 'ere. Outta... my... sight," he seethes. If it weren't for his lenses, I'm sure the look he's leveling on her would burn a hole through her skin. Saeva feels it too and spins on her heel, pushing through the cogs and retreating over the bridge to the Well.

He runs his lensed gaze over the cogs. "We're na askin' fer more 'n ta be heard. Ye can run us through now, er ye can listen fer five 'n then do it. But if ye dunna give us the five, I swear I'll take at least ten o' ye ta yer grave 'fore I'm down. Each o' my brothas'll take two. 'Tis in yer best interest ta shut 'im up instead o' us." He finishes his speech by gesturing at Endrack.

"Two's all?" I hear Evans grumble. "Thanks a lot, Fuzz."

But I don't dwell on the comment. Ronen's just sworn to kill more than half the gathering—without weapons—and the cogs don't appear to refute his ability. Even Endrack isn't arguing, but his eyes bounce between his soldiers and our group. He put himself in his predicament and likely regrets bringing us together in a public manner. He should have kept us separate and dispensed with us individually. It's too late now. He has to let us speak, and then he has to be prepared with a rebuttal.

So, my speech has to be perfect. And my rebuttal to his rebuttal—whatever I come up with—must be stellar.

"Bethy," Ronen says, drawing me in front of him. He lets go once I'm in place, but I feel his presence at my back.

"Did any of you possess knowledge about the identity of today's targets? Were you privy to details of why we were hunted for months? Or why Lord Endrack wants us dead? It's not for any crime or misdeed against Adlumen. It's simply because of our ancestry. Because we are heirs of Adlumen."

I chance a peek at Endrack, who watches me with a calculating gaze in his light green eyes. Now is when I need to lay heavily into their laws. I can't have there be any doubt as to who we are. I press a fist to my chest and say, "I am the direct descendant of Kerk Harwell and Shon Dorian. I am heir apparent to Governor Dorian, the last to bear the title of Lord Wisdom. I hold the regalia, *Dives Sapientia*," I say, reading the side of my bracelet. "And I'm prepared to swear the Governors' Oath of Leadership."

I grab Vale's arm and drag her forward before continuing to speak to the attentive cogs. "This woman is my sister and has identical ancestry. She's the heir apparent to Governor Harwell, the last Lord Knowledge. She holds the regalia in her hands."

"*Gemma Scientia*," Vale says, reading the words, and I'm grateful she says them because it's the one regalia name I struggle to remember. "And I'll swear the oath too," she adds, which strikes me as funny since Vale's just agreed to swear an oath she doesn't even know, but I keep my focus and don't even crack a smile.

"For over one hundred and fifty years, our families have hidden in Harwell to preserve our lives. The dishonorable General Endrack betrayed the governors, driving them from Adlumen under threat of death. Evans Dirby is the heir apparent to Governor Dirby, the *true* Lord Peace, and he retains the regalia."

I hear a chuckle from Evans and glance over at him. "Well, I would retain it if that guy down there hadn't confiscated it from me." The cog in question pulls the dagger from his pants and holds it up for the others to see. "*Ferrum Pax*," Evans says, and then no more.

I clear my throat to get Evans's attention. When he turns to me, I widen my eyes, pursing my lips. *Fine*, he mouths at me with a frown. "And I'll swear the oath," he finally says, in a voice barely above a whisper.

With an imperceptible shake of my head, I face the crowd. "Recall the words in your Citizen's Allegiance Vow. You are honor-bound to sustain the laws of Adlumen above all else. You promised to fortify the system with every breath and belonging. You swore to abandon personal opinion, turn away from fear, and offer up your life if necessary. We are a part of your laws and that system. We are your governors restored to you. Will you uphold our rightful power?"

I'm met with silence—a silence that stirs the fears in my stomach and inspires a throbbing headache in my ears.

Endrack steps forward, walking down the line until he's in front of me. "You've had your five minutes, and now I get mine." He turns to face his cogs. "This is foolish talk. The Endracks have ruled for over a century, instated honorably by the previous governors. I've labored alongside you to secure the borders of Adlumen my entire life. We've worked and fought together. You know me. You don't know them."

"Keine Endrack's family has ruled Adlumen without any right to do so," I interrupt. Endrack spins to look at me, but I keep my eyes on the cogs. "General Endrack was never advanced to the position of Lord Peace by Knowledge and Wisdom, who are the only ones with the power to do so." I look again at Endrack. "Your family did not have Right to Rule. Still does not. The governors didn't create the Adlumen government to be ruled by an individual. There are three— a balance of authority—and it's time to restore a stabilized government to Adlumen. We are the heirs of your governors, and we *demand* the laws be upheld."

Vale grabs my hand and squeezes it. Her message is clear— I may have gone too far. But the only way I've ever maintained control is by demanding the right. It's the only thing I'm consistently good at.

"Demand? That's preposterous," Endrack comments, moving closer to me. "You must know they won't obey your orders. They can't. *They're my army.*"

I stare at Endrack. Other than repeating the same argument, I'm at a loss for words. I've reinforced our ancestry, reminded the cogs of their time-honored laws, exposed the Endrack family's deception—both then and now—and requested a tribunal to explore our claims. I have no more tools. If they can't or won't respond to what I've given them, I have no more.

I look down at the rough cotton Harwellian clothes I've worn the last week. They're embedded with dirt from the repository and stained with the blood of old wounds. My hair is in shambles. I'm bruised and broken. My rebuttal to his rebuttal was weak—non-persuasive—and with the way I look, I wouldn't believe me either. I hardly look fit to govern.

I've failed.

Glancing to each side, I observe my companions, looking exhausted and afraid. They watch me—hopeful—waiting for my next move. They want to see me draw figurative blood from this man who's terrorized us. Instead, my eyes fall to my feet because I can barely look at them. Biting my lip, I hold back my emotions. This is more than a debate I've lost. It's more than my pride Endrack's taken. My knowledge and abilities weren't enough, and I've ruined our tomorrow, for there will be none.

Endrack senses my defeat and saunters away, smiling before reiterating loudly and triumphantly, "Yes! They are my army."

And without a beat, I hear one among the cogs call out, "Are they, though?" The comment gathers the attention of every cog, Harwellian, and Coastal, while two important questions occupy my mind.

Who is this person? And what exactly do they mean by calling into question Lord Endrack leading this army?

CHAPTER FORTY

I t's an authoritative voice, and the cogs respond to it, parting and letting the man through while he continues to speak. "Are they your army, Lord Endrack, or Adlumen's army?"

Endrack freezes, and the change in his expression can't be denied. He goes from calm assurance to panicked frustration with each syllable off of the man's tongue. "General Pruden," he says, twisting to face the man laying questions at his door. "What in the Dark are you doing here?"

"You insisted I forego this excursion, but Adlumen worries when her leader goes unprotected. It's my duty and right to monitor your safety."

I can see the man now—General Pruden—tall and lean, probably mid-forties. His hair is thick—it's difficult to tell if it's blond or gray—and a deep scar intersects his upper lip. He's dressed well, like the cogs, but crisper with not a wrinkle to be found. The general doesn't rule Adlumen, but he clearly operates high in her ranks, projecting a confident, unhurried vibe.

"Very considerate. But you're not wanted here," Endrack says, nearing the general but not getting too close.

"I sense I'm unwanted, but it appears I'm *needed*. For instance, I just cleared up a gross misrepresentation—we are *Adlumen's* army." General Pruden looks among his fellow soldiers before his attention falls back on Endrack. "Are you overextending your power?"

"You twist my words."

The general tilts his head. "I'm an agent of truth with no belief in twisting words, as any from Adlumen will attest."

He gestures to the cogs. "As the Coastals will attest." He nods toward the Dark brothers, and I look at each of them, watching them nod in agreement. It's then I realize they've had dealings with this man before.

General Pruden continues, "And it appears the girl speaks the truth. Isn't that the governor's lost regalia she has on her arm? Doesn't she recite the words of Kerk Harwell?"

"I do!" I yell, and though he doesn't look at me, the general nods evenly.

"If her actions are guided by Kerk Harwell, the very man who wrote our *Book of Adlumen Law*, shouldn't we acknowledge we're hearing unpolluted truth?"

Endrack shakes his head. "Anyone can repeat the laws of Kerk Harwell, It's not a guarantee of truth. It's a fake claim."

"Ah." The general looks away, and my stomach sinks. I've mostly ignored my body's signals, reminding me I'm unwell, but I suddenly feel my fever flare—heat burning behind my eyes—and I don't know how much more I can take. I can barely stand, and now the tiny measure of hope I gleaned upon the general's arrival is disappearing with every silent second.

I consider submitting to the blood technology machine again, but I didn't see the readout. It might say 'Dorian blood,' or it could be a series of numbers only Endrack understands.

Besides, Endrack isn't done, and he lobs his next accusation. "The regalia is equally fraudulent."

General Pruden faces us again, looking at the items. "I'm not a jeweler, so I can't swear to their validity. However, their description appears accurate. The names, titles, and customs are the ones my parents and grandparents recited to me in childhood. The same I recite to my children." The general looks over the gathered cogs. "What say you about this woman's claim? Do you find any validity in her words?"

After another long pause, one cog steps forward. Endrack

rounds on her, and even with the distance between them, she reacts as if struck, jumping back a step. I'm sure he's effectively silenced her, but discover I'm hasty in discounting the bravery of an Adlumen cog. "I've heard the stories of balanced government," she says hesitantly, keeping her eyes on Endrack. "My grandparents spoke of it, and I'd like to hear more."

"I, too, grew up with them," another cog says. "I tell my children about the balance of three and the honor of Adlumen before the governors were gone."

"I know it as well," another cog says, and the ones who have spoken discuss together what they know of the governors, but it doesn't last long.

"The girl heard the stories from an Adlumian," Endrack says, speaking over them. "She's guessing at the rest. After all, she doesn't have the book."

"It's uncommon for outsiders to know the venerated history of Adlumen—the unwritten things we speak of in private—but, yes, it is possible." General Pruden frowns, looking at Endrack, the cogs, and us. "If she had Kerk Harwell's book, her claim would be more persuasive, but we all know the book's been gone for as long as Kerk has."

The cogs are silent again, listening thoughtfully while their leaders discuss our fate. Meanwhile, I'm practically humming, the words ready to burst from my tongue. But something holds me back. It's nothing like Siman's voodoo —ideas and impressions—but is something I think of as my reckoner's instinct.

Endrack gives a firm nod. "Exactly. The book would make a difference. Without it, her claim is invalid."

"I hesitate to say invalid. Let's agree that it's... more difficult to prove," General Pruden answers, and his gaze falls on me. His blue eyes widen a fraction, and he tilts his head in anticipation.

We play a game in Harwell—usually with an apple—

volleying the fruit from one person to the next. Each time it comes into our possession, we complete a required action, take a bite, then pick someone for the next turn by passing them the apple. General Pruden's giving me control of the game—the apple is in my hands.

I twist my fingers together, eagerly announcing, "But I do have the book."

"What's that?" the general asks, though I know he heard me, and more so, he doesn't seem surprised by my answer.

This time I say louder, "I said, I have Kerk Harwell's *Book of Adlumen Law*."

Beside me, Vale clears her throat, whispering, "What are you doing?"

I blink and turn my head until our eyes meet, then smile. "I'm telling the truth."

Her green eyes go wide, but I don't have time to enjoy the reveal because my attention is back on the general who says to Lord Endrack, "Ah, so there could yet be some validity to her claim."

"She can't have the book!" Endrack exclaims, glaring at me. "No one in Harwell knows about the book." His eyes freeze, and he clears his throat, looking around the gathering. "What I mean is no one could have the book because it no longer exists."

His words make me sick. It's obvious he questioned Ennette Rennick about the book—a volume she likely didn't have knowledge of, hidden away as it was. She's probably suffered under his hands like I did under Saeva's. While I haven't always been fair in my dealings with others, I was never a coward like Endrack, speaking vaguely to conceal my actions, so it's with great pleasure I plan my words to crush his smug expression and show how little he knows.

"You're right. The citizens of my community know nothing

about Kerk Harwell's book. Even cruelly persuasive methods couldn't collect unknown facts from a person's mind." I finger the lines on my arm, wondering how much worse Ennette's had it than me—what fate I subjected her to. "None of us knew where or what it was until very recently." *This morning, in fact*, I think with some wonder. "Because Kerk Harwell hid it safely away from *everyone*."

Endrack freezes in place. A slight twitch near his eye is the only sign of his frustration. I want to pump my fist in the air, but I also want to sit down. I'm not sure how much longer my legs will support me.

"She says she has Kerk Harwell's original *Book of Adlumen Law*. What do the citizens of Adlumen say?" General Pruden asks, looking at the cogs.

One man close to me looks at my bracelet and then my face before answering, "I'd like to see her book." A few more cogs voice similar opinions. While some remain quiet, what's most amazing is that no one objects.

The favorable vote is enough to put Evans back into his normal mode. He steps forward, pulling the dagger from the cog's belt. The other soldiers watch Evans tuck it into the strap on his chest. "Thanks," he says, patting the guy on the arm.

"Get back in line! You're not free to go roaming about, gathering weapons. You're my prisoner!" Endrack's ears are red from yelling, but Evans smiles and strolls back to us.

"Actually, they aren't prisoners. According to Adlumen law, they are contenders who extended an official challenge regarding Right to Rule. After which, more than a dozen Adlumen citizens expressed concern over possible inaccuracy in the Succession of Governors. This prompts a formal investigation which will lead to a tribunal," General Pruden states. "Meaning that, as of this moment, I hold the government in stasis."

"Stasis?" Endrack turns on the general, fisting his hands.

"Then who will govern Adlumen?"

"The army will."

"You mean *you* will!"

General Pruden nods, unfazed. "Yes. Technically, I will until the matter is resolved. That is the law." He steps away from Endrack before the man can respond, approaching us and addressing our line. "There's some truth in what Keine Endrack says. You will be held—not labeled as prisoners—but your movement will be limited. Can you manage that?"

"There's little room for complaints when our choices are to challenge Adlumen's leader or die by his hand," I say. The corner of General Pruden's mouth tilts up as he listens to my reasoning, but then he clears his throat and turns away.

Endrack's behind him with his arms crossed, smiling. Apparently, our captivity—even though limited—brings him joy. But then, General Pruden faces the man and calmly states, "You will share the same restrictions."

His smile dies. "You have no right to hold me!"

"We have every right. The army doesn't misinterpret the law. We uphold it."

"You can't mean to uphold their false claim. They're ignorant community dwellers and filthy moles!"

"Ignorant or not, mole or not, it's their right to have their declaration investigated."

Endrack fumes. His fists are in tight balls at his side, and he stares at us with wild eyes, but his glare stays on me the longest. I hold the look and give him one of my own. Months back, when his army burned my community, I declared he'd made an enemy of me. Today, it seems I've made one of him. Officially. Because now it's my actions fueling his animosity and not just my birth.

"It's best to keep you separated while we determine our next steps," General Pruden declares, glancing between us.

Then with a wave of his hand, a new group of cogs comes forward.

"The Elite?" Endrack scoffs. "You mean to keep me prisoner using my exclusive security team?"

"The Elite are here to *guard and protect* you," the general clarifies. "Similarly, I'll assign a group to guard and protect the contenders. It will remain that way until we resolve the situation."

Resolve. I shake my head, wondering when that will be and not believing it will ever really happen.

As the Elite escort a reluctant Endrack from the Common, General Pruden pulls our line into a circle, blocking Janny's body from my vision—a small mercy. It's just our group of seven and him. He doesn't seem to find us a threat.

"I need to see the book," he says blatantly. "While there are other ways to substantiate your right to challenge, I hope you weren't lying about it." He looks directly at me. "I'll have some angry soldiers if you were."

I shake my head. "I wasn't." I hope we're not falling into a trap, giving up this information and the book. He's either an honorable man, or he's led us comfortably into a trap. Regardless, we're out of options. All we can do is hope he'll follow through. With no other option to aid our survival, I look at Vale and reveal, "The book's with Laso in the repository."

"My father? He's here!" A smile full of relief and joy spreads across her face.

I return the expression, nodding, before turning back to the general. "Vale can take you there. I'd rather stay here if that's okay."

I'm worn out. All I want is to sit down or maybe lie down. The sustained tension was exhausting, and now that I'm not in fight mode, the energy I had is fading fast.

"I'll go with her," Geric volunteers.

"I'll leave instructions with my soldiers, and then we'll go," the general says, and with a sympathetic nod, he leaves us.

"See here, Pruden!" Endrack resumes his yelling the moment the general leaves our midst. "It's my right to command the Elite. I selected them and are mine!"

I rub the space between my eyes, blinking wearily and barely able to keep them open. "I knew Endrack was a terrible person but didn't realize he's also a pettifog."

"A what?" Vale asks.

"A pettifog. A person invested in small, unimportant things. It's not a bad discovery. We might use it for our benefit, but it also could be very telling about the Adlumians."

"How so?" Vale asks, stepping closer. My voice isn't strong, and the more I talk, the more it softens. I'm so tired.

"A pettifogging leader is as worthless as salt with no savor," I say with a shrug while Vale shakes her head, not understanding. So instead of creating a picture, I say plainly, "A pettifogging leader has lost their primary purpose: Guiding their supporters with a firm resolve based on facts. If the Adlumians are content with a visionless leader—at least, one who has lost the larger vision of his people by focusing on his own small gains—it will cause problems for us. It would be in our best interest to hope for discontent in Adlumen, even if it's aimed at us for a while."

"Discontent," Vale murmurs worriedly. And while I stand by what I said, the discontent of an entire people also concerns me.

Vale and Geric make plans to go to the repository while Siman and Tesha are in their own world. I'm content not to think or speak, but Evans, ever the talker, breaks the silence. "Well, I guess there's no avoiding my role in this now. Thanks for that, Annibeth."

Ronen puts a comforting arm around my back, pulling me

into his side. I go willingly, and my eyes droop as I rest my head on his chest. "You're disappointed?" I ask with a grin.

"Yeah. Now I'll never have any peace."

"You can call me a bitch, and we'll call it even," I say with a grin, and Ronen growls at the suggestion.

"Nah," Evans replies. I peek through one eyelid, and he's shaking his head.

"Why not?" I ask, surprised when my voice sounds disappointed.

"It's no fun anymore, is all. Not when you don't care if I do it."

"Come on. Do it. I need a reason to put more itchy powder on your clothes." I close my eyes again, feeling Ronen's chest rumble with quiet laughter.

"I'll just smack you with more ping-pong balls."

My eyes fly open, and I point at Evans. "Hah! I knew you did that on purpose!" But I can't keep my finger in the air for long, and it drops heavily to my side.

Evans laughs. "If I really wanted to torture you, I'd burn your reading books."

I shrug. "They're not mine anyway, and they're back in Durus. Besides, that's not real torture." I finger my white-blond hair, and Evans frowns.

"Hey," he says, hunching over to get in my face. "It's a good look on you. Makes you tough on the outside as well as within."

My nose stings, and tears well in my eyes. "*Gross*," I choke out, not wanting to get emotional about compliments coming from Evans of all people. "Are you flirting with me?" I ask, trying to sound disgusted but failing epically.

"Hell, no. Though I'd be up for a game of kissing tag." Evans chuckles. "That'd bust Fuzz up."

"Bells," Ronen groans, but Evans keeps on.

"Hey! I need someone to chase. Brass and Girlie have been stuck together for months. And thanks to Number Six, I missed out on Songbird. The Shrew was all I had, and now she's clinging to you like sap on a tree."

Sap on a tree? Just like that, my tears dry up, and I'm bristling, ready to take him on. But Evans douses my fury with a simple wink, and instantly, I understand the purpose of his antagonism. It was a tool to help me abandon my useless emotions. A very effective tool.

"You know I've never been interested in you like that," he says, nudging my shoulder. "I only liked that you were unattached and miserable, just like me."

"Watch yourself, Droll," I mumble before closing my eyes.

It's been an eventful day—so much has happened—and things aren't looking so bad right now. Not great, but not awful.

"Hey. You okay?" Vale asks, tapping my arm. I lift my heavy eyelids and find her standing close and looking concerned.

"I'm good," I answer, licking my lips and realizing they're parched. "Honestly, I'm just trying to figure out how we got here. Did all that really just happen?" I look over the faces of my friends. "Did my plan really work?"

They share looks and smile at me, and I figure that's my answer.

Releasing a relaxed breath, I realize I did what my father asked of me—I used my mind to help. Then I remember my other father and the words we shared before I left the repository. I promised I'd keep Vale safe. And I did. And he told me he loves me.

There's so much crowding my mind—gratitude we didn't die and anxiety that we could still die tomorrow—but right now, his love seems the loudest. And that has me feeling... disturbingly affectionate. And even though it's going to be embarrassing, I need Vale to know I've decided I'm glad she's my sister. But instead of revealing my heart, a wave of fatigue rushes over me. And then everything goes dark, and I faint away before any cloying words are spoken.

CHAPTER FORTY-ONE

Blinking my eyes open, it takes a second to recognize the confined space of a Clinic observation room. I'm unsure how long I've been here, but I'm guessing a while since I'm flat on my back and my body aches. The beds here have never been called comfortable.

Rolling to my side, I groan as my body protests the movement. Immediately, two faces peer down at me. "Are we still safe?" I ask, the words scratching from my throat. A second later, Tesha places a cup of water in my hand.

"So far," Vale answers.

I try to drink, but it doesn't work lying down. Tesha sees I'm having trouble and takes my arm to help me sit. "Where's Endrack?" I ask while I wait for the world to stop tilting at wrong angles.

"Lord Endrack," Vale corrects while I sip water. "I keep doing that too, but we need to make it a habit to use his title. Don't want to offend the Adlumians. And he's staying in the Dark cabin with the Elite as per General Pruden's plan."

I tire of sipping and gulp the remaining water. Lowering the empty cup, my bracelet slides down my arm. It feels silly wearing a fancy bracelet on my wrist while I'm dirty and lying in the Clinic, but I don't know what I'd do with it if I took it off, so I leave it there. Besides, Vale is wearing the regalia necklace. It's probably good for us to keep them on to remind the Adlumian soldiers who we are. Hopefully, Evans is doing the same with the dagger—keeping it on him and visible.

"What about Laso and the book?"

"You're just full of questions." Vale laughs, and I grin, embarrassed. It's a strange feeling and must be because I'm so drained. "I'm just teasing. He's good. Glad to be out of the repository. And we got the book," she says, while Tesha flits around, seeing to my needs by taking the cup away to refill it. "He was here earlier while you slept. He's talking to General Pruden and Lucan now."

Lucan. My nose wrinkles. I can't believe I was so wrong about him.

Vale moves, and I get a good view of the clinician's counter. In the corner is a wooden vase with carved daisies—my birthday gift. That seems so long ago. I smile, just able to make out the cricket on the back of a petal. Next to it, folded neatly, is a light blue longcoat.

Ronen must have carried them with him while he searched for me.

A single tear rolls down my cheek, and I brush it away before taking the refilled cup from Tesha. "Have you asked about Ennette?" I ask, wanting to get fully caught up on things.

"Not yet," Vale answers, stepping up to lift my shirt and check my side. "I will soon." I can tell she's not looking forward to the conversation, whether she's nervous about the answer or unsure if she can keep her temper in check. Maybe a little of both.

"Where's Evans?"

"Lamenting his lot in life," Vale answers without a pause.

"You can't be serious." Sure, he joked about being put in the center of things and having no peace, but he can't be that upset about it.

"He's avoided this obligation his entire life. So, yeah, he's seriously discontent."

"Is he mad at me?" I ask, surprised I care.

Vale shakes her head. "No, he's upset about the circumstances. He knows you saved us by doing what you did." When I look at her doubtfully, she adds, "Don't worry. He'll figure it out."

"You were s-so brave," Tesha gushes. It's annoying when she does that, but I try to smile. After all, Tesha's pandering is better than a single moment I spent with Saeva.

Saeva. I can't help but wonder where my tormentor is. Not here, and that should be enough. And it is, for now, but I'll need more going forward.

"I could never have done what you did, s-speaking to the cogs that way and conducting the law s-so eloquently," Tesha adds, tears sparkling in her eyes.

Vale's gaze connects with mine, and seeing how uncomfortable Tesha's got me, she has mercy. "You were brilliant. And that's saying something since I'm loads smarter than you." I chuckle, then rub my face because I'm too tired to banter with her, though I appreciate the sentiment behind her put-down.

Vale flits around me like a stir-crazy clinician. As far as I'm aware, with Janny gone, there's no one more medically trained in Harwell than her. So, it's not a surprise my sister (I'm acclimating to the title) has taken on the job of caring for me.

I lie back down, tucking my fists under my cheek, just as Siman appears, strolling in with his thumbs hanging from his pockets. It's a happy sight that has my body relaxing into the uncomfortable bed.

"Hey, Heartbreaker," I mumble against my hand. I say it with a tired smile rather than my usual venom. "I wanted to say I'm sorry about not believing your intuition. Also, about being awful to you about Tesha. I hope you know I get it now."

I'm unable to look at Tesha when I apologize. Not because I hate her—no, that's not the reason—but because, well, I still don't really like her. And while I get that Nacole wasn't his person, I'm still surprised Tesha is.

Siman absorbs my perfunctory apology, raising an

eyebrow, and I prepare for him to lecture me. Instead, he says, "No worries. It's good to see you looking better."

Better, but not good. "Yeah, thanks."

"Where have you been?" Tesha asks.

"Hanging with Evans." Siman looks at me.

"Good. He can use the support of his bestie," Vale comments with a sly grin.

"Bestie?" Siman snorts. "That's laughable."

"Laughable, but true."

"Whatever. We barely tolerate each other."

"No one believes that. And one of these days, you'll admit it, Sir Cuddles," Vale says with a laugh.

"Not you too." Siman shakes his head, but the corner of his mouth lifts. For all he says, I think Vale has the right of it. They're friends now. It became more and more apparent the longer we were in Durus. Their attitude toward each other has changed, just like I changed mine toward them.

Siman sits in a chair next to me. "The girls tell you they've got us staying in the Well?" I shake my head. "We have free passage on the little island but can't go anywhere else without an escort. But Endrack has to stay inside the cabin, so I guess it's cool we've got more space. Still," Siman starts and wrinkles his nose, "Endrack has the flushing toilet and shower."

"And the beds-s," Tesha says wistfully. I agree. Though I'm on a raised bed, the hard surface is nothing like the bed I got used to in Durus or, I'm sure, the ones in the cabin.

"Oh! I'm glad you're here," Vale says, and I'm shocked when Captain Rhed walks into the room. "We'll go grab mid-day meal and leave you two to talk," she continues, shuffling Tesha and Siman from the room before closing the door and leaving me alone with the leader of the Coastal Territory.

I haven't seen Captain Rhed since spending so much time with Evans. I never realized how similar they are—like their smiles and the dark brown hair with a slight curl. Evans is a bit shorter with more muscles, but they have the same energy—the same swagger. I'm looking at Evans in thirty years.

"When did you get here?" I ask as he walks toward me.

"I came with General Pruden."

"*With* him?"

Captain Rhed nods. "We've had dealings in the past, though nothing this extensive. Although he serves Lord Endrack, I always found him fair-minded and honorable. I couldn't imagine he knew of Endrack's scheme, and he didn't. I'm glad we got here when we did. It wasn't a moment too soon."

"You saw everything, then?"

"Yes, Annibeth. You were awe-inspiring. I may have doubted your approach before—your attitude such as it was—but you're a dynamic individual. The reckoner role suits you."

"Thanks, though I think your son is upset with me." Captain Rhed tilts his head. "Since I forced Evans's hand into the role of a governor," I add when he doesn't seem to catch my meaning.

"Ahh," he draws out, then chuckles. "I couldn't figure out what you'd done to upset Ronen. You could cause a lot of mayhem, and he'd still gaze at you like you added a corner of heaven to his world." I press my lips together and look away. I'm not sure why he's saying that. Does he approve of Ronen's reaction to me or fear it? "I hope you'll treat that kind of devotion with the respect it deserves," he adds, answering my question—it's a little of both.

"I know what's required," I say, glancing up at Captain Rhed before adding, "And I know what he's worth."

Captain Rhed smiles. "I hoped that was the case." He clears his throat, standing. "And as for my other son, you forced nothing on him. Evans might say he blames you, just like he repeatedly blames me, but he's held this position since the day he was born. Now he'll do what all exceptional people do—what you did, Annibeth. He'll rise to the occasion and shock us all with the hidden depths of his character—things he's not even aware of yet."

I nod, thinking of how I've changed in the last few months—alterations developed through new situations and people.

"I have news of your parents," he says, leaning against the door.

"My parents?" I ask, pushing up in bed again and dropping my legs over the edge, eager for his words.

"Your mother's lack of energy worried me, so I asked them to go to Labrum. Of all the Dark communities, they have the most advanced medicine. They discovered she has a heart condition."

"A heart condition?" My skin prickles with worry, hearing this news. I don't even know what a *heart condition* means. It sounds dreadful, and I rub my face, distressed.

"Hey," Captain Rhed's suddenly at my side, his hand on my shoulder. "The news is actually good. They know what it is and how to help her get stronger. When you see her next, she'll be in a lot better health."

I try to blink away tears but end up wiping them with my fingers. I hate that I cry more than I used to, but even before, if there was one thing that could bring me to tears, it was anything troubling my parents. "Thanks for getting them to Labrum."

"Let's hope it's one of many things that start going our way."

I smile. We could use some positive things to get us through the difficulties ahead. I still worry our course is precarious. Will a tribunal in Adlumen help or hurt us? I hope bringing attention to our plight will help. But can we trust them?

"Captain Rhed, what do you know about General Pruden?"

He releases my shoulder and walks back to the door. He seems to enjoy leaning against the frame. "The general has served the Endrack family his entire life. His ancestors led the Adlumen army. He, like us, has a history of service in his bloodline."

My skin flushes as his words bolster my fears. "So, he's very loyal to the Endracks," I say, feeling defeated before we even leave Harwell.

"Yes, he is. But he's even more loyal to Adlumen law. And you are part of those laws. Pruden would never condone killing the governors' descendants. He didn't want to see you die, even if he's unsure about you leading Adlumen."

At that remark, a laugh bursts from me. "*Lead Adlumen?* Heavens, in all seriousness, I *never* intend for that to happen. I just want to stay alive."

Captain Rhed grins. "Well, Annibeth, you've started down this path. And if Adlumen law is followed, governing lies at the end for all three of you."

I shake my head, maybe feeling some of Evans's trepidation for the first time. "I don't think I'm prepared for that."

"Well, I'm sure the three of you will figure it out. You've gotten this far," Captain Rhed says, moving to the side and opening the door. A moment later, Ronen peeks his head around the corner.

"Ye're awake."

I'm amazed by the wave of happiness that rushes through me just seeing him. I thought I cared for Cully but never felt this way when he entered a room. With a haughty grin, I observe, "And you're peeking through doorways like a pervert."

Ronen chuckles deeply. "Nah. Saw wha' ye did ta tha' Feck fellow. I'd ne'er dare."

"I'm heading out," Captain Rhed interrupts. "I'll see you

two again. Hopefully soon, but it may be a month." Captain Rhed pats Ronen's shoulder and both look sad before breaking apart for the older man to leave the room.

"He's leaving?" I ask while Ronen closes the door.

"Goin' ta Ma in Tenebris." He rubs the hair at the end of his chin. "Tough leavin' us, but he thinks the cogs'll feel safer with 'im gone." He takes a step closer. "Seems right ta see ye wearin' pee-jamas again."

"I bet you carried me again, didn't you?"

"Aye. Number one job."

"You brought my flowers," I say, but I don't turn to look at them. My eyes won't leave Ronen.

He smiles and nods. "Couldna leave 'em there. Brought yer shoes 'n dress too, though they need cleanin'."

"Thank you." I lick my lips. "I miss Durus. Isn't that crazy?"

Ronen shakes his head. "Woulda brought books fer ye too, 'cept fer bein' so heavy."

I wish we were in the Dark with a circlight so I could see his eyes. I hate being here with the lenses and losing his gaze. Still searching his face, I tell him, "I love books, but that's not what I miss."

"Aye. Me neither, Bethy." Ronen clears his throat and steps up to the chair, taking a seat so he's only a foot lower than me on the raised bed.

"Ye were amazin'. 'Twas a perfect plan," Ronen says, reaching out to take my hand. "Ne'er seen ye more beautiful than fightin' fer yer friends."

"I had a lot to fight for." I reach out with my bare foot and rest it on his knee. Ronen stares at my toes, and his grip on my hand gets tighter, though I'm not sure he's aware he's doing it.

"Was dead petrified when ye fainted."

"But I'm doing better now." I tap my foot on his knee (it's

a nice knee) and then drop it so it dangles in the air again. Feeling bold, I ask, "Don't I look better?"

Ronen's head tilts up, watching me. A moment passes before he pushes up from the chair and stands before me. He puts his fists on the bed, one on each side of me, and leans in. "Aye, ye look better. Ye're beautiful, Bethy. No other lass has eyes as big 'n blue, 'n yer sweet li'l freckles are enchantin'." He leans in slowly and places a kiss on my cheek—just to the side of my nose, right on the concentration of freckles. My heart beats so hard, I feel like it will leap out of my chest and into his massive hands.

His thicker beard brushes my skin, but it's not uncomfortable. It's soft, and I want to run my finger over it, but I don't dare. I don't want him to stop whatever he's doing, so I lean into him. He brushes a thumb over my cheekbone. "Ye're so small. I barely dare touch ye."

"I won't break."

"I dunno. Feel awful clumsy," Ronen answers, lifting his hands and looking at them like they're capable of things he can't control.

"You're anything *but* clumsy. You're silent and sure. You never make a misstep."

"Aye, in the woods, where I know how I fit. But with a lovely lass... uh, woman... I mean, with ye... 'tis diff'rent. Ye're precious in a way tha' trees 'n shrubs aren't."

"Don't let Evans hear you say that," I say, staring at his hands which haven't moved from in front of me.

Ronen chuckles. "Ye think he'd disagree?"

"That I'm precious? I know he would." Evans and I have settled into a peaceable existence—other than me outing him as a governor's heir—but he doesn't think *that* well of me. I'm tolerable, and while I don't care if I don't meet his expectations, I wonder if it will bother Ronen. He's his brother, after all. The first people I approached when exploring my feelings for Cully were my mother and Nacole. It's natural to seek the approval of those you hold most dear.

"Wha' if I dunna care what Evans thinks? Er anyone else? Wha' if consultin' my own feelin's is all I'm concerned with?"

I tilt my head. "What are you saying?"

"Tha' I know my own feelin's well 'n dunna need ta hash it out." Ronen licks the lips hidden in his thick beard. "Tha' I've found the woman in my dream."

A picture returns to my mind: Ronen and Bethy sharing quiet, starry nights at a lake house, surrounded by dogs and children fishin' and fightin'.

It sounds like bliss. But didn't he say he was looking for a good *woman?*

"You're sure?"

"Aye." Ronen smiles.

A laugh breaks from my throat, nervous and shaky. "I'd no idea you were such an expert at flirting and collecting hearts."

Ronen's smile falters. "Cricket, I dunna collect hearts ner break 'em, 'n I dunna flirt. I only say what I feel."

"Oh, stop. Not a flirt?" I throw my hand out to tap his shoulder, but he catches it, using my fingers to pull me closer and then not letting go.

"Anyone e'er tell ye they love ye, Bethy?"

"Of course." I scoff and lick my lips, looking away.

"Yer da 'n ma dunna count." He rubs my fingers, and I look up at him. "Did Cully e'er say it?"

I shake my head and squeeze out, "No."

"Ye e'er say it ta 'im?"

My head stills. "No."

"Could ye e'er say it ta... someone like me?"

"Someone *like* you?"

"Fine, Bethy, if ye need me ta be clear," Ronen says, speaking low. "Could ye e'er feel tha' fer *me*? Could ye e'er love me?"

I slowly pull my hand from his. He watches my fingers go and sinks back a foot until he's no longer hovering over me. He's drifting away, which is not what I intended. I just needed my hands. So, I grab the collar of his shirt and pull him in, but he resists. "Gah! A little help here?" I complain.

"Ye're makin' no sense, Cricket." Ronen shakes his head, perplexed. I pull his collar again, and this time he comes forward. Putting both arms over his shoulders, I link my hands behind his neck and finally have him where I want him. "Wha' ye doin', Bethy?" he asks, inches away from me.

I recall Vale telling me it was hard for her to tell Geric she loved him, and I'm determined not to hesitate nor waste time.

"I'm trying to tell you, but it's not proving so easy, that I already do." I pull him closer, just a breath away. "I already have those feelings. I already love you, Ronen."

His hands, which Vale compares to frying pans, span my back, and suddenly, I'm no longer sitting because I'm in his arms.

"Ye mean it?" he asks, with a voice Tesha says sounds like low, rumbling thunder.

"I've always been a selfish person, and I don't think that will ever change. I don't want to see you with anyone else. Ever. I want you to be mine. Always."

"Aye, Bethy. I'm yers. I care fer many people 'n would grieve were somethin' ta happen ta 'em, but if I lost ye, I'd go mad. I did, when the cogs had ye. It tore me apart. 'Twas a shock, 'n I dinna understand at first, but quickly learned ye'd taken the first spot in my heart."

"The first spot?" I smile at the idea.

"Aye. When I found ye lost in tha' forest, 'n ye held on ta me, it's like ye crawled inside 'n refused ta leave."

"I'm stubborn that way."

"Aye. Stubborn 'n captivatin'."

I brush my hand down the side of his face, over his thick beard, running my thumb over the thin pink of his lips. "The only thing missing from this moment is a kiss from Yip," I whisper, staring at his mouth.

"From Yip?" he grits out, his hands tightening on my back.

My eyes flash to his, hating his lenses but making due as I admit, "Well, it's quite funny your dog has kissed me, but you haven't."

"Do ye mind if I do tha' now?"

I giggle. "Ronen. You need to catch up."

CHAPTER FORTY-TWO

I've kissed Cully and other boys, so I'm not unfamiliar with what it's like, but I'm shocked to discover it's different when Ronen's lips find mine.

This is nothing I've ever known.

Emotions course through me—impatience, excitement, calmness, and relief—all from the affection in his every touch. I'm exceedingly happy, but at the same time, so overwhelmed I start to cry.

Ronen's not bothered but seems to understand. He breaks between each kiss to brush tears away—his large fingers swiping them like the brush of a bird's wing.

I pull him closer, wanting more of the same feeling, only he doesn't move—just watches me. I take his face in my hands. I'd considered his beard before and how strange it might feel, but the soft bristle is like a caress, and I lean in to rub it against my cheek. His hand on my back makes me feel protected in a way I've never known or even realized I wanted. Soon he's kissing me again, but it's different this time. Not soft, but desperate. I link my hands behind his neck, running my fingers against the back of his hair. Thunder sounds in Ronen's throat, and his kisses get harder. His beard scrapes rather than soothes, and I discover I like that too.

And then his mouth is gone—his breath heavy as he tries to catch it. I'm startled to find I'm again sitting on the raised bed—so caught in the moment, I hadn't realized he'd lowered me to it. The muscle in my side complains from my lifted arms, so I slide them down, resting them on his thick forearms. We remain that way, staring at each other and grinning. Ronen's breath finally settles. Minutes pass before he places my hands on my lap and puts his fists back on the bed, caging my thighs.

"Ye're perfection, Bethy," Ronen whispers in his low rumble, and my cheeks heat.

"Hardly," I say, leaning into him. "But you kiss way better than Yip." His mouth breaks into a smile, and he watches me behind those dark lenses. The moment slows, and I remember all we've gone through. "I'm so grateful you're terrible at drawing sticks," I whisper.

"Wha' ye chirpin' 'bout, Cricket?" Ronen asks, but he's not annoyed with me—not like he usually is when using that moniker. No, he's pleased about something.

"I was referring to your terrible luck in always drawing the short stick when it comes to errands involving me."

"Ah, Bethy, 'twas ne'er any sticks gettin' drawn. This ol' dog volunteered every time." Ronen's words sink in—pleasure replacing shock—and then he chuckles, running his chin along my neck and jaw, tickling and making me giggle.

"Your face is harrier since Durus. Now's when I should call you Big Scruff."

He pauses. "Ye na like it?"

"I didn't say that. It's just different. Why'd you grow it out?"

"No time fer shavin'. Too focused on findin' ye." He brushes my cheek lightly with his finger, then kisses the spot. "Might be awhile yet." He kisses me again on my lips. "We're goin' south, 'n I made ye promises, Bethy. Ones I intend ta keep."

A slight breeze finds its way through the open window, and on the air, a yellow butterfly flits into the room, circling the space before finding its way back outside again.

"Huh?" Between the buzz in my chest from Ronen dropping kisses across my cheeks and the butterfly visiting my room, I can't concentrate.

"Was talkin' 'bout promises, Bethy." Our mouths meet again, the tip of his tongue finding mine. It's too quick, and then he's talking again. "I promised ye'd see Yip, 'n I'd get ye back with yer parents. Also, a meal o' rabbit 'n potatoes with yer ma 'n mine. I havena forgot."

I put Ronen's face in my hands and stare into those black lenses, trying to find his eyes. "I appreciate those things, but there's only one promise I truly need right now."

"Name it, Bethy."

"Promise you won't leave my side." I pull him forward and kiss his mouth, finding mostly beard, which makes me grin. It's so him. "I had a long-standing belief about my life in Harwell. I thought it was perfect. I was terribly mistaken. Life won't ever be perfect unless you're in it. I want you, and everything else can wait."

Ronen's answering smile tells me everything. Still, he says, "Okay, Bethy. They'll wait." He leans in, and I know what's coming—more kisses that make me forget every problem—and I'm eager for them. But then there's a knock on the door, and when the purpose of the noise registers—that someone's intruding on my moment—I groan and stare daggers through the door to the person on the other side. Whoever it is, I hate them.

Ronen takes a step back, putting a bit of space between us, and I hate them even more.

"Ye can come in," Ronen says, and the door pops open with force, swinging until it hits the wall. It's then I can name my newest enemy—it's Geric, sweeping in with his dark blue longcoat trailing behind him. I doubt Ronen would approve of the retribution I've decided upon for his brother's unwelcome interruption.

"Hey, you two. Looking for Vale," he says casually, but even behind the lenses, I can tell he knows what he walked in on. Evans would comment, but Geric's subtle. I'm not and feel waves of frustration rolling off me.

"Hey, brotha," Ronen greets cheerfully. "Havna seen 'er fer a bit. But will ye stay with Bethy a minute?"

A scowl pulls my brows low. Geric catches the look and pauses before pushing out a cautious, "Sure." Then we watch Ronen—the man I asked never to leave my side—walk out of the room. Obviously, I don't expect him to always be in sight, but it still strikes as contrary to my present wishes.

Geric wears a slightly panicked expression, and I wonder if he's uncomfortable being alone with me. In the past, I haven't been the nicest. (Understatement.) I also said some awkward and demeaning things about him. (Boy toy.) It occurs to me I should probably make amends. (In reckoner language: A harmonious future requires mending the perfidy of my past.)

"Hey," I say, getting his attention. "I'm sorry about calling you a Hot Little Number. It was inappropriate and, quite honestly, crass."

Geric chuckles, displaying his rare toothy grin, complete with overlapping front teeth. "Trust me. There's no reason to be sorry."

"You're sure?" I don't want him to let me off too easily. I want to put the incident behind us.

"Of course. It gave me something to hang over Fuzz's head —made him crazy jealous. And it got Vale stirred up, and I got the benefit." He waggles his brows. "Nope. Nothing to be sorry about."

"So ye dunna mind if I call ye Hot Li'l Number, then?" Ronen asks, stepping back into the room.

Geric groans. "Shut it, eavesdropper."

"Overheard, is all," he says, sounding like Evans.

"Whatever. Tell Vale I'm looking for her." Geric grins and shoves Ronen's shoulder—barely moving him—then he's out the door and gone.

"Where'd you go?" I ask while Ronen still hovers by the entrance. But then he steps to the side, and General Pruden enters. "Oh, hello," I say to the general, and he returns the greeting. While this man helped us, I'm still wary of him and unsure about what he's doing in my sick room. That is until Ronen speaks up, and I realize it's all his doing.

"Ye need to tell 'im 'bout Saeva," Ronen says, nodding at the general. My hands tighten, feeling instant panic at the prospect. At the same time, I understand Ronen's motivation. When I first met him, he was my unlikely champion, protecting me from others and often from myself. Though his protective display is no longer unexpected, it's no less appreciated, and this is an extension of that—involving others with the power to protect in situations where he has none.

So, in the small room, I show General Pruden everything —my hair, the stab wound in my side, the eight cuts on my arm, and the burn marks on my fingers. Then I talk about the moments that left a mark on my mind, not my body—the bugs, the poop, and Saeva nearly drowning me at Rocky Point. I'm sure to include she would have succeeded if not for Hersh intervening.

I'd yet to tell Ronen all that happened with Saeva, and his fists tightened with each incident I relived until the veins bulged in his arms. When he heard about Rocky Point, he slammed his fist on the counter, spit out his favorite swear, and my vase of daisies wobbled.

"Your story is appalling, and I don't condone her actions," General Pruden says, narrowing his blue eyes in thought. "But against an enemy—and Lord Endrack named you as such—it's not unusual to inflict pain to acquire information."

I shake my head. "Saeva never asked for information. Not once. Ask Hersh. He's no saint, but I believe he'll tell you the truth. She's vile and did it for her pleasure. The torture will continue if she has access to me."

General Pruden nods. "She won't be allowed near you."

"Thank you. Additionally, while you research our claim, will you investigate her? I won't hold Dennie, Pinyon, or Hersh responsible." Even though I'll never hold a good opinion of the men. "But will you question them and hold her accountable under your laws?"

The leader of Adlumen's army lets out a long breath. "You have a talent for acquiring powerful enemies."

I bark out a laugh. "It's true, though usually, I'm partly to blame for turning them into an enemy. In this case, it was all Saeva. Well, until yesterday when I punched her and knocked out a tooth."

"Aye, 'n I broke 'er finger," Ronen adds.

"Great. Thanks for not making my job any more difficult," the general says with a touch of sarcasm I appreciate since it humanizes him.

"I've also wondered what happened to another of your... soldiers." I narrowly avoid calling her a cog, which I doubt the general would appreciate. "I think her name is Eddy."

General Pruden rubs his forehead, and it's the first time I've noticed the man looks exhausted. I feel bad for laying more troubles on his doorstep, but there's not much else to be done. Now he's rubbing his chin as he says, "I was told they demoted Eddy for disobedience and dishonorable conduct."

Demoted.

I shake my head, disagreeing with the charges. "Likely, that's her punishment for being in the room when I escaped. She was on the floor, unconscious, when I left. She got hit in the head with a pot." By Janny, though I can't seem to say her name.

"I see."

"She obeyed her orders admirably, much to my chagrin, but she wouldn't allow Saeva to harm me. I don't mean to tell you your job, but you should check her story."

"I'll do that." General Pruden grins. "You know, discovering multiple military and legal issues wasn't my purpose in coming here to see you."

I shake my head, confused. "Wait. I thought Ronen went to get you."

"Sort of. I was waiting to speak with you." The general chuckles. "You have a line, but I told Ronen he could go first."

I grimace. "I'm sorry. I didn't know. What was it you wanted?"

He says nothing. Instead, he opens the door and motions someone forward. A moment later, a little round-faced boy stands in the doorway. He's about four years old with an upturned nose. I recognize him instantly.

"Higbee," I say on shallow breath.

"Who?" Ronen asks, looking down at me.

I'd forgotten about her boy. I hadn't spared a thought for him when everything happened on the Common, and the oversight is enough to knock the wind from me. Another tear —they come so easily now—flows down my cheek. I look at Ronen. "Higbee is Janny's son," I tell him, and his expression echoes my pain.

The general motions for Higbee to step farther into the room. I recall some of his family's history. His father got ill a few years back. It lasted for weeks until he succumbed. Afterward, Janny raised him alone since her parents were gone too—not walked, but deceased.

She told me she had someone in Harwell she couldn't leave behind. It was just the two of them—Janny and Higbee.

And now it's just Higbee. All alone.

CHAPTER FORTY-THREE

"**C**ome here, little man," I say. I'm not the logical one to comfort this boy, but after his mother sacrificed her life for mine—well, it's something I must confront head-on. He gets close enough to touch, and rather than waiting for him to acclimate to me, or even asking if he wants it, I have Ronen pick him up and sit him beside me. Then I put my arms around him.

"I'm sorry about your mother," I say, giving him a squeeze. "But I want you to know you're not alone. You never will be. You understand? Harwellians stick together, and we'll ensure you have a place and whatever you need."

He nods, his small chin dropping to his chest, but he puts an arm around me and pulls me tighter.

General Pruden nods. "Figured the boy could us all the support he can get." He doesn't fully understand the boy's situation. He doesn't know Vale knows him better than I do. Doesn't know that a few months ago, I would have pushed him onto someone else as fast as I could. The general only knows his mother's fate at Lord Endrack's hands. And, for my part, this boy lost his mother because of me. She risked everything and paid the ultimate price to prevent my death. There's no debating that. What she didn't know is how many others she'd save. If I hadn't escaped, I wouldn't have spent time in the repository and discovered the book. If not for Janny, I would be dead, along with my friends.

"Your mother was the bravest person in Harwell. She saved a lot of lives." I pull back, looking down at his innocent, tear-stained eyes. "I'll love her forever for what she did for me. You tell me what you want, and I'll do it. If I can, I'll do it. Anything."

Higbee's lip quivers. "I want my mother back."

I don't know how to talk to children. I'm messing this all up. I bite my lips and shake my head. It hurts, to be honest, and he may be young, and false stories may be simpler, but this boy deserves everything good and true.

"If I could, I'd do it for you in a second. I'm sorry I can't. I'm so sorry."

He nods. He knew my answer before he made the request. He's not dumb, but his appeal seemed as much of an expression of his sorrow as a test of my character. And I'm sure I'm right when he wipes his nose with a sleeve, and with confidence beyond his years, he says, "If I can't have her, then I want to stay with you."

I blink.

And blink again. Scowling, I tilt my head. "I don't understand."

"If I can't have mamma, I want you."

I'm just coming to terms with my new Rennick family—a father, stepmother, sister, and grandmother to make room for. Now this little boy is asking to join my world—an inner circle I've kept very small. But I also have a new perspective—something Ronen gave me in Durus when he told me to open myself up—and I'm just discovering I have an unlimited capacity to care about people. Who knows how Higbee might fit into my life? Maybe I'll be like an aunt or a big sister. Maybe my parents will want to help him. All I know for sure is I can't say no. I won't. Because agreeing to his request is the right thing to do. The only thing.

"Of course," I say, pulling Higbee against me. "You're sticking with me."

Higbee relaxes into my side and twists the gold bracelet on my wrist. This is so very unlike me—all this hugging and affection and saying agreeable things. It's strange, but I find

I'm developing an affinity for it.

"I want him too," Higbee says, pointing at Ronen. "Because he's big."

I grin up at Ronen, and Big Scruff breaks out into laughter. "Aye, lad. Tha' I am. I appreciate yer direct approach in expressin' the matter."

After that, the room clears because they want me to sleep. It's not a challenge to follow the order. I go under quickly and don't wake until the next morning.

I see Vale when it's time for my morning meal. She gives me food, checks my progress, and tells me Higbee's staying with her and Laso. I'm relieved to learn he's not upset over our separation. I worried he'd already think I abandoned him, but Vale insists he understands I'm not a hundred percent.

Ronen pops in for a quick visit, kissing and cuddling until he decides I need to get more rest because all he's doing is keeping me up. I can't argue his logic, though I'm sad to see him go. He promises to come back around mid-day meal, so after a morning nap, when there's a knock on the door (like a storm demanding entrance), I'm sure it's him.

Instead, Lucan files in, followed by Cully. I can't say I'm excited to see them.

"Annibeth, dear, I was so scared for you," Lucan says, taking a chair without being invited. "I'm so glad things worked out."

I push up in bed, looking down at the man. "I'm lucky I had people who cared about and supported me. I wouldn't be alive without them."

"And now, you'll be the leader of Adlumen!" Lucan says enthusiastically, completely ignoring the jab. I know he heard it—he's not that stupid—but left it unacknowledged. "We'll do so much good together. You know I've always considered you one of my own—like a daughter. My greatest hope is for things to work out between you and Cully."

I squint, glaring between both of them. At least Cully has the sense to look flustered by the baseless comment.

"I have no affection for Cully," I say without hesitation or sympathy. "Not anymore. And where do you get off thinking I'll be governing Adlumen? On the Common, I debated our situation because it was our only recourse. It gave us a slim hope of survival. The two of you didn't step in to help. So, I acted, hoping to discover the cogs were more reasonable than Endrack. We succeeded in that small endeavor, but we've by no means secured a path for our continued safety. The citizens of Adlumen might ignore the challenge, turn on us, and demand blood. Or possibly Endrack has a stronger hold on the people than I hope. Who knows how far General Pruden's honor extends? This is one step in many. There's no guarantee we'll lead Adlumen—the people may not want us, or we may decline the offer. And if we do end up in that position, working with you isn't high on my list. You, of all people, should realize that. Your actions these last months have been deplorable. All these years, I thought you had more substance and leadership ability. I now know how wrong I was."

Cully's flustered face turns into an angry frown. "You have no right to talk to my father that way," he says, putting a hand on Lucan's shoulder.

"I didn't ask you to come," I respond with finality and stare at the door. I think about Cully making deals with Malum. I think about their censure on the Common. They turned on me to save themselves. While I've acted similarly in the past, the difference is I've changed. They haven't.

I glance up to find Ronen's finally arrived. "Brought someone ta see ye," he says, and I motion for him to come inside, but he enters the room alone. When the Clarcs don't move, Ronen tells them, "Time fer ye ta leave," and ushers them out the door. I don't give them a final glance.

"I didn't mean to interrupt," someone says—someone I never expected to see in the Clinic again.

"Eddy," I mumble, startled. Without thinking, I look at her head where Janny hit her. I see nothing unusual, but, feeling embarrassed, I add, "Sorry about your head."

She rubs the back with a grimace. "Thanks. Sorry about your friend."

"Yeah. Not your fault."

"Mind if I sit?" Eddy asks, coming forward.

"Go ahead."

Ronen leans against the end of my bed while Eddy settles into the chair beside me. She stares down at her fingers, picking a piece of skin off her thumb and scratching the spot. "General Pruden restored my rank. He says I owe you for that."

"I hoped you'd corroborate my story about Saeva."

"She did," General Pruden says, surprising me by entering the room and closing the door. "Sorry, I'm late. I can't believe how small these rooms are," he says, looking for a place to settle. Ultimately, he leans against the door like so many are prone to do.

Eddy looks up, finding my eyes. "General Pruden asked me to meet with you. He'd like me to lead the security team for the governors during your trip to Adlumen."

"Trip to Adlumen? You mean, we can't hold the tribunal here?"

"No," the general says. "We must return. Our advisors will make inquiries, review the law and evidence, and present their findings to the judges for their determination. The process will take some time."

"And a group of cogs will protect us?" I ask, letting the word slip. "Why can't the Coastal guard do it?"

General Pruden chuckles and shakes his head. "First, you'll fare better if you hold off on calling Adlumen's soldiers cogs. They won't appreciate it." I nod, rubbing my eyes in frustration because I know better—it was the error of a tired mind. "Second, returning to Adlumen will be awkward with Lord Endrack accused of overextending his power and acting contrary to Adlumen law. If we arrive with members of the Coastal guard? Well, it will heighten an already tense situation."

"I don't feel comfortable going to Adlumen without their presence."

"I understand that," the general concedes. "But Annibeth, you're trying to resolve your conflict with Lord Endrack by using the power of Adlumen law. You chose the method—and it wasn't a terrible choice—but it means your protection will come from those who support Adlumen law. That's not Captain Rhed's guard. If you include them, it looks like you're bringing conflict. War maybe. Without them, you're long-lost citizens of Adlumen—heirs of the governors—returning home to your people. It's logical in your position to feel uneasy, but I don't expect animosity or anarchy upon your arrival. Indeed, I think the people will be curious."

"Okay." I hope he's right. "Is Captain Rhed concerned that none of his guard will accompany us?"

"You mean, except for his three sons?" General Pruden asks with a teasing smile.

I forget Captain Rhed's sons are part of the guard—not just members, but high-ranking leaders—but I've learned to think of them as my companions before anything else. And while some of them are, as the general described, long-lost citizens of Adlumen, others are not and that must be addressed.

"Technically, two of the sons aren't necessary to make the trip."

"Bethy," Ronen starts, but I forge on.

"They're not blood relatives of the governors, so they should stay behind."

"I won't," Ronen starts again, going silent when General Pruden shakes his head and puts up a hand to stop him.

"There were seven of you on the Common when the request for a tribunal was made. Seven of you chose death together over separation. Therefore, seven of you will go to Adlumen."

Ronen expels a relieved breath, and I'd be lying if I didn't acknowledge feeling the same way. Still, I had to mention it. I wouldn't feel right about ignoring a route for them to escape our fate. My needs and wants—it's a fine line to straddle the two.

"Returning to your initial question," General Pruden says, "Rhed indeed has concerns, which is why he wants you to have a say in those dedicated to your protection. As military men, we know it's important to surround ourselves with people we trust. In your limited interactions with Adlumian soldiers, could you name anyone you feel comfortable with?"

"I maybe trust you," I say, and he chuckles.

"You're kind, but the scope of my responsibility is large, and I must remain neutral. I can't align too heavily with a single faction."

"Faction," I repeat, not understanding the term. "What does that mean?"

"In our situation, I'd define faction as areas of individual interest. There are the three heirs and your friends, who were lined up in the Common. Your group made the challenge, creating the factions, and your main interest, as I see it, is survival. Next, there's my army. I'm asking them to do difficult things—namely, holding their leader against his will. Any honorable soldier will second guess this action." General Pruden looks at Eddy, pressing his lips into an anguished line before admitting, "I know I have." Then he looks at me.

"And, like me, they'll third and fourth guess their actions, reevaluating constantly. And while all that guessing happens —for me and others—I must maintain the integrity of Adlumen's defenses."

The general pushes off the door, approaching me. "The next faction is the citizenship back in Adlumen. They aren't aware of the confusion we're bringing into their lives. We can't hope to understand how they'll react. And last, although it may upset you, I must look out for Lord Endrack and his family. They need to be dealt with fairly."

"He has a family?"

"Yes. A wife and three children who I respect and care for. This situation will shock and confuse them, and if he's convicted, they'll be heartbroken."

"I see how it would have been easier if we'd died. No wonder Endrack wanted that."

"Lord Endrack," he corrects. "And the simplest path isn't necessarily the appropriate one. Adlumen law takes time, and I doubt any of us will enjoy the process, but I believe we'll find a solution. Until then, I'd like to return this conversation to its initial purpose. How do you feel about Eddy leading your security team?"

I glance at Eddy, who doesn't seem eager one way or the other. I'm sure she's fifth and sixth guessing right now. "I don't feel very comfortable with anyone, but there's mistrust on all sides. After all, a Harwellian hit Eddy on the head." I smile, but the others don't respond to the expression. I clear my throat. "I was around Eddy long enough to know she's fair even under pressure. I know little about her but still know her more than most of the others. So, yeah, I guess I prefer her."

Eddy nods. No spoken gratitude or look of frustration. Just a nod.

"Okay, that's solved. Now I have one more thing," General Pruden says, and I squeeze the bridge of my nose. I don't know if I can handle any more decisions. He calls for someone outside the room, and they enter, carrying the *Book of Adlumen Law*. "I couldn't decide how to secure the book during our travels, but I think you should keep it. Between your Harwell friends and Captain Rhed's sons, you'll know how to keep it protected."

The three people from Adlumen leave the room, passing the book to Ronen. "Ye got a preference on who keeps it?"

I shake my head. "Any of us can, though it is pretty big. You might be the only one capable of carrying it."

Ronen chuckles, dropping it onto the counter with a thunk, then taking a seat. "Lucan 'n Cully make ye angry?"

"No. I'm not angry. At least, not anymore."

"Thanks be fer tha'. Ye're a tad scary when ye are."

I tilt my head. "Truth is, I'm in a perfectly excellent mood."

"Are ye? Why's tha'?"

"Well, I have more energy than I've had in days." I sit up and drop my legs over the edge of the bed before hopping to the floor. Still in my pajamas and barefoot, I pad the few steps until I reach Ronen and sit sideways on his lap. He wraps his arms around me, and I lay my head against him. "And I've traded my sleeping arrangements from a hard slab to your comfortable lap." Ronen's chuckle echoes in his chest. "And I'm with you, which always puts me in a perfectly... excellent... mood."

"Wasna always so, Cricket," Ronen counters with a kiss on the top of my head.

"No, but from today on, it will always be. Because I've decided, no matter what happens to us in Adlumen, I'll never lose sight of you. You mean everything to me."

My vision was clouded for so long, but I see clearly now. There's nowhere I'd rather be. Ronen's vocal about the winning attributes he sees in me, but he's got it wrong. It's him. He's the one who's perfect and beautiful. Infinitely dearer than other things I profess to love: towels, pillows, books, and the like.

Ronen releases a sigh—a mixture of unease over the future and contentment with one another. He runs his hand soothingly over my shoulder, then wraps me tighter in his embrace before saying, "Aye, Bethy. Ye make me impossibly happy too."

VALE'S EPILOGUE

General Pruden steps from Annibeth's room. He's a determined man. I can tell by the set of his shoulders and his long gait when he moves. He's got two other Adlumians with him, but I hustle to catch up before another day passes and, with it, another missed opportunity to speak with him.

"Excuse me! General Pruden," I call out, and he stops. The others stop too, but when he sees me, he motions them to continue without him, and they enter the stairwell, leaving us alone.

"Thanks for stopping. I hope I'm not keeping you from anything."

"I have a moment. It's Vale, right?"

"Yes," I answer but say no more, unsure what holds my tongue. It could be I'm intimidated, or maybe I don't fully trust him even though I'm trying. He's done nothing untoward in our dealings, and Captain Rhed seems to trust him, but I need to be cautious, which is silly because I'm the one who stopped him.

He seems to sense my hesitation because he starts up a conversation. "You're wearing the regalia."

"Oh, yes," I say, touching the alexandrite stone hanging around my neck, sparkling green in the natural light.

"It's a wise move. I advise you to keep up the practice. It reinforces your importance among the Adlumen soldiers who feel negatively about restraining Lord Endrack."

"Some of them don't like what's happening?"

"It would be impossible to have it otherwise."

"So, you think we're still in danger?"

"Not while you're under my watch," he replies with a confident nod.

"Are you concerned *you're* in danger for helping us?" I can't help but ask, and it makes the general laugh, his blue eyes sparkling.

"I'm not helping you. I'm helping Adlumen and you by extension. Besides, my reputation is solid. Now, what did you stop me for?"

"I'm concerned about my sister." I point at her door, which is closed—just her and Ronen inside. I'm still reeling from how their relationship developed. It's not that I don't approve or don't like what's happening between them—it just seems strange. Ronen's a big softie—the gentlest and kindest man I know. Whereas, traditionally, Annibeth's been thorny and rude. She's changed a lot, but it's still hard to comprehend how they work.

I turn my focus back to the general, telling him, "I know you're eager to get back to Adlumen, but I'm worried about her traveling. Will you please keep her in mind when making plans?"

Yeah, I've changed too—worrying about Annibeth's health and well-being. Truth is, I'm warming to her and to her being my sister.

"I understand your concern. It's part of why I keep checking in with her. She seems much improved today, but we should wait another day or two."

"Thanks. I think that's sufficient."

"Is there anything else?"

"Yes, actually. Will you tell me the status of my grandmother?"

"Your grandmother?" General Pruden squints, then shakes his head, perplexed. "Why do you presume I know something about your grandmother?"

"Because she's in Adlumen."

He shakes his head, his gray hair moving with the motion. Or maybe it's blond. It's hard to be sure. "We aren't holding anyone from Harwell. This is the first time I've encountered any of your people."

"But I know that's not right. By the time we arrive in Adlumen, Gran will have been your captive for over four months."

"I'm telling you, she's not there," he insists.

My anger flares—my green eyes sparking—and I have to temper my frustration before I act stupidly. After exhaling a calming breath, I say, "Then Lord Endrack has kept it secret from you." I try not to sound accusatory, but by the frown the general's wearing, I'm sure I failed. But how do you tell a confident and influential person they're wrong? How do you tell them the person they follow has misled them? It's not easy, I tell you.

At his doubtful expression, I add, "I know he has her. He alluded as much when conversing with me on the Common."

It was clever of Endrack never to come out and talk about Gran specifically. He never mentioned her name or even identified he had a relative of mine as his prisoner. None of the cogs, or even General Pruden, would guess there was a person linked to Endrack's comments.

"I can see you were unaware he took her," I concede. "But I'll ask another favor of you. When we get to Adlumen, will you check into it?"

General Pruden doesn't hesitate. "I will."

"Thank you." At least he isn't ruling out the possibility. "I won't have a moment's peace until I find her."

"I don't mean to hinder your chance at peace, but please be prepared I might not find anything. Nothing goes on in

Adlumen of which I'm not aware."

I can't help but push his logic. "So you knew Endrack had found the governors' heirs and planned to execute them?" The general's already frustrated expression turns sour, and I feel guilty for pushing. "I'm sorry," I say before he can speak. "I know the answer to that, and I don't mean to be contrary, but I won't let this drop. Endrack hired a group led by a man named Malum. They're the ones who took my grandmother."

"*Lord* Endrack. And we have no dealings with Malum," he replies quickly. "We never have, even for covert operations."

"What about someone named Geminus? He used that name as well. The man was a beacon and took jobs under either alias as best suited the situation."

"I know of Geminus," he says with a weary sigh. "You speak of him in the past tense."

"He's dead, though some of his Six continue to work using his names."

"But you're sure he's dead?"

"Positive. He died here in Harwell. His daughter killed him. Tesha?" General Pruden nods, knowing she was one of the people lined up in the Common. "I don't believe Endrack mentioned Malum by name."

"Lord," the General interrupts to correct.

"Yes. I'm sorry. Lord Endrack. He didn't mention Malum's name but knew Tesha was his daughter. After he tested our blood, he commented on their hair, comparing the color. Did Geminus have red hair?"

I know the answer even before the general says, "Yes."

"Malum was hired for two reasons—to find the governors and the lamlight. He exposed Harwell to the outside world, delivered Gran to Adlumen, and retrieved the lamlight before he died. Gran was all the proof Endrack needed that the heirs were in Harwell. Lord Endrack, I mean. The lamlight allowed your soldiers to search for us for months in the Cliffs. Captured, they brought us here where Lord Endrack could confront us."

General Pruden looks exhausted as I finish spilling every drop of information I possess. Sure, part is conjecture, but mostly, it's fact. Mostly, they're events I lived through.

He doesn't move or speak, just stares down at me with a mild expression—whether it's thoughtful or blank, I'm unable to determine. Maybe for the first time, I see the toll this circumstance is taking on him. I can't imagine the pressure he feels to keep all the facets of this situation from caving in on him. He could end the burden now by abandoning us. He doesn't seem the type, but under the right conditions, it could happen. So I decide it's best to stop there and not add to his stress. He's heard enough for now.

"Look, I understand you're an intermediary, taking a neutral path until we're situated to figure things out. I understand the complexity of that role and appreciate you for taking it on. Accosting you and demanding things isn't the best way to show my appreciation. I'm truly sorry about that. But I tend to be pushy, and truthfully, it's a little hard not to clamor onto you as an object of hope."

General Pruden chuckles at the comment, and some of his anxiety wanes.

"Anyway, that's all I was wondering about. I appreciate your time," I say to let him know I won't be bothering him anymore and maybe to leave things on a positive note.

He seems happy to go, but before he does, he tells me one last thing. "I will check into your grandmother. You have my word."

◆ ◆ ◆

Three days later, we're preparing to enter the Dark. General

Pruden waited an extra day so Annibeth was better healed and rested for the long trek to Adlumen. She's much improved, and only a few moments have put a kink in her otherwise upbeat mood.

The first happened yesterday when Nacole Rupret arrived at the Clinic. They had a falling out—of which I'm not privy to the details—and Nacole sought her out to talk, though I don't know if any talking took place.

I was in the other room, packing clinical supplies for the trip. Nacole walked in, and a minute later, Annibeth was screaming, pushing Nacole from her room, and slamming the door in her face. Nacole retreated without a glance at me. I considered consoling Annibeth, but through the door, I heard Ronen speaking to her.

"I'm not ready to forgive her," Annibeth said.

"Ye dunna have ta," he replied in his deep tone.

It was a sweet and supportive moment, leaving me curious about what happened. I still haven't asked.

And now I'm witnessing another blow to Annibeth's pleasant demeanor. We're mounting the horses, and Annibeth's on Clod with Ronen at her back. They're accustomed to riding together, and it will be more comfortable for Annibeth's continued recovery. My sister turns, looking sunny with a smile on her lips, and within seconds, her expression turns cold and flat.

Saeva passes by—not close enough to be unusual, but near enough to set Annibeth on edge. "Morning, Beauty," Saeva says with a casual wave in Annibeth's direction. Ronen wraps a protective arm around her waist, but it's Eddy who jumps into action.

Within seconds, she's between Annibeth and Saeva, blocking them so they can't see each other. As the two women argue, I can't help but notice Saeva's bandaged finger and missing tooth. I hear nothing they say since Eddy maneuvers her away from us too quickly.

I glance over at a still-shaken Annibeth. She's petrified of Saeva, though she'll never admit it. But I've seen her scars and realize she has a reason to be scared, even though I'm unaware of everything she suffered during her time with the cogs. She doesn't talk about it, but the trauma lingers, and we all see it.

When Annibeth thought I was infringing on her and Cully's relationship, she threatened to hurt me multiple times. I wonder now if her threats were bluster. I can't imagine she'd have followed through with her ideas. Though maybe I can't see it now because she's a new person. She really has changed.

The procession starts. Endrack's in the front, surrounded by the Elite. We follow, surrounded by a group of cogs selected and led by Eddy. Behind us are the rest of the soldiers.

"I can't help it," I tell Geric in a voice I hope only he can hear. We're not sharing a horse, so it's impossible to have a private conversation, but the clomp of horse's feet and the boisterous soldier's voices should be enough to camouflage my words. "I know they're around us for protection, but I feel more like a prisoner than a guest."

General Pruden has taken to calling us that—guests of Adlumen. It's all semantics. I think he does it to make us feel welcome and remind the cogs to treat us fairly. I don't know that it's working on a deeper level, but we all play along.

"Well, for you Harwellians, it's a little of both," Geric replies. "But for us Coastals—or really anyone from the Dark territories—we lean heavily toward prisoners."

"What about Evans?" I ask, voicing a worry that's grown over the last few days. Geric shrugs. Really, there's no other answer he could give. Evans is light blind, and Adlumians look down on that. But he's also an heir. Will they accept him?

But really—light blind or not—will they accept any of us?

Are we prisoners? Guests? Future leaders?

We are all and none, and our unresolved status provides no comfort.

Regardless of what we are or aren't—we're outnumbered. I can only hope the laws and traditions of those who came before us are strong enough to protect our group when we reach Adlumen. There's no telling what will unravel in Endrack's domain.

The seven of us left Harwell to hide in Durus, and now we're leaving together again—this time under army escort. The enemy's army.

My father remains in Harwell. He'll leave to join Milany in Tenebris and keep updated on us through Captain Rhed. Though he's a spare heir, like Captain Rhed, he wasn't part of the Common showdown. He didn't take part in challenging Right to Rule. He's not a contender. Consequently, General Pruden doesn't consider him part of the tribunal. Though my father argued to accompany us, I was glad he wasn't allowed. If everything goes wrong, he'll still have a chance to escape this madness.

I think about his words as he hugged me goodbye. "Go and make Harwell safe." He told Annibeth the same thing and hugged her too. The strange part was it didn't make me upset, and she didn't seem to mind. It was a confusing moment, and I realized something. This time as we entered the Dark—Geric, Tesha, Siman, Evans, Ronen, Annibeth, and me—Annibeth's no longer on the outside. She's one of us.

And that's something.

It's something really great.

We're off to Adlumen, and part of me thinks we may never return to Harwell. But a few things I know for certain—we won't come back until we find Gran or until Harwell is safe for our families again. There's nothing to deter us from our goals —no unhinged leader or crazy cog. We're poised to fight—with weapons or words.

The seven of us will stay together until we figure this out, and when we do, we'll be safe from Lord Endrack's threats forever. As far as I'm concerned, there's no other acceptable outcome.

END OF BOOK THREE

THE STORY CONTINUES
The Soldier

Mother says I was born with a soft soul—that the moment they placed me into her arms as a newborn, she could see it in my countenance—and overcome by her feelings, she told them to me, though I was only minutes old. "Chessie Endrack, I see peace in your eyes. You are a gift and a blessing to our family. A vessel of compassion and a dealer of truth."

But my father, Lord Keine Endrack—the most exacting and wise ruler in any light bubble or Dark territory—would have none of that. He drew me from her, gazed into my fresh eyes, and declared, "Your mother considers you too much with her heart. I see fierceness and bravery. You're a soldier and a stronghold for shaping Adlumen's future. A vessel of victory and, when required, a dealer of death."

Unsurprisingly, neither has relinquished their viewpoint, always retelling my birth story with their own bias, though never while in the same room.

But I'm eighteen now with biases of my own.

"Lady Chessie," a household servant says, snapping me from my memories. The woman dips her head and stands to the side while I pass. I appreciate her kindness but am embarrassed by the honorifics. It's silly for someone engaged in a task to halt their progress merely to pay homage to a title. It's one item on a list of things I plan to change—someday, when I become the person shaping Adlumen's future.

My eyes fall on a commemorative portrait of my parents, set in a stone cove and highlighted with soft lighting. I step closer and look into their eyes—the ones that expect so much from me—knowing they'd be frustrated to learn I've developed my own ideas regarding their character observations on the day of my birth. Primarily, they'd be disappointed that neither can claim triumph for labeling me correctly... because I've discovered they're both right.

I'm the firstborn of Lord Keine Endrack, and I take the position seriously. My entire life he's demanded ferocity and courage in all I do, and I've learned those traits well. I'm his heir, eager for the day I'll guide our people's fortunes, and I'm a dedicated soldier, ready to give my life to defend Adlumen.

But as Mother predicted, I'm devoted to my family, even when they're difficult, which they often are. And in all my dealings, I prefer the peaceful path, performing my duties with precision and mercy. But if a situation evolves where precision and mercy are no longer enough?

Well, then I bring my enemy to their knees, becoming the dealer of death.

GET THE SOLDIER NOW ON AMAZON!

BOOKS BY THIS AUTHOR

<u>THE DARK SERIES</u>

The Dark

The Witch

The Shrew

The Soldier

The Prisoner

AUTHOR'S NOTE

Hmm. I feel another apology is due... sorry to those who couldn't stomach the idea of a story from Annibeth's perspective. Well, sorry... not sorry. Haha. This has been, for some time, my favorite of the first three books. It practically wrote itself with far fewer edits. Sure, some of that could be from the foundation being in place, but I believe it's mostly because of Annibeth. She's a strong character and made it easy. So, thanks, Annibeth!

Annibeth was not originally a lead character in this series. And when she was suddenly front and center (after presenting her as rather despicable in the previous books), I wasn't sure how I was going to pull it off. Truthfully, I enjoyed writing from her perspective more than from Vale or Tesha. I'm not sure what that says about me.

SPOILERS AHEAD. (So, skip to the three diamonds below unless you've read The Shrew.)

I loved bringing Ronen and Annibeth together. I don't think anyone would pick them as a match, but of their own accord, they gravitated toward one another. I knew Annibeth would appreciate his strength, which is a trait she values greatly. But what could ever cause Ronen to care for such a harpy? I didn't know. But, again, somehow it worked. I think they understand each other in a way the others don't get, but that's the thing about connection—it's not for other people to decide.

Ronen was especially enjoyable to write. I like all the Dark brothers, but when considering what's happening in a scene, his perspective is often my favorite. (Well, him or Evans.) And having some leniency with words was freeing—using adjectives as nouns or making up words for him. I read a book some years back about a large man, who was self-conscious about his motion while in public—afraid he'd bump into someone or knock something over. I liked his strong vulnerability, and it was the basis for Ronen. Luckily, Ronen's usually in a position to move around freely, since he's so often outdoors. But entering the repository isn't possible, traversing rooftops in Harwell is questionable behavior, and he has to ride Clod.

The thing I find unusual about Annibeth is she doesn't really change. Sure, she discovers she's not the level of villain she always believed she was back in Harwell. And she feels some regret about how she navigated things—like with Gran and Nacole. But, at the core, she's still herself. She still dislikes Tesha, though she treats her better. She still has a reluctant respect for Vale. She still struggles to accept Laso. And even though she's adjusted her mindset, like with Evans, she can still bring the chaos. She feels like a true representation of humanity—sure, we evolve, but most often, it's a slow process.

Endrack... It was fun to introduce the mastermind behind their troubles. Unlike Malum, I didn't cultivate a soft spot for Adlumen's leader. I think that comes across in the story. (I felt terrible about Janny. I didn't anticipate her end but realized Endrack wouldn't let something like that slide.) His character felt truly despicable and heartless to me, which paired well with Annibeth, since that's how she was frequently labeled by Harwell's citizens.

Another character that paired well with Annibeth was Saeva, for many of the same reasons. I pulled Saeva into the story to serve a few purposes, but a primary one was redemption for Annibeth. She came out more terrible than anticipated. My mother-in-law, who's read the series more than anyone, skips the Saeva chapters. And Saeva set a high standard when it came time to introduce Endrack and make him take over as the main villain in the story. Saeva is unstable and gleeful in her torture… as opposed to Endrack, who's calculating and quick to execute his will. I guess they each have their place.

Something interesting to note: After escaping the Clinic, Annibeth goes to the repository. Well, initially, it wasn't Laso inside the cave. It was Ronen's ma. I'd completed the chapters, and it hit me that the wrong character was inside the repository! *It needed to be Laso.* Duh! I couldn't believe it took so long to realize my error. But while rewriting that section, it was obvious the character change was right for the storyline.

I love this book, and I'm so pleased with how it came together. I don't know what it is about this one, but I think it will always hold a special spot for me.

Wow! You made it through book three! I'm so grateful to you for giving this series a chance. It's been a fun journey, and it's exciting to share the results. Thanks so much for reading. If you have the time, a review on Amazon or Goodreads is always very, very, very appreciated. Very.

Many thanks to Matt. Love you! And my family and friends. Figuring out this writing stuff was a huge learning curve. I'm sure many of you wondered if I'd ever finish anything. But I did! Three times now! (With just two more to go in the series.)

Thanks to my beta readers. Much appreciation goes out to: Matt, Sandi, Tara, Kirsti, and Fish. (Many thanks to Kirsti… I love that this one is your favorite… you validated for me that I got it right.)

Thanks to my fellow writers. Writing sprints got me through a lot of slumps. I might still be struggling to get down words without our regular 10am Discord meeting with Randi, Eve, and Sam. That feels like forever ago!

Prospective writers… it's time to write! Just do it. Go to NaNoWriMo now and make a plan to participate. Check out Novlr if you need somewhere to store your words. (They often run subscription deals during NaNo.) Get Grammarly and learn how to order a sentence properly. (Yeah, I never realized I was terrible at that.) And get your creative on with Canva.

Happy reading!

www.ingramcontent.com/pod-product-compliance
Lightning Source LLC
Chambersburg PA
CBHW060216030726
47499CB00004B/1066